AN ATLAS
TO FOREVER

Visit us at www.boldstrokesbooks.com

By the Author

Something Between Us

Last New Beginning

An Atlas to Forever

AN ATLAS
TO FOREVER

by

Krystina Rivers

2023

ISBN 13: 978-1-63679-451-8

This Trade Paperback Original Is Published By
Bold Strokes Books, Inc.
P.O. Box 249
Valley Falls, NY 12185

First Edition: November 2023

Credits
Editor: Barbara Ann Wright
Production Design: Susan Ramundo
Cover Design By Tammy Seidick

Acknowledgments

This book is close to my heart for so many reasons. My wife and I adopted our first dog, Jordan, the way I approach a lot of things: impulsively, wildly unprepared, and with more confidence than is prudent but with enough determination to see it through. Jordan is the sweetest dog who ever lived, and despite all the mauled shoes, DVDs, pens, pillows, etc.—in part because we didn't really know what to do with a puppy—I wouldn't change a single thing about her. She completely turned us into dog people, and we wanted to help more dogs, so we fostered a couple until we foster-failed with Clark.

Clark was the inspiration for Atlas, and he is the best boy ever, but he made us learn a lot and fast about dealing with a reactive dog. I'm pretty sure many of our neighbors thought we had a vicious dog, but really, we had a dog who was terrified of everything and tried to protect us all by barking like he was fighting off the end of the world. It took a lot of work—a lot of books, vet visits, blogs, training courses, training time with him—and a little help from the pharmacy, but I'm so proud of him and no longer feel terrified when I walk him. As he lays here sprawled on the couch next to me while I write this, I have such gratitude in my heart for everyone who helped us along this journey.

Thank you to Rad and everyone at Bold Strokes Books for everything you do to support me and allow me to continue chasing this author dream. Sandy, thank you for having patience with me when I can't decide on a title until the last possible second or ask for the impossible on my covers—which you completely delivered on. I am in love with this cover. It captures exactly what I wanted even though I wasn't terribly articulate or clear in asking for it. Barbara

Ann, thank you for being the amazing you. I love editing with you and am grateful for your witty commentary, insightful suggestions, and willingness to put up with my bouts of impostor syndrome.

I am so grateful to have you back home with me, Kerri. I thought I would write this entire book while you were deployed last year, but it turns out it's a little hard to write romance when your heart is eight thousand or so miles away. Thank you for having patience with me after you got home as I charged toward my deadline with a lot of words still left to write. And more than that, thank you for building a life with me for the last twenty-two years, for creating a family with me, for always supporting me and cheering me on. There is no way I could do any of this without you. It's always for you.

I am so lucky to have a supportive family. Mom Angel, my wonderful grandmother, and our family matriarch, I love you so much and am so proud of your strength and perseverance over the last difficult year and a half. Mom, I cannot fully express how grateful I am for you. You've always been there for me, and I know you always will be. Cheryl, best big sister and best cheerleader. Now it's time for me to be yours: I believe in you enough for both of us. You're up! Catey and Mindy, I miss you both so much, but I can't wait to be an aunt again. I think a trip to Toronto is in my future very soon. Dad, always steady and always there. All of my aunts and uncles and cousins, thank you for being so supportive too. I love this family.

Kris, Ana, Morgan…my nugs. I love you all so much and all of our fun times. I love talking books and plots and eating cheese and drinking wine with you as much as I love more eventful times like the Kit Kat. I am so grateful for your friendship and fellowship and how it makes this author journey so much more special to me. Kris, thank you so much for your mentorship as much as your friendship. Despite how confusing it is when someone also calls me Krys when we're together.

The sapphic literary community—readers, reviewers, and authors—is so dynamic and supportive, and I am so happy to be a part of it. Huge thank you to everyone who has read my books, recommended one to a friend, encouraged me, left a review, or included me on a list...You all help to make this possible and you have my unending appreciation.

Finally, thank you to everyone who picks up this book and gives Atlas and Ellie and Hayden a chance to win you over. They have a special place in my heart, and I hope they will have a special place in your heart too.

Dedication

To all the pet parents out there
who know who rescued whom.

Chapter One

E llie stared at the call button in the lobby of Iris's attorney's office, wondering if every elevator was out of service. She jabbed her finger into the already illuminated button again as if that would help. She knew it would do nothing, but she had to do something to keep her mind off the day ahead.

It was a random Thursday in June. It would be nondescript under other circumstances. She would typically be going into the office. Actually, had it been the nondescript Thursday in June that it was supposed to be, she would have landed in Nashville an hour ago. She'd been scheduled to tour two buildings down there that she was thinking about purchasing for the Geffin Family Trust, but her assistant had canceled the flight yesterday afternoon.

Nothing about this Thursday was typical or normal. Because yesterday, Iris, her best friend since Sinai Daycare, had died. No warning. No premonition. Ellie had spoken to her Tuesday night, and they'd made plans to have a happy hour with no foreshadowing of what would happen less than twelve hours later. No bad feeling. No inkling that there was no way they would follow through on their plans.

Iris had woken up yesterday like any other weekday, had gotten in the shower, and had a brain aneurysm rupture. She was gone within moments.

The police had discovered her lying in the bottom of her walk-in shower next to her cell phone. They'd theorized she'd tried to call 9-1-1 for the blinding headache that would have seized her but collapsed before she could connect the call. They wouldn't have found her so quickly except that, when she'd collapsed, she'd blocked the drain of the shower and flooded the condos below hers within minutes. The shower was still pouring on her when the building engineers had let themselves into her condo and discovered why it was raining in the condo below.

She was forty-one. Six months younger than Ellie. She was supposed to be moving into her new place in Evanston that weekend. Ellie didn't understand it, but Iris had adopted some dog who wasn't taking to condo life, so she'd decided to move to the suburbs. That path was normally for young married couples with small kids. Not an unmarried, nearly middle-aged woman with a dog she'd had for less than two months.

But it didn't matter now. Ellie's best friend in the world was gone. In an instant. While Ellie had been taking her morning jog along the lake.

She pressed the call button again. Harder. Until her fingertip turned from white to red. She kept trying to focus on anything to keep her thoughts from spiraling around Iris, and in that moment, it was the technicolor of her finger. Yet, her thoughts swirled back to Iris. Again. As they had nonstop since she'd gotten that terrible call from Iris's mother.

Finally, a ding behind her signaled the elevator had arrived. She smoothed nonexistent wrinkles from the lapel of her black suit jacket and stepped into the car. The grout in the tile desperately needed a thorough steaming. The wooden panels had gouges from careless movers or perhaps a tenant simply carrying too much. The brass rails had long since lost their luster.

It seemed odd that Iris's attorney had insisted upon seeing Ellie that morning before the service. Probate took forever, so it didn't make sense that there could be something so urgent that morning. Before the fucking funeral.

Everything was a blur, and she wasn't entirely sure how she finally ended up sitting in a chair in front of the attorney, Mr. Volpe. Wait, Bill. She was supposed to call him Bill. Her last twenty-four hours felt like she'd been seeing it through a dark haze, and she was amazed she hadn't fallen down a flight of stairs or gotten hit by a car on her way to his office since she couldn't clearly remember how she'd even gotten there.

Bill came around his desk and sat next to her rather than across from her with the large, stately desk between them. "I'm so sorry for your loss, Ellie," he said.

His face was kind, grandfatherly, but why was he calling her Ellie? It wasn't like he knew her. "Thank you. Though I must admit, I'm a little surprised it was so urgent for me to come this morning." She watched her hand tremble as she reached for the small bottle of water that she was pretty sure was hers. She couldn't remember, but that hand didn't look like hers either, so her cognition was clearly questionable. She moved slowly so Bill would hopefully tell her if she was stealing his.

"I take it Iris never had a conversation with you about what she would like from you if she died?"

Ellie shook her head.

He reached across his desk and grabbed a letter in a beige envelope that Ellie had missed lying there in plain sight. "Iris asked me to give this to you as soon as possible after her death if, and I quote, 'you seemed to have no idea what the fuck I was talking about.'"

That extricated a small laugh from Ellie. Definitely sounded like how Iris would talk to her attorney. Even if the guy looked like someone's grandpa. She silently took the letter and started reading:

My dearest friend, Ellie,

If you are reading this, it means I am gone and much sooner than I would have ever predicted. I thought I'd have time to discuss this ask with you in person, but I knew it would be a hard sell, so I might have procrastinated a day too long, and for that, I am truly sorry.

Ellie's throat tightened at Iris being afraid to ask her something. And at more glaring evidence that she was really gone.

I don't know if you've met him yet, but at the time I'm writing this, I just adopted the sweetest dog in the world, Atlas. He is amazing but had a difficult life before, and he carries the scars. But we have bonded in a way that I would have never thought possible. I can't let him go back to the pound. He doesn't do well there.

Ellie squeezed the letter harder and harder as the ask was becoming clear, even though Iris hadn't written it yet.

I can't ask Mom and Dad to take him because they are too old to care for a large dog, and I can't ask Brian as my nephews are too small to have a dog with a past go live with them. Atlas is a sweetie, but he's afraid of kids, and if they do something to startle him, well, I wouldn't be able to live with myself if something happened to either them or the dog. Ha! I'm already gone, so I can't live with myself anyway, but I know you know what I mean.

Ellie smiled at what a goober Iris had always been. Making a joke about her death in a letter to be delivered after she was gone. Seriously. And cruel. But it did make her chuckle, so maybe not so cruel.

I don't have anyone else I can ask. Please consider taking him and giving him a good home. It's going to be an adjustment for you. He is going to need some training unless it's been a while, and I still haven't talked to you about this, but he's the best dog and can't go back to the shelter. If that is where he is now, please, please get him out as soon as you can.

I know this isn't fair to you, but I can't ask anyone else. Please grant me this last wish and take care of Atlas. He changed my life in whatever time we had together. If you will agree to take him, I'm going to leave you a chunk of money. I know you don't need it, but it only seems fair given the huge ask I am making of you.

I'm so sorry to have left you and him. Please know you are the best friend I've ever had. My platonic soulmate. I'm sorry that we won't rule the nursing home together but know I'm always with you. I love you and thank you. I know you're going to love Atlas too.

Love,
Iris

Ellie wiped her tears with the tissue Bill handed her and struggled to not crumple the letter. What was she supposed to do with this? She didn't want some damn dog. She didn't like dogs. Granted, she'd never had a dog, but she'd also never wanted one either. She laid the letter down to resist throwing it and picked up her water again.

How could Iris do this to her? Her skin prickled against her clothes as anger radiated from her. She was so mad at Iris. For leaving her. For trying to force her to take some goofy dog. For guilting her into adopting it. How could she make all these plans, change her will, without talking to Ellie first? Without asking if this was okay? What was Ellie supposed to do? She didn't want a dog, and this was a huge request. A gigantic fucking ask.

"I'm sure you're shocked. I haven't read the letter, but I know what Iris was going to ask you. I encouraged her to talk to you, but of course, I'm sure she thought she had more time. But she shouldn't have asked you like this."

"You're goddamn right she shouldn't have." Ellie didn't realize how hard she was squeezing her bottle until water shot out the top and onto her leg. "What the?" She jumped up, brushing at her pants. As if that would help. As if anything could help.

Bill handed her a wad of tissues, and she tried to blot at the wet spot, but it did nothing other than leave white flecks all over her black suit pants. "You've got to be kidding me right now." She slumped back into Bill's guest chair and caught her head in her hands as a sob broke free from her chest. "I can't do any of this. I'm not ready to say good-bye, I have white shit all over my pants, and how the hell am I supposed to know what to do with a dog?" Her body shook with the tremors that accompanied the sobs tearing through her.

Bill's hand on her shoulder startled her, and she looked up. "I know. But you don't have a lot of time to think about this. Atlas is at the shelter because no one could take him when…" He cleared his throat, and Ellie was surprised to see true grief in his eyes. "When she changed her will, she told me that he was terrified of the shelter and shut down completely. She asked that if you could take him, to please pick him up as soon as possible. Technically, I think the shelter will hold him for a week or two before he'll go up for adoption, but Iris was adamant he could not stay there."

Ellie wasn't sure what she was going to do. She did *not* want a dog, but how could she possibly deny Iris this last request? Even if Iris hadn't had the courage to ask in person. Ellie was gutted and just trying to survive from minute to minute, and now Iris had thrown *this* request at her? As if she didn't have enough on her plate. If Iris had still been alive, she'd want to shake her and had to fight the surge of tears that notion prompted.

❖

Ellie walked Atlas up to the door of her condo building that evening and thought maybe this wouldn't be as bad as she'd feared. The day had been a fucking nightmare with Iris's funeral. She should be sitting shiva with Iris's family, as they were essentially sisters, but she'd apparently had to go adopt a damn dog. And she had to work tomorrow. Three days ago, she was blithely making her way through this week unaware that her life was about to be upended.

But Atlas seemed sweet, at least. He walked a few steps on his leash and looked back at Ellie for reassurance. When she encouraged him to keep going, he did. When she'd walked into the shelter, the sounds of dogs barking and howling had been nearly paralyzing, but she was only there to see one, so she'd tried to keep her time in the overwhelming space brief.

Atlas had been lying curled in the back corner of his kennel with his head buried inside the tiny blanket the shelter had given him. She'd said his name once, and he'd stayed as unmoving as a statue, other than a tiny twitch of his ears.

She'd said his name once more, and he'd lifted his head. The sadness in his chocolate brown eyes had torn at Ellie's heart, and she'd known in that moment that he would be coming home with her. As she'd walked into the shelter, she'd still been telling herself that if Atlas didn't seem like a good fit, she could turn around and just leave, but his eyes had called to her in a way she hadn't been expecting.

But good God, he'd looked a *lot* smaller curled up into a tiny ball in the back of that kennel than he did now. Ellie didn't know how to judge, but she thought that he was maybe seventy-five pounds. He seemed gigantic with his stocky body and big head, but he was gentle.

He again looked back at her with those sad eyes, as if expecting her to have vanished from the other end of the leash while they walked. "I'm not going anywhere, buddy. I promise."

He nodded like he understood and walked through the front doors of her condo building.

"Good evening, Ms. Efron," Chet, the building's evening door attendant, said. "And who is this big fellow?" He squatted in front of Atlas and reached the back of his hand toward the gentle giant. "Is this okay?" he asked, though it was kind of too late as Atlas was already sniffing his hand before giving it a little nudge with his snout followed by a tentative lick.

"This is Atlas. He's apparently mine now. It's too long of a story to tell you tonight, but he's going to be living with me." All those words weren't ones she'd ever expected herself to be saying, but here she was, feeling weirdly possessive about the dog.

"What a sweet boy," Chet said, his voice all baby talk.

What is it about dogs that makes people act like buffoons? Ellie gave the leash a gentle tug, and Atlas followed her to the elevator. She smiled at him, thinking that this might be the beginning of a beautiful friendship.

He sat next to Ellie in the elevator with his heavy body pushing into the side of her leg. A woman rushed in as the doors were closing, carrying some tiny dog, and Ellie swore she could feel Atlas tense, but he stayed pressed against her, so she rubbed his head and watched the numbers slowly climb to the top floor of her building.

CHAPTER TWO

Hayden's eyes scratched open, feeling like they were lined with sandpaper, and she was immediately disoriented. No soft lapping of waves against the side of her house. No light snoring of her cat, Chelsea. Where the hell was she? Adrenaline made her limbs feel momentarily weak as she struggled to piece together where she was and how she'd gotten there.

She reminded herself to breathe even as swallowing felt like she had a mouthful of cat litter. Finally, the events of the evening came rolling back, and it was like a weight lifted off her chest. She'd spent last night at the Scarlett Lounge, the best drag venue in the city.

She normally would have been happier at home alone with a glass of wine and a good book, but she'd been feeling restless and unfulfilled and had been hoping a few hours of debauchery might act as a balm. So she'd gone out with the goal of finding someone to spend a few pleasurable hours with. Nothing more, nothing less.

She'd chatted with a guy at the bar for a few minutes early in the evening and thought he'd had potential, but there'd been a bachelorette party full of women, and one redhead in particular had continued to make eye contact with Hayden. At first, she'd been a little shy, but as the show went on, her heated gazes had become more and more brazen.

Although pansexual, Hayden generally had a slight preference for the feel of a woman's soft skin versus the harder planes of a man. But when she was in the right mood, either could and would do the trick.

When Hayden had gone to the restroom between singers, the woman, whose name Hayden was having a hard time recalling, had followed. She'd told Hayden all about her best friend, the bride. They were from Peoria and were only in town for the weekend as the friend was getting married next weekend. There were more details that Hayden couldn't recall. Honestly, she hadn't been paying attention. She'd only cared about the desire in the redhead's eyes. She'd been looking at Hayden like she wanted to have her naked on the vanity, onlookers be damned, and heat had surged in Hayden's center. That had been exactly what she'd been looking for when she'd gone out that evening, though someplace a little more private than a restroom with four stalls would be preferable.

Hayden had asked if she wanted to get out of there when the redhead had kissed her. Clearly, she had, and that was how Hayden had ended up in a nondescript hotel room, hungover—probably still a little tipsy—with a woman whose name she still couldn't recall curled beside her. She hated sleeping someplace unfamiliar, but more than that, she hated having a stranger in her personal space, so she never brought anyone back to her place.

She wasn't sure what time it was, but she knew it was time to go. She'd been sleeping on her back, and Scarlett—as Hayden was now thinking of her since the real name was still eluding her—was wrapped around her with a leg draped over her hip and a heel tucked underneath her thigh. Her head was on Hayden's shoulder, and her hand cupped Hayden's breast in an uncomfortably possessive fashion. It was suffocating.

She gingerly lifted Scarlett's knee off her hip and used her core strength for all it was worth to slide her hips away until she could place the knee down on the bed. She froze as Scarlett let out a little grunt. Hayden watched her face, praying she wasn't waking up.

When Scarlett's breath returned to the slow, even cadence of sleep, Hayden's mission to extricate herself continued. She removed the hand from her breast. Her nipple hardened, exposed to the cool air in the room, and that made her queasy with the need to get out of there.

She was just about to slide fully off the bed when she heard a voice raspy with sleep say, "You aren't going anywhere yet, are you, baby?"

Baby? Really? She thought she'd been pretty clear about what this was and wasn't when they'd decided to go back to this hotel. Scarlett lived in Peoria for crying out loud. Fuck. Should she blatantly lie, or should she tell a version of the truth about having to get home? Hayden despised lying, but she didn't want to have to defend her decision to leave either. "Just going to use the bathroom. Go back to sleep," she said softly without looking. That was the truth. Just not the complete truth. She was going to use the bathroom as she got dressed and call a Lyft to take her home.

Scarlett's fingers grazed Hayden's back, and she mumbled something unintelligible. Hayden felt a tiny pang of guilt as she silently gathered her clothes that were scattered all over the room and tiptoed into the bathroom, waiting until the door was fully closed before switching on the light.

Hayden stared at herself in the mirror as she quickly cleaned up. Why was she still feeling so restless? Sex with Scarlett hadn't been the greatest she'd ever had, but it certainly wasn't the worst. Scarlett hadn't said anything, but Hayden suspected this might have been her first time with a woman, as she'd been pretty clumsy to start. Not that Hayden cared if she was an experiment. She was pretty sure they'd both gotten what they'd been looking for—a couple of orgasms—and that was what mattered.

Regardless, the real problem was that Hayden had been so sure a quick tryst would quell her dissatisfaction. Extinguish that feeling that something was missing. And yet, she felt worse after their few hours together.

She was still contemplating why as she walked down the dock to where her houseboat moored during all but the frozen winter months. She loved living on the water. It gave her a modicum of permanency in an impermanent world. Life had taught her that nothing in this existence was permanent. If you lost something you had relied on, it was crushing. Out of self-preservation, she'd long ago committed to never relying on anyone again. If you didn't try to hold on to anything, it didn't hurt when it was gone.

Chelsea's angry cries greeted her when she walked in. She'd known she would have to incur Chelsea's ire at being left alone for too many hours when she'd gone to a hotel with whatever her name was, but Hayden had been so sure it would be worth it. She grimaced, knowing it hadn't been.

Chelsea's cries got more insistent, and Hayden squatted to give her a little love. "What do you think, Chelsea? Are you starting to get a little restless too?"

The calico answered with a purr that was combined with a cry, which wouldn't seem possible, but somehow, Chelsea made it happen, and it was her regular, "I'm happy to see you but hate you a little bit too," sound.

"I know, sweet girl. I love Chicago too, but I'm starting to think maybe it's time to move on. Try another city. Pull up anchor and sail away. We've been here for a few years now, and—"

Chelsea's loud cry cut her off. She was a little shit sometimes, but Hayden had loved her ever since she'd wormed her way into Hayden's heart by stalking her until Hayden had taken her in during college, so she was willing to put up with her cantankerousness. After all, Chelsea was her longest relationship.

"Don't get testy, little girl. I think long-term, this might make the most sense. You know how we always get wandering feet, and I'm starting to feel them again." She scratched the bottom of Chelsea's chin, and Chelsea switched from angry crying purring to plain purring and leaned into Hayden's hand. It was a good thing Hayden knew her weaknesses. "I knew I could make you see reason."

Hayden pressed a kiss into the top of her soft head and breathed in, her scent so familiar and comforting. Chelsea was always a little cranky, but Hayden never doubted her love. She closed her eyes and tried to remember the name of the behaviorist she'd met at last year's Behavior Symposium who had told Hayden she was planning to retire in the next few years and had been looking for someone to take over her practice. Maybe she'd give her a call tomorrow.

Chelsea really wouldn't appreciate the move, as the rocking when the houseboat was traveling was unsettling to her, but once they got wherever they were going, it wouldn't really be different for her. The beauty of a houseboat.

❖

When Ellie opened the door to her condo on the eleventh day after adopting Atlas, she shrieked. It looked like someone had broken in and trashed the living room, even though she knew that wasn't possible as she had a secure building, and no one could even get to her floor.

What the hell had happened? Three couch cushions were torn up, all the books on the bottom two shelves of her bookcases had been pulled onto the floor, many of them completely destroyed, and her kitchen garbage can had been pulled into the living room and dumped.

Numb, she walked into the living room and turned to close the door. She noticed her coatrack bench was pulled on its side, three of the hooks were broken off, and her favorite plaid Burberry trench coat was missing all of its buttons, the collar nearly torn off.

"Atlas," she finally yelled.

He walked into the living room, head down, a book between his teeth. He looked so sad that Ellie's heart broke, which warred with her anger. What could have possibly happened that had turned him from a sweet, snuggly dog into a terrorist hell-bent on the destruction of her house?

"What the fuck is this?" she yelled while gesturing wildly. "Why would you do this?" She swung her arm and briefcase but realized he was cowering. He looked terrified.

She dropped to her knees, placing the bag on the floor behind her. "I'm sorry, buddy. I didn't mean to scare you." She held out the back of her hand as she'd seen Chet do and slowly crawled toward him, trying to avoid frightening him more.

He crawled, belly against the floor, and pressed his nose against her knee, so she scratched him on the head. That seemed to break the dam, and he frantically crawled onto her until he was sitting on her lap. He looked so pathetic, panting like it was one-hundred degrees and staring at her.

"What happened today, Atlas, huh? Did something scare you? What am I supposed to do? Do you not have enough toys to keep you busy?"

There was no way he didn't have enough toys, Ellie thought as she looked at his toy box full of chews and bones. Some of which she'd purchased herself and some of which she'd inherited from

Iris. She even had one of those big rubber ones stuffed with kibble, treats, and peanut butter that he hadn't touched. She would've never thought to do that except her favorite general contractor, Bailey, had mentioned it was a great treat to give dogs when leaving for a few hours. Clearly, that hadn't worked.

Ellie looked at the crate on the other side of the room that she'd taken from Iris's place along with the other dog-related stuff. She felt sick at the thought of having to stick him in there while she was at work, but if this was how he was going to act when she was away, she wasn't going to have a choice.

She didn't relish the thought of cleaning this mess up and decided to take Atlas for his evening walk first. Maybe she could also walk off some of her own frustration and confusion.

She clipped his leash on to his harness and grabbed a few poop bags before taking him downstairs. "You don't have such a bad life do you, Atlas? I walk you twice a day, we snuggle on the couch all evening." Well, all evening might be a little bit of an exaggeration since it was almost eight, but still. They'd have a couple of hours before she went to bed. "It's a better life than the shelter, isn't it?"

She was so busy looking at him as she spoke to him that she didn't register another dog approaching on the other side of the street until he started barking like someone was attacking them, and her arm was nearly wrenched out of its socket when he tried to run to get the tiny terrier who looked as bewildered as Ellie felt. The only reason she was able stop their momentum was because she caught herself on a tree in the boulevard, scraping her palm and tearing her dress pants.

"Atlas," she yelled over and over, trying to get him to come back, but he kept pulling as though he didn't hear until the woman with the terrier picked her dog up and speed-walked away.

When Atlas turned, his eyes looked flat, as though he wasn't the dog she'd been bonding with for the last week and a half. Ellie's heart was beating at what felt like two-hundred beats per minute, and she couldn't catch her breath. What if she hadn't been able to stop him? Would he have attacked that dog? Attacked that woman? She tried to suppress the tears that burned at the corners of her eyes at the terror of what could have happened.

Atlas nudged her hand with his cold nose, bringing her out of her spiraling thoughts. "Let's get you home, buddy. I don't know what's happening with you, but I think I need to find a vet. We can't behave like this. You're going to get us both killed."

Her hand was trembling so badly that she could barely hit the elevator button and pushed two wrong floors before she successfully hit her own. Shit. When they walked into her apartment, she let Atlas out of his harness and went to her wet bar, pulled out a low-ball glass, dropped one large rock into it, and poured Angel's Envy rye until it was level with the top of the rock. Probably more than was necessary, but she needed something to settle her nerves. It had been a long day, but the last forty-five minutes had her on the verge of a breakdown.

She sank onto the only intact couch cushion and took a long sip. The burn felt particularly good and helped ground her even as she felt a little hopeless, and tears began to prick her eyes again. This time, she let them flow since she was alone.

How could he have gone from perfectly behaved to demon overnight? Did he decide he hated her? Did he *want* to be bad? He climbed onto a destroyed cushion next to her and did his best to climb into her lap again. She wanted to yell at him, but those sad brown eyes did her in. He rolled onto his back, half on her and half on the ruined cushion and looked up at her. A vise squeezed her chest. She couldn't stay mad at him. She didn't understand why he'd done it, but she knew in her heart that he hadn't done it to make her angry.

As she sipped her rye and loved on him, Ellie resolved to call his vet first thing in the morning to talk. Clearly, there was something wrong with him, and she needed to nip whatever this new problem was in the bud.

CHAPTER THREE

Ellie stepped out of her cab, looked up at Ambassador Plaza, and couldn't help but smile. It was her newest office redevelopment, and it was going well. It was a gorgeous, if neglected, art deco building that she'd led the acquisition of a few months ago and would be leading the redevelopment of for the foreseeable future.

"Good morning!" Skye Kohl, her good friend and the broker heading up the leasing efforts, exclaimed as she met Ellie on the plaza in front of the building.

Ellie hugged her, then gave her a once-over. "Morning, Skye. You look amazing. Like, glowing."

Skye was always perfectly put together in a designer suit and without a strand of blond hair out of place—unlike Ellie's mess of wild curls that she self-consciously adjusted—but there was something extra today. "Oh, probably the quickie Bailey and I had upstairs right before you got here."

"The what?" Ellie could feel her eyes go wide and struggled to keep her mouth from falling open. Had Skye really just admitted to something like that on a job site? *Completely professional and in the closet until just recently* Skye Kohl?

"Oh my God, Ellie. Your face. I can't even." Skye was laughing so hard, tears were starting to trickle out of the corners of her eyes. She gasped a few times, and Ellie hoped she'd said that just to get a rise out of her. She wasn't a prude but didn't think public sex prudent. Especially not at work, where a random construction worker who worked for Bailey, Skye's girlfriend, could hear. "Priceless, Ellie, just priceless. Almost makes me wish it was true."

"Wow. And to think, six months ago, you wouldn't have even admitted to being interested in women anywhere near work, and now you're joking about sex with your girlfriend where anyone could hear you." Ellie laughed at how much Skye had changed. For the better. But she couldn't help a pang of jealousy. Not about Bailey. She was certainly gorgeous but far too young for Ellie. But about Skye finding her person. Ellie had been searching for the elusive "One" for more than a decade and was...discouraged. To put it lightly.

"No one was around to hear. And for the record, we didn't have sex here. That quickie was at Bailey's place before we left." She laughed again and linked her arm with Ellie's as she turned them toward the building.

"It's a good thing I love you." Ellie laughed but felt a tug at her heart over Iris's death. Skye was Ellie's oldest friend after Iris. They'd known each other since shortly after Ellie had graduated college, and Ellie had been a mentor to the then-teenage Skye, and she loved her dearly. But Iris had been her friend nearly from the womb, and knowing she'd never get to talk to her again felt like someone had opened her chest and poured salt all over her heart.

Skye must have noticed her somber silence as she said, "How are you doing? Really?" She had been at Iris's funeral, but they hadn't seen each other since.

Ellie wasn't really sure how to answer. Heartbroken? Lonely? Trying to figure out what her world looked like without her best friend, the closest thing she'd had to a sister? Trying to understand why Iris had forced a dog upon her? Especially a dog who seemed to have more issues than she'd originally realized. Or maybe he'd just had a bad day yesterday.

Skye stopped walking and unlinked their arms and squeezed her hand.

"I'm...hanging in there. Trying to focus on work. And dealing with this horse of a dog that she guilted me into taking." Ellie shook her head and sighed.

"I'm so sorry, Ellie, but a dog? You?" She scoffed.

"I want to take offense at your incredulous tone, but I have the same question myself." Her teeth clenched, and she relaxed her jaw as she exhaled, still exhausted over the mess she'd walked into the previous night.

"How is *that* going?"

Ellie was trying to put into words the roller coaster the last twelve—could it have only been twelve—days had been when Bailey popped out from seemingly nowhere in her typical uniform of jeans and a blazer.

"Good morning, ladies. If it isn't my favorite client and my favorite broker. Together." Her grin stretched from ear to ear. Skye must not have been kidding about their quickie.

Another bolt of jealousy struck Ellie, and she worked hard to school her face so neither of them would realize it. She laughed. "You act as though you didn't know we were meeting here. Or that you didn't arrive here *with* Skye this morning."

"How did you know?" Bailey asked, innocence in her voice.

"Please. You two basically live together now." Ellie rolled her eyes but still smiled. She so desperately wanted someone to love, but she was so busy with work, and after a difficult breakup and now Atlas…she was taking a much-needed break from dating. But her longing for someone to share her life with—a companion to walk through life beside—hadn't stopped because of it.

When Ellie thought she might actually gag if she watched them make gooey eyes at each other anymore, she cleared her throat. "Well, now that's settled, can we go see the crown jewel that your crews have been working tirelessly on, Bailey?"

Her face turned red. "Oh yes. Of course. Sorry. After you." She handed hard hats to both Skye and Ellie and gestured for them to head to the elevators. They were all awkwardly silent as the car meandered to the rooftop, but when the doors opened, Ellie gasped at how great it all looked.

Bailey's company, City Beautiful Construction, did great work, but this roof-deck went above and beyond what she'd even been hoping for. The city views were one of the reasons she'd pursued this acquisition, but she hadn't been exaggerating when she'd said this was the "crown jewel."

"I don't know who to compliment more, Skye for your vision or Bailey for your implementation, but either way, this rooftop deck is going to sell, sell, sell."

"I'll give all the credit to Bailey, but I am going to lease this building because of how much people will love this deck. Guaranteed. You've got good views of the lake, good views of the sunset. It can be used for private events, weddings..." Skye trailed off as she stared dreamily and spun three-hundred-and-sixty degrees.

Ellie was not pleased that they were behind schedule on the tenant lounge and a few of the finishing touches in the lobby, but lead times on materials couldn't be helped, and this amenity space was going to more than make up for it.

After going through her recent tours, Skye brought them back to catching up. "Tell us more about this dog, Ellie. Do you have any pics?"

Atlas looked so sad all the time that she really hadn't taken many, but she pulled out her phone to show them the couple that she did have.

"Oh my God, that face breaks my heart," Bailey said. "He's such a beefy boy." She sighed, pulled the phone out of Ellie's hand, and zoomed in on his face.

Skye joined in the lovefest. "Look at those sad eyes."

"Yeah, well, he had those sad eyes on display last night after he tore my entire house apart," Ellie mumbled.

Bailey and Skye looked up in sync, their expressions mirrors of each other with brows drawn, mouths curved down. It was almost comical. "Poor baby," Bailey said.

"Me?"

"No, Atlas."

"Why poor Atlas? He's the one who tore my entire place apart. I mean, couch cushions, coatrack, bookshelf, he pulled all the towels down—dish towel in the kitchen, hand towels in the bathrooms—and carried them into the living room." In what world was he the one to receive sympathy here? Maybe they didn't realize just how long it had taken to clean all that shit up.

Bailey gave her a sad smile and squeezed her shoulder. "Because he's had a lot of upheaval in his life, and he's having separation anxiety. He's not doing it to be bad. He doesn't understand what's going on, and he needs a release for all the anxiety. What did you do with him when you left today? Do you have a dog walker?"

A dog walker? Was that a thing? "Iris had a kennel in her condo that I took along with his other stuff, so I put him in it this morning."

Bailey winced and inhaled sharply. That wasn't good. "How did he go into the kennel?"

"He walked in and lay down. His head hung, and he had a sad expression, but he always looks sad."

"You didn't have to force him to go in?" Bailey asked.

"No, he walked right in."

"Okay, what about a walker?"

"I didn't know walkers were a thing," she said, an image of a green zombie with stiff legs walking Atlas flashing in her mind. But that was quickly replaced with guilt as she wondered how much her lack of knowledge about how to care for a dog was hurting him. Damn Iris for putting her into this position. "How do I find one? And I forgot to mention the part where he almost got us killed trying to attack another dog. If I hadn't caught myself on a tree, he would have pulled us into traffic. That might make finding a walker harder, won't it?"

"Yeah, that sounds like reactivity. I'll send you some resources. You may want to take him to the vet to see if there's anything wrong, and if there isn't, a friend of mine had a reactive dog and took him to a behaviorist. It was a huge help. I don't remember her name, but I'll get it."

A behaviorist? Wasn't there a show or something called *The Behaviorist*? No, maybe that was *The Mentalist*? Regardless, it all sounded like new age mumbo jumbo to Ellie, but she puffed out her cheeks and sighed. "Please send it over." She would do pretty much anything to improve this situation. She couldn't let Iris down. Or Atlas. It had only been twelve days, but he already had a hold on her heart.

❖

Ellie could hear rustling in her condo as she slid her key into the lock and felt dread heavy upon her shoulders before she'd even opened the door. She'd planned on slipping home to check on Atlas in the middle of the day, but the phone had kept ringing, and meetings ran over, and it somehow ended up being seven p.m., and she was still at the office.

She'd hurried out, but poor Atlas had been home alone for more than thirteen hours, and Ellie feared what she was about to walk into. She'd left him in the crate, but there was so much movement, she was sure he'd gotten out.

When she opened the door, she first felt relief. Atlas was still in the kennel, door and sides all intact. He appeared to have been turning around until she walked in, but as soon as he realized she was there, he started jumping around, trying to paw at the door.

"Hey, buddy," she said in her most soothing tone. "I'm going to let you out, just settle down, good boy."

The soothing tone did not work as he started to get more frantic, so she bit the bullet and opened the door. Pandemonium was the only word she could think as he ran around like a rabid raccoon. He jumped up and down before running into the kitchen and doing laps out there.

Ellie let him have at it as she removed first one heel then the other, alternating between flexing her toes wide and then sinking them into her plush, living room carpet. She was unclasping her second earing when she walked into the kitchen and squinted at the streaks on her light gray cabinets and slate refrigerator. What was that?

Atlas chose that moment to brush past, and as he did, he left a red streak at knee height across her cream-colored slacks. What the… Was that blood?

"Come here, Atlas."

He charged back, and she was barely able to get him to stop before he barreled into her legs. She dropped to her knees and began looking him over. When she got to his tail, she saw the tip was bloody, and all the hair had been chewed off the last quarter inch.

"Atlas, what did you do, buddy?" She sank onto her behind and swung her legs in front, allowing him to lie across her. "Did you do this to yourself?" He nuzzled into her elbow and let out a long exhale that seemed far too human. "Are you okay?"

He looked up at her with those sad eyes, and she didn't think he was. "Me either, buddy. Me either. I miss her too. So much."

Tears burned in her eyes, and her throat closed up. She panicked for a moment, afraid she couldn't breathe, but somehow, she pulled in air through the sealed passage of her trachea.

Iris couldn't be gone, and yet, she was. How had things gotten so far out of control with Atlas? How was Ellie going to live the rest of her life without her best friend in the world? And what the fuck was she going to do with this gentle giant of a dog who apparently lost his shit when he was left alone?

She couldn't stop the tears and didn't bother to try as they bubbled up, and sobs tore through her. Atlas pushed himself up until his head was resting on her shoulder. She buried her face into his neck and cried.

Chapter Four

M rs. Murphy, you have to understand that your dog has a limited physical capability." Hayden tried to keep the frustration out of her voice. This was the third time she'd seen Mrs. Murphy and Winston. Their first visit had been productive, but since then...less so.

Winston came from an unlicensed breeder who hadn't even provided a grassy patch for the chihuahuas he bred constantly. Winston kept going to the bathroom on the tile floor because it felt like the outdoor concrete on his little paws. That had been months ago, and Hayden had given Mrs. Murphy the skills to get him peeing outside consistently. But Mrs. Murphy refused to see reason.

"He's a small dog. He has a small bladder. You can't *train* him to have a bigger bladder. He can only hold it for so long."

Mrs. Murphy huffed. "That's not true, Dr. Brandt. He only does it when he's angry at me. He's acting out."

"How do you know he's mad and acting out?" Hayden took a deep breath through her nose and schooled her features. She loved animals and wanted to help them all, which unfortunately, meant training their owners to understand them better. She reminded herself that patience was a virtue. A virtue she wasn't flush with, but she was working on it.

"Well, he gets mad when I leave him home alone for a few hours." She stared like Hayden was the one missing a piece of critical information.

It was painful not to roll her eyes. "Mrs. Murphy, did you hear what you just said? It's when you leave him home for a few *hours*. He's not mad. He *physically* can't hold it. If you're going to be gone for more than a few hours, you need to either get a dog sitter or be willing to train him to go on pee pads."

"Pee pads are...disgusting."

Hayden smothered a laugh as Mrs. Murphy's face looked like she'd been ordered to clean a public restroom with her tongue. "Your other option is to hire a dog walker."

"But I don't want some stranger in my house." She nearly spat the words.

"You could take Winston with you. But if you don't want him to relieve himself on your floors, these are your options. He's doing the best he can. He's not choosing to disappoint you."

"But that doesn't..." Mrs. Murphy trailed off as she no doubt thought through everything Hayden had just said.

After twenty more painful minutes trying to tactfully convince Mrs. Murphy that she was the problem, not Winston, Mrs. Murphy finally gave in and left, and Hayden sighed in relief. She stared out the window in her office and wished people would understand that dogs thought differently than humans. She squeezed her hand into a fist. It was so damn frustrating that people assumed that the logic of a dog was the same as their own. She sincerely hoped her message would sink in with Mrs. Murphy.

Shirley, the practice receptionist, buzzed on the intercom, her voice tinny over the speaker. "Hayden, there's a Dr. Prewster on line one for you."

Excellent. Hayden had been hoping Dr. Prewster would be intrigued enough to call her back. "Thanks, Shirley. How much time do I have before my next appointment?"

"Twelve minutes."

Perfect. Hayden closed her office door. She didn't want Shirley or Britt, her resident who was getting very close to their own behaviorist certification, to hear. She settled in her chair and pressed the speaker button on her phone. "Dr. Prewster, thanks for getting back to me."

"Dr. Brandt, I'll admit, I was a little surprised to hear from you. How have you been? How long has it been? A year? Two?"

Hayden tapped a finger on her desk as she struggled to remember. "Two. I think? Maybe three? When the convention was in Salt Lake City. My practice in Chicago is so busy, it's hard to keep track."

"Oh, I'm sure. The same here."

It was heartbreaking how animals needed help pretty much everywhere. But that was why Hayden loved her job so much. She and Dr. Prewster caught up on the most difficult clients they'd had—human—and those most in need—dogs—before Hayden circled to the reason she'd reached out. "This is probably a weird question given that we haven't spoken in a few years, but back then, you'd mentioned you might be getting close to retiring. Do you still have an eye on that?"

Dr. Prewster laughed. "My wife wishes I would have retired a year ago, but I just keep hanging in there. I want to, yet I don't…but it certainly is looming."

Excellent. "Have you started talking to anyone about selling your practice?"

"Not really. I've had general conversations with a few people, but nothing serious, and I don't have any partners to sell to. It's one of the reasons I've been dragging my feet."

"I *might* be interested in the next year or so." Hayden didn't want to formally commit but open a line for a conversation as a what-if.

"Really? And move to New Orleans? What about your Chicago practice?"

She didn't want to get into her true reasons for her wanderlust and tendency toward impermanence. "Eh," she grunted, buying a few seconds. "I just feel ready for a change. I love my practice, but I'm not from here. I don't have any family or ties. In fact, I was born in New Orleans, so there's a little piece of it that pulls at me. And it doesn't hurt that I have a resident about to get their certification who, I think, would be interested in stepping in." She ran her fingers through her short hair. That was all true, other than the bit about New Orleans calling to her. It was much more of an itch to go anywhere versus an itch to go someplace in particular, and New Orleans was as good a place as any.

"Interesting." Dr. Prewster added a fourth syllable to the word as she drew it out. "I need to talk to my wife, but this could work out nicely. Would you be willing to come down here and work with me for a few months to get a feel for my clientele before making the full switch?"

"I think that'd be the best approach."

"Give me a little time to think through some more logistical issues, but why don't we plan to connect next week and discuss further?"

It felt as though a weight had been lifted when Hayden hung up. That itchiness that had been plaguing her for a couple of weeks felt relieved, almost like she'd put ointment on a rash. It still itched, but it was more a vague prickling versus angry and inflamed. That glimpse of an exit strategy relieved some of the pressure, which seemed strange since anything meaningful would still be a year or so away, but knowing she had the beginning of a plan was freeing.

"Hayden?" Shirley buzzed in on the intercom, again. "Your five thirty is here."

"Great. Please send them in." Punctual. Often, that five thirty slot was booked by someone who worked during the day, and frequently, clients didn't leave themselves enough time to leave work, go home, get their dog, and make it to her office by five thirty.

She grabbed a handful of treats and was walking around her desk to greet her newest clients, both human and canine, when the door opened, and a tall woman with a mess of wild, almost frizzy, curls tried to walk in backward.

She was clearly attempting to coax a dog into the office even though the dog was still hidden behind the wall. "Come on, Atlas. Get in here." The woman whose name Hayden should have checked before she'd stood sounded frazzled, her voice shaky.

Hayden stepped toward them. "Hi, I'm Dr. Hayden Brandt." She didn't reach out to shake since both of the woman's hands were white-knuckled on the leash—must be a pretty big dog, though he was still out of her line of sight—but she did pull a few treats out of her pocket.

"Dammit, Atlas. Get. In. Here." It looked like she was trying to drag the dog in by the leash as she leaned farther back without getting the dog to move any closer.

Hayden placed her other hand lightly on the woman's shoulder. "Can I help?" It was apparent this woman needed a *lot* of help.

"God, please, yes." The woman yanked the leash again, and again, no movement from the other end. Her voice was filled with frustration, but it was also a little sexy. Sultry, Hayden would call it if she was forced to put a name to the nearly gravely quality.

She touched the woman's forearm softly and kept her voice as low and calming as she could. "Take a step toward him and allow the leash to go slack."

The woman immediately followed instructions—admittedly, a little hot—and Hayden was able to move behind her and finally look at the dog.

Atlas was a big boy. About one-hundred pounds, maybe a little more, and it was all muscle. He looked like he had some pit bull and some boxer in him, likely with some other dogs mixed in there too. Even though Hayden was having a hard time remembering the woman's name, she remembered everything about Atlas's initial consult notes. He'd never shown aggression toward people unless they had dogs, and that seemed to be a fear response.

She turned sideways to squeeze through the blocked doorway, and her hips brushed the woman's thigh. The unexpected contact made Hayden jolt back into the door frame and rebound into the woman again. "Oh, I'm so sorry," Hayden said as she regained her balance but stayed awkwardly close as they both were stuck.

"No problem." The woman looked at her, and Hayden's mouth went a little dry. She was wearing very sexy, horn-rimmed glasses, and the dark brown eyes staring from behind them were wide and beautiful. Her olive skin glowed even in the fluorescent light of the office.

Hayden caught herself before she stared for too long. She cleared her throat. "You trying to drag him in here is only going to make him dig in more." Hayden pulled her gaze away and took a closer look at Atlas. "He's terrified right now. I'm going to see if I can coax him with some treats." She stepped through the doorway and crouched to be at Atlas's level. She brought the back of her treat-less hand toward him to sniff. He touched her hand with his nose and tentatively licked it before lying down.

"Good boy," she said softly, no inflection to keep him calm. "Do you like treats?" His ear quirked, but he stayed rooted in place, gaze averted. "I saw that ear, buddy. I know you like treats." That time, he lifted his head and looked at her with heartbreaking eyes.

She held out a treat, still giving him lots of room. He sniffed at it and took it so gently from her fingers, something cracked in her. "Yes, you're a good boy, aren't you, Atlas?" She gave him a few more treats and lured him into the office slowly, step-by-step.

The woman with the sexy librarian glasses looked at Hayden like she was a miracle worker, and Hayden couldn't help but judge a little. If that basic bit of dog training was impressive, this woman must not know a single thing about dogs. What was she doing with such a large, difficult boy?

"Please have a seat, Ms...." Hayden still couldn't recall her name and chastised herself again for not checking the file. She'd been distracted following the call with Dr. Prewster.

"Efron, but please call me Ellie." She ran a hand through her mass of unruly curls and shook it out.

Hayden was momentarily distracted watching those soft curls fluff around her face and settle into place. "Ellie, then. You can call me Dr. Hayden. Or Hayden. Either way." Why had she just said that? She always went with Dr. Brandt or Dr. Hayden. Never just Hayden.

"Dr. Hayden." Her smile was large, but Hayden could see the strain at the corners.

Hayden gestured to the visitor chair as her heart fluttered at how something as innocuous as her name sounded sexy on Ellie's lips. "Please, have a seat."

Ellie started to sit, but Atlas picked that moment to hunch and take a shit right there in the middle of the office.

Thankfully, Hayden had vinyl plank flooring for this exact reason.

"Atlas, no," Ellie yelled. "Oh my God, I'm so sorry."

Hayden couldn't help the laugh that bubbled out, even though she worried Ellie would think she was laughing at her. "It's fine. This happens all the time." Atlas was still pooping, and Hayden laughed even harder. Had he not shit in two days? She pushed the intercom to the front desk. "Shirley, can you please bring in the code brown emergency supplies?"

"On the way, Dr. Brandt," Shirley said with more cheer than was natural, given that she was about to clean up the largest pile of crap Hayden had ever seen.

Within seconds, Shirley trotted in carrying a shower caddy containing poop bags, a roll of paper towels, and several cleaning supplies so they were covered no matter what surface the mess ended up on. "Whew! Did that dog eat a dead squirrel or something?"

Ellie tried grabbing the cleaning supplies, but Shirley waived her off. Hayden used to keep supplies in her office, but Shirley liked to be useful and had asked for so little that allowing her to be in charge of something that certainly wasn't Hayden's favorite task seemed like a no-brainer. She only felt a *little* guilty about it.

"Are his poops normally this big?" Shirley said.

Ellie's voice wavered, but she said, "They're normally big, but this is excessive even for him."

Clearly, Ellie was out of her depth, and Hayden felt a mix of sympathy and annoyance. Though anything was better than Atlas being in a shelter, Hayden supposed, and at least Ellie had brought the big guy in to get help. She was trying. "Relax, Ellie," she finally said. "This isn't the first time—and it won't be the last—that a dog shits in my office."

Ellie started to laugh, and Hayden felt a little tension melt. "I just never know what to expect from him. When I first got him, he was so mild mannered. I thought this was going to be a breeze. And then his behavior when I wasn't around flipped, and I began questioning everything. Not that it helped. I've got this dog now, and that's that. But with him, it's like I have to always expect the unexpected." She snorted, and it sounded a little like a sob.

Hayden wanted to dig into Atlas's evolving behavioral issues but decided to start at the beginning. "Tell me how you ended up with him. How long has it been?" Ellie clearly wasn't a dog expert, and it was bizarre that such a novice would have adopted such a large dog with so many challenges.

"I…" Ellie trailed off, and suddenly, tears were streaking down her face.

Hayden didn't have a damn clue what the fuck to do. She must have missed the day in vet school when they'd talked about what to do when a total stranger started crying in the office for seemingly no reason.

Shit. Hayden tried to be comforting, even with her socially awkward personality. She laid a hand on Ellie's shoulder. "Whatever it is, it's going to be okay. Let's sit on the couch?" She guided Ellie to the couch on the far side of her office, Atlas following, and gently pulled on her hand until she sat—very close—on the soft leather sofa.

Hayden desperately tried to figure out what the hell she was supposed to do. Should she put a hand on Ellie's leg? Probably too intimate. Should she put an arm around her shoulders? Hell. She wanted to run as quickly as she could but settled for continuing to hold Ellie's hand and squeezing it. She'd seen that in movies, right? Why couldn't this woman have been Britt's patient? They were better with the people. She finally landed on, "Do…you…want to talk about it?" but felt completely unsure if she wanted Ellie to take her up on the offer or not.

"I—…" Ellie started, then threw her arms around Hayden's neck and began crying in earnest. Not quiet demure sobs but full, body quaking, soul shaking sobs.

Hayden instinctively wrapped her arms around Ellie and let her cry. Having Ellie in her arms wasn't unpleasant, despite the awkwardness. Rather than try to say anything she wasn't adept enough to articulate, she simply held on. She alternated between rubbing her back in small, soothing circles and lightly patting it.

Hayden's shoulder was soon wet with tears. The heat of Ellie's breath tickled her neck, and she struggled not to squirm. Ellie simply needed someone to hold her for a few minutes, and Hayden was trying to oblige. And it should have felt incredibly uncomfortable— Hayden wasn't sure if she'd ever comforted someone the way she was now—but the way Ellie melted into her side…wasn't. It was the most non-sexual contact Hayden had had with another human since her grandmother had passed away, and she didn't want to admit it, but it almost felt…good. Before she even realized what she was doing, her other hand made its way to Ellie's hair and stroked it as she made comforting sounds and pulled Ellie a little closer.

CHAPTER FIVE

Ellie had no idea what had come over her, but she couldn't stop crying. Dr. Hayden's calm voice asking how she had ended up adopting Atlas made the memories of losing Iris so poignant, and combined with Atlas's cringeworthy and enormous crap, she'd lost her ability to hold her own shit together.

As she gradually got her sobs under control, she started to realize that she felt like she was ensconced in a warm cocoon. Someone's arms were around her, rubbing her back, soothing. Around her sniffles, she could smell the faint aroma of white tea and aloe that felt clean and yummy. But why was it so all-encompassing? Who was rubbing her back and murmuring soothing words?

Oh fuck. Had she flung herself into the arms of the sexy Dr. Hayden? Had she snotted on her neck? Ellie tried not to laugh at this unbelievable situation and figure out how to move away with the least amount of awkwardness.

She couldn't come up with a way, and now that her tears had slowed, it seemed weird to keep her face buried in Dr. Hayden's neck. She took a large sniff and said a quick prayer that a trail of snot from her nose to Dr. Hayden's neck didn't exist. "I'm…uh…really sorry about that. I don't know what came over me. I don't do that sort of thing. Ever." She sniffed again, and Hayden handed her a tissue from a conveniently located box on the side table, as if she was at a funeral home, though that thought had her clearing her throat again in an effort to stave off more tears. Mortifying.

Hayden squeezed her hand and slid down on the couch, creating a more appropriate amount of distance between them. "I'll admit, I've never had someone cry in my office before, but it's completely okay. When dealing with animals, you have to expect the unexpected."

Ellie swiped her nose a few times just in case. She coughed in an effort to find her voice again and ran a hand across Atlas's head and scratched his ear. She wasn't sure when he'd put his head in her lap, but she appreciated the comfort, especially now that Dr. Hayden had moved away. "I just lost my best friend in the entire world. We've been friends for more than thirty-five years, and now she's gone, and I'm just feeling a little lost. I'm so sorry. I promise, I'm not normally like this, but I haven't had the time to just let go, and...I don't know. Shit. I'm sorry. I'm rambling. You don't need to hear my entire life story. But she's the reason I have this big guy."

"I see," Hayden said, but the furrow between her brows said she didn't see at all. She did reach out again and squeeze Ellie's forearm before saying, "I'm so sorry for your loss. I'm sure you're going through a lot. Losing someone is never easy."

Atlas sighed and pushed more firmly against Ellie's legs as she continued to rub his head. "Thank you. She was my ride or die, the closest thing I've ever had to a sister, the person I planned to room with at the nursing home when we were old and gray. And Atlas, he was her dog. Her last wish was for me to take him and not let him go back to the shelter. He apparently doesn't do well there, though when I picked him up, he didn't seem like he was doing that poorly. Just sedate and quiet. Maybe depressed?"

Dr. Hayden went to her desk and grabbed a file and pen but came back to sit on the couch, and Atlas finally lay down and seemed to relax. "Tell me more about how he behaved when you first brought him home and how and when that started to change."

Ellie told her everything from the first moment she'd laid eyes on Atlas through him tearing her house apart and his self-harm of his tail. Her stomach roiled as she spoke of how badly things had gotten, but she was able to keep a waver out of her voice.

She ended by saying, "I'm praying you can help me because he's such a sweet loving boy when it's just us at home. But out on walks or when he's alone...I just don't know what to do. I made a promise to my best friend, but I can't imagine a world where every day my house is destroyed, or he's chewed on his tail so badly that it bleeds." Okay, there might have been a waver in her voice at the end there. She hoped Dr. Hayden hadn't noticed. Though, what pride did she even have left? She just needed help.

Dr. Hayden gave her a gentle smile that settled her nerves. "First, you're doing an admirable thing, taking on a dog who has some issues and committing to work with him on them, especially when you aren't a dog person."

"What makes you think I'm not a dog person?" Ellie said with a nervous chuckle. Why was she being such a dork? There was no denying Dr. Hayden was gorgeous—she looked a little like Halle Berry in that terrible *Bond* film with her light brown skin and short brown hair in a choppy pixie cut—but Ellie lived in a world with a lot of beautiful people and had never had issues. She had to be struggling because of the emotional stress. "You're right, I'm not a dog person, but when Atlas is sweet and calm, I think I might be becoming one. And I've made a commitment."

"That's an excellent first step." One corner of Dr. Hayden's mouth started to turn up. "However, it's important to understand that, although we can do some things to make your lives better, there isn't a *cure*. You should think of his issues as a type of chronic disease. We can likely address the severity of symptoms and tone them down with medication, lifestyle changes, and desensitization, but they are always going to be there. I want you to be prepared for that. He's not going to be that demure dog that you brought home from the shelter."

Ellie's heart sank at the thought, but anything had to be better than where they were. "Any improvement sounds like a good place to start."

The other corner of Dr. Hayden's mouth curled up, giving her an almost smile. "Excellent. It's not unusual for dogs to have very different behaviors in kennels versus once they are home and comfortable. It sounds like Atlas had shut down at the shelter to the point that even his crippling anxiety was suppressed as he turned in on himself out of self-preservation."

"Anxiety?" Ellie said. She didn't realize that was a thing in dogs.

"Yes, he suffers from both isolation distress as well as reactivity, both of which are rooted, in his case, in anxiety." Dr. Hayden rubbed her index finger along her lower lip, and Ellie was transfixed watching that finger trace the plump curve before she moistened her lips with her tongue.

Shit. Dr. Hayden had just said something, and she'd completely missed it. "I'm sorry?" She tried to seem nonchalant about her lapse in concentration and hoped Dr. Hayden hadn't noticed her staring.

The corners of Dr. Hayden's mouth tightened before she said, "I'd like to start him on a couple of drug therapies to give him—and you—some relief and give us time to work on some of his other issues. An antidepressant."

"Like Prozac?" Could dogs take medicines like that?

"Exactly. Keep his stress levels lower and allow you to desensitize him against some of the things he is most fearful of, being left alone and other dogs. In order for him to make gains, he has to be calm, below threshold."

"Threshold?" This dog thing had a whole different vocabulary. As she started to feel a little overwhelmed, Atlas lifted his head, and she scratched his ear, drawing a contented sigh. Ellie's heart melted a little bit more, and she remembered why she was doing all this.

"Threshold is his emotional breaking point, where he can't cope with any more triggers or stressors and will go into fight, flight, or freeze mode. Sometimes, it might seem like something random will set him off, but it's more likely there have been multiple triggers during the day that have stacked up until he meets threshold. And then he reacts. At home, it's destructive behavior, and on walks, it's aggressive behavior toward dogs."

"Oh," Ellie said so softly she could barely hear her own voice. It sounded terrible.

"Would you be able to either work from home or take a day or two off so you can be with him the first couple of days after we start medication?"

That was going to be dicey, but did she have a choice? "Maybe, but what about starting him over the weekend?"

"That might make him suffer for three more days."

"When you put it that way…I'll figure out how to make it work."
She forced a laugh that sounded unsteady to her ears. Great.

Dr. Hayden clicked her pen several times, and Ellie wondered if
that was an unconscious tick or if Ellie was annoying her. "I would
highly recommend using some of that time to meet with a few dog
sitters. At a minimum, you're going to want someone to come by a few
times a day for the next few weeks. Ideally, they'd stay at your house
the whole time while the medication's efficacy slowly increases."

She didn't like the sound of that at all. She lived in a secure
building, but the idea of someone having a key made her uncomfortable.

"I understand that this may not be possible, but whatever you
can do to leave him alone less is going to help. Even if you swing by
a few times a day. Also, I recommend setting up a camera. It's critical
that we get feedback on how he's doing so we can adjust the plan as
we go."

Good God. Ellie had no idea how complex this was all going to
be. She thought it would be some training classes, and miraculously,
Atlas would be healed, the perfect dog. Cameras and sitters and what
the actual fuck?

He rolled onto his back on Ellie's toes, and his big doe eyes
brought her frustration down again. How could she not do everything
in her power to help him? "I guess I can do that. Seems creepy, doesn't
it?"

"Not at all," Dr. Hayden said. "You can set them up discreetly
and turn them off when you're home. Newer ones have passwords
to keep hackers out, but it's important that we be able to watch his
behavior when you're not there. Does that make sense?"

Ellie was queasy at the thought of all of the privacy she was
sacrificing for this dog, but he'd wormed his way into her heart, and
she'd made a commitment to Iris. Fuck. "Yes." She sighed.

"Why don't we start him on the medication and give him two
weeks with those and the cameras, and next time, we can watch the
footage?"

"Okay," Ellie said, trying to ignore the overwhelming waves
crashing into her.

"I strongly urge you to get a sitter to come by at least once or
twice while you're at work, ideally more in the beginning. Do you

have a friend or family member who can sit with him? Maybe a teenager or a college student on break?"

"That could work." Her nieces might be candidates; that wouldn't involve having a stranger in her home.

"Also, when you walk him, take a large handful of treats. When you see another dog, try to shower him with goodies, and that will help teach him that good things happen when he sees scary things."

"Okay," Ellie said, feeling a strong urge to go home and snuggle under the covers with him and never leave the house again.

"Let me grab some resources on cameras and sitters, and I'll get the medication, and Shirley will help you make another appointment."

Although Ellie was still stressed about Atlas—and over her small breakdown—there was something about Dr. Hayden that inspired confidence. She was *finally* feeling like she was on the right path.

CHAPTER SIX

Hayden was rubbing the bridge of her nose after Ellie and Atlas's departure when a light tapping sounded at her door. "Come in," she called. She really didn't feel like chatting, but it had to be Britt. They typically connected with her at the end of the day to regroup and discuss any difficult cases. However, they also insisted on trying to be her friend.

"Well, that session went *really* late," Britt said as they walked in, looking dapper as always in a button-down shirt with the top couple of buttons open, khakis, and dark brown wing tips. "Was that because the dog was difficult or because the human was a MILF?"

Hayden could only shake her head as Britt laughed, their shaggy brown hair bouncing. "I don't think MILF is an appropriate term for a client, Britt." Not that they would ever say something like that when anyone else was around, but if they were going to give her a hard time, she'd give them a hard time right back, so she tried to use a stern tone.

"Whatever." They flopped in the guest chair Ellie had barely sat in before Atlas had taken that massive shit in the middle of the office. "But you haven't answered my question."

"I cannot deny that she's hot, but that certainly isn't the reason we went over. That was a literal shit show from the moment the dog pooped all over the floor until the client looked at me like I had three heads when I told her she should get a dog sitter. Oh, and including the ten minutes she cried in my arms."

Britt gaped. "She cried? In your arms?"

Hayden shook her head, her brain still refusing to fully process the fact that she'd held Ellie for more like fifteen minutes. And although the embrace had been awkward and uncomfortable, Ellie's hair had smelled amazing, like a field of strawberries. It had probably been the longest embrace she'd ever had since she'd never had a serious girl or boyfriend. *Not* that she would tell Britt any of that. That was way too personal. "Yes," she said simply.

"Have you ever had someone cry in your office before? I certainly haven't. We aren't those kinds of vets." They wrung their hands as though they were the one who'd had to deal with all of that emotion rather than her.

"I had to euthanize a few family pets in general practice, but even then, it wasn't like this. Normally, family members hold on to each other. Not me." Hayden felt the back of her neck and palms grow damp just thinking about all of that emotion. She wiped at her neck as though the emotional residue was still there. "Do you want a drink? You know emotions make me twitchy. I need to take the edge off."

Britt snorted. "What are you offering?"

Hayden didn't drink at the office regularly, but sometimes, while working on paperwork at the end of the day, a nice glass of something strong and brown really hit the spot. She opened her bottom desk drawer and took out two low-ball glasses and a bottle of Basil Hayden dark rye, turning the label so Britt could read it.

"Sure," they said. "But do you have a little club soda or something to cut it with?"

"Don't be a baby. You can handle it." She smirked. "Do you want it on a big rock? That'll help."

"Fine, I guess," they said on a long sigh. "If you're going to force me to go pro in my drinking game."

Even with as much as Hayden tried to avoid emotional connection, Britt always made her smile. Even if just on the inside. But she didn't want them to know she mostly liked them. That might encourage them to try harder at the friendship thing. The emotional wherewithal required to sustain a true friendship was more than Hayden could fathom, and she was unwilling to expose herself to the potential crushing pain when it was inevitably lost. Exhausted at the thought, she plinked two large rocks from her office freezer into both their glasses, then filled them until the dark brown liquid reached the middle of the ice cube.

They clinked their glasses and took a sip. Hayden loved that little burn in the back of her throat. The hint of spice from the rye lingered on her tongue. She was sure Ellie would taste a little spicy too. Whoa. Where had that come from? Britt was planting ideas.

They grimaced when they swallowed the first sip, their freckled white face flushing instantly. "Tell me more about this woman and her dog. Why'd she break down?"

"That's a long story, but the short of it is, her best friend just died and asked her to take care of Atlas, the dog, even though Ellie, the client, isn't a dog person. She's never had a dog and has been saddled with a difficult but very sweet boy. She's overwhelmed and grieving, and I get the sense she'd been bottling all of those emotions since her friend passed away very unexpectedly."

"That's gotta be hard."

"Yeah. She seemed so confident one minute and hopeless the next. Truthfully, I kept wanting to pull her into a hug, she looked so sad." The confession of how good Ellie had felt in her arms was on the tip of her tongue, but she swallowed it. She was surprised at her own candor but refused to share more.

"She was hot. Any chance you might pursue something?"

"Absolutely not. I don't get attached and definitely not with a client. It's bad for business. And that poor dog is going to need a lot of help. Today, we started with the basics and some medication, but he's going to need a lot more work."

"It's not like you're *her* doctor. You're going to work with her dog for a few months and go your separate ways. Why not have a little *fun* along the way?" Britt's eyes sparkled.

"It's unprofessional. And even if it wasn't, this woman drips of lifelong commitment. She's gorgeous, but one look at those earnest brown eyes, and you can feel that she's not 'one night of fun' material."

"Who says it has to be one night?" Britt winced as they took another sip, and Hayden bit the inside of her lip to keep from laughing again.

"Me. I say so," she said forcefully. "I don't do anything more than that. I've had more than..." She trailed off as she again almost shared too much about her past. "It doesn't matter because it's not going to happen. Feel free to ask her out if you want in a couple weeks." She threw her pen at Britt for fun.

They caught it just before it hit them in the chest. "You're going to have to do a better job than that if you want to actually hit me. I'm a wuss with drinks, but you're the wuss with anything requiring hand-eye coordination. But going back to your client. Ellie, was it?" At Hayden's nod, they continued, "She isn't my type, but damn, she looked amazing in that suit. She was like every thirsty sapphic's dream."

Hayden couldn't dispute that.

When she got home later that evening, she kicked off her shoes and greeted Chelsea, who began weaving between her legs. She fed her a can of wet food and made herself a quick veggie stir-fry, all the while thinking of Ellie and Atlas. She told herself it was because she felt bad for them. It was horrible to lose someone close to you—she certainly knew that from experience—and Ellie and Atlas had both lost someone. But Atlas was going to be a real challenge for a novice dog owner. Though Ellie was clearly committed, and Hayden respected that. A lot.

She tried to read a book but struggled to concentrate on the main characters and their struggles on the slopes of Mt. Everest, so she decided to do a little yoga and meditation before bed. That was her surefire way to clear her mind and her go to for self-care, but for some reason, she couldn't get a pair of chocolate brown eyes out of her mind. And that mass of unruly chestnut waves? She'd had a thing for women with long wavy brown hair since she'd had a bit of a sexual awakening at thirteen from both Maggie Gyllenhaal and Julia Roberts in *Mona Lisa Smile,* and a pleasant chill ran down her back thinking of both the women on-screen as well as the beautiful woman who'd been in her office a few short hours before.

As she listened to her guided meditation app, her damn brain kept turning the narrator's voice into a sultry one that she listened to for a long time before throwing in the towel on meditation and just letting the sexy voice lull her to sleep.

❖

It was three in the afternoon, and Ellie could hear Once Upon a Wine calling her name. She had a call scheduled with Skye to review leasing activity at Ambassador Plaza at four, but a stroke of inspiration struck her.

"Skye Kohl," Skye answered her phone efficiently and apparently without checking the caller ID.

"What do you think about changing venues for our leasing call this afternoon?" Ellie said, knowing Skye would recognize her voice.

"I could be in favor. What do you have in mind?"

"I have got to get out of this office, but I can't be out too late because my niece Andrea can only stay with Atlas until six thirty. Do you want to convene at Once Upon a Wine instead of Zoom?"

"I'm in. Do you mind if I invite Bailey?" Ellie could hear the smile on Skye's face through the phone.

"That works. I can tell you both about *the behaviorist* that I took Atlas to yesterday."

Skye waved when Ellie walked in forty-five minutes later. In typical Skye style, she was early and had already snagged a table. "I just ordered a bottle of our favorite cab. It should be here in a minute." She greeted Ellie with a wide smile as she stood to hug her.

"How'd you know I needed that?"

Skye squeezed her shoulder. "You wanted to do our leasing call at the wine bar. That's a pretty good indicator of how your day has been."

"Guess I wasn't being particularly elusive." Ellie felt her smile grow as the server brought their bottle along with three glasses. "There's my friend."

"Glad to see you value that wine more than you value me, Ellie."

"Entirely untrue. But both that wine and your company are salves for my tortured soul. Just wait until I tell you what this doctor has me doing. But let's talk marketing and leasing first."

As Skye spoke, Ellie realized how nervous she still was about this acquisition even months after the close. It was the largest value-add deal that she had purchased for her company, and it was risky. It wasn't necessarily career making or breaking, but the company was investing a lot of capital, and if this building fizzled rather than took off, she'd have a lot of explaining to do.

It was one of the reasons she was taking a short break from dating. She needed to be able to focus on work and not worry about disappointing someone because she wasn't around often enough.

Though as Bailey walked up with eyes only for Skye and they kissed sweetly before Bailey took the last empty seat, Ellie felt a tug in her heart that felt an awful lot like envy. But good God, if she didn't have time before, now that she had Atlas, she certainly didn't have any. And her heart was still bruised over Jessie, who'd left almost a year ago but had recently gotten married.

"What are you looking so pensive about, Ellie?" Skye asked.

Shit. She certainly wasn't going to tell them she'd been a little envious of their domestic bliss. She went with the still embarrassing but slightly less so, "I was thinking about Jessie. Did you hear she got married last month?"

"Ugh, I hadn't, but she wasn't right for you anyway. Even though I liked her, your personalities never felt like forever to me."

"On paper, she was perfect for me. Right family, right career, but it just…I don't know. Were my expectations too high? I know I worked a lot, but I tried to make time for her too." A painful burn tightened in her chest as she remembered when they'd broken up.

Jessie had been the one to end things—not surprising since she'd already started seeing someone else—and Ellie had swallowed her pride and tried to salvage the relationship, even though she'd known it wasn't right. She hadn't wanted to fail at *another* relationship. "Regardless, it still stings. She was the third woman I was serious with who left me for, or immediately met, the person they married. How is that the person I've become? I take care of myself, I work out, I eat healthy, I make good money. I'm a catch, aren't I?" How much had she had to drink that that just popped out of her mouth? She took a sip of wine and had to swallow around the lump that had suddenly blocked the wine's path.

Luckily, Skye and Bailey were quick to jump in. "You are an absolute catch," Skye said as Bailey said, "Of course you're a catch."

"I'm so sorry. You did *not* come here to listen to me whine about my love life or lack thereof. I swear, I'm not this pathetic." Ellie closed her eyes and took a deep breath and let it out slowly. Like in yoga. Exhale the negativity or something. She should find time to squeeze in a yoga class. Yeah, right. As if she had time for that with work and now this dog.

"You absolutely have the right to feel whiny and sad right now," Skye said. "You have a lot going on. We're your friends and are here for you when you're happy *and* when you're sad."

They laid their hands on Ellie's forearms and squeezed. They were assimilating into the same person in their coupledom. "How's Atlas doing?" Bailey said.

"We'll see when I get home. My niece is with him now, so he should be fine. He also started on doggie Zoloft today, which is supposed to help a little. Or make it so I can start helping him help himself. There's a lot of lingo, like thresholds and triggers, and I don't know. I spent half the office visit crying. It was perhaps the most embarrassing day of my life, so I couldn't fully pay attention to everything Dr. Hayden was saying, other than give him these meds, have someone come into my house and stay with him, and come back in two weeks." She swirled her wine and tried to ignore the burn in her gut at how her emotions had poured out that day in front of a complete stranger.

"I'm pretty sure I mentioned a dog walker or a dog sitter the other day," Bailey said with a self-satisfied smile.

"Well, yes, but I didn't have time to find one before I went to see her." Ellie huffed. How was she supposed to find time to search for walkers or sitters when she had to work all day and deal with Atlas at night? "Luckily, I remembered Andrea, my brother's older daughter, was home for the summer and probably didn't have a job. I gave her a call in the hope she could squeeze in some Atlas time between visiting her friends, but she's why I can't be out late. She's going barhopping with some friends in Fulton Market." Ah to be young and have the energy to barhop. "Oh, I forgot, Dr. Hayden also told me to put a bunch of creeper cameras all around my house so we can watch the videos of him when he's home alone. Can you believe that?"

Bailey said, "It's a good idea, and a lot of dog parents have them. It's nice to be able to look in on your baby while you're at work and make sure they're okay, especially with a new dog who has separation anxiety."

"You don't think it's weird the good doctor wants to watch the film with me when I go in?" It felt a little…intimate that she would be sitting next to Dr. Hayden watching video filmed in her own home, almost like having Dr. Hayden in her house. That thought made her uncomfortable and yet had little fireflies dancing around in her lower belly. It wasn't an unpleasant sensation.

"No," Bailey said and paused, pursing her lips. "And what does this *good doctor* look like?"

Ellie could feel her face starting to go warm as Bailey said "good doctor" like…*that*. "Uh, what do you mean?" She tried to play it cool, even though she knew her face would give her away.

"Is she a *good-looking good doctor*?" Skye smirked.

"I…" Ellie stammered. "I guess she's good-looking. If you go for that sort of thing."

"Hmm," Skye said. "Bailey, would you say you go for a good-looking type of thing?"

Bailey looked at the corner of the room and tapped her index finger against her lip. "You know, I think I do go for the good-looking type of thing. What about you, sweetheart?"

"Just shut up, both of you," Ellie said but couldn't help a laugh. "You don't have to be assholes. She is attractive. *Very* attractive. Picture a young Halle Berry but with fuller lips. Very full lips. And one of those weird nose rings. You know, like the one that they put in bull's noses?" Skye laughed, and Bailey snorted when Ellie squeezed her septum. "But young. Way too young for me. Not that I'm looking right now anyway."

"How young? She can't be that young if she's a vet, and that behaviorist piece had to take longer. And if you aren't looking, what would be the harm in a little fling with *the good doctor*?" Skye said.

"Don't plant that idea in my head! I need to focus on helping Atlas. I don't have time for any extra bullshit."

Skye gave her a knowing look, and Ellie's heart skipped a beat thinking about the peek of a tattoo that she'd seen along the edge of Dr. Hayden's collarbone in that button-up she'd been wearing yesterday. Skye was probably right. Dr. Hayden couldn't be as young as she looked, but it still didn't make her relationship material. Best to keep the good doctor Hayden firmly as a professional consultant. Maybe with a side of eye candy.

CHAPTER SEVEN

When Atlas and Ellie arrived for their next appointment, Hayden was impressed. Atlas was still clearly terrified, but Ellie was convincing him he wanted to come into the office with treats. Hayden had meant to mention that specifically but had forgotten.

She came out from behind her desk and squatted halfway between the desk and the door. "Hey, Atlas," she said calmly and held out the back of her hand while still several feet away. His ear twitched when she said his name, but he only had eyes for Ellie. So far. "Hey, Atlas, I've got some of those treats you liked last time."

He slowly turned his head toward her at the word treats and took the few steps to the back of her hand. When he nudged her hand gently with his cool wet nose, she opened it and gave him the treat. "Good boy." She stood and said, "Sorry about that. Sometimes, it's easier to put the dog at ease first, but it looks like he's doing at least a little better, yeah?" She stumbled over the last few words as her hand slid into Ellie's, and they shook. Her skin was cool and so soft, Hayden wondered how often she had manicures. Yet her grip was firm. Commanding. Hot as hell.

"Definitely a little better, and Atlas is, and should be, the star of the show here, so I am not offended at all." Ellie's face was more relaxed today, and when she smiled, her eyes lit up in a way they hadn't the previous visit, despite the small strain still present.

Hayden's heart quickened, and she quickly tried to redirect the conversation. "Excellent. Please have a seat." She gestured at one of the chairs on the near side of her desk. When Ellie sat and Atlas lay at her feet, Hayden sat in the second guest chair rather than behind her desk. "How is Atlas, and how are you?" She normally asked this question trying to determine the dog's progress as well as how the human was handling the experience because both factors were crucial to the dog's future. However, she realized her question now was focused on Atlas as well as how Ellie was handling the grief. Ellie looked like she was doing fine, but Hayden knew looks could be deceiving, and she genuinely wanted to know if Ellie was okay. And it wasn't as if anything about Ellie last time had said, "I'm about to dissolve sobbing into your arms."

Ellie stared at Hayden for two beats longer than decorum would dictate, and she felt the tips of her ears go hot under the scrutiny. Finally, Ellie cleared her throat. "He's doing better. I don't think I'd say a lot better, but better."

"Better is good. Even if it isn't much. Have you been treating him on walks? Has it been working?"

Ellie scratched his ear. "Yes, and yes. I'll admit, I didn't think it would help, but truly, it's made an impact. I can't always get his attention with the treats and sometimes have to catch myself on a tree before he pulls us into the street, but I'd say we have success sixty percent of the time, maybe? We also avoid other dogs like the plague." She shrugged.

"Sixty percent is better than zero. You could also consider having treats of different values. Something lower value for a small trigger and something higher value, like pieces of a hot dog or lunch meat, for dogs that he is particularly afraid of or anything he can't redirect himself from easily."

Ellie pulled a leather notebook out of her bag and started writing. "Hmm. Okay."

Hayden's mouth went dry when Ellie looked up and adjusted her glasses higher on her nose. She cleared her throat. "How is his new routine? Do you have a sitter? Or is he still by himself all day?"

"Oh no." Ellie's neck flushed, and her hand drifted to her throat. "I've had my niece come stay with him since our last visit. She couldn't make it on Monday, but I met with one of the services you recommended and liked their walkers, so I had someone come twice on Monday, and he seemed okay. No major destruction that evening—either to himself or my condo—so I think that's a good sign."

"That's great." Hayden noticed Ellie didn't comment on how she herself was doing, but she let it go for the moment. "Were you able to record him?"

"Yes." Ellie pulled a laptop out of her briefcase and opened it on Hayden's desk. It was already queued up to the video, and Ellie hit play.

The video started just as a front door closed. Atlas was lying on a couch that seemed to be missing a few cushions. Odd choice of decor. He lifted his head when the door closed and let out a half-hearted bark but lay right back down. So far, reasonably good. "Do you see how even lying down, his ears are pointed straight up, and his forehead is wrinkled?" Hayden pointed at the screen.

"Yes," Ellie said quietly.

"Those are signs he isn't as relaxed as he looks. He's stressed, but he's holding it in. Oh see, now he's starting to self-soothe."

"Hmm?"

"Licking his paws, doing what he can to feel less stressed. Let's watch this on a faster speed." Hayden reached toward the laptop but was so focused on the screen, she didn't realize Ellie's fingers still claimed that real estate. Before she'd realized what was happening, their fingers were interlaced. She looked to Ellie, whose eyes had gone wide, and jerked her hand away. "Shit. Sorry." Hayden cleared her throat and pointed at the screen. "Click there twice."

She focused on Atlas and tried to tune out the buzz she felt from sitting so close to Ellie. She had a job to do, and Atlas's health was most important. At about three hours in, Atlas got up and started pacing from the living room into the study and back. He stared at the door and licked his nose for a moment, then went back to pacing. "So this is where his anxiety is starting to ratchet up. The pacing, the licking. Do you see?" For the first time since the hand incident, she looked at Ellie, who nodded a little faster than seemed normal. "I'd recommend not letting him go more than three hours before you have a walker or a sitter come by. It's going to be important to monitor his progress, and you may be able to start extending this time, but for now, I'd keep three hours max."

"Not a problem." Ellie scratched Atlas's neck, and his back leg was moving in time. He was a handsome boy, and Hayden didn't know why, but that reflexive action always melted her heart.

They watched the rest of the video, and nothing else jumped out as concerning, other than how Atlas behaved when the walkers arrived to take him out. "Does he always act like this when anyone gets there?" she said. He was jumping into the walkers, spinning, and jumping into them again.

Ellie sighed. "Yes. He's a little frantic when I get home too, and that's pretty much always how he is. Even when my niece has been there all day."

"How well-trained is he otherwise? Can you get him to sit or lie down and stay?"

"Um. Not exactly. Sometimes, he'll sit, but that seems to be his only command, and it's pretty hit-or-miss." Ellie averted her eyes.

"It's nothing to be embarrassed about, Ellie." She laid her hand on her arm. "Seriously, you've had him a few weeks? And your friend had him for a few weeks before that, right?"

"But I don't know what to do to make him listen." Ellie's voice was small, but she did bring her gaze back to Hayden's. Behind her glasses, her eyelashes were dark and long and framed deep brown eyes. They looked so sad, and Hayden used every bit of self-control to not run her thumb along Ellie's jaw and instead found her way back to professional, nearly detached Dr. Brandt.

She realized removing her hand from Ellie's arm was also crucial in that endeavor, so she squeezed gently, then released and grabbed her mug of peppermint tea from the desk. "You're doing the right things. You brought him to see me, but he's also going to need basic obedience training."

"Aren't we working on that here?" Ellie's fingertips grew white, and she clutched the armrest as panic flashed across her face.

Hayden gave her a soft smile, trying to calm her. "Not really. I'm going to work with you through medication and counterconditioning. However, it's important that you learn how to communicate with him and that he learns to listen to you."

"Can I send him to a trainer? A friend of mine has an ugly little chihuahua, and she sent him to a summer camp for dog training."

"You can, but it's hard to find a trainer who will commit to only training one dog at a time on their campus. And a lot of those don't use the force-free training method, which could be dangerous, especially for a dog like Atlas, who already has underlying reactivity issues." In a perfectly timed shuffle, Atlas harrumphed and rolled onto his back, giving Hayden an adorable upside-down sharky face smile. "I know, buddy, you're not aggressive, are you? Just misunderstood." She rubbed his belly, and he shimmied a little closer on his back.

Ellie's shoulders slumped. "Oh," she said. "I'm not sure how to find time for everything."

"It doesn't have to be a huge time commitment. Maybe an hour a week with an instructor, then fifteen minutes a day for the rest of the week, practicing what you've learned. Also, doing the training with him will help you bond and establish trust, which will help with the anxiety. And his understanding basic commands will help facilitate the counterconditioning we're going to work on."

"That doesn't sound too bad." Ellie's lips curved up into a half-smile.

"I'll give you a list of trainers who would be great."

"Not…you?" Ellie asked.

Was Hayden imagining it, or was that hurt on Ellie's face? "I'm a behaviorist. I'm sorry, Ellie. It's not my wheelhouse." It wasn't until her hand landed on Ellie's that she realized what she'd done, but it would be weirder to touch her and pull away, so she gave in and laid her hand lightly on top of Ellie's.

"You say that, but you also said it wasn't that big of a deal. The basics of obedience training, right? I'd pay you, of course." Ellie flipped her hand and interlaced their fingers. Squeezed. Holy shit. "Please."

Hayden's tongue felt swollen at the pleading in Ellie's eyes. "Um, you'd be better served with a trainer. Also, your wallet would appreciate it. A basic obedience series with a trainer is probably less than one session with me. Even if you had a trainer come to your house." There was no way spending more time with this woman was going to be a good choice. Ever.

"Money doesn't matter. Whatever you want to charge is fine. I'll pay you double. Or triple. Or whatever you want since it isn't really what you do. Atlas and I know you. He's comfortable with you. He isn't comfortable with many people. And we have a route that we walk to get here that has the fewest number of dogs. I've scouted it without him. I don't have time to figure out another route to another place." Her palm was so warm. She squeezed Hayden's hand again and added a swipe of her thumb across the back. The little thrum that had been jittering in Hayden's heart turned into the beat of a drum line. *Tat-tat-tat-a-tat-tat*, beating at the speed of hummingbird wings.

The answer was categorically no. Absolutely not. She'd spent too many years in vet school to spend her precious free time, of which she didn't have enough, training a dog. Her few free hours were better spent with a good book and a glass of wine. "I guess I could do that. Atlas is a sweet boy."

Before Hayden could even process what was happening, Ellie had used their joined hands to pull Hayden up and into her arms. "Thank you. Thank you. *Thank you!*"

With heels, it felt like Ellie was a foot taller, but it was probably more like five inches. But that meant Hayden's face was pressed into Ellie's neck. How could she smell so good? It was like strawberries and sunshine and the cleanness of the air after a summer rain. Okay, so maybe her face didn't *have* to be pressed into Ellie's neck, but she was caught off guard, and that was the way it was facing when Ellie had embraced her. Despite calling herself twenty types of bonehead, she couldn't turn away. She could have rested her chin on Ellie's shoulder and faced the wall. But she didn't.

And good lord. Ellie rubbed a hand up and down Hayden's back—twice—and Hayden finally relaxed, tightening her embrace until Ellie let out a puff of air that ruffled through Hayden's short hair. She knew she needed to let go. Push back. Step away. Anything to end this hug. One more breath, though. One more second. After one more beat, she was going to step back.

But one beat bled into two and three, and Hayden lost count. Her hands ached with the need to move, but she pressed harder into Ellie's back to try to prevent it, but those traitorous fingers of hers started to move anyway. Just a little, but she couldn't help herself. She *needed* to feel the silkiness of Ellie's suit jacket beneath her fingertips.

Thankfully, Atlas jolted them out of the moment, unfroze them in time with a low grumble. Hayden started to step away when Ellie fell forward into her arms again. If Hayden hadn't been holding on, Ellie surely would have fallen.

"Sorry. So, so sorry." Ellie stepped to the side and stared at Atlas, but Hayden still caught a hint of pink in her cheeks. "And what did you mean by that maneuver, sir?" Atlas let out another grumble and rolled onto his back, giving them the most hilarious grin. If Hayden hadn't known better, she would have sworn he'd done that on purpose. Hayden stepped back. She needed to create a little distance. She clearly couldn't think when they were that close. "That was, um…"

Ellie saved her from trying to figure what the hell she was going to say next. "I'm really sorry for the hug. I was just so excited that you agreed. And I'm really, really sorry about the tumble near the end. I've no idea why he thought he should roll into the back of my legs." She shook her head and rubbed the back of her neck, also adorably red.

"No problem at all." Hayden took another step back, and Ellie bent and rubbed her shin. "Oh, no. Did you hit your leg on the chair?"

"I did, but I don't think it's that bad." Yet she continued rubbing.

"Here, sit down, and let's take a look at it."

Ellie tried to protest, but Hayden basically pushed her into the chair easily, even though Ellie was quite a bit taller because she was already folded in half. "Oof," she said as she landed.

Hayden knelt and placed Ellie's heeled foot on her knee, sliding the pant leg up. When she skimmed her thumb over the angry red oval starting to swell, Ellie winced. *Oops.* "Ouch. Sorry. Let's get some ice on that to curb the swelling. You'll thank me tomorrow."

Ellie's face was fully red now. "Oh, no need, I'm sure it'll be fine when I get home."

Hayden ignored her and made an ice pack. Despite her protests, Ellie stayed put in the chair with Atlas's head in her lap until Hayden brought back the zipper baggie filled with ice and wrapped in a few random fast-food napkins. Ellie gasped when Hayden lifted her pant leg again and gently applied the ice to her shin.

Ellie tried to pull away, but Hayden kept her foot rooted firmly in place. "Do you mind if I slip this shoe off? Your heel is digging into my thigh a little." Oh. My. God. What was she doing? She could not take a client's shoe off in her office like a reverse Prince Charming. She should not be holding the very soft leg of a very sexy client in her office.

It was a relief when Ellie said, "You don't have to sit on the floor and hold the ice pack. Since you insisted on making it for me, I can hold it." She slid her hand between Hayden's and the ice pack, and Hayden had no choice but to release it or make things really weird.

She let go and stood. "At least let me pull this other chair over so you can prop your leg up."

"You don't hav—"

But Hayden was already pulling the chair around Atlas so Ellie could put her foot on it. She felt a little manic, but she needed to move to stop focusing on how perfect Ellie's calf had felt beneath her hands. Ellie deftly slipped off her heel before placing her foot on the chair. "You don't like being the center of attention, do you?" Hayden said.

"Not when it's because of my clumsiness." Ellie cleared her throat as she looked away.

"Sorry if I made you uncomfortable." Hayden had made *herself* uncomfortable, and she definitely shouldn't have touched Ellie without her permission. They'd been so inadvertently touchy for the whole appointment, but that didn't mean Hayden hadn't overstepped. "I have no idea what came over me, manhandling you like that and forcing you into icing your leg." Hayden wondered if her face was flaming as Ellie's was. She hoped not but suspected she'd have no such luck. She wanted to crawl under her desk and hide until they left.

"Don't think anything of it. It was fine. I'm just glad I shaved my legs this morning." Ellie laughed, and it was enchanting.

Hayden's knees swayed, and her mouth felt like a piece of leather left in the sun for a century. She coughed. She needed a drink. Well, shit. She'd already crossed so many lines with Ellie… "Can I make up for my inappropriateness with a drink? I don't have a huge selection. Okay, I only have one bottle, but it's a lovely rye whiskey. Well, technically, it doesn't have quite enough mash to be considered one, but whatever. It's tasty. And interesting."

"A woman after my own heart. I'd love a glass. What is it?"

As Hayden pulled out their glasses she said, "Basil Hayden dark rye. Neat or rocks?"

Ellie's shiny lips parted and then puckered, and Hayden swore her heart might have completely come to a halt. "Color me intrigued. Rocks, but only two or three."

She needed to look anywhere other than Ellie's mouth, and thankfully, the ice gave her an excuse. When she turned back, she kept her gaze averted, fascinated by the rye in her glass, apparently. Until Ellie's finger brushed hers as she handed over the glass. For fuck's sake. She should have used Ellie monopolizing both the guest chairs to sit behind her desk, but she wheeled her desk chair around to the front, silently chastising but unable to help herself.

"Dr. Hayden secreting a bottle of Basil Hayden in her desk." Ellie tipped her head from side to side as if weighing the play on words. "I like it."

"Please just call me Hayden at this point." Around her laughter, she managed to say, "I mean, if you call me Hayden, I can pretend like we're friends, and as such, I'm not so unprofessional."

Ellie's hand went to her chest as she laughed with Hayden at the perfect absurdity of the situation. "I promise not to post about any of this on Yelp. I'm quite grateful for this glass of rye. Coming to see you with Atlas is stressful, and this is taking the edge right off. Though, what about Atlas *isn't* stressful? He's such a good boy, but he's turned my life completely and entirely upside down." Atlas lifted his head when Ellie said his name and licked her hand a few times before adjusting himself so he could curl up beneath her chair as much as his bulk would allow. It was both comical and sweet.

"I'm sorry you've found yourself in this situation on all levels. You don't have anyone at home to help you? A significant other or kid or anything?" Hayden hated herself for using Ellie's stress to pump her for information about her home life. It wasn't like it mattered. Even if Ellie was gay and single, she wasn't short-term material.

"No, it's just me. My last serious girlfriend and I broke up about a year ago, and I haven't quite gotten back on the horse in the dating scene. At this point, I definitely don't have time for anything serious between the arrival of Atlas and all of his *complications* and my job."

Hayden pressed her hand to her throat to try to stop the quivering at the news that Ellie was queer. Or was at least into women. Of course she was.

"And no on the kids front too. I always wanted a couple, but I didn't want to do it alone, and the older I got without getting married, the less I wanted them. Me and my man, Atlas. That's it." She leaned forward and rubbed his head, and Hayden was again struck at what an amazing woman Ellie was for taking on Atlas without a second thought, even though she'd never had a dog.

Hayden coughed to cover up a sigh at the charming sight in front of her. "I see." She had no idea what else to say to all of that information, especially when all she felt like doing was swooning. But at Ellie's next words, she wished she'd said something else. Anything.

"What about you? Anyone at home?"

Alarm bells severe enough for impending nuclear disaster went off in her head. Deflect. Abort. Divert. Change the subject. Knock over her glass. This was getting way too personal. Yet, instead of doing any of those diversionary tactics, Hayden gave her the truth. "I'm not exactly the relationship type. I've got a geriatric cat named Chelsea, but that's it." At least she hadn't brought up her sexuality.

"Ah." Ellie's face had fallen slightly when Hayden had said she wasn't into long-term, and she didn't like it. She wasn't surprised by Ellie's reaction, more by her own pang of regret that Ellie couldn't be interested in something short-term. As she'd told Britt, Hayden could see she had long-term written all over her. It was for the best. And the more she thought about it, the better it was that Ellie knew Hayden wasn't long-term material. It would cut off any possibilities, and maybe they'd stop having those...*moments.*

"What is that tattoo on your chest?" Ellie pointed to her collarbone as she asked.

Great. Hayden was *not* going to talk about the meaning behind that tattoo, but to appease Ellie, she pulled her shirt away to expose the top of the three cardinals in flight that stretched from her sternum, across the top of her left breast, to just below her collarbone. "Just a few birds that I thought were cool when I was young." She dropped her shirt back into place and took a sip to avoid looking at Ellie for as long as possible. She didn't want to watch Ellie concentrate on her chest. Nor did she want to answer any more questions. "What do you think of the almost rye?"

Ellie took a sip and, of course, Hayden's gaze was drawn to her mouth. Again. As if she needed any incentive. But those perfect lips curled into a smile as she said, "It's tasty. Different than what you'd expect. A little sweet, but…" She took another sip, and Hayden watched the column of her throat as she swallowed. That shouldn't be alluring, but it was. "Interesting. Which is, I think, what you called it."

Hayden squeezed her hand into a fist until her fingernails dug into her palm, and she almost yelped at the pain. She needed to focus on something—anything—other than this inappropriate and impossible attraction. She took another sip and finally squeaked, "I'm glad you like it."

Why had Britt planted the idea that Ellie was a dog MILF? If not for that, Hayden certainly wouldn't be thinking of a client like this. And yet. She was…So. Fucking. Screwed.

Chapter Eight

The moment Ellie walked in the door of her condo with Atlas after her session with Hayden, she pulled out her phone and started to dial Iris. Shit. Iris wasn't taking calls these days. She closed her eyes when they started to burn and willed the tears back inside. She could not let the sadness in right now. She needed to talk about the sexy Dr. Hayden. Or just Hayden now that they'd had a drink together. And now that Hayden had run her hands all over Ellie's calf. She could feel herself starting to flush just thinking about those fingers again. A featherlight touch but the way her body reacted to it? Good lord.

She flopped onto the only remaining cushion on her couch— she really needed to get to a furniture store as soon as possible—and sighed the longest sigh of her life. "Come here, buddy," she called to Atlas. If Atlas hadn't been the reason for the lack of cushions, she would feel bad for him having to lie on the couch frame, but now he was going to have to deal with it.

She started laughing at that bananas thought—she didn't even recognize herself anymore—and pulled out her phone to text Skye.

Ellie: *Still up and have a few to chat?*

Skye: *Ooh. You just finish with Dr. Hottie? Getting ready to leave an event. Call u from Lyft in five.*

Ellie sent her the thumbs-up emoji, and seconds later, the phone still in her hand started ringing. She'd been spacing out and staring at the dark screen, picturing Hayden's hands again. Her fingers were long, but her nails were trimmed in short blunt ovals. No polish but the pads of her fingers were soft yet firm, and the way they'd so delicately held her leg, as though Ellie's entire shin might crumble into ten thousand pieces, started another fluttering in the lowest part of her belly.

The phone vibrated again. She swiped to answer.

"So tell me all about the appointment with Dr. Hottie," Skye said before Ellie could even say hello.

"I don't even have words."

Skye chuckled. "You've got to have some because you texted me to talk."

"Okay, truth. I want to talk about it, but I don't even know where to begin." Ellie did want to talk to Skye, have a sounding board for all the madness, but truthfully, she'd texted before she could even process the evening enough to describe it.

"Start at the beginning. I believe a beautiful woman once said that the beginning was the perfect place to start. Or something like that."

"Misquoting Julie Andrews. You know the way to my heart. And would you please stop calling her Dr. Hottie? It's weird. And she has a name. Hayden." Ellie couldn't disagree with the moniker, but Hayden was distracting enough without it.

"You literally just purred her name. Hayden," Skye said breathlessly. "And wasn't it *Doctor* Hayden last week?"

"Yes, but that was before…" Ellie put a hand on her forehead and wondered if it had gotten a lot hotter in her living room. "Jesus."

"Before Jesus? That was a long time ago."

If Skye was standing there, Ellie would have thrown something at her. "Don't be obtuse. You know I didn't mean it that way."

"Then what was before your sudden trail off?"

Ellie took a deep breath and recalled every perfect moment of her time in Hayden's office. "Before I accidentally grabbed her hand and interlaced our fingers. Before I pulled her into a hug. Before Atlas rolled into the back of my legs and almost knocked me over. I smacked my shin on a chair, and I would have fallen except Hayden caught me."

"Oh?"

"You know I'm not the most coordinated, and Atlas is a big boy, so it was a recipe for disaster. But somehow, Hayden noticed I was in pain and forced me to sit and ice my leg. But good God, she felt compelled to examine my contusion herself. Her fingers..." Ellie started to get dreamy thinking of Hayden's hands again and shook herself out of it. "Needless to say, they were cool and soft and heavenly, even when running over the quickly forming bruise. I was so embarrassed by the way she was fawning over me that I took the ice pack out of her hands and pushed her away despite how much I wanted to pull her hand into mine."

Skye didn't say anything for a long moment. Which was surprising. She was rarely without words. "Wow."

"That's what you've got for me? Wow? No sage words?"

"Well, what happened next?"

"I don't even remember exactly how it all played out. She tried to bribe me with whiskey to not post on Yelp about how unprofessional she was, which is ridiculous. All I could think about was jumping her, so clearly, I was also beyond the point of professional myself. The problem is that it came up that she isn't interested in anything long-term. And you know I can't waste any more time on someone who isn't my forever person. If a relationship has nowhere to go, I don't have time for it."

Skye chuckled. "Well, it may be true that you are on the hunt for Mrs. Forever, but you have told me several times that you don't have time for a relationship right *now*, so maybe what you need is a little sexual reset."

"Have you lost your mind? A sexual reset? You Millennials." What the fuck was that even? Ellie didn't normally feel old, but Skye's terminology made her feel like an actual dinosaur.

"It's not a generational thing. It's a literal thing. You've been burned, and are still licking your wounds—"

"I am *not* licking my wounds," Ellie said indignantly.

But Skye continued as though she hadn't said anything. "You're busy as hell right now and don't have time to commit. So why not have a little fun with a Mrs. Right Now to take the edge off and remind yourself that you're still a sexual being?"

The concept felt unnatural. Like petting a cat from tail to head. Yet there was something there. But that wasn't her. She didn't have casual affairs. She didn't want casual. She wanted forever. Soon, but not now. "I don't think that's something that I can really…I don't know. Comprehend? It's so outside my wheelhouse."

Skye scoffed. "What would you need to comprehend? And what about any of this *is* within your wheelhouse?"

"That's fair. I can't deny that she's hot as hell, even with her nose ring. She has this fucking sexy tattoo on her chest. I asked her about it and then ogled her when she exposed part of it. She had the decency to pretend not to notice. But I could tell she did because of her blush."

"She's definitely gay, then? Or bi or pan or something?"

"I don't know. I came out to her intentionally to gauge her reaction, but I couldn't be certain. Though it seemed like she *may* be interested. She didn't return the disclosure. Unfortunately." Ellie thought for sure that outing herself would make Hayden either reciprocate or quickly bring up her straightness. Neither of which had happened, which was abnormal. Hayden gave off the vibe, and sometimes, the way she looked at Ellie made her think Hayden had to be gay—or at least somewhere on the queer spectrum—but the fact that she hadn't said anything when Ellie had intentionally mentioned her ex-girlfriend made it harder to tell.

Not that Ellie was interested. No matter what ideas Skye tried to plant, Ellie had no interest in a casual affair with an unavailable woman. Regardless of how gorgeous she might be.

❖

Hayden called herself one hundred kinds of fool as she stood outside Ellie's condo building, trying to convince herself to walk in the door. She'd already walked past the building three times and was pretty sure the doorman was about to call the police because he thought she was casing the building. Which she wasn't. She just didn't understand why she'd agreed to go to Ellie's residence to train Atlas. It didn't make a damn bit of sense.

It wasn't like she needed money. She was a behaviorist because she loved helping animals, and the only upside to being an orphan was that her parents and grandmother had all had insurance policies that set her up for life as long as she invested wisely and didn't live too extravagantly. Luckily for her, she had always invested very wisely and benefited from good market timing.

So why was she at Ellie's apartment on a Tuesday night at seven? After her last actual patient of the day. And she was charging Ellie triple her normal rate for both travel time and the lesson. She'd been hoping that would convince Ellie to find another trainer, but Ellie had latched on to her "bargain" like a shipwreck survivor on to the only life ring in the ocean.

Even though she'd had enough time to circle the block three times—she despised being late—she still had a few minutes before she needed to go in. It wasn't like she could avoid it. She'd committed to meeting with Ellie, but the sticking point was why? She wasn't a damn trainer, but something about Ellie's earnest eyes…

Hayden's mouth had moved without her brain engaging. She was horrified at herself. But Ellie did something to her, and even though she knew she was making a mistake—Ellie sparked a dormant need in Hayden to feel a connection that was inherently dangerous to her well-being—she couldn't stop herself.

So here she was. Pulling open the door to Ellie's bougie-ass building. With a concierge. And although it wasn't like Hayden was impoverished, her blue-collar roots had a hard time comprehending the poshness of this condo building.

"Good evening, ma'am. How can I help you? Are you here to visit?" The concierge could apparently tell she didn't belong.

She looked at her clothes and shoes self-consciously, wondering what glaring faux pas she'd committed. She'd thought a burgundy sweater and white shirt went quite well with her pin-striped charcoal pants and black wing tips. She cleared her throat. "Yes, I have an appointment with Ellie Efron." She adjusted her shirt and hated herself for doing it. She belonged here as much as anyone, and no pretentious doorman was going to make her feel like she didn't. Except he did. She felt as much of an outsider as she always had.

Fuck.

"Of course, ma'am. Let me just call up." He adjusted his bowtie, and Hayden wanted to knock the fresh-cut flowers on his desk onto the floor. She knew intellectually that no one could demean her without her permission, but the way he looked at her—so snooty as his gaze roved over her while she spoke—made her want to throw in the towel on this visit, but she wouldn't give him the satisfaction.

Ellie must have answered immediately and given him the all clear because he hung up and ushered her to the elevator bank. When the door opened above, there was a small lobby that seemed almost pointless since there was only one door. But since the alternative was the elevator opening right into Ellie's home, it probably did make sense. At least, she hoped it was Ellie's door.

Hayden had barely stepped out when Atlas's loud barks announced her arrival. She wanted to talk and comfort him but that felt a little weird, so she knocked instead.

Ellie opened it at once. Although she'd had warning, it was still a little startling. "Hi," Ellie said, still in the navy-blue skirt suit that she must've worn to work that day. She swiped a few strands of hair from her forehead. She looked a little frazzled, and Hayden wondered if Atlas had had a particularly difficult afternoon. "Please come in. Sorry about the mess. I want to say Atlas destroyed all this today, but it was weeks ago, and I haven't had time to replace everything. If you give me two minutes, I'll be right with you. Please have a seat." She pointed to a couch and laughed a little manically. "On the one cushion that Atlas *hasn't* destroyed." She laughed again as she walked away, shaking her head.

It seemed strange that she would be frazzled at having Hayden in her space since she was the one who'd suggested it, but she was terribly adorable trying to tame her unruly curls that seemed even less under control than normal. There were stirrings in Hayden that she definitely wasn't comfortable with.

She sat on the lone cushion lying there like the sole survivor of a vicious battle and surveyed Ellie's house. She wasn't sure how minimalist Ellie had been before Atlas, but what was present was tasteful. The photos on the mantel showed a seemingly loving family. Atlas—surprising, given Ellie was in the kitchen making his dinner—jumped onto the springs of the couch, lay down, and placed his head on her lap.

"Hey, buddy," she said, rubbing the top of his head and jostling his floppy ears. "Are you the reason for this stark living room?"

"He absolutely is," Ellie said as she returned carrying Atlas's bowl in one hand and two low-ball glasses with a delightful looking brown liquid in the other. Ellie's fingers seemed impossibly long holding the two glasses in one hand.

Hayden had somehow missed that this was going to be a cocktail dog-training session. Though she was quickly distracted by Ellie's more relaxed appearance. She'd lost the heels but still looked delicious in the suit. Those fingers and the juxtaposition of her sexy business suit paired with casual bare feet and perfect toes sent the rational part of Hayden's brain on vacation.

"I hope you don't mind that I took the liberty without asking if you wanted one of these." Ellie nodded to the glasses still secured between those dexterous fingers. "I desperately needed one after my day and thought maybe you did as well."

In an entirely unprofessional move, Hayden reached out to grab the glass. She couldn't help herself. There was something about Ellie that continued to silence her voice of reason. "Thank you. But only as long as we both swear to drink slowly."

"Deal." Ellie laughed.

"It *was* an odd day."

"Another gigantic dog took a huge poop in your office?"

"Worse." At Ellie's lifted eyebrows, she said, "Really. It might be hard to believe, but Atlas's oversized shit wasn't even in my top one hundred most difficult work moments. That was basically nothing."

"It felt like a tad more than nothing." Ellie pulled an uncomfortable-looking and oddly shaped wooden chair a few feet closer to the couch and sagged onto it.

Hayden suppressed a laugh at the way she contorted herself. "That chair is…"

"Don't get me started on this weird thing." Ellie shifted again and tried to drape her arm around the back, but that apparently wasn't comfortable as she quickly removed it and shifted to the other side. "It was a gift from an investor after a particularly lucrative deal. Their money came from some fancy hand-carved wood furniture that they've mostly gotten away from, but apparently, if they're extra happy about something, they send one of their 'favorite pieces.' I've hated this chair since it arrived, but I can't get rid of it because they always ask how it's doing. Every. Single. Investor. Meeting." She huffed and took a very large sip of her drink. "However. It doesn't have any cushions, so it made it through relatively unscathed from Atlas's episodes. If I didn't have this chair, I would have no other seating in this living room."

"Thank goodness for ugly, uncomfortable gifts." Hayden sucked in a breath as Ellie barked a laugh. "Oh God. I didn't mean to call your chair ugly. It's…not…the worst." She tried to find the least offensive words to describe the least attractive chair she'd ever seen.

"'Ugly as fuck' is what you're looking for," Ellie said.

Hayden choked on her drink. "You said it, not me."

"It's terrible. Would you like to try it out? It's like sitting on a crooked piece of driftwood."

"Although you make it sound so appealing, I'll pass, but thank you. I sincerely appreciate the offer." Hayden chuckled and took a sip. "What is this? I think rye, but I've never had it."

"Yep. It's Redemption's ten-year high rye. It's a little indulgent, but it's my current favorite for bad days."

"Hmm." Hayden took another sip and let the liquor roll over her tongue. "I've had Redemption's younger bourbons and ryes but not this one. It's delicious."

The hint of pink that graced Ellie's cheeks was glaring, but Hayden pretended not to notice. She took another sip and pointed to Atlas. "How's he doing?"

"Better. Not great. I dread every single walk with an anxiety that makes me want to throw up, but he isn't always horrible. And I don't really cry anymore." Ellie was adorable as she cleared her throat and took a sip.

"That's something. Progress is progress."

Ellie coughed as she said, "You think that's progress? It doesn't feel much like it."

"Not crying is a great first step. It means that Atlas is getting a little better. Sometimes, it's hard to see the incremental steps, but your subconscious knows. How have the sit commands been coming?"

"Good." Ellie jumped up and grabbed a canister from her fireplace mantle. "Do you want to see?" At the jingle of treats, Atlas's eyes got big, and he also popped up. Ellie pulled out a treat and held it in her fingertips, palm up, in the universal sit gesture. Without a word, Atlas's butt hit the ground.

The immediate response was impressive. Ellie had clearly been working with him. "Nice. Ready to learn some more?"

"Let's do it." Ellie ran her fingers through her hair, and the chestnut curls bounced and cascaded around her face. She glowed as though Hayden was watching her through a sparkle filter. Hayden took a large sip in the hope that the sting in her throat would distract her from the burn of desire flooding her belly.

Hayden worked with them for forty-five minutes on the basic commands of watch, down, shake, and leave it. "As you continue to work on these, the first step is making sure Atlas can do them all consistently at home. Then take him to a public place with distractions, staying well away from any dogs, of course."

"He seems to love doing the work at home. I'm afraid to take him in public still, but I know we have to do it."

"It's scary, but the better trained he is at home, the greater the chances that you can break him out of any reactivity while out. Trust in the training as well as the effects of the medication," Hayden said and realized she was nearing the end of her glass. She should definitely wrap things up and head out. And if Ellie asked her if she wanted another, she needed to say no. She was resolved. *Say good night within the next ten minutes.* It was late. Chelsea was at home, and Hayden couldn't keep her waiting for dinner.

"I know. It's funny, I'm so confident at work, but you'd never know it from how timid I feel with this dog." Ellie took the last sip from her glass and shook her head.

"He can sense when you're nervous, which is going to make him nervous. Just channel some of the 'fake it till you make it' energy." Ellie shook her hair again, and Hayden ached for her fingers to be the ones running through her tresses. Yup, she needed to get the hell out of there.

Ellie winced. "I know. I know how to feign confidence when I don't feel it. I'll work on it. And on that terrifying commitment, can I get you one more?" She pointed to Hayden's glass.

Just. Say. No. "Sure, that would be great." *Why the* hell *had she said that?* It was like all of her long-ingrained protection mechanisms went out the window whenever she was with Ellie. The smile that blossomed across Ellie's face had ten thousand flutters starting at the juncture of her thighs. She *knew* she needed to go but felt rooted to the spot. And she'd lost her chance to leave as Ellie walked away with their glasses in hand. Perhaps she could just sneak out. That wouldn't be weird at all.

Instead, she sank onto the floor next to Atlas. "What is it about your mommy that causes me to throw caution to the wind, buddy?"

He scooched over on his belly and laid his head on her leg.

"I don't know either, dammit." She leaned to his ear and whispered, "I need to get a handle on this inappropriate crush."

CHAPTER NINE

Ellie tripped over her own feet walking out of the kitchen when she saw Hayden with her face buried in Atlas's neck. She knew Hayden had to love dogs—why else would she have become a vet behaviorist—but that moment of unselfconscious affection struck Ellie hard. She took a sip to quench her dry throat and continued into the room. "He's such a sweetheart, isn't he?"

"Definitely the sweetest." Hayden's skin was even more radiant with a hint of rose in her cheeks. Ellie wondered what embarrassment had led to the heightened color, but whatever it was, Ellie appreciated it.

"Here you go." Ellie handed her a glass. However, when Hayden tried to shimmy out from under Atlas's head, he grumbled and pushed forward until as much of his body as possible was lying on her legs.

"Looks like I'm stuck down here," she said and chuckled.

Ellie couldn't let her guest sit on the floor alone; as gracefully as she could manage, she lowered herself to the floor and prayed she wasn't giving Hayden too much of a show of her thighs. Her knees didn't bend comfortably enough for her to sit on her heels, so she stretched her legs in front of herself and crossed them at the ankles. Trying to bring a little more flexibility to her feet after wearing her favorite navy Manolo Mary Jane pumps all day, she alternated between pointing and flexing her toes.

Hayden seemed transfixed by the motion, her gaze locked on Ellie's feet rather than her face when she said, "Oh no, you don't have to sit on the floor with me. Please sit in the chair. Or on your couch. Atlas and I are fine down here."

"Well, now that I'm down here, it's easier to stay than to try to get back up in this skirt."

Ellie stopped flexing her Achilles, and Hayden finally looked at her face rather than her feet. Ellie wanted to laugh, as it was such a ridiculous notion that Hayden was fascinated by her feet, but she managed to hold it in. "Tell me why you wanted to become a veterinary behaviorist."

Hayden took a sip and rubbed the back of her neck. "That is a very long and uninteresting story. I don't want to bore you."

"I promise, it won't bore me. I want to know." Ellie wasn't sure why she had this driving desire to know…she just needed to know Hayden better.

Hayden looked away and cleared her throat.

"Please?" Ellie tried again. She needed to understand the woman sitting in front of her.

❖

Hayden did not want to talk about her past. She did not want to talk about why her past had driven her to become a veterinary behaviorist. She did not want to even think about her past. So why was she feeling compelled to spill everything. Maybe she could tell a bit of the story, enough to satiate Ellie without saying everything. There was no way she could tell everything. No one knew that story.

"Both my parents passed away when I was quite young, and I started living with my grandmother at thirteen."

"I'm so sorry." Ellie placed a hand on her forearm for a moment and squeezed. That warm touch sent a small shiver of pleasure down Hayden's spine.

She tried to give Ellie a reassuring smile. "It was a long time ago. And anyway, we lived in a really nice suburb just west of Cleveland. It was right on the lake—idyllic, really—but I never fit in all that well." She couldn't believe she was saying all of this. She wanted to stop and pivot, but the earnest look on Ellie's face encouraged her to keep going. "I'm not sure if you're aware, but Cleveland is one of the most segregated cities in the country, and I didn't fit in. I lived with my grandmother in a white subdivision in a predominantly white town.

My high school had a handful of Black kids. The white kids bullied us, but—and I don't know if it was because my grandmother was white or if it was because my skin was lighter—I still never felt like I fit in with the Black kids, either, even though the bullying should have brought us closer. I was just…adrift in a sea of people who looked nothing like me."

Hayden couldn't bear the thought of looking at Ellie and seeing pity, so she stared at her legs, mostly covered by Atlas, and picked a few stray dog hairs off. It was a losing battle, but it kept her fingers busy while she summoned the courage to keep going without the grief of her childhood swallowing her whole.

"It wasn't all bad. My grandmother loved me to the ends of the earth, and we had such a great time together. But it was really animals for me. My grandmother rescued senior dogs, essentially for hospice care, and I loved being with them and helping them live their best lives for however many months or days they had left." At the burn in her throat, she paused and took a sip. Why was she exposing herself like this? Ellie was a client. That was all. Yet, she couldn't stop. "And I still do that now. Sort of. But now it's helping troubled animals get past the most daunting psychological issues and allowing good families to love them for the rest of their days."

"I'm so sorry. Feeling like an outsider, especially when you're young, is brutal. I went to a Jewish elementary school, but once I got to high school, I went to a secular private school where almost everyone was Christian. I became this outcast with glasses and frizzy hair who didn't celebrate Christmas. I know it isn't the same at all, especially with the community I had around me, but I understand a little, and honestly, with the rise and seeming acceptability of antisemitism now, I can probably understand a little better and am really sorry you experienced that." Ellie squeezed her hand, and Hayden finally looked up. Ellie's face was full of compassion as she said, "Do you have any pets of your own? You mentioned a cat?"

Hayden couldn't help but laugh. "Yes, Chelsea, my cat, but it's not like she's *my* pet. It's more like I'm hers."

"You're…her…pet?" Ellie's head tilted, and she pursed her lips.

"You aren't familiar with cats and their personalities, are you?"

Ellie chewed on the inside of her cheek and shrugged one shoulder. "Not really. My parents weren't the animal types."

"Some cats, including my Chelsea, are like miniature terrorists. They force you to take them in and then act like everything nice you do for them is deserved but also that you don't do nearly enough."

"If they're so terrible, why did you adopt one?"

"Not totally terrible. And technically, I didn't adopt Chelsea. That's where part of the 'I'm her pet' comes into this. When I was working on my undergrad in Portland, she showed up on my back patio one day and wouldn't leave until I paid attention to her. This went on for a few weeks, and as winter came on, one day, she ran through the door when I opened it and refused to leave. I tried to convince her. It wasn't like I had a litter box or cat food or anything, but she refused, and keeping her seemed like the path of least resistance."

Ellie belly laughed. "The path of least resistance...you kill me, Hayden. You really do. So has love blossomed in your forced marriage?"

The thought of Chelsea forcing her into marriage cracked Hayden up too, and before either of them knew it, she and Ellie were laughing so hard, their cheeks had become damp. "It took a little while, but *some* form of love truly blossomed. It could be Stockholm Syndrome, and she's definitely a pain in my ass, but the feel of her purr when she lies on my chest as I fall asleep at night is calming. Like a mini massage."

"A massage is all it takes to get into your heart?" The moment the words came out of Ellie's mouth, her eyes went as huge as saucers, and she started to stammer, "Uh, that's not what I meant. Sorry, please ignore me and pretend I didn't say that at all. I didn't mean...I mean what that sounded like wasn't...Uh. Just please ignore me." Ellie set her drink on the floor and buried her face in her hands. A muffled, "Please just pretend the last fifteen seconds never happened," came from behind those hands.

Panic bubbled at the thought of Ellie developing romantic feelings for her, but Hayden had been clear that day in her office that long-term wasn't her thing. She didn't even date. She was sure if Ellie knew that her entire romantic life consisted of an occasional one-night stand, she wouldn't want to touch her with a ten-foot pole. She wasn't going to fess up to that, but there was no way Ellie was interested. Ellie had made it clear she was looking for Mrs.

Right—eventually—which Hayden certainly wasn't. Maybe she was simply a harmless flirt? Hayden would do as requested and not think anything of it. She definitely was *not* going to obsess over how hot being with Ellie might be. Hell no. "Of course. Think nothing of it. I've already forgotten what you said."

Ellie spread her fingers so she could look at Hayden through them. "You promise?" She was adorable. Fuck.

"I promise. No weirdness."

"Thank you." Ellie adjusted as she spoke, and her skirt crept up a little higher on her thighs, and Hayden struggled to look anywhere but at that new expanse of skin. Ellie started to flex and point her feet again. As if it wasn't bad enough the first time. Hayden wasn't sure why watching the little muscles around her ankles and in the lower part of her calf was so enthralling, but it was.

She didn't have a foot fetish, but that contrast of sexy business clothes and casual feet continued to cause a slow burn in Hayden that was distracting. Ellie had taken off her suit jacket when she'd gotten them their second drink, so now she was sitting in a white blouse with the sleeves rolled up to her forearms. Even that was sexy. She had to get out of there. Now. She'd let them get too close with all her sharing this evening, and now she was starting to have fantasies about those forearms pressing against her back and holding her close.

Fuck. She took a long swallow, consuming about half of the liquor still in her glass. Her eyes burned a little, but the panic seizing her was real. What the hell was she doing? She'd already allowed them to get too close. She had to go.

Ellie didn't seem to notice Hayden's frantic drinking and asked, "What's your favorite part about being a behaviorist?"

Without thought, Hayden said, "Helping animals who have experienced trauma recover and have a chance of having a happy, stress-free life—or as close to it as possible—for whatever they have left without getting emotionally attached."

Ellie's eyes went wide again. "What?" she said softly. "No emotional attachment at all? You don't care how they do once you're done with them?"

Why had she spoken thoughtlessly like that? She did *not* do emotional attachments period, neither animal nor human. But she didn't need to share that as that made her seem heartless. She drained the rest of her drink. "That's not what I meant. I care about them. I want them to have happy lives. They are all sweet babies who deserve happiness. However, it's easier for me to help them and let them go home to their forever families so I don't have to go through the life cycle with them."

"Life cycle?" Ellie asked, but Hayden ignored the question and stood, placing her empty glass on a coaster on Ellie's mantle after making a big show of looking at her watch.

"I'm sorry. I didn't realize how late it had gotten. I need to get home to feed Chelsea, or she's going to make me pay. Do you want to work on these new commands for a couple of weeks, and we can schedule another obedience session in a week or two?"

"Uh, sure?" Ellie said. She tried to push off the floor, but in that pencil skirt, her movement was really restricted.

Hayden wanted to watch Ellie's legs as she struggled to stand without flashing her but instead offered her a hand and focused intently on Atlas as Ellie rose. Once Ellie was standing, however, she adjusted her skirt, and Hayden stared the entire time like the perv that she was turning into. What was wrong with her? "So sorry to leave so abruptly, but Chelsea has a strict routine, and she will angry-cry all night if I don't feed her on time. I'm so glad to see Atlas is doing well, and I'll see you next week for his next behavioral visit," Hayden said and nearly ran out the door.

What a coward. But she'd found herself opening up to Ellie, and it was terrifying. She wiped her sweaty palms on her pant legs once she was in the elevator and tried to settle her racing heart by slowing her breath. She had strict rules about not making connections for a reason, yet a part of her had been ready to tell Ellie everything—every piece of her history that she never talked about—despite the rules she'd implemented to protect herself. She hadn't experienced that desire to share since her grandmother had passed away sixteen years ago and didn't know what to do to rebuild the defensive walls Ellie seemed able to blow over like they were a house of cards.

CHAPTER TEN

It was Sunday morning, and Ellie had been working diligently on all of Atlas's new tricks since Wednesday when Hayden had been over. It was six a.m., and she felt reasonably confident that if they went over to the Lake Front Path, she could walk Atlas and have him practice in an unfamiliar environment, as Hayden had suggested, without a plethora of other dogs around. However, she'd also asked Skye and Bailey to meet her so she would have backup in case anything went awry.

She was trying to project a confidence she didn't feel, per Hayden's recommendation. She hoped it was working. "You want to go for a walk, Mr. Atlas?"

He ran to her and flashed a rare doggo smile. He loved his walk time. Even if Ellie was a nervous wreck the entire time. But Sunday mornings had always been good, and she prayed the City of Chicago continued following the trend this morning.

"Good morning," she called to Skye and Bailey as they walked toward each other on the path.

"It's a morning, and you dragged us out of bed at five thirty, so I don't know if I'd call it good or not," a grumpy Skye said.

"Oh, don't listen to her," said Bailey. "We stayed at her place last night, and it was a short walk to get here. And we're almost always up this early to watch the sunrise when we stay there."

"Yeah, watch the sunrise. Relaxing, drinking coffee. Not putting on clothes and dragging our asses out for exercise."

"You're still getting the sunrise, and she's a beaut this morning." Ellie pointed east at the few inches of sky holding a compressed rainbow, the promise of a gorgeous sunrise. "Regardless, thanks for being my backup. Having you here makes me feel better."

Skye squeezed her arm. "Not sure what we can do either other than run interference, but I'm happy we can be moral support." Skye laughed. "And hear all about what went down the other night with the sexy Dr. Hayden. It's really the only reason we were willing to come out so early."

Ellie's jaw dropped just before Bailey said, "Don't listen to her, Ellie. We're happy to hang with you and finally meet the very handsome Atlas."

"Thank you, Bailey. At least I know I have one true friend here." Ellie squeezed her arm and started walking down the path.

"But we still want to hear how things went with Dr. Hottie." Bailey grinned, and Skye gave her a high five. They were disgustingly cute. But her time with Hayden this week, though abrupt, had been... yummy. Until it wasn't.

Atlas pulled on the leash to sniff at a suspicious lump that might have been a dead bird. Ellie quickly said, "Leave it," and miraculously, he did. She didn't even have to pull on the leash. He really was a good boy, just misunderstood and a pessimist. Thank goodness they'd found Hayden.

"I can't believe he just listened." Bailey pointed at the likely dead bird. "Impressive."

Ellie nodded. "I know. If not for his anxiety, he'd be the perfect dog."

Skye refused to let them move away from the subject of Hayden, however. "Yes, yes, good dog. Anyway, how was having Dr. Hayden in your house?"

"Clearly, Atlas is getting a lot out of her lessons. He didn't even know that leave-it command four days ago. At least, I don't think he knew it. Maybe he did, and Hayden is just training me." When Skye and Bailey both started giggling hysterically, Ellie said, "What's so fun—oh...for fuck's sake. Not training me like...I don't even know what. You two are perverts."

Over her laughter, Skye somehow managed to snort. "You said it, not us."

There was nothing to do with the two of them until they stopped laughing, so Ellie called Atlas over and had him go through a sit, down, sit, shake progression while shaking her head. They were still laughing, so she went through it twice more as four runners jogged past. Thankfully without dogs. "Are you two about finished?"

Bailey said something like, "Almost," but her words were almost completely drowned out by the gasps for air.

It wasn't that funny. Ellie decided to leave them doubled over and started walking Atlas again. After only a few steps, she saw an almost familiar silhouette jogging toward them. Was that? No, it couldn't be. The woman in burgundy knee leggings and a light gray sports bra with several burgundy splashes had abs that Ellie could see popping even at that distance. Did Hayden?

As she neared them, Ellie was able to make out her high cheekbones and elegant jawline. Definitely Hayden. She had started to veer toward the water, no doubt to give them a wider berth when her steps faltered, likely when she recognized them.

She took out an earbud and walked to them. "Good morning," she called and waved. "Atlas looks good. He doesn't seem to be reacting at any passersby."

Ellie was a little surprised—but pleasantly so—at the enthusiasm with which Hayden approached, given her weird and abrupt departure a few nights before. Ellie had been worried she'd done something to offend or had asked too many questions that evening and was concerned they would lose their easy camaraderie.

She told herself to look at Hayden's face and not the athletic frame that her running outfit put so perfectly on display. She felt like she was seventeen again, trying to come to terms with her sexuality while watching the cheerleaders bouncing around in their short skirts at the football games. "Morning, and yes. He's been on his best behavior in unfamiliar settings. I thought it would be better to come out early. Hopefully before any other dogs are out. You know?"

Hayden's face glistened with sweat, and Ellie squeezed her hand into a fist, resisting the urge to swipe at a bead of sweat running from Hayden's right temple. She took care of it herself with the back of her wrist. Ellie prayed Skye and Bailey, still behind her, stayed back there and remained oblivious to Ellie's current interaction.

"That's perfect. You want to continue to train him in unfamiliar areas but where he can stay below threshold. Eventually we'll work on proximity, but for now, staying away from triggers is the best course of action whenever possible." Hayden's chest rose and fell noticeably as she continued to breathe hard, and Ellie again reminded herself to focus on her face. It didn't matter what was going on with her chest. No matter how enticing it looked in Ellie's peripheral vision.

"I'm trying to listen to everything." Ellie's laugh sounded nervous, and she prayed Hayden couldn't hear it.

"You seem to be doing an excellent job." Hayden smiled, and Ellie's knees felt weak.

She was far too old for her body to react this way to a smile and a kind word. Even if that smile and word came from one of the most beautiful women Ellie had ever seen. And even if that woman happened to be part of Ellie's support through a difficult emotional time without realizing it. But she needed Hayden's expertise with Atlas. "Oh, thank you. We're doing our best." She stumbled over the words.

"Hi," Skye said to Hayden as she walked up to them and extended a hand. "I'm Skye Kohl, friend of Ellie. And Atlas too, of course. This is my girlfriend, Bailey, since Ellie isn't going to introduce anyone." She pointed her thumb at Bailey, who also reached out to shake.

Of course *this* was the moment that the lovebirds managed to stop laughing and crash the conversation. Perfect timing to embarrass Ellie more.

"Lovely to meet you. I'm Dr. Brandt. Uh, Hayden, I suppose... here." She rubbed her earlobe and looked toward the lake.

"Dr. Hayden." Skye smiled and nodded knowingly.

Ellie coughed sharply and gave Bailey and Skye a look that she hoped communicated how much she did not find them amusing in any way. "Sorry, but you two were cackling back there like a couple of old hens, and I didn't realize you were walking back up. Hayden, Skye and Bailey are friends and colleagues."

"We're also apparently doggie backup on Sunday mornings." Skye pointed at Atlas and looked between Ellie, Hayden, and Atlas.

"But it doesn't look like anyone needs backup right now. Bailey, come look at this." She grabbed Bailey's hand and pulled her toward a section of the seawall.

Ellie was grateful she'd realized they were making everything incredibly weird. When they were out of earshot, Ellie said, "Sorry about that. I've known Skye since she was an awkward high schooler, and sometimes, she's still awkward without realizing it."

"She wasn't really that bad," Hayden said and choked out a chuckle.

Ellie wasn't sure how. "No need to lie. She's been trying to ship us for weeks now and apparently thought this was the time to jump in. Thankfully, she realized how ridiculous an idea that is and scuttled off." Ellie couldn't believe she'd said all that and wished she could rewind the last five minutes. Why had she said *anything* about shipping? Firstly, she was too old to use that phrase. Secondly, she didn't want Hayden to think she'd thought about anything relationship-y between them. At all. Because she hadn't. That would be embarrassing.

Hayden cleared her throat and rubbed her earlobe again.

Shit. Ellie wanted to apologize for the ill-timed comment but decided calling more attention to it would be more uncomfortable than just moving on. "Anyway, even if Skye is awkward, it was still kind of her and Bailey to help me find some confidence this morning."

Hayden smiled again as she looked at Atlas. "Totally. You're looking confident, so even if you don't feel it, you're doing a good job of faking it. Atlas looks relaxed too." She squatted and presented the back of her hand for him to sniff. "Sorry, buddy, I don't have any treats with me today." He answered that by licking her hand, placing one paw on her knee, and using it as leverage to lick her face.

Ellie was mortified. "Shit. Sorry about that."

Hayden giggled and said, "No worries. He's a dog, and I came down to his level, after all."

Atlas picked that moment to place his other paw on her chest and knocked her onto her butt.

"Atlas! What's wrong with you? Come here." He returned to Ellie's side as she reached a hand to help Hayden up. "I'm so sorry. Are you okay? I don't think he realizes how big he is sometimes."

"Oh, no problem," Hayden said as she stood with Ellie's assistance. "I'm not made of glass." Hayden looked at her, their hands still clasped. They were standing too close, but neither of them took a step back. Hayden's breath was a gentle puff across Ellie's chin as her eyes flicked to Ellie's lips.

The moment was broken when Atlas sat against the backs of Ellie's legs, pushing her. She wanted to savor the seconds that Hayden's arms were around her, but that jolt seemed to snap Hayden out of a trance, and as soon as Ellie had her balance again, Hayden placed her hands on Ellie's hips and took two steps back.

The muscle in her throat spasmed several times before Hayden said, "Atlas keeps trying to knock you over, doesn't he? You'd better watch out." She smiled nervously.

"That would be a good idea, wouldn't it?" Ellie took her own step back, stumbling over Atlas in the process but catching herself before disaster ensued. She was going to make a note to start watching where he lounged at all times. Clearly, he was trying to kill her. Or at least maim her enough that she couldn't go into work anymore. That would make a lot more sense.

"I would recommend it. Doctor's orders and all." Hayden rubbed her bottom lip with her thumb and said, "Well, this run isn't going to finish itself, and Sunday is chore day, so I'd better keep going and get back to my to-do list."

"Of course. Sorry to have kept you, but it was lovely seeing you." Ellie was embarrassed to admit even to herself how true that was. Seeing Hayden was always lovely, and when she was glistening from her workout and in such revealing running attire, well, that was in a category all its own. She resisted the urge to fan her face, which felt excruciatingly hot.

"Likewise. I'll see you later this week." And she was off.

Ellie waited for a count of five before she turned and watched Hayden as she ran away. She placed a hand on her chest and willed her heart to slow back down.

She jumped when Skye said, "I can see why you have a thing for her. She's hot, Ellie."

"I don't have a—"

"Really?" Bailey said, eyes wide.

"I don…" Ellie started, but with Bailey and Skye both staring, she couldn't get the denial past her lips. "Fine, I may have the tiniest of harmless crushes on her, but I don't have a real thing for her. It's a fleeting little physical attraction. It can't go anywhere. She's probably not even thirty. And she's commitment-phobic. It's a nonstarter."

"Technically, you're not looking for a relationship right now either, right? But with all of your stressors, you could use a good fling, my friend." Skye shoulder bumped her as they started walking.

"I need her too much for Atlas. I can't fuck that up by fucking her. Even if I'm sure the fucking itself would be amazing." And, my God, Ellie was confident the fucking that would never happen would have been off the charts.

Chapter Eleven

Hayden placed her phone in the cradle just as Britt walked into her office. Thankfully, they hadn't come in seconds earlier and heard her talking with Dr. Prewster about the New Orleans practice. Dr. Prewster was on the fence about her timeline, but she'd called Hayden to let her know she was definitely open to selling and wanted to make sure Hayden was still interested.

But she wasn't ready for Britt to know any of that.

"Do you have a few minutes, Hayden? I have a case I wanted to discuss with you."

Hayden waved for them to have a seat while they laid out all the issues a new dog was experiencing and how he'd responded to treatment so far. Hayden thought they were doing all the right things but gave them a few additional pointers. However, when she thought Britt would get up and leave, they stayed in her visitor chair.

She really needed to use the restroom before her next patient and was hoping to have time to grab a cup of tea as well. "Is there something else I can help you with?" she finally said.

"Uh, yes." They ran their finger around the inside of their collar. "If you have a moment."

She really didn't, but she felt a little guilty about the possible move and blindsiding them. "Sure, but I really need to use the restroom. Is it something we can walk and talk about? I don't have a lot of time before my next patient."

"Sure." As they both stood, Britt said, "There's a woman…that I want to ask out."

"Oh-kay." Why were they talking about their dating life? They weren't those kinds of friends. "Why do you think there's a problem?"

"She's a little older, like, maybe forty or so." They waved in the air.

"So ten-ish years. I don't see that as a problem." She walked into the common restroom, and Britt followed. She was hopeful she wouldn't get stage fright while Britt slowly got to the point.

They turned their head away and mumbled something she couldn't hear.

"Sorry, what?" Hayden paused with her hand on the stall to make sure she could hear that time.

"She's kind of a client," they blurted.

Oh.

"But," they continued, "only for a few more days. Her little Frenchie is doing great, and Thursday *should* be his final visit. I was thinking about asking her then. At the end. Like, after the appointment is over, you know? But before they leave, and I never see her again." Their voice was adorably squeaky.

"I don't normally condone dating clients, but there isn't anything prohibiting it in the code of ethics. Especially if your treatment of her pet is concluding. I don't see an issue."

"What about the other thing? About, uh, me, and who I am?" they said from the other side of the stall.

"I'm not sure what you mean. One sec." She flushed and went to the sink.

When she looked at Britt again, they said, "The non-binary thing," and pointed at themselves from head to toe and back up again. "And she's a little older, so I don't know if it's something she'd understand or be open to."

"Ah. Well, firstly, forty isn't *that* old." Ellie jumped to mind. Hayden thought she was probably around forty and seemed pretty progressive. And hot. *So damn hot.* "I don't know this woman, so it's hard to gauge. As a pan woman, I wouldn't have an issue, but some people might. Do you know how she identifies?" The warm water was delightful on her cold hands.

"I don't." They winced. "But she gives off a bit of a queer vibe."

Hayden dried her hands and gestured for Britt to head toward the door as a quick check of her watch reminded her she only had a couple more minutes to make tea before her next appointment. "Well, that's positive. Do you think she's into you? Has she said or done anything to make you feel like she is?"

"Kind of. Like, sometimes, I catch her staring. Or sometimes, I feel like she asks questions that she already knows the answers to just to have an excuse to stay longer. She's also asked me some general personal questions like, what's my favorite dessert." They shrugged.

"Okay, so she gives off a queer vibe, seems to be into you, and your pronouns are on your business cards and in your signature block. I'd guess she probably knows, and it isn't an issue. I'd say be confident and go for it." She squeezed Britt's shoulder as they walked into the kitchen. She didn't envy them having to come out daily both with their gender identity and their sexuality. Hayden used to hate defending her pansexuality back when she cared. Now that she neither cared nor had any close relatives or friends, it didn't matter, but always having it assumed she was gay when she was with a woman or straight when she was with a man had been exhausting.

"Thanks, Hayden. I appreciate it. Really. Will you give me another pep talk on Thursday morning? Say, around eleven fifteen?" They flashed their brilliant smile, and Hayden was certain whoever this woman was, she didn't have a chance with that smile and those light blue eyes.

"Speaking of romance…" Britt bounced their eyebrows a few times. "I've noticed you've had the hot mom on your calendar a lot over the past few weeks. Even an appointment at her house last week?" They smirked, and Hayden shook her head.

"Don't go there. Nothing untoward is happening. Her dog just has a lot of special needs, and she's really inexperienced."

"Sure," Britt said with a half-smile. "And you're just the one to make sure she gets that *experience*."

"It's true. I'm just trying to make sure no one gets hurt as they find their way together. Either themselves or an innocent bystander." That was a completely truthful answer. Hayden was worried that Atlas might react at the wrong moment, but she also couldn't deny how nice spending time with Ellie had been. Although they were focused on

Atlas at the start of every meeting, once they finished with the lessons, they always ended up talking for at least an hour. Sometimes several. Hayden tried to steer clear of her past, but she enjoyed hearing about Ellie's. Some of the shenanigans she and Iris had gotten into were hilarious.

Being with her simply felt so…normal. Like they were best friends, even though they weren't. Their relationship revolved around Atlas and his needs.

"She's on your calendar today, right? Last appointment of the day? Again." Britt asked the second question like there was some hidden meaning. Like she was doing it on purpose for some reason. Which was ridiculous.

"She has a full-time job and needs to come after work. That's it. No nefarious reason."

"However, you never seem to be finished by the time I finish inputting my notes. That's normally about an hour after the appointments for the day should be over. But you're still in your office with the door closed, and I can hear you talking."

"That was, like, one time." That was a complete and total lie. It was every time. But Hayden knew that a couple of the times had been Hayden's late nights, when she'd started later and worked two hours after Britt finished.

Though it didn't matter. After Hayden had overshared about her childhood and outcast status the other night, she needed to back off. Cool things down. She was getting far too comfortable with Ellie, and that simply came with an unacceptable amount of risk. Especially after she ran into Ellie over the weekend.

Ellie had looked at her with a hunger that had made Hayden go warm all over. As if she wasn't already warm after having run two miles. Ellie looked as good as always, even though she'd been more casual than Hayden had ever seen in leggings and a long-sleeve shirt that rested off one shoulder. But it was the way Ellie had looked at her that had her reeling. And turned on.

And that comment about her friends shipping them. Ridiculous. Neither of them was interested in that, but Ellie must have been talking to her friends about her. And that all signaled trouble. So she would do the only thing that made sense. Put the kibosh on anything not related to Atlas: no personal chats, no staying late, and no hanging out as though they were friends.

If only it was as easy to do as it was to think it.

❖

Ellie arrived with Atlas at exactly six o'clock—punctual as always—looking even hotter than normal in another power suit. She seemed to normally prefer skirts, but today she was in a double-breasted charcoal pantsuit. However, it wasn't the color that pulled Hayden in but rather the appearance of no shirt below the suit jacket that had her mouth watering. The cut of the jacket wasn't revealing in any way, but Hayden couldn't help but wonder what would be beneath the jacket if she flicked those two buttons open. Would it be a camisole that was simply hidden? A plain black bra? Something red and lacy? Maybe a print or—she swallowed at the thought—perhaps a sheer black bra that would give a glimpse of dusky nipples, erect from the intensity of Hayden's gaze before she even had a chance to touch them.

"Come on, Atlas." Ellie said, pulling Hayden from her intense appreciation of the outfit. So much for playing it cool. Thankfully, Ellie was mostly paying attention to Atlas, so she *probably* hadn't noticed Hayden staring at her. She could only hope. "You know this isn't a scary place. You like Hayden." She held out a treat, and he moved into the room to take it.

Be cool.

When Atlas walked into the room after getting his treat, he looked more confident despite his reluctance. "Hey, buddy. I promise, nothing scary is in here waiting for you." Unless you counted Hayden's completely inappropriate thoughts about his mother, which were *very scary* to her.

"You won't believe what happened on the way over here. I am still walking on air thinking about it." Ellie's smile was so bright, it was almost blinding, and she was radiating enthusiasm.

"What happened?"

"We passed another dog on the opposite side of the street, and Atlas didn't react at all. Not even a little grumble. He saw the dog and looked at me, so I gave him a treat. Then about seven more as he continued to walk. I couldn't believe it. I was preparing for him to lunge, but I also pulled out his extra-special hot dog treats, and that got his attention completely. I'm still in shock. But the best kind of shock."

"Excellent. Nice job, Atlas." Hayden squatted and held out her hand with a treat in it for him, even though she knew he wouldn't associate getting a treat now with anything that had happened on their walk over. But she was still proud of him, and he deserved a treat for being such a good boy, even if he didn't know it. If dogs knew what a high five meant, this would be a high five moment. She rubbed his ears after he took the treat and looked up to see Ellie staring at her again with that hungry look in her eyes. *Shit.* "Let's sit."

She pointed to Ellie's normal chair but rather than sit next to her like she usually did, she went behind her desk and sat. Ellie had a puzzled expression but shrugged and sat where Hayden had pointed.

"How did the rest of your walk on Sunday morning go?"

"We didn't see any dogs, thank God, but Atlas was great. He sniffed new things, watched the waves lap against the seawall, and followed all my commands. Didn't you, Atlas?" She leaned over and gave him a kiss on the head.

"Excellent, Ellie. I am so proud of *both* of you. Because you've been putting in the time. This progress doesn't happen without a commitment from you too." If Hayden had been sitting next to her, she would've placed a hand on Ellie's knee and squeezed. Thank God she'd put the desk between them. She was in dire need of better impulse control.

"I am nervous about next week, though. I have rescheduled or canceled several business trips since Iris…uh…" Ellie cleared her throat and looked away. "And Atlas came into my life, but next week, I have to go back on the road. I have a project in Denver that I have to go visit, and I am going to be gone for three full days and two nights, and I'm terrified about what that's going to do to Atlas. He has such a fear of abandonment."

"You're not putting him in a kennel, I hope?" That would be traumatizing for him with all of his issues.

"Goodness, no. I have the service coming to stay in my apartment with him. They'll be there all night both nights and most of the day every day. He's met the sitter and seemed okay with her. Hopefully, he'll be fine, but I just worry. There's no way around traveling for my job, so I'm praying this works for him." Ellie started to fidget with the pendant on her necklace again, which it seemed like she always did whenever she was nervous.

"It sounds like you're doing everything right. Do you want me to give you a prescription for some sedatives just as a precaution? It's the same prescription we started him on in the early days. But it's important while you're away that he not continuously go over threshold, or he may start regressing. The sitter knows how you work on counterconditioning on every walk?" She wouldn't tell Ellie, but she was worried as well. Atlas was making progress but only because of consistent training and counterconditioning and being comfortable and relaxed enough to make progress. So much could go wrong, but she wanted Ellie to not be a ball of stress worrying about him.

"Yes. I also showed her what we've been working on with the obedience, so she'll continue it with him." Ellie continued playing with her necklace but also started chewing on her bottom lip.

It was like she was trying to kill Hayden.

They went through relaxation exercises to use when Atlas was already feeling relaxed to teach him to relax on his own or on command. Even as she tried to be cool and have a professional distance, Hayden struggled. She didn't manage to stay behind her desk for long as she moved to demonstrate the exercises. Which put her at Ellie's feet. At least she wasn't wearing a skirt, but it still put her at about eye level with the top button of *that* suit jacket.

As the top of the hour approached, Hayden knew she needed to say something to set up the expectation that they couldn't sit around chatting for hours as they had on previous visits, but she didn't want to be weird or bitchy about it. She agonized for longer than she probably should have but finally said, "I'm sorry, but I'll have to run as soon as we wrap this up. I have an appointment this evening, and I can't be late."

"Oh, okay." Was that disappointment on Ellie's face? Dammit. *Stop.*

"Do you want to check in late next week when you're back on how he did and if there's anything we should alter to make future trips easier?" Hayden knew that was the right thing, but she still felt a lead weight in her gut as she asked, knowing she'd be fighting the same attraction next time. And every time.

"That would be great." Ellie smiled, and the lead in Hayden's stomach miraculously got a little lighter. "He's probably due for more obedience training, right? Do you want to come to my place again, and we can discuss how my trip went?"

Terrible idea. "Sure. That'll probably be the most productive."

"Friday evening? I can order some food if you'd like so we aren't too famished."

And just like that, Hayden was going back to Ellie's house. On a Friday night. For dinner. Fuck. Hayden hated her inability to find her self-control around Ellie. She knew what she needed to do but found it impossible to fight the urge to do whatever her libido wanted. She was like a dog with no impulse control, and it was embarrassing. And didn't bode well for her.

CHAPTER TWELVE

Chelsea batted at Hayden's face until she woke up enough to push her away and under the covers. Chelsea loved to snuggle into Hayden's chest under the warm comforter, but even that didn't appease her, so Hayden finally grunted. "Fine, fine. I'll get up. What time is it?" As though Chelsea could answer. She squinted at the clock as her eyes tried to adjust to being open and was not impressed.

"Are you aware, my little princess, that it is only four thirty in the morning?"

Chelsea looked at her and produced a strangled cry that made Hayden's ears feel like they were going to start bleeding. That was the cry of intense displeasure.

"Fair enough. I know, I was out late last night." She hadn't been able to get Ellie out of her mind after the appointment a few evenings before, so she'd gone out to her drag show bar and ended up at the hotel of a nameless woman with long, wavy brown hair. It wasn't until she was sneaking out of the woman's hotel room—after faking an orgasm because she couldn't get into it, and the woman passed out—that she'd realized how much that woman resembled Ellie. She was pathetic.

So Chelsea might have a case to be pissed off. Hayden had fed her before she'd left, had given her some treats and a new catnip toy. But it had taken her longer than normal to find someone at the bar, and then it had turned out they were staying in a hotel on the opposite side of town, so it had been almost one a.m. when she'd gotten back.

Chelsea followed her around the house, crying like she was being murdered until Hayden put some wet food into her bowl and topped it with a tablespoon of tuna. She thankfully plopped her slightly round body in front of the bowl and went to town.

Hayden tried to start her very early morning off by meditating, but that wasn't nearly as easy as it sounded. Her conversation with Ellie about never having fit in anywhere echoed around her otherwise empty mind. She still couldn't believe she'd said all that. And how Ellie had kindly understood and commiserated. Was that what having a real friend would feel like? Someone to laugh with but also someone to give her the grace and understanding she needed when at her most vulnerable?

Everything felt so domestic when she was in Ellie's house. Like she could come home from work and just relax with someone. She'd never had that before and hated admitting it, but she *liked* the feeling. More than she was comfortable with. It exposed her to the possibility of too much hurt. Yet even though she wasn't friends with Ellie and certainly wasn't Ellie's girlfriend, the little glimpse of how that might look distracted her so much that there was no way she was going to get through her morning meditation.

For fuck's sake.

She decided to go for a run along the lake since at least her body would be moving and distracting her. Maybe.

❖

When Ellie opened her door on Friday evening, Hayden's first words were, "You still haven't replaced that couch?"

They both laughed, and Ellie stepped aside to let Hayden past. It probably seemed weird that she hadn't replaced it yet, but that was low on her priority list. "Yeah, I'd like to make sure Atlas can be trusted alone before I spend the money. And also, it's hard to find extra time in my life to go to multiple furniture stores and find a couch to last me for at least a decade. I hope."

"Whew. A decade? That's a very permanent fixture."

"I like a little permanence. I love this condo. It has the best views in the city." She gestured to the north where the lights of Grant Park and Buckingham Fountain twinkled in the evening twilight and to the east where the full moon glowed nearly fluorescent white behind the Adler Planetarium. "I love this neighborhood because it's so vibrant— though Atlas does struggle with it sometimes—and I'm ready to make another ten-plus year commitment on my couch because I'm certainly happy to commit to this location for another ten years. Most likely, anyway."

Every time Ellie said permanence or years, Hayden's lips seemed to tighten a little more, and Ellie wondered what was wrong with those words. Was she really *that* afraid of any type of commitment?

Haden cleared her throat and stepped to the window. "The views are great, no question. Anyway, how did Mr. Atlas do this week while you were out of town?"

Ellie hadn't gotten home until a little after ten the night before. It had been a long but productive trip, but she was ready to sleep in her own bed again and had been desperately hoping everything would be okay with Atlas and the house when she'd opened the door. Her dog sitter had texted at five saying she was heading out, but Ellie's flight had gotten delayed three hours, so she was a lot later getting home than she'd planned. She had let out a huge sigh of relief that he was curled up on the lone remaining couch cushion, snoozing away, though that only lasted until she closed the door before he was up and over the armrest and spinning on his back legs in front of her.

When she walked into her dining room, however, she'd discovered that Atlas hadn't been quite as good of a boy as she'd thought. "Things mostly went okay. When I got home last night about five hours after the sitter left, I discovered he'd had a little trouble. He was sleeping peacefully on the couch when I walked in—well, what's left of it—but at some point, he'd taken it upon himself to rearrange all the towels from every bathroom and the kitchen and leave them in a pile in the middle of the dining room. He didn't chew them or anything, so there's that, and neither the towel bars nor the hook that my robe hangs on in the bathroom had been pulled out of the wall, but it was weird that he collected them all." She pointed to the spot where they'd been.

"It shows he had anxiety, but at least he wasn't destructive. Did he revert to any of his self-harming behaviors?" Hayden crouched and looked at Atlas's nose and then his tail.

"No, thankfully. It seems like he survived okay-ish for the three days I was away."

"Great news." Hayden sat on that remaining couch cushion, and Ellie couldn't help a little chuckle at how pathetic her furniture was. And how embarrassing it was to have a guest again without having replaced it.

"Oh, one weird thing. He did start following me around last night, and he's kept it up today. If I go to the kitchen, he's stepping on my heels. If I try to go to the bathroom, he lies on top of my feet. He was like that when I first got him, but he settled down. Now it feels like he's afraid if he loses sight of me, I'm going to disappear." She gave Atlas an ear rub before taking a seat on the least comfortable chair in the world. She really needed to get a throw pillow for this damn thing. She adjusted three times trying to find the best position, but there wasn't one. It was horrible. When she got a new couch, she should also get a new chair and throw this damn thing away but knew she wouldn't.

Hayden ran her thumb along her bottom lip. "We may need to up his dosage, but let's see how quickly he returns to normal over the weekend and into next week. How's he been doing with his down, shakes, and leave-its?" Atlas looked at her when she said familiar words, but he just cocked his head as if trying to figure out what she wanted.

"Excellent. Do you want to see?"

Ellie started to stand, but Hayden waved her off. "No, that's fine. We're going to start working on impulse control today to teach him that if he is patient and gives us what we want, he'll get what he wants. We'll work on wait, place, and drop it. These will naturally give a little impulse control by themselves, and we'll build off them in future weeks."

After working with Atlas for forty-five minutes, Ellie's phone rang. "Oh, that's probably dinner," she said. "One sec." She answered and told Chet to send the delivery person up. Back to Hayden, she said, "Sorry about that. It is dinner. I remembered you saying the other evening that you like Indian food, so I ordered a bit of a selection since I didn't know what you like."

"I'm a vegetarian, but otherwise, I eat almost everything." Her eyes got wide when she watched Ellie take four large bags from the delivery person. "Did you purchase one of everything?" Ellie laughed nervously. "Not quite. Mostly vegetarian. I did get a few meat dishes, but I can give those to Chet. Do you want to come into the kitchen where I have room to lay all this out, and we can sort through what we might like to try?"

"Sure."

Ellie led the way. She was slightly embarrassed as she pulled container after container out of the paper bags and gave Hayden a sheepish grin. "I'm not normally this indecisive, but I wanted to make sure you didn't leave hungry."

"I appreciate your concern. Though, I think you have enough to feed both of us for at least a week." She laughed, and Ellie felt a flutter in her throat again.

They both made plates with a little bit of almost everything, and Ellie grabbed them glasses of wine before they settled at her dining room table.

"How was Denver? Did you have free time to do anything fun?"

Ellie wasn't surprised by the questions. Hayden seemed to do that to avoid talking about herself. But Ellie was happy to talk. Normally, after a bit, Hayden warmed up and spoke a little more freely, but perhaps Ellie's free-flowing wine would lubricate the process this evening. "It was good. Long days visiting a couple of properties that my company owns, touring a couple of buildings we're looking into acquiring, and I met with the investment manager of one of our largest investors, a public worker's pension fund. A lot of boring but necessary stuff." She laughed because it was funny how boring her days on the road often were.

"What about in the evenings?" Hayden took a sip, and Ellie caught herself staring first at Hayden's throat as she swallowed and then at her lips as she sucked the bottom one in and cleaned off the sheen of wine.

Her head felt half filled with cotton as she struggled to remember the words Hayden had said. "Oh, uh, well, I had a business dinner Tuesday night, which was fun. It's always good to relax with the people that I half battle and half work with during the day. Wednesday night, I had dinner alone, which I honestly enjoy as well. There's something really lovely about taking yourself out on a date. Hanging out at the bar, reading a book, chatting with the bartender. It's going to sound a little bizarre, but sometimes, that's my favorite part of being on the road. I never do that at home."

"Why not? Enjoying your own company is something to treasure." Hayden's lips turned up in a half-smile. Ellie wondered if she was thinking of alternate definitions to "enjoying your own company" like Ellie was. She had to fight not to smirk at the thought of taking care of herself later to visions of Hayden.

Why on Earth had she gone *there*? She swallowed the sly smile that so badly wanted to be let loose. "That's true. I don't know. I feel like, when I'm home, if I want to enjoy my own company, I just stay home and order in. Especially now with that lovable oaf." Ellie smiled and shrugged and tried to ignore the warmth percolating in her lower half as Hayden returned her smile. Was it that smile, or was it the wine making the heat radiate through her? Ellie tried to convince herself that it was the wine, but she didn't believe her own lies. "What about you? Do you like to take yourself out?"

Hayden chuckled and took another sip. "I do, though I never call them dates. I don't call them anything. I just go out on my own and enjoy a nice dinner, bar conversation, and then go home. Mostly alone, though sometimes, I go with someone else for a little while." Her eyes went huge, as though the words she'd just said sunk in. She quickly said, "Sorry, ignore all that. Not a clue where that came from, but I didn't say it. At all. I'd never do that as Dr. Brandt."

"Ignored." But absolutely not for forever. Ellie was going to tuck that nugget of information away to be examined at a later point. For now, she was too relaxed from the wine, the food coma, and the company to spend any time on it. She tried to give Hayden her most reassuring smile. "I promise," but she crossed her fingers under the table and then topped off their glasses with the rest of the wine. "And regardless, I think we're past Dr. Brandt and into Hayden territory anyway."

"True, but thank you. And you know, I'm a bit of a loner, so me going out alone is the norm. I'm not a total introvert. I like to chat with people." She grimaced. "I just don't form close attachments."

"Never?" Ellie couldn't believe she didn't have anyone she was close to. She seemed like an amazing person, even if she wasn't interested in relationships.

"I think I told you I moved around a lot as a child? Well, that hasn't really changed. I went to undergrad in Oregon, did vet school here in Illinois at Urbana-Champaign, spent some time in general practice in Kentucky, and then, made my way up here to Chicago. I don't grow deep roots."

"Do you ever go back to Ohio?"

"No, there's nothing there for me."

Ellie couldn't decide if it was coldness or sadness that wrapped those words, but she desperately wanted to reach out and hold Hayden. Despite her curiosity, however, whatever happened in Ohio obviously wasn't something Hayden wanted to talk about, and Ellie didn't want to dwell on something that clearly upset her. Ellie was just happy she was being a little more open again this evening and wanted to change the subject enough to keep her talking without sadness clamming her up. "How long have you been in Chicago? Do you like it?"

"About six years. And yeah, it's fine. I live on the lake in the summer and the river in the winter, and either way, you can't beat the scenery."

"Your house can move?"

"Yes." Hayden laughed, and Ellie kept squinting at her because nothing was making sense. She hadn't had enough to drink to be this confused. "I live on a houseboat. So from the late spring through the late fall—essentially until just before it gets so cold that the lake starts to freeze—I dock at the 31st Street Harbor. Then, once the weather starts to turn, I move to River City on the South Branch, which is the only marina that keeps the water from freezing and provides year-round services."

"Huh. We're basically neighbors. In the warmer months, you flank me on the east, and in the winter, you flank me to the west." That seemed like a peculiar way to live, but being right on the water could be appealing. Maybe. But Ellie was certain her views were better.

"Pretty much. Though I'm a bit south of here right now."

"So you hate permanence so much that you own a home that you can move whenever the whim strikes?" Ellie said before she'd even thought about the words. *Damn you, cabernet.*

Hayden's jaw went a little slack as her eyebrows shot up, and Ellie tried to backpedal as she realized how what she'd said might have come across as rude or judgmental. She hadn't meant it that way. But before she could take it back, Hayden said, "I haven't ever thought about it that way, but sure. That seems a little oversimplified, but you're not wrong. I don't want to be tied to any one place or thing or even person. So it's me and Chelsea against the world. One marina at a time." Hayden smiled and shrugged, a little sheepish.

Ellie couldn't comprehend living that way. She was so tied to this area, to her family, to her friends, to her career. She couldn't imagine just pulling anchor and sailing into the sunset. Or sunrise. Or however someone could possibly sail away from Chicago since it was in the middle of the country, but water seemed to be everywhere. Yet, she was also a little fascinated about how a person could live in such tight quarters and have such a nomadic mindset. "I'd love to see it—your houseboat, I mean—sometime. If you wouldn't mind, of course. I'd never want to impose."

Hayden looked at her for an uncomfortably long moment, and Ellie again wished she hadn't been so forward. But she'd said it and now really wanted Hayden to answer. She could only hope that it wouldn't ruin whatever tenuous friendship they were forming. Even if it might be against Hayden's will.

Ellie realized too late that she should've taken the question back immediately, but it was too late now. She'd definitely overstepped, and when the heavy silence became too much to bear, Ellie spoke so fast that she almost slurred her words: "A houseboat is just such a novel concept, you know? Like that classic movie, *Houseboat* with Carey Grant? But I've never known someone who owned one."

"Um, yeah, that could work sometime. When things are a little calmer. Maybe." Hayden averted her eyes and took a large sip of wine. Ellie's throat burned watching her. She was quite certain Hayden didn't mean what she'd just said and knew she'd never take Hayden up on it unless she brought it up first. But living on a houseboat was so far out of her normal life that she was fascinated.

Trying to smooth the uncomfortable moment, Ellie said, "No pressure. Seriously."

Hayden nodded several times and took another large sip. Her face was still red from earlier but slightly less so. "So you know *I* don't date. And now you also know too much about why. But you said dating is also something you aren't interested in right now, right? Why?"

That was the most personal question Hayden had ever asked, and Ellie wavered on how to answer. Hayden had been pretty candid, but Ellie didn't want to sound like the gigantic loser that she was. Her heart felt like it was beating a thousand beats a minute as she tried to figure out how much to share. But the pause she took to contemplate was taking too long, and Hayden was watching her over her wineglass. Hell.

In a fit of panic Ellie said, "There are a lot of reasons. Work is hectic. We just bought a big art deco building in Chicago that was essentially vacant and had been run into the ground, and Skye and Bailey are helping me reposition it, and it's a huge undertaking. The building is going to take a lot of work, but she's going to be so beautiful when she's finished."

"So just work? That's the only reason?"

"No." Ellie took another sip for fortitude. "It's also a few other things. Atlas, for one. He's upended my very orderly life. My very orderly house." She chuckled as she pointed to her sparse living room with the one-cushioned embarrassment. Just looking, Ellie was distracted by the beautiful view out the windows. "Do you want to go sit out there to enjoy the rest of the wine? It's a beautiful night."

"Why not? That's a hell of a view. We may as well appreciate it."

They were silent as they moved to the balcony. Atlas followed and flopped at their feet as though having to move outside was the most trying part of his entire day. Ellie's balconies weren't terribly wide or private, but they were designed for enjoying the view that was spectacular that evening. The sky was clear, and she could see more stars than normal in the middle of the city. But better than the view was the fact that Ellie sat on her patio love seat, and Hayden sat next to her. The love seat was so short, their arms nearly pressed together. Ellie could feel the warmth emanating from Hayden and resisted the urge to lean closer until they touched.

Hayden finally broke their comfortable silence. "Good call moving out here. It's beautiful."

Ellie sighed contentedly. "Is that Mars?"

Hayden leaned out. "I think that's Jupiter. Though, Mars and Saturn are out here somewhere." They both relaxed against the couch, their shoulders brushing that time.

Had Hayden moved closer? Had Ellie? Had they both? Ellie didn't care. The point where they were touching, even through their shirts, was vibrating.

The silence surrounding them for several minutes was like being wrapped in a warm blanket together. A world only their own, with the muted sounds from the street hundreds of feet below. Until Hayden brought their earlier topic back. "So just work and Atlas?"

"No, not just those, either." She took a sip. "Uh, I've also had a bit of bad luck in the dating department. I'd kind of already committed to taking a break from dating before either the work stuff or Atlas. They just confirmed I needed one." Another sip. She was going to need to detox her liver after this conversation.

"You can tell me to shut the hell up or just not answer, but what went wrong in your last relationship?"

Ellie had never wanted to deflect so much in her life. Iris had known, plus Skye—and Bailey by extension—but that was it. And yet, she wanted to share. Hayden had been pretty open, and Ellie had this undeniable pull to let Hayden know the true her. She sighed and jumped in. "Honestly? I probably waited too long to change my focus from work to a meaningful relationship. I was entirely career and corporate-ladder focused until I was about thirty, when I finally realized work wasn't everything. I'd achieved so much by then, but I hated coming home to an empty house. I wanted to find that forever person who would be there at night to cook with me and give me a hard time on the nights I had to work until nine or ten."

"Mmm," Hayden said and nodded. That wasn't great encouragement. But she didn't look disgusted, at least.

"In the last slightly-more-than-a decade, I've had three long-term relationships. We didn't live together but were serious. Like, spending most nights together—at least for a while—serious. I thought they were all going somewhere. I thought marriage, but apparently, I was the only one because all three left me for someone else. Someone they eventually married."

She squeezed her eyes shut, not wanting to see the look in Hayden's eyes that confirmed just how pathetic she was. "The last one, Jessie, well, she broke up with me for someone else and got engaged less than three months later. Looking back, I knew we weren't perfect, but fuck. That hurt a lot. How fast she found the actual one and moved on? I don't know if we ever had anything real or not." The lump in her throat swelled, and she took the last sip in her glass.

Her eyes were still closed when Hayden shifted next to her and the warmth of her hand appeared on Ellie's forearm. "I'm sorry you've gone through that so many times."

"I just have this fear of dying alone. I know I'm not *that* old, but…Iris and…Fuck. I'm sorry. I keep dumping on you, don't I?" Her skin was itchy as mortification raced through her. "I'm sure you don't want to hear about all my woes. We should talk about something fun. Like, what do you have going on this weekend? Or—"

"You don't have to pretend everything is great, you know?" Hayden squeezed Ellie's forearm, and somehow, their fingers ended up interlaced on Ellie's thigh. She liked how their hands looked together. "I know you're going through a hard time right now, and keeping that mask on has to be nearly impossible. Grief is like a wildfire. Just as you think you're maybe getting it under control, it can pop up anywhere without warning."

"I haven't really lost anyone close since I was a kid. My parents are both getting older, but I still have them, and we're very close. But since my grandmother passed away when I was seventeen…I just don't really know how to deal with all this." She ran her free hand through her hair. "Fuck, that sounds like I'm whining about how fortunate I've been. I'm sorry, you don't need—"

"Stop." It wasn't a request. It was a command and got Ellie's attention. As did a thumb and forefinger against her chin that guided Ellie's gaze back up. "You shouldn't feel guilty for how you grieve. Or for being lucky. Or unlucky. You need to give yourself a little grace and grieve and feel how you need to feel. Grief sucks. I've dealt with enough of it to last a lifetime, and you deal with it how you deal with it. There isn't a right or wrong way. If you need to cry, you cry. If you need to go talk to someone, you go talk to someone. If you need to cry into Atlas's neck, I'm sure he won't mind."

"It just feels so narcissistic, and…I don't know, poor little rich girl."

Hayden laughed, and Ellie's heart dropped. Her expression must have been plain as Hayden quickly said, "I'm not laughing at you. It's just a ridiculous notion that because you're fortunate, you can't grieve. I've lost…" Hayden cleared her throat and finally looked away. Ellie missed the intimate connection, even though their hands were still intertwined. "Well, a lot of people in my life, and as a result, I'm very comfortable financially, but that doesn't mean it doesn't hurt—even still today, years later. Losing people sucks. Your life suddenly looking very different than you pictured. Well, it's horrible. Please believe me. You have a right to grieve however you need to."

When Hayden turned back, the sadness in her eyes broke Ellie's heart anew. She wanted to ask more about who Hayden had lost that left her looking so sorrowful but intuitively knew Hayden didn't want to talk about it, so instead, she said, "Thank you. I…I'm sorry you've experienced so much loss."

Ellie hadn't realized how closely they had drifted together until she felt Hayden's breath against her face, and her eyes flicked to Hayden's lips. Before she even had a chance to think it through, she leaned in closer. Slowly. Painfully slowly. She looked back up as the train carrying her thoughts pulled back into the station. She desperately wanted to kiss Hayden—so much more than a silly crush would justify—but she didn't want to cross that line unless Hayden wanted it too.

Hayden was staring at Ellie's lips, and Ellie hoped that meant she had a green light, but Hayden leaned back instead. "I'm sorry, I should go."

Ellie stared at Hayden's chest as it rose and fell, not sure what to say.

"Chelsea is a needy girl." She cleared her throat and turned to grab her wineglass as she stood. "I need to feed her, or she'll keep me up tonight."

Hayden's nervous laugh was like an ice pick into Ellie's chest. "Of course. Sorry, I didn't mean to keep you."

"Thank you." Hayden took the last sip as she walked back into Ellie's apartment and looked around as if searching for someplace to sit her glass.

"Here, I'll take it." Ellie reached out. Their fingers brushed. Hayden paused. Licked her lips. A flutter jumped into Ellie's throat for a fleeting second. This was ridiculous. She couldn't take this any longer and broke eye contact, walking to the door.

After an awkward pause at the door, Hayden waved and was gone.

Ellie sank onto the floor next to Atlas. "What in the actual fuck was that, buddy? How can I have such a massive crush on your doctor?"

He didn't have any sage wisdom but rolled onto his back with his head on Ellie's lap. She rubbed his belly, and he sighed and shimmied his shoulders up higher.

"Well, I certainly can't ruin our professional relationship because you're doing so much better. I don't want to have to take you to someone else. Get you to trust someone else and could I even find someone as good as she is? Especially not for someone so emotionally unavailable. I'll just have to figure out how to keep my feelings in check. That shouldn't be too hard, should it? The attraction is just a chemical thing. I can ignore it."

Chapter Thirteen

"What's got you so quiet, Hayden? You're not ever a Chatty Cathy, but it seems like you've been extra contemplative this entire week," Britt said.

They had insisted on Hayden accompanying them out to a happy hour after they closed the practice for the evening. Hayden had wanted to say no, but they were persistent, and she thought it might be faster to just give in rather than keep fighting. So with dreams of snuggling on her couch with Chelsea, a glass of wine, and a good book, she'd acquiesced, hoping she could have one drink and then get home.

Yet, here she was, trying to avoid talking about the reason she was so quiet. Probably the real reason she'd been reading suspense novels every night. They were the only thing that could keep her mind off Ellie's lips. Her *very* kissable lips. The lips that had been a hair's breadth from Hayden's two weeks before. How she'd longed to move those last millimeters. She'd done nothing but dream of those lips every night since. Hell, when she wasn't engrossed in work or a book, she'd done little else other than think of those lips.

"Hello? Earth to Hayden. Do I still have you?" Britt waved in front of her face.

She shook her head and tried to focus. To not think about Ellie. "Yep. Right here." She stared into her frosty mug before she took a sip.

Britt bumped her shoulder. "What's going on with you?"

If she'd given herself a moment to think about it, she probably wouldn't have said anything—confiding personal details about herself wasn't her MO—but before she could second-guess herself, she said, "Ellie. And Atlas. But Ellie is the problem. Atlas is coming along great. Mostly great. Two steps forward. One step back. But that's normal."

"Ellie?" Britt rubbed their earlobe and squinted one eye. "Oh! The dog MILF."

"Please don't call her that." The term made Hayden feel skeevy. And like she was definitely having impure thoughts. Which she was, but they felt even less appropriate when Britt called Ellie a MILF.

"Sorry. Fine. So anyway, what's going on with her?"

"Ellie." Hayden had to stop herself from sighing the name and mentally tried to slap herself.

"What's going on with Ellie and you? Because something definitely is."

"I…" She closed her eyes and squeezed the bridge of her nose. "We almost kissed." She turned her head just in time to see Britt's eyes go wide as saucers.

"Why almost? She's hot. For an older woman."

"She is, and Jesus, she's *not that old*. But it's a bad idea. She's a client. Conflict of interest. A compromise of ethics. Plus, it's not a good idea to hit-and-run where you work."

They rolled their eyes up and scratched their head. "Hit-and-run…oh. I see. Wham, bam, thank you, ma'am."

She shook her head in disbelief that they had actually just said that. "What is it? 1989? And you called Ellie old?" She snorted, her IPA bitter on her tongue as she took a sip.

"I'm an old soul."

"Speaking of, how are things going with your *lady love* client?"

The blush that stained their cheeks was adorable. "She's good. Really good," they said softly. "We went out again last week."

"Oh? No issues with…anything?"

"Nope. She'd seen my business card, is bi, and was very—" They cleared their throat and ran a finger around the inside of their collar. "Very interested." They smirked and avoided eye contact.

"Oh *really*?"

Britt shrugged sheepishly. "Yeah. So are you exclusively a hit-and-run kind of girl?"

"Hey, you can't change the subject here. We were talking about you and the Frenchie's mom. How many times have you two been out?"

"Five or six. And we were talking about you first, for the record, so I'm not changing the subject. Just reverting. And I've answered all your questions. So answer mine."

"For frick's sake. Yes. I don't get involved. Occasionally, I'll look for a little hookup but am mostly an island. That can't be much of a surprise."

"Ah, so I shouldn't take your standoffishness personally?" They laughed, and she felt a little weight lift off her shoulders. Weird.

"No, you shouldn't."

"Good. Because I just assumed you're grumpy by nature." They punched her in the arm and laughed. "So you don't date, and she's a client anyway. Why can't you wait until her dog is almost ready to stop seeing you and have your fun?"

"Because she's not a quick release kind of girl. She's a wine and flowers and forever type. She's searching for Mrs. Right and has had a lot of heartbreak. I can't lead her on when I'm only interested in a few hours. It's why I pulled away before we could kiss." It was the absolute hardest thing she'd ever found the willpower to do. Looking back, she was surprised she'd been able to stop. "I so wish it wasn't the right thing to do, though. Her lips were…enthralling."

She didn't realize she'd said that until Britt said, "Really?" *Shit.* "Enthralling? That sounds serious."

"It's nothing." But it wasn't nothing. She'd made their visit on Wednesday ridiculously uncomfortable. She knew it. She'd tried to keep things completely professional, but the hurt on Ellie's face still made Hayden squirm when she thought of it. They'd been developing a friendship, but even that was too dangerous, so she'd done what she always did. She'd shut it down and backed away. "I just need to stay away from her. Stop having social hour after Atlas's sessions and go back to what any normal professional relationship would look like. And stop going to her house to train him."

Britt choked on their beer they were laughing so hard. "Hold everything. Do you mean obedience training?"

"Yes, but she's paying me a lot of money. Like, three times what we charge for a behavioral session. I didn't even want to take it, but she was so insistent that she didn't have time to see someone else or acclimate Atlas to someone else. I felt bad for them." It sounded very rational when she said it out loud, yet she knew the only reason she'd accepted those extra sessions was because she genuinely liked Ellie and wanted to spend more time with her. She sometimes had this fantasy of what it would be like to actually be friends with someone like Ellie because she did *want* to spend time with her. Simply being in her presence *felt good*.

She wondered if they could hang out and have a glass of wine and laugh about nothing. She'd never really had that, but no, they couldn't. Clearly, they had too much chemistry to spend time alone. The thought of a friendship was scary, and the thought of a relationship had Hayden's throat feeling like it was going to close up. She took a sip of beer to wash away the bitterness. Her own self-preservation came first; she couldn't risk another loss. She knew she'd never be able to come back from it. "And the home visits are over now."

Britt stared with raised eyebrows and smirked.

"They're stopping." Hayden was adamant. They'd gotten too close to something real, and she wasn't going to let that happen.

❖

"Were you a good boy while Mommy was away on business? Were you?" As she said it, Ellie realized how she'd just slipped into referring to herself where Atlas was concerned and acknowledged that *mom* didn't feel all that weird. Certainly not as weird as she'd thought it would. It felt natural, although that was bizarre in and of itself. But after three months, he was her baby. As much as she'd never thought that'd happen.

Baby or not, as she walked farther into her condo, she was dismayed to find that he had rearranged all the towels in the house again, chewed up a new throw pillow she'd gotten for the world's least comfortable chair, and had been chewing on his tail for long enough that it had left red streaks on the cabinets again.

"Shit, Atlas. What happened today? What set you off?" She'd had a business trip earlier in the week, but she'd had a sitter stay with him. Though it was late now. She'd gotten caught up working on a returns analysis for a pension fund. She looked at her watch. Eight p.m. She really hadn't realized how late it was.

It wasn't infrequent for her to get caught up at the office, but she needed to get better at not doing it for Atlas's sake. She also needed to spend more time in the evenings working with him. She'd been skipping his training at night if she worked late and was too tired, but she could tell the difference in his behavior when she did.

She knelt, grateful the pants of this suit were a little loose and gave her the freedom to sink down. "I've got to do better with you, don't I?"

He rolled onto his back and wiggled until his head was resting on her thighs. "You *are* a good boy, aren't you? Are you ready for some dinner?" At the "D" word, he jumped up and ran into the kitchen. "I'm so sorry I've been starving you tonight, mister. I promise I'll do better."

She was going to have to talk to Hayden about this new development when she went to see her this week. But things had been so awkward since their almost kiss. Hayden had become tight-lipped and focused only on Atlas at their one session since. They hadn't shared a drink after, and Hayden had made something up about having plans. Maybe she really did, but Ellie didn't think so. Her excuse had come suspiciously late in their discussion, and Hayden had been really twitchy when giving it. That was going to make for an interesting visit this week when she took him in again.

❖

"Was there a change to the routine when he engaged in destructive behavior again?" Hayden asked, pointedly staring at Atlas rather than glancing between them like she normally did. But she was still running her thumb along her bottom lip as she often did in contemplation.

Ellie tried to force herself not to stare, but it was a struggle. At least Hayden was unlikely to notice. "Sort of. I had a business trip this week, and a sitter stayed, and he was fine with that. But then a day later, I got caught at work and didn't make it home until after eight. He'd had a walker come around lunchtime but ended up being alone for about eight hours…" She trailed off as embarrassment crept along her skin like an army of ants heading to a picnic. She already knew exactly what the problem was and knew it was her fault. But she also didn't want to *not* tell Hayden since she was his doctor. She needed to know about any setbacks. Including her own, as much as Ellie didn't want to admit to them. "It might have been ten hours. It was a really long day, and I got caught up dealing with a situation…sorry, I'm sure you don't care about any of that. I overshare a lot, but that has nothing to do with Atlas or how I left him alone for way too long." *Shit, shut the hell up.*

Hayden stopped running her thumb along that perfect lower lip, still looking at Atlas like he was the most interesting creature she'd ever seen. "That's good that you recognize it. You can make whatever changes are necessary so that you don't do that to him again." *Ouch.* "How's he been since?"

Ellie wanted to crawl into a hole. He was such a good boy when she didn't set him up for failure. He needed her to be better for him. She wanted to do it. But it was hard in the moment. She rubbed the back of her neck. "He's been good. He seems really calm when I get home from work. I've been walking him twice a day—long walks— plus the one or even two walker visits every day, depending on how long I expect my workday is going to be. When I walk in, he's just chilling on his cushion on the couch. Like the king of the castle."

That got a quick glance from Hayden and a quarter of a smile. Ellie wanted to shake her head at how pathetic it was that the tiniest smile from Hayden set a flutter of butterflies loose in her stomach. She was pitiful. "That's great that he was able to rebound so quickly. How many days ago was that?"

"Three." Ellie rubbed Atlas's ear for comfort. It was like silk between her fingers.

"And he was fine the next day?"

"Yep."

"That is remarkable that he came down so quickly. Those adrenaline responses can sometimes take a couple of days to recover from. How has he been doing with obedience when distractions are present?" Her professionalism, given they had almost kissed a few weeks ago, was driving Ellie to the edge. How could she ignore her like this?

"That is still a struggle. It's hard to get an environment where there are distractions we can control. There are so many damn dogs in this city. And many of them are tiny, with pointy ears, the type that drive him completely wild. It's ridiculous how afraid of ten-pound dogs he is." She laughed to release the simmering frustration.

Hayden gnawed on the inside of her cheek and pursed her lips. She stared at Atlas for what felt like three hours before looking up and saying, "So your largest issue is that you can't get enough distractions while being able to control his proximity to the dogs?" As soon as she finished talking, however, she looked right back at Atlas. *Seriously? What the hell?* "I hadn't thought about it like that, but, yeah, that's about it."

Hayden pinched her lower lip and sighed. Ellie wanted to say something but couldn't come up with anything intelligent, so she waited for Hayden to break the silence.

She sighed again. Ellie was beginning to wonder if a pallet of invisible bricks had been set on her legs. "The weekend after next, a few Chicago-based trainers, two other behaviorists from Milwaukee, and I are having a retreat. It was completely booked, but I saw this morning that one dog had to drop out. Only seven dogs and all in need of behavior modification as well as obedience training. If you're available, he could get some intensive training, but we could also set up a few exercises where we could control his proximity to dogs and other stimuli. It isn't a cheap retreat, and it certainly isn't a vacation but—"

"I can make that happen. Anything to help my big guy." She couldn't believe Hayden hadn't brought this up before. Well, it *had* been full but still. Even just a wait list? Perhaps this was the magic class that would fix Atlas. She knew it was a process, but this could be a shortcut. "Just next Saturday and Sunday?"

"It starts Thursday and goes through the following Wednesday."

Crap. She was going to have to take off work. Though it wasn't like she didn't have the vacation days.

"But you don't have to come for the full time," Hayden said.

Apparently, Ellie had taken too long to respond. Oops. It felt like every step was a misstep when it came to Hayden. "Oh no. I can make it work. I have vacation time." Even if Iris would never know whether Ellie had succeeded or failed, she couldn't let her down.

"Okay." It was such a simple word, but the small smile that Hayden flashed made Ellie warm all over. Did Hayden really want her to come? The eye contact was making Ellie's palms clammy. Hayden clearly had a lot of relationship issues. Yet, despite those red flags, Ellie was drawn to her like Atlas to dish towels.

"I probably should have asked this already, but where is it?" She'd drive wherever Atlas needed to speed his progress along—and also see Hayden again in a less formal setting, though she didn't spend more than a fleeting moment thinking about that—but she hoped that didn't mean driving to Utah or something.

Hayden laughed, and now that she'd made eye contact, real eye contact rather than just fleeting glances, she seemed reluctant to look away. "Near Lake Geneva, Wisconsin. Some colleagues from vet school have a facility up there."

Ellie wanted to ask her to ride up together, but given how she'd run away after their near kiss, pushing anything beyond professionalism for now seemed like a mistake. How had things gotten so out of control?

Ellie committed to no more long glances, no lingering touches, and absolutely no near kisses, and hoped they could get back to being friends. It was all they could ever have, and Ellie missed it.

❖

"You did what?" Britt's mouth fell open as Hayden dropped into a chair in their office for a change while they sipped a post-workday, wind-down rye.

She'd gone to Britt's office to have someone else tell her she was being ridiculous, and yet, she also didn't want to hear it. She was being a complete and utter blockhead and knew it. But the retreat would really help Atlas, and a slot had opened unexpectedly right before their visit. "I know. I can't believe it either."

"What happened to little Miss No More Outside of Work Interactions? She fell off the wagon already?" Britt snorted.

"I'm not addicted to her. This will really help Atlas. It has nothing to do with how I feel about Ellie." And if she kept saying that, she might eventually believe it.

"Okay, say we buy that. How do you see this little retreat to Wisconsin with Hot Mom and Troubled Son going?"

"Like it will with every other dog and parent. The team will help Atlas make as many improvements over the weekend as possible." She swirled her glass until the big rock clinked against the edge several times. It was a soothing sound and sensation. She took a sip and remembered the first time she and Ellie had shared a glass of the rye together after Atlas had knocked Ellie into her chair, and Hayden had forced that ice pack on her. She'd been the one to initiate their friendship. All of this was her own damn fault, and she hadn't even realized it.

"Do you actually believe that? That you can go and be in the middle of nowhere with five staff you don't really like—except for the one I'm pretty sure you've slept with—and seven strangers with their dogs and *not* spend time with a woman you like? Someone you are clearly attracted to? I'll venture to say you'll have a hard time staying away."

"I'm an introvert. Everyone annoys me. I'm happiest on my couch with my cat, but I can deal with people I'm ambivalent about—"

Britt snorted and whispered "Ambivalent," but Hayden continued, pretending she hadn't heard.

"You know the animals come first for me. The humans they love are tangential. And it's no different with Atlas." Helping animals had driven her entire professional career. They'd always been her refuge, even if she hadn't had any other than Chelsea.

But did her attraction to Ellie play a role in inviting her to the retreat? She would be lying if she said it hadn't, but Atlas was exactly the type of dog who would benefit from that training environment. In fact, her invite had been *despite* her attraction to Ellie, not because of it.

Or at least, that was what she kept trying to tell herself anyway.

CHAPTER FOURTEEN

Atlas lifted his head and grumbled at the crunch of tires on gravel as Ellie turned onto the unpaved road for the Best Friends Animal Behavioral Center. "It's okay bud. We're here to help you. I think you're going to love it." She took her eyes off the road for a second as she rubbed behind his ear. "I really think the wilderness is going to be your thing."

He sighed and lay his massive head back on the seat.

Ellie whistled through her teeth as a beautiful log and stone cabin came into view. No wonder this retreat was costing an arm and a leg. The upkeep had to be massive. The area around the cabin was neatly manicured, even in the fall, and was framed by hundreds of trees changing from green to blazing orange and red. The setting sun burned the sky a stunning scarlet and pink and shimmered off the lake. But it was the sight of the woman she hadn't been able to get out of her mind waiting for her in a small parking lot that had Ellie's mouth going dry. She assumed Hayden was waiting for her, anyway.

"Hey, you," Hayden said, a smile on her face as Ellie slid out of the smooth leather seat of her Range Rover, doubly happy that Hayden seemed to have warmed up since their last session.

Atlas went on high alert, jumping to stand. "It's okay, Atlas. Everything is okay. I'm going to let you out in one sec," Ellie said in her most soothing voice. She couldn't stop a smile as she walked around the front of her car and looked at Hayden. "Hi," she said quietly, barely recognizing her own voice.

Hayden tipped her chin toward the car. "You let him ride in the front seat, huh? Softie."

"I tried to make him sit in the back, but he refused. As soon as I walked around to get in, he jumped between the seats and settled in the passenger seat. I tried buckling him in the back, but he howled so badly that I pulled over after ten minutes and just let him sit up here. He curled up into a ball and went to sleep so peacefully." She clipped his leash on to his harness, and he jumped out of the car as gracefully as a hippo trying to run an agility course.

"Sounds about right for this lug." Hayden squatted, and after shaking so hard to loosen up that he almost knocked himself off his feet, he walked over to her. She held the back of her hand out to him like always, but rather than sniff it, he barreled right into her, knocking her onto the ground, and licked her face. Hayden shot one hand out to catch herself and used the other in an unsuccessful attempt to hold him off.

"Atlas," Ellie said, using her sternest voice. She knew he could hear because his ear twitched, but he didn't come back, so she tried again. "Atlas, come here." She clapped, and that finally did the trick, but she was so embarrassed at his terrible greeting. "I'm so, so sorry, Hayden. I don't know why he's such a ball of energy this evening." She reached to help Hayden up, who laughed as she stood.

"I guess one of the things I'll tell your trainer to work on is polite greetings. And a reliable recall."

Ellie's breath caught at Hayden's nearness. Her gaze was held hostage by Hayden's lips, glossy and full. Her heart was pounding so hard, Hayden had to be able to see it in the pulse at her throat. Yet she couldn't look away. The white tea and aloe scent Ellie remembered from when she'd cried in Hayden's arms was pulling her in until Hayden cleared her throat.

She took a step back and brushed her hands against the back of her pants before clearing her throat again. "All the other attendees, human and canine, are already here."

"What? Am I late?" Ellie looked at her watch, panicked that she had the wrong time. She was never late. Never.

"No, not at all." Hayden reached out, and Ellie thought she was going to touch her arm, but she diverted at the last minute and bent to pet Atlas instead. Was that what she'd been meaning to do the whole time? "We stagger the arrivals intentionally as we don't want six reactive dogs to run into each other in the parking lot."

"Oh, right." Ellie's head was still foggy as she tried to move past the moment they'd shared and the panic she'd felt at having been late. Even if she wasn't.

"Let me show you to your cabin. You can get settled, and then we have you scheduled for dinner at seven."

They hopped into Ellie's Range Rover, Atlas apparently content to lie in the back seat when Hayden rode with them, and she directed Ellie to the cabin they'd be calling home for the next week. It was gorgeous, if a bit of a tiny house. However, it had a lovely deck on the back that was fully enclosed, with two Adirondack chairs and a small love seat on the other side. Ellie imagined sitting out there during their down time and watching the sunset with a glass of wine or reading a book during sunrise with a cup of coffee. It seemed so peaceful, and she could easily get lost in the beautiful blue ripples across the small lake.

"We have a few ground rules for everyone's safety and an overview of what to expect," Hayden said, startling her out of her enrapturement.

Ellie jumped, Atlas immediately by her side. Her heart lodged in her throat, and she was surprised she was able to squeak out, "Of course. Yes."

Hayden cocked her head and narrowed her eyes. "Are you okay?"

Ellie forced a smile and tried to settle her jumpiness. "Yes. You just startled me is all. I was enthralled by the beauty. I don't often get into nature, but I love it." She pointed at the horizon that was still a deep orange but was about to be outrun by the pursuing dark blue.

"Wait until nightfall, and you can see all the stars out here. It's like a whole different planet. Probably too cloudy tonight, but I'm sure one night while you're here, you'll be able to see them." Hayden stared at her intently, and Ellie struggled not to squirm. What was it with this woman?

Trying to act a natural she didn't feel, Ellie said, "I look forward to it. Tell me about these safety ground rules."

Hayden sighed in what Ellie assumed was relief that she'd gotten them back on track. "First, please remember every dog here is like Atlas to some degree. Some may not be as reactive, but you should always assume that they are. We try to schedule things so that no dogs run into each other going to or from lessons or mealtimes, but it's important to be alert when walking. Either to and from the main building or along the many trails. Feel free to walk around the grounds when you don't have an active session, but be alert and give ample space to anyone you come upon."

"Got it and of course. I do that at home too." That was going to be a lot easier here, where she and Atlas could dart off the trail to give both dogs plenty of space. In the city, she'd had to turn around, jaywalk, or dart down an alley.

"Second, it may feel a little lonely, but we ask that you don't leave your dog unattended in the cabin or elsewhere. Since all the other dogs are also reactive, it isn't safe to have group meals or group lessons. You'll meet all the other behaviorists and the trainers this evening at dinner, but after today, meals will probably just be you or you and one of the staff, but let me know if there is anything that you need."

Ellie spent so much time with people during the day that a little time away seemed wonderful, though she wondered if she would be a little lonely by the end of the week. She nodded.

"Third, we'll start tomorrow with a schedule I came up with based on where I think Atlas's baseline is, but every evening, I'll meet with the staff to discuss how he did that day, and we'll schedule the next day based on his needs. Tomorrow, you're doing behavior training with Jared in the morning and—"

"We won't be working with you for everything?" Ellie tried to school any disappointment.

"No, but I will be working with you on his DSCC, desensitization and counterconditioning. Basically, what we've been working on already so he begins to feel neutral toward other dogs or even begins to see them as good because he knows they equal treats. In this controlled environment, we can test his threshold safely with dogs the trainers have brought who are very calm and relaxed and work to raise that threshold. We can typically make more progress than out in the real world where you can't control everything. We'll start on that tomorrow afternoon with Molly and her very chill pit bull, Daisy."

"Okay." Ellie knew she shouldn't feel disappointed, but she did and hated herself for it. She was still almost certainly going to be spending a lot of time with Hayden, but she'd been hoping they'd be spending every waking moment together. Which was ludicrous. They had *very* different romantic goals. And even if they didn't, Hayden had shot her down a few weeks ago, a clear sign that nothing would ever happen. She was hopeless.

"I'll leave you to get settled in. You can drive back over to the main building, or you can walk Atlas over on the path just to the left of your parking pad. It's only about a five-minute walk." She rocked back onto her heels, almost looking nervous. Which left Ellie...conflicted. "So, I'll, uh, see you at seven." It should have been a statement, but Hayden said it more like a question, so Ellie felt compelled to confirm.

"We'll be there with bells on." She laughed and wondered why she'd said something so foolish, but Hayden laughed too, so maybe it wasn't so bad.

❖

At six fifty-five, despite her best efforts, Hayden was pacing around one of the dining rooms, but she couldn't decide if she was stressed because she couldn't wait to see Ellie or because she didn't want to see her. Scratch that. Was afraid to see her. In the days leading up to the retreat, she'd been trying hard to reinforce her defenses, but from nearly the second she'd laid eyes upon her, it was like those defenses went on vacation. She'd even lost the aloofness she'd been able to hold on to the last couple of times they'd met. What was it about Ellie that had her dropping her walls without even realizing it? Ellie seemed more dangerous to her self-control in their every interaction, yet she couldn't stay away. The comfort she felt in her presence had her longing to be able to call Ellie a friend, even when she knew she didn't have it in her to let someone in.

Ellie had helped her stand, folding those warm soft fingers around her hand, and Hayden had forgotten every shred of resolve. And certainly, ending up mere inches from Ellie had not helped. Not kissing her had taken a colossal effort, and Hayden was just grateful she'd managed to do it. But God, she'd wanted to. Desperately.

"What's got you walking around here like a soldier on camp patrol?" Molly asked.

Hayden feigned innocence. "I'm just ready for this meet and greet to be over. It's been a long day, and I'm ready to crash." She also didn't want to be in the same room with any of these people. Chuck, in particular, who was a jerk. Given the choice, she'd always rather be alone, especially when the alternative was hanging out with seven other people, including Molly, whom she'd slept with once last year.

Not that she didn't like Molly. She was laid-back, funny, and had the sweetest pit bull, Daisy, as an assistant. And Molly was cute. With her short blond hair, vibrant blue eyes, and white skin with nary a blemish, she turned heads everywhere she went, but Hayden regretted sleeping with her. They'd both known what it was and what it wasn't, but Hayden preferred her encounters with anonymous strangers, not people she saw several times a year.

Now that they'd had their fun, Hayden was really uncomfortable spending time with her.

Molly didn't seem to notice. "It's been a long day. But I'm looking forward to meeting Ellie and Atlas. On paper, he sounds like a real sweetheart."

Hayden couldn't deny that. He definitely owned a little piece of her heart. "Oh, he is. And he's been making so much progress."

"I'm surprised you've been so successful with such a difficult dog, Hayden," Chuck chimed in.

What a dick. She did not have to put up with his bullshit. "What's that supposed to mean?"

"Oh, nothing." He laughed, and Hayden's teeth were on edge. There were very few people that she actively despised. A few politicians, some famous people who went on safari and poached wild animals, and Chuck. And it was neck and neck who was at the top of that list.

"Don't listen to him. He's just pissy because he considers himself a sex god, and even though he's set his sights on you, you won't worship him. Such an ass," Molly whispered.

"I know. I just don't know why he has to be such a prick. And why do Randy and Leila keep inviting him back?" Hayden knew Randy and Leila from vet school, and they'd remained in distant touch after graduation since they'd all gone into the same specialty. Randy and Leila, however, had gotten married and now owned this retreat.

"Probably because they choose not to see it. And he knows not to bite the hand that feeds him, so he hasn't harassed Leila." Molly rolled her eyes and made a face behind Chuck's back.

When the door opened and Ellie walked in with a reluctant Atlas in tow, Hayden felt the corners of her mouth twitch. Ellie was so beautiful, even in a hat and winter coat with a few specks of snow on it. In early October, it was always impossible to know how the weather was going to be in Wisconsin—or anywhere else in the Midwest—but Hayden hadn't realized it was supposed to flurry that evening. "Hey, Ellie. Welcome. Glad you found us."

"Thanks. Just straight along the trail as you said." Ellie stamped her feet, slipped out of her coat, and pulled off her hat. She ran her fingers through her hair and shook it.

Hayden loved watching her curls bounce, so before she could get too entranced, she bent to greet Atlas. Despite his too-warm greeting earlier, he was much more reserved this time. Likely because of all the new people. However, he still sniffed her hand and licked it. "Good boy," she whispered and scratched behind both his ears.

When she stood, she gave Ellie a small smile and guided her into the room with a light hand at her back. This was always such an awkward night. They were trying to introduce every dog and human to the staff at once, but it wasn't like they could have a nice buffet because they couldn't have all the dogs together, so Leila and Randy had decided the best choice was this weird gathering where the guests ate dinner, and everyone else had a small snack.

Hayden didn't agree. She started by introducing Ellie to Randy and Leila since they owned the center and then Chuck to get the most obnoxious person out of the way.

He reached to shake and gave a smile he probably thought was sexy. "Ellie, the pleasure is all mine." He held her hand too long, and Hayden watched the muscles in Ellie's arm flex as she pulled her hand away. Typical. "I'm looking forward to working closely with you and Atlantis this week." He didn't even look at Atlas when he said the wrong name.

"It's Atlas. And same."

Hayden could see in Ellie's posture she didn't mean it at all. She also didn't miss her surreptitiously wiping her hand on the back of her pants. She would apologize for him later and assure Ellie that she didn't have to work with him if she didn't want to. Hayden really didn't want her to, and if Ellie agreed, that would make things much easier.

She quickly steered them to Jared, a typical dog person, who shook Ellie's hand and bent to greet Atlas. "Hey, buddy," he said. "I'm looking forward to working with you tomorrow. I hear you need to work on your polite greetings, but this seems pretty darn polite to me. I'm going to tell Dr. Hayden to stop making up lies about you." He looked up at Hayden and winked, even though she'd already known he was kidding. He'd been around long enough to know this greeting was just because Atlas was nervous.

"Looks like Atlas might have a new best friend," Ellie said when Jared dropped to his knees, and Atlas bumped him in the chest with his nose.

"I can be his second-best friend," Jared said. "You'll obviously be his first." He smiled as he stood.

Suck up. Good thing he was actually a good guy. And was incredibly patient with difficult dogs. It was why Hayden had scheduled Ellie's first training session with him. He was a dog whisperer for sure, even if his man bun looked silly.

"What about me, handsome?" Molly was apparently tired of Jared monopolizing Atlas's attention. Though from the way she was looking at Ellie, maybe it wasn't *Atlas's* attention she was after, even though she greeted him first. She took a minute or so with Atlas, who was eating up all the attention, but quickly stood.

"Ellie, this is Molly, she's one of the dog trainers," Hayden said, trying to be polite as she fought the little twinge of jealousy at the look Molly was giving Ellie.

"Great to meet you, Ellie. I've heard wonderful things about you and Atlas from this one." She hooked a thumb at Hayden.

"Oh really?" Ellie said, eyebrows raised.

"Well, she didn't tell me how delightful you are, but she did talk extensively about what a good boy Atlas is." Molly smiled her typical bubbly smile, and Ellie smiled back. A full, radiant smile. Not the half-smile she'd given everyone else, and Hayden was surprised by a strong surge of jealousy. But Ellie wasn't looking for a relationship. Not that Hayden would be interested even if she was, she reminded herself. The thought of forever had a cold sweat breaking out on Hayden's lower back, and that wasn't going to change. She had nothing to be jealous of.

"He is a very good boy, but a lot of that is Hayden's handiwork. When I first got him, we were both a mess." Ellie shook her head as her knuckles turned white on the leash.

Molly squeezed her arm. Hayden squeezed her hands into fists. "Don't sell yourself short. Reactive dogs are difficult. I'm sure Hayden gave you and Atlas a lot of tools, but you two are the ones who did the actual work."

Was her hand lingering on Ellie's arm? Why wasn't Ellie pulling away like she had from Chuck? And was that a blush creeping up her cheeks? For crying out loud, was anyone going to be a professional other than her? Hayden almost laughed out loud at her absurd hypocrisy.

The rest of the evening went as awkwardly as the introductions had, with the team pretending to eat while basically watching Ellie and peppering her with questions for thirty minutes. When she finally managed to finish her meal, Hayden was quick to say, "It's getting late. Why don't I walk you back to your cabin, Ellie? Mine is that way too."

"Oh, sure. Thank you."

Molly jumped up, and Hayden wondered why. Ellie wasn't her client, after all. "It was nice meeting you, Ellie. I truly look forward to working with you and the big guy here," Molly said, looking gorgeous with her bright eyes and perfectly straight teeth. Hayden needed to find some fault with her and decided that her teeth were too perfect, like flawlessly lined up little Chiclets.

"Likewise." Ellie smiled back, and Hayden wanted to scream. She needed to get out of there and back to her room so she could process what all this possessiveness was and where it was coming from.

Once she'd finally bundled the three of them out the door, Hayden felt like she could take a deep breath again. Finally. They walked in silence along the packed dirt path for a few minutes with the light snow swirling around them. Short path lights illuminated their way in the otherwise very dark evening.

Hayden finally got her thoughts together enough to say, "I'm sorry that was all so weird, but sadly, Randy and Leila don't listen when I tell them how uncomfortable it is to have one person and one dog feel like they're under scrutiny from six people at once."

"It wasn't that bad," Ellie quickly said.

"Really?" Hayden simply stared as they walked.

"Okay, fine. It was weird as fuck." Ellie laughed. "But everything with Atlas is weird. You probably won't believe this, but in the real world, I am a confident badass. But somehow, anything that has to do with Atlas is turning me into this unsure little…I don't know… dumpling." She threw her free hand into the air, letting it slap her thigh when she dropped it. "I feel so pathetic. But that was really uncomfortable. And what's up with that Chuck dude? He's a jerk."

"Ugh, I am so sorry about him too. I really don't like him and have tried to get Randy and Leila to find another trainer, but they apparently haven't noticed his weird party trick of making everyone uncomfortable. But if you don't want to work with him, just say the word, and I will make sure it doesn't happen."

"I'd definitely prefer not. He didn't do anything wrong, per se, but he gives me the creeps, and I wouldn't want to be alone with him." She shivered and pulled her coat tighter.

"Understood. I will make sure that doesn't happen." Ellie let out a long breath, and Hayden hated that Chuck existed. "I asked you earlier, but we got distracted. How was your ride up?"

"It was good. A little traffic on the Eisenhower, but otherwise, no issues. And Atlas was a prince once I let him sit up front." She was such a softie, and Hayden loved it.

"Good. And how are you finding the accommodation? The cabin is a little small, but it's well-furnished, right?"

"Yes, I tried out one of the Adirondack chairs and had a glass of wine before I came for dinner. I wanted to take in the view before the sky went totally dark. That electric heater mounted to the ceiling worked great." She shivered again, and Hayden quickened her pace.

"When I'm not working, my back deck is my favorite place to spend time up here. It's so peaceful and beautiful. I love being close to the water. Pretty much any type of water. Lake, river, ocean. I've lived near all of them before and love every bit of it."

"Lake, river, and ocean, huh? All at the same time?"

"Sort of, but that's a story for another day," Hayden said as they approached Ellie's cabin. "Are you going to be okay for the evening? Do you need anything?"

"No, I think I'm fine...unless..." Ellie sucked half of her bottom lip into her mouth, and Hayden feared her legs might give out. "Unless you wanted to come in for a glass of wine and to hang out on the back deck for a bit?"

Hayden wanted so badly to say yes but instead said, "That is a very enticing offer, but I'm pretty beat. It's been a long day, getting set up for everyone's arrivals, making the schedules, and enduring all six of those terrible *dinners*. My bed is calling my name." While that was partially true, she could have very happily spent at least a couple of hours with Ellie, but it wasn't the prudent choice. "Plus, you probably don't have enough wine for both of us."

Ellie chuckled. "You must not know many people in real estate. We *always* have enough wine for any and every event."

"I think you're the first person in real estate that I've known, so I didn't know that was a rule. But now that I do, rain check, perhaps?" Dammit. Why had she said that?

When Ellie's face lit up, she knew exactly why. Britt had been right. There was no way she was going to be able to stay away from this woman for a whole week. "I'm going to hold you to that."

As Hayden walked back to her own cabin that night, she both hoped that Ellie did and didn't.

Chapter Fifteen

Ellie awoke the next morning feeling refreshed and more alive than she had since Iris had passed away. She was eager to start the day, but she wasn't sure what had changed. Certainly nothing between her and Hayden. It *had* felt good to have Molly flirt with her, even if it was meaningless and wouldn't go anywhere. She still wasn't in a place to explore anything, but it always felt good to be desired.

Unlike with Hayden, where she felt like she was walking on eggshells to be friends but not too friendly. To have fun and laugh without being too flirty. Because those heavy moments when they got too close—either emotionally or physically—were just too damn hard.

She couldn't believe she'd asked Hayden in for a nightcap. She'd known it was a bad idea as she'd done it. The last thing the two of them needed was any more alone time. They'd proven time and time again that they couldn't be trusted.

And yet, Hayden had said she wanted a rain check.

Those two little words had nearly stopped Ellie's heart. Did she want a rain check? Yes and no. Her libido said, unreservedly, yes. Her head, on the other hand, was somewhat rational.

When she and Atlas walked into the main building for their morning obedience session, Ellie was surprised to see Molly rather than Jared.

"Good morning," Molly yelled from the other side of the training room. "I know you were expecting Jared, but he texted this morning and said he was a little under the weather, and I was extra excited to see you sooner than anticipated. Spoiler alert, my girl Daisy and I will be working with you, Atlas, and Hayden on the desensitization this afternoon."

Ellie didn't know what to say even as she felt herself blush. Molly was an attractive woman—very attractive with a fresh face, bright blue eyes, and dimples that popped the second she even half smiled—but Ellie was way too old for her. Based on the smoothness of Molly's white skin, she was probably in her mid-twenties, making her at least fifteen years younger. And Ellie had lived nearly a third of her life before Molly had been born.

Molly either didn't notice Ellie's discomfort or didn't care because she moved on. "I believe the plan this morning is to work on polite greetings and recalls."

Ellie sighed in relief that they were moving on to a safe subject as she nodded. However, during their fifty-minute session, dog obedience training didn't feel as platonic as she'd hoped. Molly never did anything rude or inappropriate, but she found a lot of reasons to stand close and touch Ellie. Though she also touched Atlas quite frequently too. Maybe she was just a hands-on type of person. Ellie convinced herself she was imagining the flirting since Molly certainly wasn't flirting with Atlas every time she touched him.

"That should do it for this morning. Atlas did *amazing*. Tomorrow, we'll introduce new people to the polite greeting and work on the recall with some planned distractions, but for now, give your big guy a break. Maybe a good walk letting him sniff whatever he wants and a nap before the afternoon session. Do you have any questions?" Molly was so upbeat and perky that Ellie couldn't help but smile.

"No, this was great. Thanks." Ellie attached Atlas's leash and shook her hand.

"Wow. Your hand is so soft." Molly turned Ellie's hand over and examined it, running her fingertips over Ellie's knuckles and up the bones. "Not rough and calloused like mine from working with leashes all day."

Ellie was speechless. The feel of Molly's hands wasn't *unpleasant*, but it certainly wasn't expected. She stared until, thankfully, the door opened and interrupted the moment.

Or maybe not so thankfully. "Jared, how'd the morning session go?" Hayden asked, stopping as she looked them over. "Well, you're not Jared, and the morning session apparently isn't over."

Ellie loathed seeing the tightening of Hayden's lips and jaw. She was still speechless as Molly dropped her hand as though they'd been caught kissing.

"We were just wrapping up," Molly said. "We started a few minutes late, but we're all done now."

"Yes, Atlas and I were just heading out. If you'll excuse us." Ellie smiled at Hayden and Molly and fled before things got any worse. She hadn't done anything wrong, but her actual crush seeing her nearly flirting with another woman made her queasy.

❖

"You know she's not the vacation fling sort," Hayden said as soon as the door closed behind Ellie and Atlas. She squeezed her hands inside her jacket pockets until her fingers ached, protectiveness and jealousy burning in her veins.

"You don't know what I'm looking for. When we hooked up, I knew it was just one night, but that isn't who I am. I don't want to be single forever, jumping from hookup to hookup. That's a little sad, don't you think?" Molly must have seen Hayden's jaw clench. "I don't mean for everyone, but I want someone to come home to. Someone to share a life with. And Ellie is hot. And established. And the way she—"

"So you're trying to get with her so she'll take care of you?" Hayden couldn't believe that. She felt nauseated at the idea, and her protective instincts kicked up another notch.

"No! She's also kind and loves the hell out of that dog. Seeing that makes my heart go all aflutter."

Well, shit. Maybe Molly wasn't as conniving as Hayden had guessed. She might be trying to pursue Ellie for genuine reasons. Hayden tried to force her irritation and jealousy away. "Look, she and I are friends. Sort of. She's had a rough year. Her romantic life is in the toilet, she lost her best friend a few months ago, which is how she ended up with Atlas to begin with, and work is demanding. She's sworn off dating for the foreseeable future. Would you please, even if as a favor to me, lay off the full-court press?"

"But I really like her. Maybe she'd consider dating again to go out with me." The earnest and hopeful look in Molly's eyes tugged at something in Hayden.

And she didn't want to seem controlling or like she was warning Molly off. If Ellie wanted her, Hayden wouldn't stand in their way. She just didn't want Ellie manipulated or embarrassed. "Maybe have a candid conversation with her when you're alone. Rather than the blatant flirting like a high schooler. She's too polite to say something, but I worry you made her uncomfortable." Hayden sighed and looked away, not willing to see any more hope dance across Molly's face. She didn't want to picture them together.

"Wait. Hold everything." Molly stepped back into Hayden's line of sight. "You like her, don't you?"

"I just told you we're friends. Of course, I like her."

"No, no. You, like, really like her. Like, want to date her, like her." Molly nodded in slow motion as she appraised Hayden.

Was she that transparent? What should she say? What *could* she say and still be honest? "I do, and I don't. She's amazing, but I can't see a future where I settle down with anyone, so it wouldn't be fair if I pursued her. Just for one night or even a fling. It's not her style, and I'd never want to hurt her. I…care about her." Hayden was shocked at her candidness, but it felt so good to say it out loud. And it reinforced why she couldn't be with Ellie. Despite how much she wanted her. Despite how much the thought of Ellie and Molly together made her want to claw her own eyes out. Not a typical response for someone adverse to commitment.

"And you'd still be okay with me talking to her in a less aggressive way?"

"I want her to be happy." And that was true. She wanted Ellie to be happy, even if it would hurt. Which made the need to get away even stronger. She was going to email Dr. Prewster that evening to check in.

❖

Ellie had a lovely few hours with Atlas, walking the trails of the retreat, the crisp October air in her nose, and dry leaves crunching beneath their feet. She was the big spoon as they slept soundly for two hours. She didn't normally let him sleep in bed with her, but since they were away from home, she figured she wouldn't be setting a bad precedent. And she needed a little comfort after her tense moment with Hayden that morning, and Atlas gave her exactly what she needed.

Hayden was a little cool but still friendly when they arrived for their desensitization session. But Ellie was jealous of all the free love Atlas got, whereas she was getting reserved-Hayden again. She really hated reserved-Hayden now that she knew open-Hayden. But it had been a tense morning. Ellie wasn't going to push it. She would have to let Hayden warm back up in her own time, as she had the previous times Hayden had pulled away following a "too close encounter," as Ellie had started thinking of them. She'd push Hayden's boundaries a little, and Hayden would pull back, but before long, they'd be back to where they were. Ellie could wait it out.

"This afternoon, we're going to start by figuring out exactly where Atlas's threshold is for other dogs. It's critical that we keep him under-threshold the entire time, so we're going to start by having Molly walk with Daisy on the other side of this enclosure. She'll go back and forth while we take one step closer every pass. We'll watch for any sign that Atlas is starting to get uncomfortable, okay?" Hayden looked at Atlas the entire time she was talking again. Ellie hated that game but wanted to give her the space she needed.

"Sure. We trust you and Molly. We're in your hands." She gave a reassuring smile and hoped Hayden could at least see it out of the corner of her eye.

Hayden either felt her stare or was reacting to her words because she finally met Ellie's gaze. Her lips quirked, and she mumbled so softly, Ellie could barely hear. "You're in my hands, huh?" She shook her head and looked to Molly on the other side of the room. Louder, she said, "Okay, let's get this going. Ellie, bring Atlas to a seat, give him a couple of treats, and talk soothingly. Once he's settled, we'll have Molly begin."

The session went smoothly, and both Molly and Hayden said how well Atlas had done. While counterconditioning with treats, they were able to get Daisy several paces closer than where she'd started, which, for the first day, was great, they'd said.

She'd also noticed a marked change in Molly's behavior. When she and Hayden had switched places being Daisy's handler, Molly had still been flirty and batted her eyes once or twice, but it felt more lighthearted than that morning. And there'd been a noticeable difference in touching. Molly didn't causally touch her arm or brush her shoulder like earlier. It was a welcome change.

Ellie was putting on her coat when Molly ran up. "Hey, do you have a sec? There's something I wanted to talk to you about."

"It's Atlas's dinnertime, so we need to get back." Ellie really didn't want to have another awkward exchange. That afternoon had been so lovely compared to the morning.

"Would it be okay if I walked you back to your cabin? I promise, it won't take long."

Hayden looked like she'd eaten something that wasn't sitting well in her stomach, but she shrugged at Molly and turned away.

What was all that about? "Okay, I guess that's fine."

Once they were outside, Molly said, "I'm really sorry if I came on too strong before. I didn't mean to, and if I did anything to overstep, please accept my apologies. I get a little excited, and I'm not always great at reading the room."

That was unexpected. "Thank you. It was...weird."

"Got it. I won't overstep again. Look, Hayden told me you've had a rough year."

She did, did she? Why would she do that if she had no interest in Ellie at all?

"She said you weren't dating right now because you needed a break. But I just wanted to tell you that I like you. Quite a bit. I think you're sexy and funny, and I love how much you love Atlas. But I get that maybe you're not interested. *Now*, anyway. But if that changes or if that could change at any point, I'd love to stay in touch. I live in Pilsen, so I'm nearby. If, after we get back, you'd like to meet up for a drink, I'm happy to."

"That's really sweet, Molly. I like you too, but Hayden is right. I'm not in a place to even *consider* dating. Eventually, that's going to change, but you're honestly a little young for me. You're what, twenty-five?"

Molly looked down and mumbled, "Twenty-four," so softly that Ellie could barely hear.

"Oh God. I feel so old right now. I like you, Molly, but I was old enough to drive when you were born. I don't want to string you along, I'm sorry. But I enjoy your company, and I hope we can be friends. And maybe when we're home, I can hire you to teach Atlas some advanced tricks when he's ready. Okay?"

Molly's shoulders slumped slightly, but she said, "I can accept that. But maybe I'll change your mind in a few months. I'm not giving up."

"Ha. That's okay. It's good for my ego."

"Ready to serve, ma'am." Molly gave her a genuine smile and straightened again.

That went better than expected. One less weird thing at dog camp.

CHAPTER SIXTEEN

The rest of the week went almost in a blink, with each day being similar to the last, and before Ellie knew it, it was their final night. Molly stuck to her word and flirted lightheartedly but without the pressure from the first day.

Hayden slowly thawed and by the third day was walking Ellie and Atlas home from dinner every night. Which was funny because Ellie never felt afraid of walking alone in the dark. She had one hundred pounds of dog to chase any potential evildoers away. But having company was still nice.

She hadn't asked if Hayden wanted to redeem the rain check she'd offered the first night, though she'd thought about it every evening. The entire time they walked, Ellie had gone back and forth over whether she should. She wanted to. They'd had wine plenty of times in the past. Though, not since they'd nearly kissed.

"I hope you feel your time here has been worth taking off work," Hayden said as they neared Ellie's cabin.

Was that insecurity in her voice? "Of course. It feels like Atlas has made huge strides this week." Even without the enjoyment of being in Hayden's orbit, she was happy she'd brought Atlas.

"I'm glad you can see it too. I think we were able to make improvements that would've taken months to achieve at home." She gestured for Ellie to walk up the porch steps first.

On the landing, Ellie turned. "You really think so?"

"You would've gotten here eventually, but it would've taken longer."

Ellie's heart floated at Atlas doing so much better. "He's a pretty special dog, isn't he?"

"He is."

Ellie wanted to bring up the rain check, yet also didn't want to get shot down. But what the hell? It was their last night. "Any chance you want to redeem that rain-checked nightcap? It's our last chance."

Hayden pinched her bottom lip, a move that always sent tiny jolts through Ellie. "I…"

"You'd be doing me a favor. I have about a bottle and a half left, and if we drink them tonight, I won't have to lug them home." That was basically the truth, though the concierge would be the one to bring her luggage up. "Not that we have to drink a bottle and a half. Sorry. Should've been clearer. We can have whatever amount you'd like. I'm not a pusher." She needed to stop the rambling.

"You know what? Why not? I don't need to lay out a training plan, and it is a beautiful night."

"With the electric heater, it should be lovely sitting on the deck. And it looks like a clear night. If we walk around the back, I bet we'd have a great view of the stars."

Atlas happily trotted to his water bowl once they were all in the cabin and loudly drank at least half. "I don't know why I find that sound so soothing, but I do. It's like a water feature in a Zen garden," Ellie said.

"I don't know if I'd go that far, but it's cute."

"Everything about him is cute. Atlas, come here, buddy." He ran to her and dropped to a seat. She bent to give him a little love, kissed his head. "Are you mama's good boy?"

He barked once.

"Yes, you know you're mama's good boy." She gave him a treat for being the best boy and found Hayden watching her with an unreadable expression. "What?"

"The two of you together are just…I wouldn't have predicted it based on your body language the first day you walked into my office." A hint of a smile played along her lips.

"Really?" Ellie didn't like the sound of that. What was wrong with her the first time? Oh, maybe it was the breakdown she'd had in Hayden's arms.

"You were timid. Like you were afraid of him and completely overwhelmed."

"Well, that's entirely true. I still feel a little timid when it comes to him, but he brings something to my life I didn't know I was missing." Ellie had finally accepted that she'd fallen completely in love with Atlas. He was a pain in the ass and complicated the hell out of her life, but the love he gave her made up for the extra complexities. She finally understood Iris's ask.

"He's special. Every dog is, and every dog deserves a happy life, but—don't tell anyone—I have a soft spot for him. More so than other patients." She shrugged and smiled. "Come here, Atlas." He ran to her, and she kissed his head. "But don't let it go to your head, big guy. Now, I think I was promised some wine, wasn't I?" She pursed her lips, and a charge danced its way along Ellie's arms.

"Of course. One sec," Ellie said and headed to the kitchen. She grabbed two stemless glasses, checked to make sure she'd cleaned them, and poured the remainder of the bottle of wine she'd opened the night before. "Although I normally stick to cabs, this is one of my favorite old vine zinfandels. It is on the drier side of zins, but it is still pretty jammy and fruit forward."

"Perfect, thank you."

Ellie found herself watching as Hayden swirled the wine and took a sip. It was ridiculous that such a simple action could be so sensual. Her long delicate fingers wrapped around the glass, the workings of the little muscles in her jaw and throat, the little peek of her tongue along her bottom lip.

Ellie quickly closed her eyes and took a larger than advisable sip of her own. She masked the reflexive cough by walking into the kitchen and getting them both a glass of water. "Shall we head out to the deck?"

Hayden, seemingly oblivious to Ellie's attention, said, "Sure."

Ellie flicked on the heater behind the Adirondack chairs before sinking into one. They were a lot more comfortable than she'd expected. She stretched her legs in front of her before planting her feet on the ground.

The silence around them was comfortable. Ellie didn't feel a need to fill it with chatter and took in the crispness of the air and the peaceful sounds of the woods at night. The north woods in October were magnificent. There was a frog croaking somewhere down by the lake and a few crickets chirping. The eerie call of a bird startled Ellie, but a light reassuring hand on her arm calmed her.

"Just a loon," Hayden said. Her hand was gone so quickly, Ellie wondered if she'd imagined that it had ever been there at all.

"I know. But they're a little freaky, aren't they?"

"Now that it's faded into the beautiful soundtrack of the woods, I like it."

They slipped back into silence, and Ellie took a sip of wine. It felt so good to just relax. She rarely gave herself the time to simply sit and let her mind be silent.

As they neared the end of their first glass, Hayden said, "Are you close with your family?"

Ellie sighed, content. "I am. I just spent Yom Kippur with them. I mean, it's not exactly a fun day because we fast and spend most of it in temple, but it is nice for us to all be together. And when we break the fast at nightfall, everything feels so much lighter. It is sometimes my favorite evening of the year."

"I didn't realize that you were practicing. Not that there's an issue with that. I just…didn't know," Hayden stammered.

"Oh, I wouldn't say I'm practicing, exactly. We are ethnically and culturally Jewish, but we aren't necessarily believers. But the rituals are important. They remind us of who we are and where we came from. What we've lost and what we have. You know what I mean?"

"Sort of. But I'm the opposite. I grew up very Lutheran. My parents were, my grandmother was, but it never made sense to me. Now that they're all gone, I don't practice any of the traditions anymore. In fact, I try to leave the country for the last two weeks of the year and the first few days of January because I don't want to be surrounded by it all. All the holidays are just bullshit made up by big commerce to sell more food and cards and electronics." Her tone of voice was so cynical, it drilled a hole into Ellie's stomach, and she ached to give Hayden a hug.

"What about Thanksgiving? It's secular."

Hayden scoffed. "Please. A made-up holiday to give thanks for colonizers coming to America and doing their damnedest to destroy the indigenous population? We've embraced it as a way to sell overindulgence. It should come with a warning label, 'sponsored by America's turkey farms.' I spend that week on a beach in Costa Rica or Belize. I don't need to be surrounded by all that. I don't get the sense that most people even like Thanksgiving. They're obligated to go to a relative's house and spend time with people they don't even like. Thanks, but no thanks. I'm thankful that I have the means to escape the commercialized hullabaloo."

Ellie was a little taken aback. She wanted to know more, but it felt like too touchy a subject, and she couldn't help but wonder if Hayden hated holidays so much because she didn't have anyone to spend them with. Lacking any words, Ellie placed a hand on Hayden's knee and squeezed. "Are you ready for more wine? I saved my favorite bottle of cab for last." She'd saved it because she'd been secretly hoping she'd be sharing it with Hayden, though she hadn't admitted that to herself at the time.

"That would be great. Thanks." Hayden ran her middle three fingers across her forehead several times. "And I'm sorry. I didn't mean to get so irrationally angry about holidays. They just don't... resonate with me."

"Not at all." Ellie gave her what she hoped was a reassuring smile and squeezed her knee once more before walking in to open the last bottle of wine. When she brought it back out, she was hoping to steer clear of any touchy subjects. "On a lighter note, what do you have going on this weekend once we get home? Are you seeing patients Thursday or Friday?"

As Hayden took the wineglass, their fingers brushed. Ellie held the glass for a beat too long, enjoying the brush of Hayden's skin before she released it. Embarrassed, she sat quickly, but from the corner of her eye, she saw Hayden take a slow sip, as if settling herself. Ellie followed suit.

Finally, Hayden said, "No patients or anything exciting, but I'm moving from the lake to the river. I could push it another couple of weeks, but this weekend is convenient."

"I was going to say, 'that sounds like fun,' out of habit, but I'm actually not sure." Ellie laughed and swirled her wine around.

"It isn't bad. Going through the lock is always kind of cool, but I have a pretty big houseboat, so maneuvering it in the river is awkward at times. Though at this time of year, there are a lot fewer pleasure boats out there and basically no kayaks, so it's fine."

"I've lived here my whole life and haven't ever gone through the lock."

"What? There's no way." Hayden stared, brows furrowed.

"It's true. My mom is afraid of water, so we never did any boating when I was a kid, and that just stretched into my adulthood as well." She shrugged. She didn't think she'd been missing anything, but maybe she was wrong.

"You've *been* on a boat, though, right?"

"Uh." Ellie scrambled to think of a time she'd been on a boat and couldn't come up with anything.

Hayden laughed. "You must remedy that. The city you live in is on a massive lake, and a river trisects it. There's water everywhere."

"I suppose I probably should." It wasn't that Ellie was afraid of boats, but they were simply not on her radar. She wondered if Hayden might offer to go out on a boat with her to rectify the oversight. She wasn't surprised when that invitation didn't happen but still felt a pang of disappointment. She sighed and took a sip to cover it up. "Will you tell me why you hate New Year's? It isn't an occasion for cards or gifts or being gluttonous, with anything other than alcohol anyway. It's mostly just a party. Something to say good-bye to the previous year—good or bad—and hello to the new one." That question must have come from the wine, as Ellie knew she wouldn't have asked it earlier that evening.

"It's complicated. Or maybe not. But not fun."

"We don't have to be fun all the time. I like to laugh with you, but I also want to know you." Ellie was afraid to look. Afraid to see the rejection she feared she would find. "If you'll let me."

Hayden sighed. "I lost my grandmother on New Year's Eve when I was seventeen. It wasn't long or painful. She had a stroke when I was at work. When I came home, I thought she was sleeping on the couch. I tried to wake her up to watch the ball drop, but when

I tried to shake her…" Hayden's voice cracked, and she wiped at her eyes. Ellie sat her glass down and crouched in front of her, grabbing her hands. "She was only sixty-two."

"I'm sorry, I didn't mean to bring up a difficult subject." Ellie knew there weren't words that could make the pain less, but she wanted to comfort her somehow.

"I still wonder, what if I'd stayed home that day with her as she'd asked? Would I have noticed what was happening in time to call 9-1-1? Even if she'd still passed, at least she wouldn't have been alone. I hate knowing she was alone at the end." She cleared her throat, and Ellie could see she was holding back more tears.

"I'm sure she knew how much you loved her, Hayden. I'm so sorry you had to go through that at such a young age. What about your mother? Was she around?"

Hayden choked a laugh and sniffed. "No, she died when I was thirteen. Car accident on an icy road two days before Christmas, so you can probably see why I hate that time of year." She shook her head and wiped away a few more tears that had crept out. "My grandma was the last. My last relative keeping me from being an orphan." She released one of Ellie's hands and grabbed her wineglass, taking a long sip.

Ellie was a dumbass. Why had she pushed Hayden to tell her all this? Callously dredging up Hayden's worst memories wasn't how she'd seen the evening going. She wanted to change the subject, say anything to make this moment easier, but her brain was blank.

Atlas saved them. He started with a grumble from where he was lying, and when Ellie and Hayden both looked, he walked over and headbutted Ellie, knocking her off balance. She tried to catch herself, but her hand slipped off the arm of Hayden's chair, and she landed on her butt.

Hayden gave a watery laugh. "Clearly, we've been neglecting Atlas for too long." She wiped her eyes again and took another sip of wine, finishing it.

"He probably needs to potty." He spun around at the word. "Yep. Do you want to stay up here while I take him out?" She gestured toward the field beyond the deck.

"No, I'll come with you. Stretching my legs sounds great." Hayden stood and stretched her back, bending forward and touching her toes, and then, placing her hands on her hips, she arched backward. Ellie's mouth went dry watching her svelte form, so she took the last sip of her own wine before leashing Atlas to take him into the yard.

She was silent as the gravity of everything Hayden had shared weighed upon her. She wondered if Hayden had shared that much with anyone in a long time. It seemed like she had a lot of repressed emotions. Or at least a lot of grief.

"Have you looked up?" Hayden said.

Ellie hadn't, but she did, and the sky took her breath away. She knew that the light pollution masked the majority of stars in Chicago, but the twinkling in the sky was like fairies had sprinkled stardust in wide swaths. "Wow. I always forget how many stars there are."

Hayden pointed almost directly above. "That's Cassiopeia there. The sideways W or M. It's supposed to be a beautiful queen chained to her throne because she betrayed Poseidon."

Ellie stepped closer to better follow her finger. With so many stars, the brighter ones still sometimes faded into the mass. "I don't see it."

Hayden wrapped her other arm around Ellie and pulled her in front of rather than beside her. Ellie resisted the urge to sigh as the full length of Hayden pressed into her back. Her arm against Ellie's shoulder, her mouth so close to Ellie's ear that she could feel the warmth when she spoke. "Follow my hand. Do you see it? It's like a slightly wonky M rotated ninety degrees."

"Oh, yeah. There it is. Do you know any others?" She didn't want Hayden to step away.

"Not really. Not sure why Cassiopeia stuck with me. Maybe because she's easy to spot. Or maybe because my queer little brain had a fantasy of rescuing a queen tied to a chair."

Laughter overtook Ellie as she envisioned a teenage Hayden in astronomy class, fascinated with light bondage. As her body bounced against Hayden's, that joviality quickly turned to lust when the hand Hayden had around her middle brushed the bottom of her breast.

Hayden cleared her throat and turned them to the right, pointing at something lower on the horizon. "That's Jupiter. Remember, we saw it from your balcony?"

Ellie could barely find her voice. "Yeah." She hated it when Hayden dropped her arm and stepped back.

"And that's the end of my astronomy lesson because we've reached the boundary of my knowledge. Sorry."

Ellie checked to make sure Atlas was okay, and when she saw him snuffing the grass a step away, she looked at Hayden. "Thank you. Even if it was just two celestial bodies. It's more than I knew before."

"I'm sorry I got so heavy earlier. About my family and all. I never share that story. I never talk about my past to anyone, really."

"I'm sorry I pushed, but I'm not sorry you told me. I want to know you. I know Atlas is your patient, but I feel like we're becoming friends. I like you."

"I don't really have friends. Everything in life seems so impermanent, which probably makes a lot more sense now that you know I'm an orphan. I don't trust that anyone can stick around. Even if they want to."

Ellie's heart dropped. "Oh, Hayden." When she saw tears shimmering in Hayden's eyes again, she pulled her into a hug. The hug she'd been wanting to give all evening. Atlas pulled at the leash for half a second before lying against the back of Ellie's leg, pushing them closer. "Everyone has to die, and we can't choose when, but it doesn't mean they didn't have value in our lives. It doesn't mean we should walk through our lives as an island."

When Hayden's shoulders began to shake, Ellie rubbed her back. A reversal of the first time they'd met. She made soothing sounds and hoped that it helped. Hoped Hayden was getting out the good cry that she clearly needed. Atlas occasionally adjusted but seemed content to stay in the grass.

"Thank you," Hayden said when she lifted her head from Ellie's shoulder. "I'm sorry. I don't cry like that. I think the last time I cried in someone's arms, it was my grandma's right after my mom died more than twenty years ago. I apparently needed a little comfort."

"Happy to be of service," Ellie said. Hayden didn't step away, and Ellie swiped a couple of lingering tears from her face. "You've held me while I cried, so I just returned the favor." Hayden's beautiful topaz eyes had little flecks of brown and were more mesmerizing than the sky above.

Ellie knew the smart move was to step away, but she didn't. It had to be the relaxing effect of the wine. When Hayden's gaze dropped to her mouth, her heart began thundering loudly. It was all she could hear. She thought she was imagining it when Hayden started to gradually move forward. She had to have been imagining it. Hayden wasn't interested. Yet, she felt the friction of Hayden going to her toes to bring them level and knew her eyes weren't playing tricks.

Ellie couldn't be sure who brought their lips together at last. The softness was perfect. Hayden smelled like heaven and tasted like the sweetest wine. Ellie's hands tightened into her heavy sweater, pulling her closer. Their tongues touched, and the groan Hayden released sent shockwaves reverberating between Ellie's legs.

Hayden's fingers slid up Ellie's side and over her shoulder. They caressed Ellie's neck and finally landed on her cheek. The kiss was gentle yet urgent, and Ellie was desperate to feel her skin. She slid her hands under the bottom of Hayden's sweater until her thumbs found the smooth skin of her hips.

"Wait." Hayden pulled back. Took a step away. *Fuck.* "Should we be doing this?"

Ellie was breathing hard, and her body felt cold without Hayden against her. "No." She closed her eyes and massaged her forehead with her thumb and index finger as she tried to think. When she looked back up, the naked lust in Hayden's eyes did her in. "But I don't care. I've wanted you from the second I saw you. It's a terrible idea, but what would the harm of one night be? We're both single and not looking for commitment. Just a one-time occurrence. An OTO, if you will."

She swallowed hard. "Do you really think we can do this and not have anything change? We can go back to being sort of friends tomorrow?"

"I think it's safe to say we *are* friends, even if you don't see it, and yes, I'm confident we can go back to normal tomorrow. We can be better because we'll burn off some of this heat between us." Ellie's hands shook with the need to pull Hayden close again. To find out what was beneath that chunky sweater.

"Maybe you're right. By tomorrow, we'll be little spent briquettes." Hayden nodded too fast, but Ellie was willing to go with any excuse they could come up with to justify what they both so badly wanted.

"So we're doing this?" Ellie said.

"Okay. But let's go back inside where it's warm. Getting naked in this field sounds cold and might startle an unsuspecting passerby."

Ellie grabbed Hayden's hand and pulled them toward the house.

Chapter Seventeen

Ellie didn't allow herself to think of a single reason why this was a bad idea. In fact, she told herself repeatedly that it was the only thing that made sense. But she didn't want to assume Hayden was playing the same game with herself. "You still good?"

Hayden smirked. "Abso-fucking-lutely." She grabbed Ellie by the front of her jacket and pulled her in, claiming her lips. Ellie's hands went to Hayden's hips, holding her close. The gentleness they'd been ensconced in outside made way for raw passion as their hips began to move slowly together.

Hayden reached into Ellie's hair. She broke their kiss just long enough to whisper, "I've wanted to run my fingers through your hair since the first time I saw you." When their lips met again, Hayden's tongue brushed Ellie's, and she was frantic to find skin beneath Hayden's clothes. She finally found the bottom of Hayden's sweater and yanked it over her head.

Lips free momentarily again, Ellie said, "So this hasn't just been one-sided the entire time? I thought I might have been imagining things." Perhaps Hayden wore sexy lingerie all the time, or maybe she had a premonition about ending up topless that evening, but the nearly translucent black bra sent every drop of available liquid in her body to the juncture between her thighs. The dark nipples silhouetted behind the lace drew Ellie in like a bee to the sweetest flower in the garden.

"Are you kidding?"

"What?" Ellie was so taken by the need to draw those gorgeous nipples into her mouth that she hadn't a clue what Hayden was talking about.

The corner of Hayden's mouth turned up. "You're adorable." She wagged her finger between them. "You thought this was one-sided? Even for a second."

"Oh, uh, yes. I mean, I wasn't sure." Ellie's brain felt like she was trying to get through a maze. "You seemed interested, but you pulled away. I thought I must be misinterpreting your body language."

Hayden chuckled. "I just...I only do this with people I don't know. And only once. I didn't want to hurt you because I know that isn't your style, so I tried to stay remote, but holy fucking hell, you'd look at me like you're looking at me now, and I forgot the reasons it was a bad idea. Until I remembered again."

Ellie's heart was racing, afraid Hayden was going to pull away again. "Well, thank goodness we figured that out, but"—she held up her index finger—"one, I'm only looking for this exact second." She lifted her middle finger. "And two, this *is* a good idea. We're going to get it out of our systems so we can go back to being friends. Right?"

Hayden's eyes darkened. "Fuck yeah." And she yanked Ellie's jacket and Henley shirt over her head, and her nimble fingers were at the button of Ellie's jeans. Hayden pushed until the back of Ellie's knees hit the mattress, and she tumbled onto it.

Hayden stood over her for 2.3 seconds until she grabbed Ellie's socks, along with the bottoms of her jeans, and pulled them off. Ellie sat up and took one of Hayden's breasts into her mouth through the fabric of the sheer bra. Hayden's groan and the hand at the back of Ellie's head encouraged her to suck harder until she felt the nipple harden beneath her tongue, and a new surge of wetness flooded Ellie's slit.

She switched to the other nipple, needed to give it the same attention, but also pulled the cup of Hayden's bra down and squeezed the first nipple as she lightly bit the other.

"Ellie, please. Take my pants off," Hayden pleaded.

Ellie continued sucking while she fumbled with the buttons. "Didn't these fucking button flies go out of style in the early two thousands?"

"Don't make fun of me. They're comfortable. They're my go-to jeans in a hands-on environment," she panted.

"I am very happy to be having a *hands-on* session this evening." Ellie pressed kisses just below Hayden's bra and down to her belly button. Finally, she got the last button on the tormenting pants free and slid them down Hayden's legs. She pulled her onto the bed and moaned when Hayden's knee applied the absolute perfect pressure to her center. When she opened her eyes, the sight before her took her breath away. Hayden's eyes were closed, and she was riding Ellie's thigh like it was what she'd been born to do. Her eyes were closed, one hand on the breast Ellie had bared, squeezing her own nipple, the other hand braced on Ellie's hip.

Ellie nearly came at the sight. And that bra—that Ellie wanted to have framed—was half-on and half-off. Somehow, it made the entire scene sexier. Ellie wished she could take a pic and remember this moment for all eternity.

Until Hayden slid one hand between Ellie's thighs. Then all she could think about was how long she could hold off coming and continue savoring this snapshot in time. She wanted to wait forever, but her body had other ideas, and a telltale tightness started in her chest. She cried out as her orgasm roared through her, and as she lost contact with her functioning brain, the last thing she was aware of was the sound of Hayden calling her name.

Chapter Eighteen

When Ellie woke the next morning, she knew the time had come to let Hayden go. But she didn't want to. She hated the thought.

But they weren't a thing. They would never be *a thing*. She needed to slide off Hayden and sneak into the bathroom to shower before Hayden woke up. Maybe if she was in the shower, Hayden would do the sneaking instead and leave. It was a weird position to be in because all she wanted to do was shimmy their hips so she could spoon Hayden until they both woke up with the sun and have her one more time before they had to say good-bye. But that was a slippery slope. They'd both agreed to one night. One and done.

Fuck.

She'd rather have one night of memories than nothing, but walking away was going to be hard. But didn't one night extend into the next morning? Maybe not the full day, but it *could* mean one other encounter. She did shift, exactly how she wanted until she was the big spoon, and Hayden's hips were nestled snugly against her own.

❖

Hayden awoke to the sound of a dog barking. A big dog. Other than the incessant noise, she felt surprisingly amazing. The room smelled delicious. Like strawberries and summer rain and sex.

More barking. What the fuck?

"Lie down, Atlas. Just five more minutes. I swear." *Ellie.* An arm Hayden hadn't realized was there pulled her hips tighter.

She sighed and relaxed into Ellie before she realized what she was doing. *Shit.* "I should go." She hated saying it, and even more, she hated meaning it. But she really didn't want anyone to see her leaving Ellie's cabin in her clothes from yesterday. It wasn't likely to happen given how secluded the cabins were, but it was possible, and the earlier she got away, the better.

"Just five more minutes. Even Atlas agrees," Ellie said, her voice gravely and rough. "See? He's not barking anymore."

Hayden knew she shouldn't but allowed herself to be sucked back into the vortex of Ellie's warmth for five minutes. Which turned into thirty before Atlas roused them again. "I want to stay in this warm cocoon and keep sleeping, but we said one night. And we're getting into dangerous territory by not keeping that bargain," Hayden said.

"Do you have one more go in you before you leave?" She moved her hips slowly against Hayden's backside, awakening every pleasure cell in her body.

"Mmm. Now that sounds—"

Atlas barked again. More insistently and he started jumping, his nails making a *click-clack* sound every time.

"I think he's telling us he's had enough of our 'in bed' time today," Hayden said.

Ellie groaned. And not the good kind. "I know." Hayden rolled to face her. "This was our night. Our one perfect night. And now you need to go before one of us turns into a pumpkin."

"You look sad. Do you regret it?"

Ellie smiled, but it didn't reach her eyes, and Hayden hated it. Ellie traced a thumb along Hayden's lip, and Hayden resisted the urge to draw it into her mouth. The time for that was over. "Not even a little. If we hadn't, I wouldn't know how this perfect lip tastes. I wouldn't know how much you like it when I kiss your collarbones. I wouldn't know the beautiful sounds you make when I make you come with my mouth while fucking you with three fingers. And those are things I would never take back. Even if I'll never have the chance to do them again."

Heat flooded Hayden's center at the thought, and the corners of Ellie's eyes crinkled. Hayden finally believed she was smiling. Believed she'd meant the words she'd just said.

"Do *you* regret it?"

"I've enjoyed every moment I spent with you this evening. Will I regret it tomorrow or next week or a month from now? I hope not. I am worried we won't be able to work well together anymore. I'm worried the only thing we'll be able to think about is this." She waved in a circle over their bodies.

"If I could put the fantasies of what this *would* have been like on a shelf before, I can certainly put it aside now that I've satisfied this need."

Hayden sighed. The relief turned her muscles to liquid. "Good. I don't want to stop seeing Atlas."

"I don't want Atlas to stop seeing you. I also don't want to stop being your friend."

Hayden doubted that staying friends was a good idea. It was true that she'd told Ellie things the night before—hell, in the weeks leading up to last night—that she'd never told anyone. She hadn't even talked to Chelsea about them. But that was what made Ellie so dangerous. Hayden had never meant to tell her ninety percent of the things she had, and she *couldn't* come to rely on her. "Do you want to come with me this weekend when I move to the river? It could satisfy your curiosity about the houseboat concept, it will get you on an actual boat, and you'll even have a chance to go through the lock."

What the actual hell was wrong with her? She'd just finished telling herself that she didn't think they could still be friends, and now she was inviting Ellie into her home? She was a masochist. It was the only explanation.

Ellie chewed the inside of her lip. "Do you really mean that?"

No. But Hayden decided to follow up that ill-thought-out invite with more reasons why Ellie should come over. She couldn't stop herself. "I do. You can bring Atlas if you want. Chelsea doesn't love dogs, but she tolerates them. I've fostered several particularly difficult dogs while I've had her, and she generally ignores them and looks down on all of us. She doesn't run, so she doesn't set off their prey drive. And if it doesn't work, I can leave her in her bedroom."

"Thank you." Were those tears shimmering in her eyes? *Shit.* Could Hayden somehow rescind the invitation? If Ellie was already emotionally attached, this was never going to work. "Saturday is Iris's birthday." *Oh.* "Well, would have been her birthday." Ellie swiped at the tears breaking loose. "She would have been forty-two on Saturday. We always spend each other's birthdays together. Spent." Ellie closed her eyes and took a deep breath. "We always spent. I didn't know what to do this weekend, but maybe the novelty of all the boat stuff will keep my mind occupied enough that I won't dwell on my loneliness all day."

Hayden felt like a narcissistic asshole assuming Ellie's tears were because of her. "Well, in that case, you have to come. We'll make a day of it and drink to Iris. Okay?"

"Okay. Thank you. Really. I'm already dreading the weekend less."

Atlas barked again. Hayden was surprised at how long he'd given them that time. "And that's my cue to go. You need to take him out, and I need to take my walk of shame."

Ellie laughed and pulled Hayden against her. She knew that this was the last time their skin would touch like this. The last time they would hug and their breasts and stomachs and thighs could come together with no barriers between them. And she appreciated every single second of it.

On her walk back to her cabin, Hayden was surprised that she didn't feel any regret about the night. She'd been more vulnerable than she'd been since she was a teenager, and Ellie had given her exactly what she'd needed. A hug, a comfort, a distraction. A part of her longed to be Ellie's friend. She hated admitting how much she enjoyed spending time with her, but she did.

She allowed herself a brief moment to think about what having a friend like Ellie would be like. They could have a glass of wine together at a bar and laugh about whatever a challenging dog parent did that day. She could open up about the nightmares she sometimes had about waking up alone in a world where all of humanity had vanished.

When her heart started to pound at the thought of letting someone close to her—even Ellie—she took a deep breath and shook her body to release the tension, the fear. Despite how much she liked Ellie, there was no way she could let herself grow attached to her. It was a recipe for disaster, and she needed to protect herself from it.

Molly's voice rang out, calling to Daisy in the fog, and Hayden quickened her steps. The last thing she needed was for Molly to find out she'd spent the night with Ellie. Especially after their talk.

Admittedly, what she and Ellie had shared didn't feel like a one-night stand, even though they'd gone into it knowing it was. But it had been a conscious decision to give each other what they'd needed in that moment. Hayden wondered if part of the reason she'd been willing to go there was because of how jealous she'd been seeing Molly flirt with Ellie. Hayden had no claim over Ellie, but seeing Molly all over her made a primal part of her rear up.

Hayden didn't love what that said about who she was; she'd never been the jealous or possessive type. But Molly had made her blood boil.

And it had been such a delicious night. Ellie had a *very* talented tongue and loved to use it. Neither of them had gotten much sleep, and the absolute perfect soreness of Hayden's muscles meant she'd had a fucking amazing night. No matter what happened next, she resolved to look back on last night fondly. A memory she could take out, dust off, and relive whenever she needed a lift. Even if she was in New Orleans or wherever else the wind blew her.

Chapter Nineteen

Ellie, Skye, and Bailey took off their hard hats when they reached the front doors of Ambassador Plaza and headed toward Wok of Fire for lunch.

"How was the doggo retreat, Ellie?" Bailey said.

"Atlas made so much progress. He's learning to greet people politely like a champ. And we worked on his reactivity. It was great. Amazing, really." She'd been back for twenty-four hours, yet her cheeks hurt from how much she smiled every time she thought about that week. And Atlas's progress. And Hayden.

"Amazing is a strong word for a retreat that involved work the whole time," Skye said.

"Not all the time. We had down time too." She bit her lip to keep from smiling at all the "going down" time she'd had.

"And how was the sexy doctor?" Skye said, a knowing smile on her lips as they settled at their table to wait for a runner to bring their food.

Ellie felt the heat of a blush roar up her face. She took a sip of water.

"Oh. My. Fucking. God. You slept with her," Skye cried. "Didn't you?"

"Please keep your voice down," Ellie whispered loudly. "All the kids in here do not need to hear about my sex life."

"Fine," Skye huffed. "But you did, didn't you? How was it?"

"Yes, and it was sensational. I still have a few sore muscles that I didn't even realize existed until this week."

"Whew." Skye fanned her face with a napkin. "Glad to hear you're back on the horse. But I thought you weren't dating. And that she didn't do relationships."

"It was a one-time thing. We both needed a little something, and so we gave it. And took it. And it was the perfect night. But it's over now, and life is going on. I think we've agreed to be actual friends. She invited me to her houseboat this weekend. It's going to distract me from a day I've been dreading for months."

Bailey squeezed her hand. "I'm happy you have something to look forward to. We were going to invite you over, but—"

"You clearly have plans," Skye finished for her. Bailey rolled her eyes, and Skye pressed a quick kiss to her lips. "You know you love me," she whispered.

"Despite my efforts otherwise." Bailey was clearly trying to keep a straight face, but the corners of her mouth kept twitching.

"Luckily, I'm very charming." Skye smiled at her. To Ellie, she said, "Now, these plans. Are you sure both of you don't want anything else to happen? Because you're going to be in her home. In what I would assume is a romantic location." Skye bounced her eyebrows. "Do you really think you aren't going to have a little *lusty temptation*?"

"For crying out loud, Skye. We are adults. We can spend time together without it morphing into sex. We've been doing it for months."

Ellie felt surprisingly optimistic about being able to spend time with Hayden without the sexual tension between them. When Hayden had left the morning after, although she'd wanted her one more time, it was like the fog of tension that had been making it hard for her to think around Hayden had lifted, and everything felt clear. In that moment, she'd known they'd done the right thing in sleeping together, and everything between them from there on out would be smooth sailing.

❖

Ellie parked her car at the marina by the lake and wondered how she was going to get it back. It wasn't like she could just take an Uber with Atlas in tow. Hopefully, Hayden had a plan. And they *could* walk it if it came to it.

"Come on, big guy." Atlas jumped out of the car at her command, and although she could tell he was on alert from his posture and the wrinkles in his forehead, he looked to her for a treat and walked without pulling or barking. The true test came when they reached the start of the wharf, but he even did okay with a nearby German shepherd. Once clear of the shepherd, she pressed a kiss to his head and walked to the pier Hayden was docked at. She punched in the code Hayden had given her, and as she approached the slip, she double-checked the text several times, but there was no mistake. "This isn't a houseboat like in the movie, Atlas. This is a cruise ship."

"Hey, Ellie. Over here." Hayden was walking along what Ellie assumed was the second floor of the boat, waving at her. "Give me one second, and I'll be right down."

Moments later, Hayden was opening the sliding door on the back of the boat and reached out to help Ellie aboard. Atlas was a little reluctant to take the step onto the back of the boat. "Come on, Atlas. You can do it." Ellie held out a treat, but he still didn't budge.

"I have a secret weapon." Hayden held out a brown stick about eight inches long but only about the width of a pencil. "Do you want a special treat for good boys, Atlas?" She waved the stick at him, and he leaped across the small gap and sat politely in front of her. "Yes, good boy." She handed him the stick, and he took two steps before plopping down and going to town on it.

"What was that?" Ellie needed to stock up if it got him to do what she wanted that quickly.

"It's a bully stick. And don't ask what they're made of. Trust me. You don't want to know." She shook her head and made a gagging face.

"Got it, never research that information." Ellie made a show of looking around. "So *this* is your house? I was expecting something more like the one from that fifties' movie."

Hayden scoffed. "That thing was a piece of junk."

"At the end it was all spiffed-up. It was nice but boxy."

"You just don't realize this one is boxy because you can't see the front. It's quite rectangular."

Ellie pointed down the side of the boat where the wall was almost entirely glass. "But this is sleek. Classy. Looks like a yacht. Not like something the Simpsons would live on."

Hayden's brow creased. "You think I would live on a boat that the Simpsons would live on?"

"The *Cape Fear* parody episode actually started my interest in houseboats."

Hayden laughed. "It's hard for me to imagine you watching *The Simpsons*."

"I am a woman of many surprises, I guess."

"I am starting to understand that."

Relief rolled over Ellie like a warm blanket at Hayden's easy smile. Although things the morning after had felt comfortable, she'd harbored a slight fear they would be walking on eggshells, mired in uncomfortable tension.

"Regardless, I'm happy to show you your first houseboat. And take you on your first trip. Even though it's going to be short. If it was warmer and we had more time, we could cruise on the lake for a bit, but the moving process takes a while, so after I give you a tour, we should get going before it gets late."

"Sure. I guess when Atlas finishes his…" Ellie trailed off because he had already finished it and was licking his massive paws. "Well, I guess we're ready."

Ellie was amazed that there could be this much luxury on a boat. There was a small stone fireplace in the living area just inside the sliding doors. The kitchen had a gas stove, granite countertops, and even a dishwasher. The walls on both sides were reflective glass, so she could see out, though there wasn't a ton to see in the marina.

"Where's Chelsea?" Ellie didn't want to happen upon the cat and startle Atlas.

"In her bedroom with the door closed." Hayden pointed to a door on the right as they started down a narrow hallway. "The best way to introduce them is through a closed door where they can hear and smell each other but not see. Let them get used to the idea of the other first."

"That makes sense, but what I'm mostly curious about is, your cat has her own bedroom? On your boat?" Something about that entire situation struck her as hilarious.

"Why is that weird? There are five bedrooms, including some little cubbyholes below deck, but I wouldn't stick her down there. She normally sleeps in my room, but her litter box, food bowl, etc. are all in her room. It's also her safe place when I rudely bring home a dog she isn't sure about."

"Oh wow. I'm going to need to meet this cat. She sounds incredibly spoiled." *And she* was supposed to be the woman of many surprises? Who would have seen Hayden spoiling her cat that much?

"We'll see if we can get there today."

Atlas sniffed at the door and pushed at it with his nose. Chelsea cried on the other side, and there was a brushing sound that Ellie assumed was her rubbing against it.

"Those are all good signs." Hayden smiled and pointed down the hall. "Here's my bedroom." She opened the door, and Ellie's jaw dropped.

"I had no idea you could have this much room on a boat. Or this many windows. I was envisioning a little cave-like room with a porthole. But there's so much light."

"I like the light. I do have blinds if needed. Ziggy."

An automated male voice with a British accent said, "Good afternoon, Hayden."

Ellie's jaw dropped.

"Close the bedroom shades." Mechanical blackout blinds slid down each window in the bedroom. As the light was slowly extinguished, Ellie realized exactly how close she and Hayden were standing. It hadn't been intentional, but now the nearness set every cell in her body on high alert. Her skin felt needy for the touch of Hayden's fingers, soft and cool.

They stared at each other long after the blinds reached their termination point, the only light in the room coming from the hallway. Ellie tried to tell herself to step back. Move away and out of the orbit that always drew her in.

Before she had a chance, Atlas bumped into the back of her legs and forced her into Hayden, who caught her before they fell back on her bed. That would have been a disaster. A lovely, pleasurable, wonderful disaster but a disaster, nonetheless. Because Ellie did not want to ruin their friendship. Or their ability to work together.

Hayden huffed when Ellie's chest hit her.

"Sorry about that. I guess Atlas couldn't see where I was standing. He's a bit of an oaf, as you already know."

Hayden hadn't yet dropped her hands that were delicately holding on to Ellie's hips, but they'd long since passed any attempt to steady her and had moved into "making her more unsteady" territory. "Yeah, it's pretty dark in here," Hayden said.

Ellie was pretty confident she was staring at her lips, though she couldn't be certain because they were in shadow. *Stop it.* Ellie closed her eyes and took a deep breath in before she stepped away. "Yeah, poor guy probably couldn't see a thing."

"Ziggy, open the blinds," Hayden said.

As warm light flooded the room again, Ellie felt a harsh pang of loss. That was annoying because she hadn't *lost* anything. But she also didn't want to lose something now by making a mistake.

"If you head back the way we came and look to the right, you'll see another bedroom, a bathroom. There's a bathroom in my stateroom too, but it's a little too cramped in there right now."

Hayden showed her the cubbyhole bedrooms in the "basement" before taking her onto the upper deck to find another fireplace, some lounge chairs, and a small round hot tub. "You even have your own Jacuzzi? Your home is amazing, certainly not what I was picturing."

"Is that a good thing or a bad thing?" Hayden nibbled the inside of her lip, and in the surprisingly bright afternoon light, Ellie was struck by how perfectly chiseled her cheekbones were. They were high and proud and gorgeous.

She needed to answer, though. "Uh, an indifferent thing?"

"I'll take that. Let's head up to the flybridge and get out of here."

They made their way up another narrow set of stairs with Atlas surprisingly in tow. Ellie thought he would be too afraid to climb the treacherous steps. As they pulled out, she was amazed at how masterfully Hayden handled the massive ship. "How did you learn to drive a boat like this?"

"Oh, my mom—my parents, I guess, before my dad died— were boaters. My grandma had a boat on Lake Erie when my mom was growing up. It's how she met my dad. My parents had their honeymoon on a catamaran somewhere down in the Caribbean and fell even more in love with each other and boating. After my dad died, my mom had a hard time at first but felt like boating brought her closer to him, and she started taking me out all the time. So it's kind of in my blood, I guess."

"That's cool that it was something you could bond over."

"It was much smaller than this but the same feeling. It was hard to give it up when she died, but my grandma had already gotten rid of her boat when I moved in, and she felt like she was too old to buy another. After I lost her…" Hayden shrugged, and Ellie thought she was pretending to be less affected than she actually was.

"You don't have to answer this, but what happened to your mom?"

Hayden cleared her throat. "She was killed by a truck. I was thirteen. It was two days before Christmas. It was Seattle, and it was unseasonably cold. The roads were icy, and the truck driver wasn't paying attention." She flipped her sunglasses from the top of her head down onto her eyes as they exited the marina.

Ellie laid her hand on Hayden's as it rested on the throttle. "I'm so sorry, Hayden. That had to have been hard." It was no wonder Hayden was afraid of commitment. Everyone in her life had left her.

"It was a long time ago. Actually, it's going to be twenty years this year." She licked her bottom lip and pushed the throttle up as they pulled farther away from the marina. Ellie could have pulled her hand away, but she squeezed a little tighter so her hand wouldn't fall. "Truthfully, the reason I was able to afford college, vet school, this boat, was because of the insurance settlement my grandma got from the trucking company that she put in a trust for me. And some life insurance money from my dad, mom, and grandma. And I've invested well. I might be an orphan, but at least I'm a comfortable one." They approached the locks, and Hayden throttled all the way back before pulling her hand from beneath Ellie's. "Can you stand up for a sec? I need to grab vests from in this bench." She pulled out three vests and handed one to Ellie.

"Do you really have a life vest for Atlas?" It seemed ridiculous. He was a dog; he had to be able to swim.

Hayden laughed. "Ours are required by the coast guard, but Atlas? Have you seen him swim?"

"I guess not."

"Then it's better to be safe than sorry. Come here, Atlas." He walked to Hayden and let her put that ridiculous looking shark-fin life jacket on him.

Ellie wanted to take a picture but was having a hard time getting her own vest on. Where the hell was that last clip? She fumbled until Hayden stepped very close and reached around her with both arms to find the wayward straps. The maneuver brought her mouth dangerously close to Ellie's. Luckily, she managed to get the strap and pull it around to the front. She was still so close that Ellie could feel little wisps of breath as she threaded the one strap through the loop and clicked it into the clasp.

"All set," she said.

Ellie's mouth was as dry as a muscadet wine as Hayden sat back in her captain's chair and headed toward the locks again as though nothing had happened. As though their mouths hadn't been separated by mere inches. Ellie tried to shake off her inner reaction—especially since Hayden obviously hadn't been nearly as affected—but it was hard seeing Hayden standing at the wheel looking so confident with her wide stance and those aviator sunglasses. Ellie wasn't sure what it was about a woman in aviators, but it always set her heart pattering. It probably dated back to Kelly McGillis in *Top Gun*, who was absolutely one of her roots. Either way, Hayden rocked them harder than anyone she'd ever met.

She watched Hayden command the boat into the lock and expertly hold on to the "mooring line" to keep the boat in place as the water level slowly fell from the level of Lake Michigan down several feet to the level of the Chicago River.

When the gates fully opened and all the boats in the lock slowly filed out, Hayden said, "Once we're out of the lock, you can take that back off." She pointed at Ellie's chest. Was it Ellie's imagination, or did she check out her cleavage—that admittedly looked more impressive than usual due to the snug fit of the vest? "I'm assuming you'll be able to get it *off* without any assistance." She smirked.

"I'm pretty sure I can manage."

But did she want to? That wasn't a question she was willing to answer in that moment.

CHAPTER TWENTY

Hayden thought Ellie must be bored watching her chat with the harbormaster, then watching her dock *Mobile Home* and hook everything up, but she seemed fascinated, watching Hayden intently with Atlas at her feet.

"Sorry about that. Shall we see if Atlas and Chelsea can tolerate each other? Then I can make up for all the boredom with a bottle of wine, and we can sit out here on the stern and watch the sunset."

"It wasn't that bad. Atlas and I have never seen anything like... well, any of this." She waved at the boat, the marina, and the river before rubbing the back of her neck. She stared out at the river as she said, "It was fascinating, really."

"I'm not sure I believe you."

Ellie looked back. Was that a little blush on her face? Hayden was pretty sure it was.

"But either way, let's see how Chelsea and Atlas do together, okay?" When Ellie nodded, Hayden said, "Will you put him back on his leash, and we can walk by the door again to make sure they both seem chill?"

Atlas seemed curious at the door but calm. Hayden didn't want to leave Chelsea locked up any longer than necessary, so she had Ellie take Atlas to the sofa to sit and wait. "Hey, pretty girl." Chelsea rubbed against Hayden's legs as she came out of her bedroom, but when Hayden went to pet her, Chelsea hissed, likely to say she wasn't pleased about having been locked up for hours. But it also could have been because she wasn't happy about having Atlas in the house. Hayden sank to the floor with her legs out in front of her and let Chelsea decide when she wanted to come closer for love.

"I'm sorry, my sweet girl. I didn't mean to make you angry." She took a few minutes to make up for her transgression by giving Chelsea several treats and loving on her while she strutted back and forth over Hayden's legs. "Are you feeling better? Do you want to go to the living room and meet our guests?"

As though she understood, Chelsea turned and walked down the hallway toward the living room. Hayden called, "Incoming." She was a little anxious about how this meeting would go, but given Atlas's reaction at the bedroom door, she was cautiously optimistic.

"So far so good," Ellie said when Hayden walked back into the room. Atlas had lain down, facing Chelsea, who'd stopped two feet away and stared. She angled her head to the right and then to the left and took a step toward him.

Ellie's shoulders tensed, and Hayden wished she could tell her to relax so Atlas wouldn't feel her tension, but there was no way she could do that without disturbing the introduction, and so far, Atlas still seemed relaxed. No wrinkly forehead, no pink nose, no whale eyes. He just lay there watching Chelsea size him up.

Hayden was surprised when Chelsea took the last step and leaned her head close to his. When he lifted his head, she started purring and headbutted his jaw.

"I can't believe he's so damn relaxed," Ellie said. Her shoulders dropped.

Hayden smiled at the scene. "I was hopeful that they'd be okay with each other, but this is great. She's never initiated a friendship with a dog like this. She normally tolerates them, but this headbutting thing is new."

When Chelsea lay next to Atlas, Hayden decided it was safe to leave them with Ellie for a few minutes. "Ready for some wine?"

"Sure."

Hayden flipped on the fireplace in the living room and stepped out onto the deck to light that one as well. It was a lovely evening to sit outside for the sunset, even though it was October. "When I come back, we can go sit outside, but if you don't mind keeping an eye on them now, that would be great. It looks like Atlas is fine, but Chelsea can, on occasion, be unpredictable, so be alert."

"Okay, but is it safe to have a fire on a boat? And you have two, which seems like a lot."

Hayden laughed. "Do you think I'd have any if it wasn't safe?" Ellie chewed the inside of her cheek. "I guess not. It just seems odd. Fire on a boat. Where you can't escape if there's an accident. A little scary, don't you think?"

"There are a lot of extra rules to have them on a boat, but it's allowed per code and completely safe. Don't worry." When Ellie nodded, Hayden ran to the wine cellar, also known as the cuddy cabin, where she stored her wine and grabbed a full-bodied cab. There was a little chill in the air, but she was sure the cab, along with the fireplace, would help stave off the cold. She quickly went up to the kitchen, opened the wine, and sliced up some cheddar and blue cheese for them to snack on.

While grabbing crackers, however, she was seized by panic. What was she doing? When had she decided it was okay for them to hang out? And drink wine and do romantic things like watch the sunset? She knew she was sending major mixed signals. Especially when she had no intention of them being more than friends. She hadn't intended for them to even *be* friends.

Her chest was tight, but it was too late to turn back now without being a total bitch, so she tried to ignore the alarms going off, and, when the pressure in her chest loosened some, she somehow managed to carry two wineglasses in one hand and the platter with the cheese and crackers in the other.

"Will you open the sliding door? It looks like the sunset is going to be gorgeous."

Atlas stood to go outside, and Chelsea joined her new best friend. "Is it okay to let her out on the deck?" Ellie hesitated with the door open a fraction.

"Yes. She started as a stray and made the decision to become an indoor cat. She'll wander around, but she never makes any motions to jump off, so she's fine. She'll scratch at the door when she's ready to go back in."

Ellie sat on one side of the L-shaped couch around the fireplace, and Hayden sat on the other, leaving plenty of space in between them. She even set the platter on the cushion to encourage them to stay far apart.

"Thank you," Ellie said when she took her glass. Their fingers brushed, and a tiny firecracker went off in Hayden's midsection. Shit. She tried to slide a little farther away. "What are we drinking?" Ellie asked, seemingly oblivious.

Hayden coughed and wished she'd brought some water. "One of my favorite cabs. It's my 'nicer than daily drinking but not a special occasion' wine." That was a lie. It was totally a special occasion wine, but she didn't want to further complicate things by telling Ellie she'd pulled out the good stuff. "I can't believe how calm Atlas is. So chill about being on a boat, going through a lock, meeting Chelsea."

"I know, right? I'm a little surprised too, but we've never really spent any time away from home other than when we went to the retreat. And when we spent the holiday with my family. He's a champ." She leaned over to pet him, and he rolled onto his back for belly rubs. He really was adorable. Also adorable was how Chelsea had to adjust herself to keep snuggling with him when he moved.

They'd finished the cheese by the time full dark had come around. A couple of hours later, only a sip or two of wine remained, and the slightly chilled air had formally turned cold. Hayden was feeling a pleasant buzz, and Ellie had somehow ended up with her arm pressed to Hayden's on the sectional, ostensibly conserving heat.

Even buzzed, Hayden wasn't willing to admit to anything else, though it wasn't just their arms. Their feet, propped up on the edge of the firepit, were also touching, but since they were both wearing shoes, that felt a little less intimate.

As if reading Hayden's thoughts, Ellie dropped her feet and turned. Hayden's arm felt cold without her. "It would probably be best if Atlas and I headed home. It's getting late and cold."

Hayden looked at Atlas and Chelsea, still spooned around each other. "Probably not a bad idea. I'm guessing Atlas has an important bedtime routine that he's late for, judging by how tired he looks."

"He's moments away from turning into a pumpkin I think."

Neither of them made any motion to stand. Ellie took a last sip of wine, and Hayden couldn't look away. That tongue that she'd been fantasizing about since it was last on her skin peeked out. Ellie leaned closer, and Hayden gravitated in too.

It was a bad idea, but Hayden couldn't stop herself and laid her hand on Ellie's cheek. Rubbed her thumb along Ellie's lower lip. "What do you do to me, Ellie?"

"I think you have that backward," Ellie breathed.

"This is a terrible idea. You still want forever."

"I do." The wedding terminology wasn't lost on Hayden. "Though not tonight."

There was that, at least. "And I'm still not open to anything long term."

"And we promised that the last time was an OTO." Despite her words, Ellie leaned closer.

"And it's not good to break our word." But Hayden didn't want to stop. "Maybe we need one more time to exorcise it. We were better for a while, right? Then the draw came back. I think one more time will burn it out."

"Yeah, that makes a lot of sense." Ellie caught half her bottom lip between her teeth and stared unabashedly at Hayden's mouth.

Heat surged in Hayden's belly and down to the juncture of her thighs. "So…a TTO? A two times only occurrence?"

Ellie nodded as though weighing the words. Perhaps weighing the wisdom. Hayden prayed she threw caution to the wind because she couldn't handle the thought of going to bed cold and alone after the heat that felt like lava boiling in her veins. "I'm in favor." Before Hayden could take another breath, Ellie surged forward, closing the gap between their mouths and capturing her lips in a searing kiss that felt seamless from a few nights before. A continuation of kisses rather than something new.

Hayden pulled her closer by her hips, and Ellie planted one knee on the side of Hayden's thigh and swung the other leg over, straddling Hayden's lap. Her cold hands found their way under Hayden's shirt. She shivered from the icy contact, but when Ellie deepened the kiss, she forgot all about the cold. The fleeting thought of wanting to stay like that and kiss Ellie forever floated into her mind, but she quickly pushed it out before it had a chance to take root and focused on the silky feel of Ellie's skin beneath her hands.

"Wait." Ellie used Hayden's shoulders to push herself back.

"Wha...what?" Hayden tried to blink away the haze. "You want to stop?"

"Yes." Hayden's stomach plummeted until Ellie continued. "Just for a few minutes. I need to walk Atlas. He needs to go to the bathroom once more, and I know I'm not going to want to take him later." She flashed a sexy smile that did unmentionable things to Hayden's insides.

"Excellent thinking. I'll clean this mess up, turn off the firepit, and we can move inside. Before I'm too embarrassed to see any of my neighbors for the rest of the winter." Hayden hadn't really been thinking that her neighbors might be watching until Ellie had paused and was relieved Ellie had been more aware than she was.

Ellie stood and extended a hand. Once standing, she gave Hayden a kiss hot enough to scorch neighboring boats.

"Don't be gone too long," Hayden managed. "I'll be impatiently waiting."

Once Ellie had left with Atlas, Hayden quickly loaded the dishwasher. If she gave herself too long to think, she might question the wisdom of what they were about to do, and that was the last thing she wanted. She didn't want to give her brain the opportunity to plant a seed of doubt, so she focused on the tasks at hand and fed Chelsea. Once the kitchen was sparkling, she went to her bedroom and turned down the bed and turned on the fireplace.

Neither of them would much notice the ambiance, but she wanted everything to be nice since this was the absolute last time. She brushed her teeth and washed her face, then went back to the living room to wait. Pace. Obsessively clean. Anything to keep from thinking about anything serious.

When Ellie and Atlas walked in, Hayden squeezed the duster in her hands to keep from throwing it to the ground and jumping Ellie before she could even take her shoes off. That would probably scare Atlas and would give Ellie way too much information about how badly Hayden wanted her. Instead, she calmly asked, "How was the walk?"

"He did a great job. He saw two big dogs across the street and did just as he was trained. It was amazing. Such a smart boy." She ruffled his ears. "You deserve all the treats."

"I have more bully sticks. Let me grab one to keep him busy." The last thing she wanted was for Atlas to try to join them in bed or get bored and get into something. She wasn't sure if Ellie let him sleep with her, but she didn't want to take any chances.

CHAPTER TWENTY-ONE

When Atlas was settled with his chewy, Hayden looked at Ellie and said, "Would you like a more in-depth tour of my bedroom?"

Ellie had no idea how Hayden was so calm. She was trembling with nerves, but Hayden filled a glass of water like she had all the time in the world. Ellie was starting to wonder if Hayden even still wanted her until she mentioned the bedroom.

"I can't think of anything lovelier," Ellie said, pretty sure she'd kept the tremble out of her voice, proud of herself for sounding so casual.

Hayden smiled as she took her hand and led her down the hallway. "That door is the bathroom. The door to the left is the closet. The television is behind that cabinet. And *this*." She pointed to the king-size bed behind her. "Is the bed. I'd love to get your opinion on the sheets. There will be a survey sent out tomorrow, so please take note."

Ellie's heart fluttered thinking about the two of them in those sheets, regardless of how soft they were. "I will dutifully note the texture against my skin and provide a full report."

"Excellent." Hayden hooked a finger in Ellie's shirt and pulled her down until their lips met. Hayden's full lips were so soft as they moved over Ellie's. She moaned, and Ellie deepened the kiss, desperate to taste her.

Hayden pulled out her hair tie and ran her fingers into Ellie's hair, massaging her scalp. Ellie ached to feel skin against skin, so she slid her hands under Hayden's blouse and pushed it over her head. Her breasts weren't large, but they were perfect. Her dark brown nipples were already erect through the thin fabric of her bra. Ellie quickly unclasped it, slid it down her arms, and took one of those delicious nipples into her mouth.

Hayden groaned but said, "Not so fast," and brought her hands to Ellie's head.

"Hmm?" Ellie hummed, unwilling to release her.

"I want your clothes off. Now. I want to feel your skin, see your body. Need to see it." The huskiness of her voice was so sexy, there wasn't a single thing Ellie wouldn't be willing to do for her.

She dutifully released the nipple, though she did press her closed lips to it one last time before standing and pulling her sweater over her head. Before it even hit the floor, Hayden was reaching to release her bra and moved quickly to the button on her jeans. She pushed the jeans past her hips, and Ellie slid her hands into the waistbands of Hayden's leggings and underwear. She happily knelt and slowly shifted the pants down inch by inch, claiming each bit of newly revealed skin with her mouth, her tongue. "I'm so happy I don't have to battle a button fly this time."

She thought Hayden chuckled, but her hands were buried in Ellie's hair, massaging. When she got Hayden's pants to mid-thigh, she pressed a kiss to her neatly trimmed curls before dipping her tongue briefly between the folds. Hayden's legs tensed, and Ellie shoved her pants the rest of the way to the floor, impatient to be able to taste her in earnest without any barriers to restrict their movement.

Hayden sat on the bed and looked at Ellie kneeling in front of her. "You are so beautiful," she whispered. "Those dimples might be my undoing."

Ellie had always thought her dimples one of her best features, but hearing that Hayden loved them made her heart swell. "It's your cheekbones for me. You are so beautiful, but they make it hard for me to think about anything else whenever I'm around you."

Hayden ran her hand across her cheek. "Really?"

"I've always been a sucker for high cheekbones, but yours seem like they were sculpted by a Renaissance artist." She stood and placed a hand over Hayden's, caressing her cheek with her thumb. Ellie reluctantly took her glasses off but knew that they would only be in the way after this.

"I also love those glasses. You're hot without them, but with them on? You're in sexy librarian mode."

Ellie felt self-conscious because her glasses were so much a part of her, and she felt at a disadvantage when someone could see her better than she could see them. "I can try to keep them on, but we'd need to be really careful, or I won't be able to find my way home tomorrow."

Hayden laughed. "They'll only slow us down," she whispered and slid backward on the bed, pulling Ellie on top of her.

There were few things more erotic than the slide of naked skin against naked skin. Especially the rub of nipples back and forth. By the time they were both lying on the bed, Ellie's nipples were so hard, they hurt. Thankfully, Hayden seemed to know they needed a little more attention and cupped her breasts before gently squeezing her nipples.

Ellie's hips jerked on Hayden's thigh. The pressure was so delicious that she began to slide back and forth, giving her clit the stimulation it was pleading for.

"Come up here?" Hayden said.

"Where?"

"Up here. I need to taste you," Hayden said, her voice hoarse.

Oh. "Happy to oblige." Ellie crawled and planted her knees on either side of Hayden's head and allowed Hayden to guide her hips down. The breath passing across Ellie's labia before Hayden even touched her had her thighs tensing and nearly collapsing, and she caught herself on the headboard. When Hayden used her thumbs to part Ellie's folds, she thought she might die, and when Hayden brought her mouth to her clit, she thought she must have died and gone to heaven. There was no way anything on earth could feel that good.

Hayden pulled her hips firmly until Ellie relaxed and allowed Hayden to support her. She didn't want to let go, but Hayden didn't give her a choice. She was normally self-conscious riding a partner's face, but Hayden slid several fingers into her, and she couldn't think about anything past or future. All she could do was experience that perfect moment. It was like there was an invisible string connecting the nipple Hayden was pinching, her clit, and the fingers buried deep inside her, and that string pulled Ellie closer and closer to the beautiful edge and—

The sound of something dying pierced Ellie's building orgasm. "What the fuck was that?" She lifted her hips, worried that something was wrong.

"Please ignore her."

"What was it?"

"Fucking Chelsea."

Ellie opened her eyes and saw Chelsea sitting on the bed about a foot from her right knee, staring at them with true malice. "She doesn't like not being the loudest cat in the room and was trying to drown us out."

"Is she going to murder us?" Ellie asked.

"Definitely not. She knows where her next meal comes from." Hayden let go of Ellie's breast and pushed Chelsea off the bed. "And if she wants to have another meal *ever* again, she'd better stay on the fucking floor."

Ellie laughed, but it didn't last long as Hayden's fingers began their insistent motion again, and she pulled Ellie back onto her mouth. Ellie slipped right back into the pre-orgasm build, and almost immediately, she was calling Hayden's name as the world shattered into ten thousand pieces.

She fell forward and rested her head against the headboard. Still breathing hard she said, "I don't know how you make me feel so good, but what the hell is wrong with your cat?" Hayden laughed, and the vibration against Ellie's clit was too much that close to her orgasm, so she slid down until she was lying with her head on Hayden's shoulder. "Seriously. Does she do that every time you have someone over?"

"I don't actually know," Hayden whispered. "You're…the first person I've ever had over like this."

❖

When Hayden awoke before dawn, she knew exactly whose shoulder her head was resting against and felt a strong reluctance to move. A panicky feeling overtook her chest. Was her airway closing? What the hell was she doing sleeping—actually sleeping the full night—wrapped around another woman? A woman she'd now slept with more than once. In her own home. Breaking every rule in her rulebook.

She started to push off Ellie so she could use the bathroom and clear her head, but when she tried to pull away, Ellie's breast lifted until gravity pulled their skin apart. Ellie grunted and tightened her arms, holding Hayden in place. Rather than lying back down, Hayden looked at Ellie. She was so peaceful in her sleep, her chestnut curls fanned around her head like a halo, contrasting against the light cream of Hayden's sheets. The flickering light of the fire only made her more beautiful.

Get a grip. This sentimental shit wasn't who she was. She needed to figure out a way to get out of bed, so she tried whispering, "Ellie, I have to use the bathroom."

She wasn't sure if Ellie woke up or just reacted instinctively, but she pulled Hayden back down and mumbled a barely audible, "Shh."

Hayden tried in vain to resist but finally gave in and fell back asleep.

The next time she awoke, it was to the sound of Atlas grumbling. He sounded way too close. When she opened her eyes, she realized Ellie was now the big spoon, cradling her, and she was staring directly into the eyes of Atlas, who had his head resting inches from her face. "You have stinky breath, Atlas. Have you heard of a mint?" He grumbled. "No? Well, why don't you lie back down." The motivation she'd felt earlier to escape was nowhere to be found in her sleep-clouded brain as Ellie shimmied her hips tighter against Hayden's, and she quickly drifted back to sleep again.

When she awoke the third time, it was to the delicious feel of Ellie's deft fingers moving between her thighs. She was still the little spoon, but the hand that had been at her hip was now gliding back and forth along the length of her clit. Given the sensitivity from the athletic night they'd had, Hayden's climax came quickly.

Ellie bit her shoulder and whispered, "Good morning," her voice gravelly and sexy with sleep.

"A good morning it is."

"I don't want to say it, but I should get going. Atlas is restless and wants his breakfast. He probably also needs to potty."

"Cockblocker," Hayden said to Atlas while fighting the unnatural urge to get Ellie to stay. "Do you think he has a few more minutes in him? You woke me up so nicely, I'd like to do one more thing before I take you back to your car." She reached behind her and found Ellie's delightful wetness one last time.

❖

Knowing Ellie wouldn't be able to take Atlas in a taxi, Hayden had moved her car yesterday morning so she could take them back to Ellie's car after she'd moved the boat. She hadn't realized it wouldn't be until the next day, but she was glad she'd planned ahead. Ellie was grateful, and Hayden was finding there wasn't much she wouldn't do for her.

That was a problem. Because she didn't get emotionally involved. Heartache was inevitable, and Hayden had already had more than a lifetime's worth and wasn't keen to survive it again. So it was just her and Chelsea against the world. And she knew she wouldn't have Chelsea forever—she was about twenty already—but for now, Chelsea was her only companion on the island of her life. And that was okay by her.

And so far, she hadn't *really* done anything to break that routine with Ellie. Probably, they shouldn't have had sex again that morning. They definitely shouldn't have had sex in the shower while poor Atlas was doing the potty dance. Okay, the repeat performance in and of itself perhaps was a poor choice.

Fine. Hayden couldn't deny that Ellie was a dangerously slippery slope, and the last thing she wanted to do was hurt her with her inability to commit. Or get her own heart, the heart she'd spent a lifetime trying to protect, hurt. Hayden ground her teeth as she realized in a moment of—rare when it came to Ellie—brutal honesty that after all the time they'd spent together, after the two nights they'd slept together, there was *some kind of* a relationship between them. They weren't just acquaintances. They were friends even if Hayden didn't want to accept any friends into her life. They were apparently friends with benefits after fucking twice. And this was not going to work. She *would not* get close to someone again just so they could die. Or leave. Or whatever. Life was a fleeting thing and couldn't be relied upon.

She was going to harden her defenses, and not see Ellie socially anymore. Seriously. Inviting Ellie to her home? Had she actually believed that they could hang out in her house as *buddies* a handful of days after they'd had some of the hottest fucking sex of their lives? She was being naive or intentionally oblivious. Or she was in denial. Regardless, she would not see Ellie other than for official appointments for Atlas. At her office. This would stay a TTO as promised.

CHAPTER TWENTY-TWO

The server at Once Upon a Wine brought their bottle, and Skye went through the motions of tasting and approving it. Her timing in reaching out for drinks had been serendipitous because Ellie had been meaning to tell her about everything that had happened with Hayden, but it had been a busy week. And in the past, she would have talked to Iris, and going to Skye right away because Iris was gone felt...disloyal, maybe? So she'd been putting it off. She had to suppress the bitterness of how unfair this entire situation was.

"When we're leaving, will you remind me to go to my dry cleaners before I go to Bailey's for the night? I have a big pitch tomorrow, and my favorite suit is at the one by my house. I think." Skye rolled her eyes and took a sip.

Ellie laughed, not envying the logistics of trying to live in two places. "Sure, but what's going on with your living situation anyway? When are you moving in together?" She knew it was only a matter of time.

"We're enjoying the floating back and forth for now. We never stay apart, but we love both neighborhoods. She loves her backyard, and I love the views from my condo. We aren't sure how we're going to compromise, but in the interim, we're enjoying both. We'll figure it out, but if you promise to keep it secret, I'll tell you the reason why I invited you to drinks tonight, and why we'll be more motivated soon." Skye's smile turned a little self-satisfied.

"As if you even have to ask. Of course."

"Bailey and I are going to Hawaii next month, and I'm going to ask her to marry me."

"I'm so happy for you, Skye." She felt a tiny twinge of jealousy at their happiness but couldn't hope for better for them. She could find that too. Soon. When she was ready. She hoped. "And to think, a year ago, you weren't even out at work. But you and Bailey are so cute, it's disgusting. Have you decided how you're going to do it?"

"I have it all worked out with the resort. We're going to take a helicopter to the top of a mountain to watch the sunrise. We'll have a breakfast picnic and a hike to some nearby falls, and somewhere in all that, I'm going to ask her. She'd better say yes, or it's going to be a long trip." Skye ran her hand through her hair and shook it as she often did when she was a little stressed.

"Of course she's going to say yes. She loves you to infinity."

Skye's face took on a dreamy expression. "I know. I'm just ready to be her wife. And I'm ready to be Patsy's mom."

"Patsy the…dog?" Ellie still couldn't imagine Skye being a dog lover. Then again, she'd had a dog for months and still couldn't imagine being a dog lover, yet she was. Or at least, she loved one dog.

"Yep. Weird, huh?"

"Totally."

"Speaking of dogs, how is Atlas's sexy doctor? Did you help her move her houseboat this weekend?"

Ellie's skin went hot thinking of Hayden. Thinking of riding her with reckless abandon and how hard her resultant orgasm had been made Ellie want to press her glass of ice water to her face to counteract the heat. "Help her is an overstatement, but yes, Atlas and I went with her on the big houseboat move."

"Oh my God. You had sex with her again?" Skye's eyes went wide as her mouth dropped like a cartoon character. "You had sex with her twice now? During your self-imposed moratorium?"

"Yes." There wasn't much else for Ellie to say. She knew it had been a mistake, but if she was going to make one, at least she'd enjoyed every second of it. Both in the moment and every moment she'd thought about it since

"Are you okay with all that? What changed? Last time, you swore it was a one-time thing."

"It was an accident. But this time was *definitely* it."

Skye scoffed. "How do you *accidentally* have sex? Did you trip?"

Ellie almost snorted wine out of her nose. "So crass. It's not like I slipped and fell on her face. We just had a little wine, drifted a little closer on the couch, and the next thing I knew, we were kissing. It wasn't a good idea, but it felt amazing, like, best-sex-of-my-life amazing, so I'm having a hard time regretting it, even though I know it wasn't my smartest move."

Skye pursed her lips and stared, brows furrowed. "Why not?"

Ellie huffed. "You already know. Because I've sworn off dating and even if I hadn't, she's more commitment-phobic than a black widow."

"You think she's going to murder you if you sleep together again?" Skye's head tipped back as she laughed at herself.

She shook her head and chuckled. "For frick's sake, Skye. She's not going to murder me, but like a black widow, she doesn't mate with someone more than once."

"Interesting that you just referred to what you did as *mating.*"

"You're missing the point," Ellie said, exasperated. Why was she being so obtuse?

Skye sobered and gave Ellie a level look. "I'm not. I'm just teasing you because all of this is so out of character for you, but I think it's exactly what you need. You are so penned into your vision of a perfect mate and a perfect life. But life isn't perfect. And maybe what you're meant for is a meaningless fling with a hot doctor. You're allowed to do anything that makes you happy."

"I'm not the sleeping-around type, and you can't have a fling with someone who isn't interested."

Skye nodded and pursed her lips. "Fair, but you said the sex was mind-blowing, right?"

Ellie wasn't sure if words existed in the English language to describe how incredible the sex with Hayden had been. "It was like she had a user's guide to my body. She homed in on every erogenous zone. She figured out exactly how much pressure I like and where and when, and…whew." She fanned her face. She wished they'd had time to try out the hot tub. *No, that will be better somewhere out on the lake with a little privacy. Wait.* She had to mentally correct herself. It would have been better if they could have tried out the hot tub someplace secluded. They were never having sex again. "And sex on a boat is hot. The gentle rocking is relaxing and romantic."

"This may sound wild, but why don't you convince her that a little fling is exactly what you both need? You aren't going to get attached, and neither is she. It would be a shame for you to never have that most spectacular sex again."

Huh. It went against everything Ellie generally wanted, but maybe—just maybe—Skye had a point. The sex was fucking fantastic, and a little physical release seemed to be just what the doctor ordered. But could Ellie do this? And could she convince Hayden that it was a good idea? She was going to need to give the idea some time to marinate. But the thought of a short-term fling did have some appeal.

❖

It had been almost two weeks since Hayden had last seen Ellie and Atlas. Since he was doing well and making huge improvements, Hayden had dropped the frequency of their visits and switched to giving them more homework. She'd done it before they'd slept together, but having an excuse to see Ellie less felt like both a benefit and a curse.

She hadn't been able to think of much else in the last twelve days, not that she'd been counting. That would have been pathetic. They'd texted a few times about how she was settling into her new boat slip and how Atlas had dealt with Ellie's trip to Boston earlier in the week. Mostly superficial, but Hayden couldn't help but wonder if she was as present in Ellie's consciousness as Ellie was in hers.

So as she walked up to Ellie's condo building, she took a few mindful breaths to clear out the clutter and reminded herself that she was Atlas's veterinarian first and foremost. She and Ellie were friends who had shared a few intimate moments, but that wasn't what defined their relationship. She was a professional, and she was there to work. Nothing else.

Although a small part of her fantasized about what it might feel like to actually date Ellie, to spend time with her and enjoy it without feeling guilty about what lines she was crossing or what rules she was breaking. How amazing it might feel to come home at night to a woman like her. Spend the evening together with a meal and maybe a television show or two. Snuggle on the couch with a glass of wine before they went to bed and had more amazing sex.

But that could never happen. Hayden had lost too many people in her life much too early and couldn't deal with losing anyone else close to her. She would be completely crushed and had to avoid it at all costs. She started to hyperventilate at the thought of losing someone else and paused before getting in the elevator to find her meditation breathing before she passed out. She'd learned early that her own self-preservation was crucial. So she squelched that idea every time it crept into her mind.

Ellie opened the door, and Hayden wondered if she realized how hot she was in this half-work, half-casual mode with her slim-fitting navy slacks and white blouse with the sleeves rolled up, and her feet bare. But when Hayden realized where her mind was going, she forced herself to be a professional. "Hey, Ellie. Good to see you."

"Likewise. Come on in. Sorry, I was about to change, but time evaporated." Ellie backed up to let her in, and as Hayden was walking by, Ellie hugged her. It was a quick hug she'd no doubt give to a sister or an aunt, but Hayden's senses went on high alert, and she forced herself to think of anything other than the feel.

And thus, the second thing she noticed was the furniture. "You got a new couch."

"Ha. Yes, I finally took the time last weekend to go shopping. Atlas has been doing so good that I thought it might be time. I'll be very regretful if he regresses and tears this one up." She looked to Atlas. "But you aren't going to do that, are you, my good boy?" He looked up from the bone he was chewing, licked his lips, and went right back to the bone. "That means he agrees. We've worked extensively on what his soulful looks mean while we've been bonding."

Why did she have to be so damn adorable? "I'm glad to hear that you've worked so hard on your nonverbal communication skills," Hayden said, deadpan. "It's important."

"Don't I know it. Every little sound can have a meaning, can provide guidance, for what someone needs." Her voice dropped, and

Hayden was certain she was also thinking about nonverbal cues in a different context. A horizontal context.

Hayden shook her head and took a step back in an effort to rein in her wandering mind. The only things still between them were Atlas and friendship. "Uh, why don't you go get changed, and I'll hang out with my boy?"

Ellie swallowed hard enough that Hayden could see it, even though she was now standing a couple of steps away. "That's perfect. I'll be right back. Do you want something to drink? Water? Booze?"

With as dry as Hayden's throat already was, a drink would be ideal. "Sure. Whatever you're having." She sat next to Atlas on the couch, excited that there were actually multiple cushions now and took a few more cleansing breaths. She was in control of her mind, thoughts, and body. She could choose how she wanted to react. She kept petting Atlas and went through that over and over.

However, when Ellie appeared again holding two bottles of water between her deliciously long fingers, along with two tumblers of whiskey, Hayden forgot all the things she'd been telling herself since before she'd arrived. Those fingers were so very lovely. And talented.

"How do you like the new couch? It's comfy, isn't it?"

"Uh, yes, it is." Hayden bounced a couple times. "It's got good support." Why had she done that? Said that?

Ellie smirked. "Atlas and I have been enjoying snuggling on a full-sized couch again. He also told me he appreciates being able to stretch out rather than just lie like a doughnut on one cushion. And he promised not to eat them."

"Well, as long as he promises, I'm sure he can be trusted."

With Atlas stretched on the chaise side of the couch and Hayden in the middle, the only area available for Ellie was right next to Hayden. She watched her look back and forth between her bizarre wooden chair and the couch a few times before settling on the couch. Most of Hayden wanted her to pick the horrible chair even though she knew Ellie would be terribly uncomfortable the whole time, but a small portion of her was happy.

"How's your week been?" Ellie asked.

"Good. Busy. Lots of new patients, which require longer appointments."

"Ah." Ellie winced and looked away. "Especially when the dog takes a massive shit, and your client breaks down in tears. Any of those this week?"

Hayden laughed, the tension broken. At least on her part. "No, but I did have a dog start humping my leg in the middle of a session, so that was a fun one. The owner swears he has never done that before, but I don't believe him."

"That makes me feel a little better." Ellie chuckled and looked at her.

Hayden took a sip of her drink. "Mmm. What is this? Some kind of rye? I like its spiciness."

"Yes. It's a bottle that one of my investors sent as an early Thanksgiving present or something. No real clue why, other than the last time I was in town, we went rye tasting. But I thought this would be the perfect time to try it as rye tastes better when shared." She took her first sip. "Spicy. I like it."

"Is that a new rule? Rye tastes better when you don't drink alone?" It sounded like an excuse to get them both drinking, but that first sip had taken the edge off the tension, so she was on board.

"Most things are better with friends, aren't they?" Ellie arched an eyebrow.

Heat blazed through Hayden's chest. She could think of *at least* a few things that would be better with a friend. This specific friend. Otherwise, she'd prefer to do those things with strangers.

Nope, not going there. "Perhaps," Hayden said neutrally. "Shall we work on training?" She was desperate to change the subject, even though she didn't have any specific lessons in mind.

"Okay." Ellie's shoulders dropped almost imperceptibly, but Hayden noticed and didn't like it. But she needed to get them moving, or only bad things would happen.

"Is there anything in particular you want to work on? It seems like he's got most things down pretty well. For tonight, distractions are going to be tricky, other than the fact that I'm here. How's his recall?"

"In the house, it's hard because nothing really distracts him besides food, and I don't have a safe place to do it outside."

Hayden worked through a few ideas and decided on one that wasn't going to be terribly challenging but would work. "Why don't I go somewhere else in the house and convince him to come with me? You can work on calling him back. We'll start with a really high-value treat. That way, you'll be teaching him that the best reward is always to come back to you."

She lured Atlas with some treats and went farther into Ellie's condo than she'd ever been. She hadn't realized how large it was. She stood in a bedroom and had Atlas go through the sit, watch, wait commands. When Ellie first called his name, his ear twitched, but he still played with Hayden. But the second time she called for him, he turned and ran to her. Perfect.

They did that a few more times before Hayden said, "Okay, let me get some of the hot dogs to feed him and see if you can get him to come. I might also stand in your bedroom if you're okay with it so he's in a room he spends a fair amount of time in."

"Sure."

She felt uncomfortable when she walked into Ellie's bedroom. There was a hook on the wall with a silky robe hanging from it that called Hayden to touch it. She resisted the urge but just barely. She started Atlas on the sit, watch, waits again and gave him hot dog pieces every few seconds to keep him invested. His focus was amazing, and when Ellie called his name, his ear didn't even twitch. She called again and still nothing. After the third time, Hayden stopped giving him treats, and he stayed standing in front of her.

Well, hell.

He finally turned his head when Ellie walked into the bedroom. "Guess that move needs a little work still, huh?" Ellie said, and they both laughed.

"Treats are good motivators for most dogs. Unfortunately, I was using his treats for evil rather than good." She shrugged.

"I don't think you could have evil motivations in any context."

"You have too much faith in me." She became very aware of the large bed just steps away. "Do you mind if I wash my hands? I have hot dog juice all over them. It's a little gross."

"Of course. It's right there."

Hayden thought Ellie would step aside and let her use the guest bathroom off the living room. But she pointed to the en suite. That was fine. The sink there would work just as well. She didn't bother to turn on the light, and as she soaped her hands in the dark room, Ellie walked in and squeezed past to get to the farther sink. Did she intentionally brush her hips against Hayden's ass? It felt like she might have gone slower than was necessary too.

Maybe it was the darkness that made her bold, but Hayden had to know. "Did you do that on purpose?" The thought that she had been intentional had butterflies zooming in Hayden's stomach, but an alarm also started screaming in her head, but for a change, she told the alarm to shut the hell up.

"Do what?" Ellie seemed to avoid making eye contact in the mirror. Suspicious.

"Brush so closely past me." Hayden turned and rested her hip on the sink counter. She crossed her arms. Not because she was irritated but because she wanted to control where her hands wandered.

"Can I plead the Fifth?"

Hayden's breath caught, yet she took a step closer. "I'm not sure. How are you going to make it up to me?" Traitorous mouth. Traitorous thoughts. But were they traitorous? Hayden chose to not get attached, but that didn't mean they couldn't do this one last time, did it? She'd already violated her own rules once—okay, twice—but at this point, what was the harm of once more? If this was the absolute last time, of course.

Ellie mirrored Hayden's stance, but she was squeezing the countertop with one hand. "I'm open to suggestions."

"I have a thought. About our rules. And TTOs."

"Oh really?" Ellie's lip quirked up.

Hayden swallowed and went for it. "I was thinking, the numbers two and three both start with the letter T. So TTO could just as easily mean three time only occurrence. We wouldn't even be breaking any rules. Because we clearly could have meant three times only." She was impressed with her creativity on that one.

The look on Ellie's face would keep her from even considering retracting the comment. "Interesting. Were you an attorney in another life?"

"Why?"

"I've never met anyone other than attorneys who take as many loose interpretations with rules as you do," Ellie said flatly.

Hayden's old friend, disappointment, landed heavily in her lungs. Was Ellie going to turn her down? She couldn't come up with a retort before Ellie broke into a radiant smile.

"But like when my own attorneys contort meanings or revise interpretations, I like your new interpretation. Because they all work to my benefit."

"So?"

Ellie nodded, her brown eyes sparkling, a sexy half-smile playing at her lips.

CHAPTER TWENTY-THREE

When Hayden awoke the next morning, she was alone in Ellie's bed, and she didn't like it. She'd been hoping for another morning delight, but Ellie apparently had other plans. She tried to squelch her disappointment and stretched her tired muscles. When she pushed herself up, she saw a robe lying across the bottom half of the bed and a travel mug on the nightstand with a sticky note that said, "For You."

That was odd to wake up to but surprisingly not unpleasant. Even though a niggling fear of Ellie developing feelings tried to take root. She muffled it—or tried to—as she pulled on the robe Ellie had left for her and took a sip of coffee. The robe felt warm—as though she'd just pulled it out of the dryer—and smelled so much like Ellie, Hayden had to force herself not to sigh. And how did Ellie know how she liked her coffee? This cup was perfect, with a touch of cream and no sugar.

"Good morning," Hayden said when she shuffled into the kitchen and found Ellie leaning over a cutting board slicing cherry tomatoes.

The full smile that spread across Ellie's face set off a flurry of activity in Hayden's belly that she was unprepared for. "Good morning."

"Thank you for the robe. And the coffee." She wrapped both hands around the cup, absorbing the warmth.

"My pleasure. I thought maybe you'd like to have breakfast together since I don't have to rush off to take care of Atlas. We've gone for a walk, and he's already eaten."

Hayden's mind began to race with conflicting thoughts of whether or not that was a good idea, but before she could decide, Ellie said, "There is a little thing I wanted to talk to you about. Well, before that, do you eat eggs? I was going to make omelets, but if you don't, I can pivot and make a tofu scramble. Or polenta scramble. Or scrap it altogether."

She appeared to be breathing hard in her nervous chatter, and Hayden had the urge to wrap her arms around her. She didn't—she wasn't willing to let their relationship go there—but it wasn't as easy as she wanted it to be. "Omelets are fine. I don't eat a lot of eggs, but I do eat them occasionally."

Ellie sighed. "Good. You have perfect timing as I've already cut up all the vegetables." She pointed at several bowls sitting neatly in a straight line on the counter behind her: peppers, onions, mushrooms, spinach, small broccoli florets, and a mound of a shredded white cheese. "Anything you don't like back there?"

"Hold the fungus for me, please. Everything else looks great." She sat on one of the stools on the other side of the island. As Ellie started to pull out pans and olive oil and got the stove going, Hayden said, "Do you have two pans specifically for omelets?" Was she that domestic?

"They are multipurpose. I like to cook, so I have lots of pots and pans, and this small size is perfect for a lot of things, omelets included." She started to heat the oil and dumped in all the veggies.

"I didn't know you liked to cook." But Ellie clearly knew what she was doing as she swirled both pans simultaneously to keep the veggies moving. Competence and confidence were things Hayden had always found sexy.

"I don't have a lot of time for it, but I love it. And I really love cooking for other people. So *you* get to reap the benefits. I will admit that I have cheese and crackers for dinner as often as I have real food. Sometimes, work is a bitch, and the last thing I feel like doing when I get home is cooking."

Watching her was fascinating. Hayden had discovered she was at least a little ambidextrous after their nights together, but she seemed completely capable of cooking with both her left and right hands as she poured the eggs into both pans at the same time.

"How's the coffee?" she asked. "I thought I remembered how you take it, but I wasn't certain. Feel free to dump it down the drain and make yourself fresh if it's not right. There's plenty more in the pot, and I have oat milk and creamer in the refrigerator. Sugar in the cabinet over the pot."

"This is actually perfect, thank you." Was Ellie trying to woo her? Or convince her they should try dating, even though Ellie wasn't currently dating, and Hayden didn't date? Hayden's fingers tightened on the mug until they ached as an unfamiliar tightness seized her throat. If Ellie was trying to woo her, giving her perfect coffee and food would be a good way to start, but Hayden couldn't do it. Relationships were for fools. It didn't matter if her heart quickened every time Ellie walked into a room. She could resist it. Would resist it. Had to resist it to protect herself.

Hayden wondered if Ellie was reading her mind when she said, "So what I wanted to talk to you about—and you can absolutely say no—is…neither of us is looking for something serious right now. I'm not sure when I'll be ready. But that doesn't mean I'm not interested in sex or in having a good time. Sex has never been the most important thing in a relationship for me, but I've enjoyed every second we've spent together, uh, like that." Hayden couldn't see her face, but she could see the redness in her ears, and it was endearing.

"The sex has been fantastic."

"Exactly. And we have some serious chemistry, so if neither of us is looking for something serious, we could give something super casual a go."

Hayden sucked in a breath; her knee-jerk reaction was "run far and fast," but the last thing she wanted to do was hurt Ellie. Plus, she was in a bathrobe. Where the hell was she going to go?

"Not like going on dates. Just, you could text me, or I could text you if we're horny. The other could opt out at any time. No hard feelings. You'd keep seeing Atlas as his vet, and anything we did off the clock would be just that."

As if on cue, Atlas walked into the kitchen and laid his head on Hayden's thigh, buying her a few precious seconds to think. "Good morning to you, sir. How did you sleep?" He sighed, and after she rubbed his head a few times, he lay at her feet.

Ellie expertly put cheese into the middle of the omelets and spread it around until it melted just a little. She simultaneously flipped both pans to fold the omelets in half. She cleared her throat loudly. "Nothing to say to that, huh? Guess that's a no." She still hadn't looked back, but Hayden watched her shoulders slump.

"Oh gosh, not no. I'm sorry. I was just processing," she said quickly. "And then I got a little distracted by Atlas's good morning and mesmerized watching you fold the eggs with just a flick of your wrist. I didn't mean to not say anything. I…I'm not sure. But it's not a hard no."

Ellie finally glanced over her shoulder before turning back to her pans, but the look on her face was smoldering.

Given her body's reaction to that look, Hayden wanted to shout yes, but that would still be a big change. She never ever slept with anyone multiple times. In college, she'd gone out with one woman a few times, but after they'd slept together, she'd realized she was giving the girl too much power to hurt her. So she'd been a total cad and dumped her amidst a lot of tears and name-calling. That was the last time she'd gone out with someone without being completely up-front about her intentions.

That being said, she'd already broken the rules with Ellie more than once. But unlike all the others, she *wanted* another time and another, like Ellie was some kind of drug. Addictive. Hayden certainly hadn't come there the night before with the intention of ending up in bed again. It had just happened. Because they'd both wanted it. And now…God help her, she still wanted Ellie. After three amazing nights. Three nights where neither of them had gotten much sleep because every time they woke up, their hands or mouths found each other.

And that was precarious. Hayden had spent her entire adult life protecting herself from getting hurt, and she wasn't about to let her guard down. She couldn't—wouldn't—give Ellie that power.

Yet, was there a downside if they tried it for a bit and realized it wasn't working? At least she'd be having regular sex, and if she was going to have a casual fuckbuddy, it should be someone with whom the sex was electric, and Ellie checked that box with a fluorescent pink check.

She felt confident she could continue fucking Ellie while keeping her walls up, but could Ellie actually do it too? She didn't seem like the type. "Are you sure that's something you can do? I mean, you told me before you were searching for your soulmate. Are you sure you can just casually fuck around without getting attached? Without growing feelings? I can't—I won't—do long-term. Can you promise you aren't going to fall for me?"

Ellie sat a plate in front of her and leaned on the island until their faces were level. "You're pretty cocky thinking I won't be able to fuck you and *not* fall for you." She smirked.

"Not cocky. Just worried. I like you. I think you're an amazing woman, Ellie. *I* don't want to hurt *you*. And my commitment baggage could fill a cargo plane. I want to keep doing this with you, but if there's any chance I'm going to hurt you, I'd rather walk away now." She hoped Ellie could understand, but more than she'd wanted anything in her adult life, she wanted Ellie to promise not to let Hayden hurt her.

Ellie bit her lip. "I'm responsible for my own feelings, for making sure I don't get hurt. Especially since this entire thing is my idea. But I promise, I know you're not the one for me. If I start to feel like I might be falling for you, I'll end it, okay? You have my word. No hurt feelings."

Despite the feeling in the pit of her stomach that there was no way this would ever work—no way they could both emerge on the other side pain free—Hayden couldn't resist Ellie's smile. Her magnetism. *Their* chemistry. "Okay."

CHAPTER TWENTY-FOUR

Ellie was on the conference call from hell with a development partner who spoke at half speed and somehow managed to use three times the words needed to get his point across, so everything he said took six times longer than necessary. When her phone buzzed, she looked down, grateful for any interruption. Perhaps it would be an emergency that she'd need to hang up for.

When she saw who it was, she couldn't stop a smile, and she was grateful this was just a conference call rather than a video meeting.

Hayden: *Are you busy tonight?*

She was meeting Skye and Bailey for a glass of wine at happy hour but was free after. *By some miracle, I'm free. Heading to Portland tomorrow for a few days, but it's an afternoon flight, so I don't need to do anything tonight. You?*

Hayden: *Hoping to be making plans right now.*

Ellie: *Already so tired of me that you're looking to hook up with someone new?*

Hayden: *Silly. I'm hoping I can convince you to come over tonight. I'll order food. Hot tub?*

It'd been nearly a month since they'd decided to casually fuck, and they'd been doing it very regularly. When Ellie was in town, they spent a lot of nights together. They didn't go out. They got together at the condo or the boat, maybe had a quick meal, and hopped into bed as soon as possible, given Chelsea's and Atlas's needs.

The night before had been the most romantic evening they'd spent together. Other than perhaps the night they'd looked at the stars in Wisconsin. Not that any of this was about being romantic. It was about casual fucking. And some flirting.

After dinner, they'd turned off all the lights on the boat and snuck up into Hayden's hot tub. Her most immediate neighbors in the marina had gone south for the winter, and there wasn't anyone else close, so they'd gone skinny-dipping. It was a clear night, and although they couldn't see nearly as many stars as in Wisconsin, they'd seen a lot by Chicago standards.

Ellie's nipples tightened thinking about what they'd done. What they might do in that hot tub again tonight. She hoped no one had been watching them with night vision goggles, but even if they had, it was worth it.

She hoped her analyst was taking notes because this guy was still droning, and Ellie had no idea what was going on. That was becoming a regular occurrence. Head in the sexy clouds. Wondering what delicious underwear she might find under Hayden's clothes. To be sure, she shot her analyst Brad an IM to verify and told him she'd gotten another call and had to put this one on hold.

She was losing her mind, but it was awfully delicious. She had a vision of Hayden straddling her while sitting in the hot tub, her pert breasts at Ellie's eye level. Perfect for kissing.

Ellie: *Perfect. I have drinks with Skye at 5 but I can pick up Atlas and come over after? 7:30?*

Hayden: *C u then.*

❖

Hayden had almost canceled on Thanksgiving twenty times. She didn't know why she was going. Okay, she did. Ellie had asked her to go to help make things a little easier without Iris. It was the only reason she'd agreed. She didn't want to actually spend this day—or any day—with a hoard of people, but the thought of letting Ellie down felt…wrong.

But to her, Thanksgiving was a day like any other. There was no need to make some huge feast so everyone could reflect on what shit their lives were while pretending they had so much to be happy about. With a four-day weekend, she could spend loads of time on her couch with a book and a glass of wine. She could probably read at least four books if she called a Lyft right then and went back home.

When Ellie squeezed her arm and then opened the door to the pandemonium of Thanksgiving at the Efron house, every reason Hayden had for not going came flooding back. It felt like there were two hundred people in the house, half of whom were screaming children, and Hayden's instinct to run battled against her commitment to attending this boondoggle and had her frozen in place.

Ellie smiled. "It looks worse than it is. I promise. Just come inside. If it's too overwhelming, I'll take you home. I can't stay late anyway since I didn't bring Atlas."

"Okay. Let's dive in." Though Hayden was already calculating how long she needed to stay before she could make a polite exit.

She was introduced to Ellie's parents, brother, nieces, Iris's parents and brother and nephews, three sets of neighbors, Ellie's aunts and uncles. She wished everyone had a name tag because for the love of everything, how was she supposed to keep everyone straight? The only ones she felt confident in were Eva and Levi, Ellie's parents.

Her head was spinning when Eva touched her shoulder and said, "Hayden, dear, you're looking a little overwhelmed. Do you want to help me in the kitchen?"

Hayden sighed, relieved. "I would love to. But I need to warn you, I'm not much of a chef."

"Just keep me company."

Ellie was busy crawling on the floor with Iris's nephews playing *WrestleMania*. She certainly didn't need Hayden's moral support in that moment.

When the door swung closed behind them, Hayden said, "Thank you for saving me. It's refreshing to be around this many people but also draining. I'm better with animals than with humans." That was about half-true. It was twice as draining as it was refreshing.

"You know humans are just animals who can talk? Otherwise, they're all the same. Driven by primal needs like food and comfort." Eva laughed and went back to doing something with pecans on a flat pan.

"You're probably right. But the fact that they can't talk makes animals a lot easier."

"I can't disagree with that. If you try to tell anyone this, I'll call you a liar, but I actually spend most of the day in the kitchen so I can have a little peace and quiet. No one needs that much yelling. Don't get me wrong. I love Thanksgiving. I love a day that reminds me to be thankful for all the gifts I have in my life and being able to host our family and friends. It fills me with love to have our family so close." While continuing to stir a dark brown glaze with a metal whisk, Eva used her shoulder to push a few strands of hair off her forehead. "But, wow, can they be overwhelming."

Hayden thought she was the only one feeling overrun. Not that they weren't all kind and funny. It was just *a lot*. "Thank you for allowing me a few moments' reprieve."

"No thanks needed. You were looking a little like a deer in headlights with Ellie crawling around on the ground with those boys. Honestly you would think she was twenty-two not forty-two. If I crawled like that even twenty-five years ago—hell, thirty-five years ago—I'd never have been able to get back up."

"It's nice that she's still close to the boys even after Iris." Hayden realized too late that was really insensitive but wasn't sure how to fix it, so she just let the words hang for a moment.

"Of course they're still close. They've been our family for the last forty-plus years. That doesn't just vanish. The family you choose is just as important as the family you were born into. I don't know if Ellie told you, but we had a second son, a year and a half younger than her. He died when he was just a toddler.

"Levi and I were lost for a little while. The pain of losing a child is something that can't be described, but life…went on. We filled it by loving on Ellie and Isaac to the point where they were probably ready to run away in annoyance, and my parents and grandparents also reminded us of everything our relatives lost in the Holocaust and encouraged us to take solace in the embrace of family. Sorry, don't mind my rambling. I get a little extra sentimental on Thanksgiving. It's silly."

"Not silly at all. Really." Hayden wasn't sure if she meant that, but it seemed like the right thing to say. The idea of a chosen family was so foreign to her. She'd made the conscious choice to rely only on herself after being orphaned at seventeen and had lived her entire life believing no one could be trusted to stay.

She'd inherited a fair amount of money from her grandmother, but she'd learned to invest it herself. Figured out how to survive off a small portion of it during college. Learned how to fix things that broke on her boat. She'd never sought out anyone for anything. Other than Britt to be her partner at the practice.

And even that wasn't entirely true. Britt had sought her out as a mentor and to do their residency. Now Hayden was planning to try to convince them to buy her out of the practice once they sat for their certification exam in a few weeks. A little twinge of guilt rippled through her, but she reminded herself that it wasn't like she was keeping something from a girlfriend. She and Ellie were friends. Sort of. She didn't need to tell Ellie about her every career move before she made it.

"Thanks, dear," Eva said. "I'm never happier than I am with my whole family together." Eva had a tear in her eye, and despite her cynicism, Hayden found herself oddly moved.

She'd never had these types of moments on a holiday with her mom or grandmother. There'd never been a slew of people. As far as she could remember, it had been the three of them. And then just two. And then one. What was the point of big dinners then? But there was something that warmed Hayden's being in this delicious-smelling kitchen with Ellie's mom. Watching her cook and pretending to help.

Stop it.

"I don't know if Ellie told you that I don't have any family, but it's sweet that you all get together like this. Thank you for allowing me to be a part of your day." She was surprised at her actual gratitude. The camaraderie kind of made up for the paralyzing number of people. Maybe.

"Well, I'm so happy Eleanor brought you." She squeezed Hayden's forearm. "Happy we could spend the day together and that you didn't have to spend it alone, dear."

"Wait, Ellie's name is Eleanor?" Hayden laughed. She hadn't realized Ellie had such an old-fashioned name.

"I know, I know. She should probably be a seventy-year-old woman with that name. I suspect it's why she embraces Ellie, but I just loved Eleanor Roosevelt. She reformed the role of First Lady from being a hostess to being an activist and fought for the rights of women and minorities and spoke out strongly against antisemitism. And I wanted to give my baby girl a strong name. A name that let her know she could do anything she wanted to. And she has."

The pride in Eva's voice constricted Hayden's throat. After a moment, she managed, "She is a badass isn't she?"

"That she is."

After Eva and Hayden rejoined the bedlam, the urge to run didn't reappear. Something about sharing that hour in the kitchen with Eva had settled her nerves. She ended up talking to Isaac, Ellie's brother, and Brian, Iris's brother, about the Bears and how it sometimes seemed like they intentionally got rid of every player with a modicum of talent. Luckily, although Hayden watched football, she wasn't a rabid Bears fan, so she didn't have to endure the crushing disappointment each season.

She also spent a while talking to Iris's sister-in-law, Martha, discussing yoga and meditation before she found herself pulled into a lengthy game of *Hungry Hungry Hippos*—more like ten games in a row—with Ellie and two of Martha's triplets. Though she had no idea which two. They looked identical and were dressed the same, so no one could tell them apart.

By the time she and Ellie left, Hayden was full, a little buzzed from the wine that Martha had continued to top off, and exhausted, and in desperate need of sleep and maybe some yoga to help all this heavy food digest. Definitely some Chelsea snuggles.

"Do you want to head back to my place? Maybe have a glass of limoncello?"

That sounded delightful too. "Sure, but can we swing by the boat to feed Chelsea and give her some snuggles?" Hayden was surprised that her desire to be alone wasn't stronger, but the thought of a few orgasms to cap off a surprisingly pleasant day was more appealing than the rest of the evening alone on her couch. Even with a good book. "Or, actually, maybe bring her with us? She's not a spring kitten, and I'm trying to give her lots of extra love. And she and Atlas really seem to love snuggling, so we'd hit a few birds with one stone." Chelsea's vet had reminded her at their last visit that, although her bloodwork all looked okay, Chelsea was getting older, and Hayden should start preparing herself. It seemed ridiculous because Chelsea was great, but Hayden couldn't deny that the calendar years were ticking up.

"Of course." Ellie smiled as they approached a stoplight. That completely relaxed look of hers always seemed to do Hayden in.

"Eleanor Roosevelt, huh?"

"Ugh. Was it my mother who told you that?" Ellie playfully dropped her forehead onto the steering wheel and looked at Hayden from under her arm.

"It was." Hayden smirked. "But seriously, that's awesome. Eleanor Roosevelt was an amazing woman."

"I know." Ellie sighed and turned into the parking lot at the marina. "It was hard growing up with the name Eleanor. Everyone made fun of me. But as an adult, it's pretty cool to be named after such a pioneer. But I was so used to being called Ellie that I never went back to Eleanor, even now that I'm a forty-year-old woman." She shrugged.

"Do you think she knew Eleanor was probably a lesbian or bisexual when she named you after her?"

"Eh, probably not, but who knows. Just fate, I guess." Ellie chuckled, and it was adorable.

"Luckily, you are just as impressive as dear Eleanor with your work and kind soul, but..." Hayden waited until Ellie parked and looked at her. "You're a lot hotter."

"Charmer," Ellie said and pulled her in for a kiss that was a little too steamy for the parking lot, but Hayden was buzzed on wine and life and didn't really care.

CHAPTER TWENTY-FIVE

Hayden flopped in Britt's guest chair with two tumblers in hand, waiting for Britt to grab one. "How was your Thanksgiving? You spent it with Shauna and her family, right?" It was a full week later, but their schedules had been booked solid, and they hadn't had a chance to catch up.

Hayden paused when she realized she had started to look forward to their catch-up sessions. Not just the professional aspect but the actual talking about life. It was an odd feeling. Was this what a genuine friendship felt like?

Britt finally took their glass, and relief flooded Hayden's arm like a tidal wave. "Yeah. Shauna's family was less stressful than expected. They were hilarious, and Shauna must have coached them because they all used the right pronouns and seemed totally cool. Then Friday, we went with my family and did some hiking at Kettle Moraine. It was all pretty perfect."

Hayden didn't think she'd ever seen Britt look so happy. "That's great. I'm glad all your stressing was for naught. And Kettle Moraine is one of my favorite places to hike. Did you freeze?"

"Surprisingly, no. It wasn't bad. I mean, it did snow on Saturday but just enough to make everything beautiful, not so much as to ruin our fun or require snowshoes." They took a sip of rye and smacked their lips. "I think I love her. I haven't ever said that to anyone other than family, and I haven't said it to her yet, but the words are tumbling around in my brain like Ping-Pong balls in one of those bingo barrels, you know? Like, I'm afraid the words are going to be called before it's the right time to say them, but I don't know how much longer I can keep them inside."

"That's so sweet." Hayden's heart squeezed. She did believe in true love. She believed her parents had it. She believed her grandparents had it. But she just didn't believe it had any permanence for most people, herself included.

"What about you?" Britt said. "I can't believe that you spent Thanksgiving with the dog MILF...I mean Ellie. Sorry. I know how you feel about that word. Plus, I have a girlfriend now. I can't be talking about moms I'd want to fu...uh, you know."

Hayden rolled her eyes. "My Thanksgiving was surprisingly lovely. I also can't believe I spent it with her and her family, but it was nice. And we had a lot of sex for the rest of the weekend. It was a delicious way to spend four days." She couldn't stop the smile thinking about having sex on Ellie's ridiculously horrible wooden chair. It was still a horrible chair, but she'd never be able to look at it the same after lounging on it while watching Ellie go down on her. The angle was perfect for her viewing pleasure. She felt a surge of heat between her legs and looked forward to their plans that evening.

"Are you sure you're not actually dating her? It seems like you spend a lot of time together. And holidays are, like, different." They shrugged.

"Totally sure. We haven't even talked since Sunday." That was almost completely true. They'd texted a few times because Ellie was in Orlando for some type of convention. But even if they texted every day, it didn't mean anything. "I mean, she's coming over tonight, but just for some delivery food and sex. It's not serious."

Britt just nodded and took another sip. "Mmm-hmm."

Hayden could no longer deny that they weren't friends, but she and Ellie were being very careful about it just being friends who fucked—it wasn't dating. Other than Thanksgiving, which was purely as moral support, they'd never spent time together outside of their homes.

Did she enjoy spending time with Ellie? Of course. Was she spending a lot of time with Ellie? Yes. Maybe too much, but Hayden was enjoying the sex too much to do anything about it. She was certain they'd fizzle out within a few weeks, but until then, she was going to enjoy the ride.

❖

When Ellie walked up to Hayden's houseboat with Atlas at seven, she was surprised to see that only the living room light was on. Normally, Hayden had her "porch" light on, along with several in the kitchen and upstairs. She wondered if Hayden had gotten caught up somewhere, but when that had happened before, she'd just texted.

"What do you think, Atlas? Is she not home? Should we go check?" Ellie felt weird creeping onto Hayden's boat in the dark, but she didn't answer her call, and Ellie was getting worried.

She knocked lightly on the back door, and when no one answered, she cracked open the unlocked door and peered in. She hurried in at the sight of Hayden on the couch, hunched over. Ellie was pretty sure she was crying. She sat beside her and put an arm around her, pulling her close, terrified of what was wrong. "What is it, Hayden? What's wrong, sweetheart?"

Hayden started crying harder but sat up straighter so Ellie could see the cat bed in her lap, and Ellie's heart broke. "It...it...it's Chelsea," She sobbed burying her face in Ellie's shoulder.

Chelsea, beautiful and cantankerously sweet Chelsea, Atlas's surprise best friend, was curled up peacefully on the bed with her eyes closed and her head resting on a small pink bunny toy that Ellie had seen her play with almost every time she'd been here. She wasn't breathing.

Tears pricked at the back of Ellie's eyes. "I'm so sorry, Hayden." She wrapped her other arm around Hayden and held her while she sobbed. Atlas slumped on their feet, seeming to know that something was very wrong.

"I...I came home, and when I opened the door, she didn't run to meet me like normal, so I called for her, but she didn't come." Hayden took a quivering breath in and hiccupped a few times. Ellie squeezed her tighter. "I was starting to worry. I thought maybe I'd locked her in a closet this morning or that she'd gotten out and decided for the first time in her life to jump off the boat. I didn't even look in her favorite bed nestled in the corner of the window ledge in her bedroom. That was her favorite—"

She dissolved into tears again, and Ellie held her, rubbing her back, trying to give Hayden whatever comfort she could. "I'm so sorry." She wished there were better words at times like this, but there weren't.

When Hayden got her sobs back under control again, she said, "That was her favorite spot in the whole house. And that's her favorite toy." Hayden's shoulders shook with a small sob.

"She looks like she went peacefully. Like she just wanted to be surrounded by her favorite things and take a nap." Ellie was crying now too.

"I hate that she was alone when she died. I should've been here with her. She should've been on my lap or something, so she knew she was surrounded by love."

"She knew you loved her. You took her in, you gave her gourmet food, you gave her all the pets she ever asked for…well other than that *one* time she tried to join us, but I'm sure she got over that snub."

Hayden's laugh sounded watery, but at least she'd laughed.

"She was a sweet girl, and you gave her an amazing life. And you said she was about twenty, right?"

"That was our best estimate, given that she was a stray." Hayden curled her fingers into Ellie's shirt before letting go and running her hand across Chelsea's head.

"She's known nothing but love for more than half of her life. I don't think she could have had a better one."

"I know." Hayden sniffed. "I just can't believe she's gone." She wiped her tears away with one hand as she continued petting Chelsea with the other. "You and Atlas should go home. I need to take care of her, but I'll text you later."

Ellie struggled to wrap her head around the words, Hayden wanted her to *just go home*? "What?"

Tears were still running down Hayden's cheeks as she sniffed and said, "There isn't anything you can do right now. I need to get myself together and then take her to the vet. I'm sorry I didn't text you to save you a trip."

"Hayden. I am not leaving you to deal with this on your own. I'm going to text my niece to pick up Atlas and stay with him, and then, when you're ready, I'm going to take you to the vet." How could Hayden think she could just send Ellie away? Well, she didn't care what Hayden thought, she wasn't leaving her. She texted Andrea one-handed, pretty sure she was still home from college and would be able to come pick Atlas up.

"I…appreciate the thought, but I can handle everything on my own."

Ellie touched her on the chin and gently guided her until she was looking Ellie in the eyes. "No one disputes that you *can*. I'm sure you're more than capable. However, you don't *have to* handle everything on your own when you have friends to lean on. It's not going to make you soft. And you'd better get used to it because Andrea is on her way over to pick up Atlas and stay the night at my house. I'm *not* leaving you, and you can't make me."

Hayden broke into full tears again as she buried her face in Ellie's neck. But this time, she wrapped an arm around Ellie and held on tight as she cried. Ellie was pretty sure no one had held her as she'd cried in a very, very long time. Well, other than when they were in Wisconsin. Her heart fractured a little thinking of Hayden never having anyone to lean on for emotional support. Ellie had leaned on her parents, her brother. She and Iris's parents had leaned on each other, holding each other up. She couldn't imagine going through life not having anyone to just *be there* for her. She squeezed Hayden tighter.

Andrea texted that she was there, but Ellie waited ten more minutes until Hayden's crying had eased up before she whispered, "Andrea is here. Let me go run Atlas out to her. I'll be right back, okay?"

She felt her nod but made no other move to let her up. It was like she was afraid to see Ellie's face and stayed buried in her neck. It took Atlas sitting up and laying his head on Chelsea's bed before Hayden moved.

"You're a good boy, Atlas." He whined and pressed his nose against Chelsea. "I'm sorry. I know she was your cuddle buddy."

Ellie rubbed his head. "Let's go, bubs." She was so worried about Hayden that she'd never even taken him off his leash. To Hayden, she said, "I'll be back in a minute, okay?"

Hayden nodded.

Ellie ran out to meet Andrea, not wanting to leave Hayden alone for any longer than necessary. Andrea jumped out of the car. "I'm so sorry, Auntie El. Please tell Hayden I'm thinking of her. She seemed super cool at Thanksgiving."

"Thanks, Andrea. And sorry to keep you waiting. You don't know how much I appreciate you taking care of Atlas tonight. I owe you one. I'll text you in the morning. Call if you have any problems, okay?" Ellie hugged her, and Andrea packed Atlas into her car and drove off.

Ellie jogged back to the boat. When she walked in, without looking up, Hayden said, "Okay. I think I'm ready."

Ellie sat again. "Okay, but no rush. I'm not in a hurry."

"I know, but I think it's time. Would you…would you sit with her while I go put my shoes on and grab a blanket? I want to keep her in her bed because it was her favorite." Hayden swallowed hard. "But I don't want her being a spectacle. I also want to call the vet and let them know we're coming."

"I can call while you're getting ready." Ellie hated feeling powerless. She knew there wasn't anything that she could do to ease Hayden's pain, but if she could do anything to take a little off her plate, she'd do it without a second thought.

"It's fine. Thank you, though." She slid Chelsea's bed onto Ellie's lap and touched her cheek. "Thank you. Really." She looked like she wanted to say more but walked away instead.

Ellie helped Hayden wrap Chelsea and the bed inside of a blanket and held Hayden as they walked out to Ellie's car. She held Hayden's hand the whole ride to the emergency vet. There really weren't any words to say, so they rode in a silence that was comfortable but for the heavy fog of sadness that wrapped them both.

When they arrived at the vet, it was thankfully a slow night, so they escorted them back into a treatment room right away and got them seated.

"Thank you again for coming. I know I told you not to, but I don't know how to do this." Hayden's eyes filled again as Ellie pulled her closer.

"One step at a time, okay? Don't think too far ahead." Ellie squeezed her shoulder and picked up the trifold card that had all the different memorial options.

When they were finished, Ellie drove Hayden back to the boat and stayed all night. It was the first night they'd spent together without having sex, but Ellie was content to hold Hayden and be whatever she needed in that moment.

CHAPTER TWENTY-SIX

After a long couple of weeks, then an afternoon of her ex's bullshit, Ellie was still fuming when she met up with Skye and Bailey, and she apparently wasn't hiding it well.

After hugs were exchanged, Skye said, "Why do you look like you're about to murder someone?"

"I ran into Jessie today while shopping. She foisted herself on me while I was trying to get a coffee and proceeded to tell me that the reason she started an emotional affair with her now-wife while we were still together was because *I* was never home."

Ellie hadn't believed it when Jessie had walked up and started talking, but she really hadn't believed it when Jessie had said, "Honestly, I came over here because I wanted to apologize. I never cheated on you physically, but I had started to cheat on you emotionally." She'd grimaced as if she actually cared. "Mentally. Before we broke up. This was my fault. I chose to not talk to you about how unhappy I was and instead confided in another woman, Mari. I'm so happy with her—I know she's my soulmate—but I'm also the bad guy in your story, even though I never slept around. I doubt any of that helps, but I wanted you to know how truly sorry I am." Jessie had taken a sip of her coffee, and Ellie had fought the urge to slap the cup out of her hands. She doubted Jessie was sorry at all living her new life.

"Uh, thank you. I guess." Ellie had mumbled. Jessie was right. Knowing she hadn't actually fucked someone else while they were dating wasn't much of a consolation. Her mind had raced, trying to figure out how to get away. She'd considered abandoning the coffee.

She didn't care if Jessie was sorry or if she knew she was the bad guy. She hadn't wanted to be confronted with any of this.

"Well, look. Regardless of whatever happened between us, I'm glad to hear that you have a dog. It must mean that you're making a more concerted effort to be home at night. You're funny, attractive, great to spend time with. You're a catch. The only drawback—and it was one I obviously couldn't get over—was you being gone all the time."

Again, was that supposed to make her feel better? That she was a catch? Just not someone Jessie had been willing to work to keep? Ellie had envisioned shoving a handful of napkins from the table into Jessie's mouth to shut her the hell up.

Bailey whistled under her breath as Skye said, "What a bitch."

Ellie was grateful they broke her out of reliving that unpleasant scene. "She then implied that now that I have dog, maybe I can find my forever person because I'm home at night for him. Can you believe that?" Ellie took a large sip of water to try to cool down as Bailey and Skye exchanged a glance. What was that about? They certainly couldn't be siding with Jessie.

Skye spoke first. "I definitely don't agree with her—she's a bitch—but you do seem to travel less now, and you don't email me at ten or eleven at night anymore. I could see how a partner might have gotten frustrated with your schedule. And you have always worked a lot. If I hadn't asked you what was wrong when you first got here, your first question probably still would have been, 'How is leasing going?'"

"That's...hmm..." Ellie wished the server had already brought them some wine but took a sip of water again to give herself a moment to think. "Okay, maybe some of that is true, and I do want to know how leasing is going. And my roof-deck and amenities. But that doesn't make me a workaholic." Ellie didn't like the defensiveness sprouting in her. She tried to tamp it down.

"I'm not saying you were doing anything wrong. Jessie should have talked to you about how she was feeling, but Atlas has helped you make some positive changes in your life that maybe will help you in your next relationship. That's it." Skye held her hands up in a harmless gesture.

Ellie took that as a sign to move on. She really didn't want to discuss her shortcomings. She'd been obsessing about them all day already. "Well enough about my shitty day. I can't believe this is the first time I've seen you since Thanksgiving. Tell me about your amazing trip. I think I saw on Instagram that a couple of someones should be wearing some new hardware on their left ring fingers."

Smiles popped up on both Skye's and Bailey's faces, and they lifted their hands that were sporting very similar diamond solitaires.

Ellie grabbed them. "I love you so much, and I'm so happy for you both. So tell me all about it."

Her chest tightened as Skye and Bailey told her about their adorable dual proposal and how Bailey had tried to steal Skye's scene when she'd dropped to one knee on the top of the mountain before Skye had the chance to, even though she'd planned the whole morning around her own proposal. It was completely perfect, and Ellie was happy for them. She really was.

Except for that little knife in her side because her current non-relationship would never lead anywhere, and she was probably going to die an old spinster. They bickered over who hijacked whose proposal, and Ellie took a long sip of wine and reminded herself not to be bitter. She had faith things would work out. They always did somehow. Seeing Jessie and having her flaunt Ellie's shortcomings had done a number on her. But that did not mean she wasn't happy for Skye and Bailey.

When they finally agreed that it didn't matter who got credit for proposing first, Skye gave Bailey a quick peck before she looked back at Ellie, apparently remembering she was there. "So how are things going with the hot doctor sex friend? Still sexy? Still casual?"

"Still going and all of those things. I'm actually going over there this evening after dinner."

"Ooh, a booty call," Sky said.

"Is it a booty call if you plan it in advance?" Bailey asked. "I thought that was a more spur-of-the-moment thing?'"

Ellie laughed, and Skye said, "You might have a point. I think planning in advance does sound like more of a date."

"Ugh, it's not like I invited her to dinner with you two. Though she does have Atlas at her place and has had him all day today so

I wouldn't have to go home to get him and bring him over." Skye and Bailey shared a glance again, so Ellie tried to explain further. "She's really bonded with him in our sessions, and she just lost her cat a couple of weeks ago, so her place feels really empty. It's nothing serious."

"Oh no," Bailey said. "I'm so sorry. Losing a pet is the worst. How's she doing?"

"She's struggling. She doesn't really let anyone in, but she'd had that cat for fifteen years, so she'd really bonded with her. I took her to the vet and held her hand while she chose the urn and everything. It was horrible."

Skye and Bailey shared another look.

What the fuck? "What's with your secretive couple's glances?"

Skye sighed. "I'm a little worried you might not be feeling as casual as you want to believe."

"It's not serious. I'm still too busy, and Atlas is a handful. And Hayden doesn't do anything more. Sure, we're going to Michigan for the last two weeks of the year, but just as friends with benefits. I hadn't made my year end travel plans yet because I didn't know what to do about Atlas, and she didn't feel like going to Costa Rica anymore because she's in the doldrums after losing Chelsea, so she invited us to come with her. No big deal. Not a date. Just friends sharing a cabin during the holidays that we don't celebrate. That's all."

Skye's and Bailey's raised eyebrows told Ellie they really didn't believe her, and a tiny bit of her questioned it too, but she wasn't ready to admit that. Not even to herself. She was sure she was still only thinking of Hayden as Ms. Right Now.

"Ellie," Skye said, "going away with someone for two weeks does *not* sound like casual." Bailey's face was tight, like she was in pain as she nodded along. "I'm just worried you're going to get hurt."

"You have absolutely nothing to worry about. Hayden and I are completely and entirely on the same page. Nothing has changed since we talked about this possibility months ago. I'm just having fun, sowing the last of my wild oats, and having the best sex of my life before I settle down. You're the one who said I should just have some fun."

"Ellie, you took her to the vet and held her hand through one of the most difficult things pet parents have to do," Bailey said.

"That was just human decency. She needed a friend. Nothing more. We aren't girlfriends."

"That's fair, but you really believe you can go away for two weeks and stay at a romantic cabin without any inappropriate *feelings?*" Skye said.

"Yes. My heart is not in play, and that's not going to change," she said emphatically and hoped she was right. And could keep it that way. She knew that if she started to feel *things*—real things—for Hayden and couldn't get them under control, that would be the last she saw of Hayden in the bedroom—or the living room or the hot tub—and she wasn't ready for this to end. She'd gone into this with her eyes wide open, fully aware that Hayden would never *care* for her. At least not as anything more than a friend.

And that stung a little bit—okay, a lot—but Ellie liked spending time together, and until she was actually ready to step back into the dating world, she didn't want to lose what they had. Now, if she was being honest, she *possibly* was starting to feel a little something. But it was manageable. It was also *possible* that she could be close to being ready to date again, but she wasn't there yet, and she definitely wasn't ready for things with Hayden to be over.

So she'd continue to deny any inconvenient truths and maintain the status quo.

CHAPTER TWENTY-SEVEN

The cabin was gorgeous, nestled in the trees and blanketed with a fresh coat of snow. It was even better than the photos Hayden had looked at online. Atlas seemed to be loving being able to run around in the fenced yard, and Hayden enjoyed the easy camaraderie with Ellie. They went snowshoeing every day while Atlas frolicked, they played board games or put puzzles together in the afternoons, and spent at least some time every afternoon in the hot tub watching the sunset.

Hayden was also terrified, even as she loved how it felt. As she stood at the kitchen sink that overlooked the lake, she allowed herself the luxury of imagining this being permanent. Of spending endless days with Ellie, just being them. Not just for the sex—which they had pretty much every night in the hot tub, sometimes on the couch, in bed, first thing in the morning—but for the everything else of it.

Sharing meals and hikes and games. Hayden had never felt this way, but she didn't want to give it up. She knew she was going to have to, but she also didn't *want* to. But that was the danger of their situation. Nothing had changed about her desire for a relationship. She didn't think she could handle it if anyone else she came to rely on deserted her, yet she was growing closer to Ellie every day. Getting closer to that point of too much reliance. She'd known she was playing with fire when she rented this cabin, but she couldn't imagine two full weeks without Ellie and Atlas.

She was terrified about what that meant in the moment. She'd committed to not focusing on it. She was appreciating everything as it came. She refused to taint the time they still had together with anything. And their time was definitely limited. Once Britt passed their exams the following week, the clock would really start ticking on her departure. And Hayden's own feelings were coming into play, and that was too risky to her self-preservation, so she really couldn't delay.

"Are you almost done there?" Ellie mumbled against her neck, warm arms wrapping around her waist.

Ellie had been a little quiet all day, so Hayden was relieved she was back to normal, and nothing was wrong. She pushed her hips back and moved them slowly side to side. She quickly finished washing the last pan. "I just might be. What did you have in mind?"

Ellie kissed a path up her neck and nibbled on her earlobe. "Well, I just lit a fire, and it's really roaring. I was thinking maybe you, me, and a blanket on the couch?" She reached under Hayden's shirt and cupped her breasts, her thumbs rubbing back and forth across Hayden's quickly hardening nipples.

Hayden turned in her embrace, missing the nipple contact but wanting to taste her. The kiss was soft but urgent. Ellie's lips parted, her tongue soft, yet Hayden could taste her impatience. She didn't want to go fast but could sense Ellie's need, so she increased the intensity. Ellie pulled them out of the kitchen, walking backward until she sank onto the couch, pulling Hayden on top of her.

Ellie had Hayden's shirt over her head before she was even settled, her mouth peppering her chest with kisses. There was something frantic in Ellie's movements, and Hayden was having a hard time getting into it, so she stilled Ellie's face and forced her to look at her.

Was that panic? Hayden kissed her softly. "You are so beautiful, Ellie. Will you talk to me? What's going on right now?"

Ellie closed her eyes, and when they opened, they were glistening with tears. She pressed up until Hayden got the hint and slid to the other end of the couch. She felt suddenly exposed, even though she was still in her bra and grabbed her shirt off the floor, pulling it on quickly. Her heart was in her throat as she waited for Ellie to explain.

"I'm sorry about that." Ellie waved between them. "I've been struggling with something for a while now. Before we even came up here, but since we've been here together twenty-four seven, it's gotten worse, and I can't ignore it anymore." She ran her fingers through her hair and shook it as she always did when she was nervous. "Everything feels so perfect, but I can't seem to keep denying that I've broken my word."

"I don't think you've made me any promises." Hayden was afraid she knew where all of this was going but didn't want to admit it. She didn't want to consider what might be happening. She'd always known this was temporary, but…

"It's been in the back of my mind for a while, but I convinced myself that I had it in hand. We didn't act like we were dating. I was fine with it just being sex, but somewhere along the way, it started to be more. Maybe it's always been, and I was just in denial." She was talking so fast that Hayden's brain struggled to keep up. She didn't want to keep up.

"I promised you in that first conversation about turning this"— she pointed between them—"into more than just a TTO, that I wouldn't fall for you, but I have. I'm so sorry. And it's not just that. I've been in denial about not being ready for a relationship. The thing is, my ex-girlfriend, whom I ran into a few weeks ago, made me face some hard truths. I convinced myself she was full of shit at first, but she was right. I was never home because I never *wanted* to make time for her. But I've done it for Atlas. And I've done it for you. Because I *wanted* to spend time with you. I wanted to be *close* to you. Even if it was just as friends. But that's not enough now. I'm forty-two. I can't spend time pining over you when yourself, your future, aren't things you're willing to share."

Hayden couldn't breathe. Her heart was thundering like galloping horses at the Kentucky Derby. She'd known this would happen, but she didn't expect it to hurt like this. Didn't expect to feel like she was being trampled by the horses that had broken out of her chest. She swallowed, tried to take a breath.

"I'm so sorry I broke the rules, Hayden. There is nothing in this world that I want more than to pick up where we left off a few minutes ago, but my heart can't take it. I'm going to move into one of the other bedrooms for tonight. I know you've paid for a few more days since tomorrow is New Year's Eve, and I know the timing is shit, but I think it would be best if you took me someplace to rent a car tomorrow so we can drive home. Come on, Atlas." He jumped up from the floor and followed her down the hall.

Hayden opened her mouth to speak—to call and beg for her to come back—but didn't know what to think, no less what to say. She hadn't felt this sense of loss since her grandma had passed away. This was the reason she didn't get involved. This feeling of having the thing she needed ripped out of her grasp was the reason she didn't make friends or take lovers for more than a night. She'd almost forgotten how bad it felt. But she'd brought it on herself. Her need for Ellie had overpowered her need for self-preservation.

She should have never gone down this path.

Yet, the idea of never seeing Ellie again other than for Atlas's last two appointments felt devastating. She'd grown to rely on Ellie despite her best efforts. Would that go away if they never saw each other again? She feared it wouldn't. She feared she'd be heartbroken for a long time after this.

If she could get her heart broken without even being *in* a real relationship, would trying and failing at a relationship be any worse? Trying a real relationship and then one of them leaving or dying?

She still wasn't sure if she believed in forever, but how could she ignore something that felt so right? Life since she'd met Ellie had been so much brighter, more than she'd believed possible. But could Hayden give her what she needed? She'd never even had a real relationship. Could she figure it out as she went, or would she inevitably hurt Ellie again anyway? Maybe it would be easier to work through the pain and let things go now. Hayden sat numb, staring down the hall where Ellie and Atlas had disappeared as she tried to figure out what she should do. What would lead to the least amount of devastation for them both.

❖

Ellie lay in bed, spooning Atlas and trying unsuccessfully not to cry. She hadn't meant to say anything to Hayden today. Even though this realization had been building almost from the moment they'd arrived. But a seed had planted itself that morning when they'd watched the sunrise after hiking up above the tree line. Everything had felt so perfect in that moment, holding Hayden's hand with Atlas at their feet.

And Ellie had realized she was living in a fantasy world.

This little island that they were living on this week wasn't real. What she was feeling wasn't reciprocated. But she'd planned to wait until they were back in Chicago to say anything so they could enjoy their last few days at the cabin. Yet, as the day went on, it became harder and harder to pretend nothing had changed.

She'd tried to distract them with sex, but Hayden could clearly tell something was off, and when she'd stopped them, there was nothing Ellie could do to hold in how she was feeling anymore.

In the end, it was for the best. Now that she'd stopped denying she was ready to start dating again, now that she'd realized what she'd been doing wrong before, the only choice was to stop before she wasted any more time with someone who absolutely couldn't be her One. Someone who refused to be anyone's One. And it hurt like fucking hell because she loved being with Hayden. And it still felt like they were together, even though they weren't. And Ellie could only imagine how much worse it would be if she'd kept going down this path for weeks or months more.

She squeezed Atlas tighter. "It's going to just be you and me for a while, buddy. I'm sorry." She buried her face in the scruffy hair at his neck. She loved the way he smelled there. Like Fritos and love.

She thought she was imagining it when she heard a soft tap at the door. But when that tap returned, louder, she pushed up onto her elbow. When the tapping came a third time, she croaked, "Come in."

Hayden was framed in the light of the hallway. Ellie couldn't see her face but heard her sniffles. "Do you mind if I come in? I want to talk."

What could she want? Ellie prayed she wasn't there to try to convince Ellie to keep being casual. There was no way she could do that. At the same time, she couldn't help feeling a small kernel of hope. "Come on in." She pushed up and crossed her legs. Atlas rolled over and put his head in her lap. She ran her hand over his head and ear, his fur soft and comforting beneath her fingertips.

Hayden sat at the foot of the bed. "Is this okay?" Ellie managed a nod. "I…I've never believed in forever. I'm still not sure I really do." Ellie's heart fell. "But I can honestly say that what's going on here isn't just sex. I don't think it's *ever* been just sex. From the moment you walked into my office with this lug." She affectionately rubbed his back leg. "I've been drawn to you. I tried to fight it, to deny it. I tried to pretend we weren't friends. And I tried to pretend that all I wanted was sex. But you took me to Thanksgiving. You've been my rock since I lost Chelsea. Then you came here with me…and you've made it impossible for me to deny that I have feelings, genuine feelings, for you. Whether or not I want to."

Ellie laughed, but it was brittle. "It doesn't sound like you really want something else."

"That was true. It's been true. I've been sitting in the living room trying to decide if I should let things lie and walk away like you suggested, but I can't. I can't promise you forever. I can't promise that we're going to want to be together in six weeks, but I also cannot imagine life without you. I kept thinking this thing with us would burn itself out, but it just keeps getting stronger. You are the only person who has *ever* made me want more. Made me consider pursuing more. Maybe we date and in six months you're sick of me. Maybe not, but I can't sit here and let you walk away without telling you how I feel and begging you to give us a try. A real try. Please?" Her face was hidden in the shadow from the light trickling in behind her, but she ran her fingers under her eyes and sniffed again.

Ellie hadn't dared to hope that Hayden might want to try for more, but now that she was facing it, she was worried Hayden didn't mean it. Or she meant it in that moment but wouldn't once she'd realized what she'd done. "Are you sure? Like, really sure you want to try this? You have always been so adamant about not wanting commitment. How do you know you aren't going to change your mind next week or next month and decide to go back to being alone?"

"I can't imagine walking away from something that feels so right. I never wanted to consider having someone in my life before, but now I can't imagine my life without you. It feels bleak and bland. Can I promise I will always feel that way? No, but neither can you.

What I can promise you is to be honest. To tell you when I'm scared or need you."

Ellie's heart started to beat again. "You won't run away if things get hard?"

Hayden nodded.

How could Ellie resist? She was pretty sure if she wasn't fully in love, she was awfully damn close. She crawled toward Hayden and took her hand and kissed it. "How did this all happen to us?"

"I don't know. But let's go to bed."

"We're in bed already," Ellie said and smiled.

"This is the small bed. And Atlas has claimed seventy-five percent of it. Let's go back to our bed, where there's room to maneuver." She reached out a hand to help Ellie up.

Ellie was still afraid that Hayden was going to hurt her somehow, but knowing that her feelings were reciprocated, knowing that there maybe could be a future that involved them together had her heart swelling so huge that it might burst from her chest. It was everything she'd been secretly hoping for in the recent weeks without even realizing it.

CHAPTER TWENTY-EIGHT

Hayden guided Ellie into the room they'd claimed as their own and ignored the slight quiver in her knees. She'd already crossed a lot of firsts with Ellie, but this was absolutely the biggest. The scariest. Yet knowing she was going there with Ellie made it feel less scary. Ellie was like a security blanket. She'd been there for Hayden in the most difficult time since her grandma had passed away and had just stepped in like it was nothing. Like it was just what friends did. And maybe that was what she'd been missing.

Since those moments, it had been harder to pretend they were just friends. Well, it had been hard before that, but that was when the switch had flipped. Every minute they'd spent together since then had been building toward this.

When they neared the foot of the bed, Hayden went up on her toes to bring them closer to eye level and cupped Ellie's chin.

"Are you absolutely sure this is what you want, Hayden? I want it so badly, I don't even have words, but I don't want to pressure you. I don't think I'll recover if you change your mind tomorrow." Ellie's eyes were so vulnerable. Hayden knew she'd been having second thoughts on their walk over. Maybe that was why she'd paused.

"I'm absolutely sure." She looked into the deep umber pools of Ellie's eyes, drawing her in. She prayed Ellie could see the honesty, the sincerity, in her own. Still cupping Ellie's cheek, she ran her thumb over Ellie's lower lip and moaned when Ellie swirled her tongue over the tip. She lost her balance and rocked onto her heels. She had a fleeting thought she should work on her balance more in yoga, but that thought was quickly wiped away when Ellie's fingers dug into her hips and pulled their bodies together.

"Okay," she whispered before crushing her mouth to Hayden's. Her tongue was insistent but yielding when Hayden pushed back. Ellie pulled her in as tightly as their clothing would allow, and they both became impatient with the barriers. Hayden wasn't sure who allowed a small amount of distance to open between them, but they both quickly pulled off their own shirts the second space was available.

Hayden loved this red satin bra of Ellie's. She loved every bra Ellie owned, but the feel of this one was…extra. She blazed a path along Ellie's chest with her mouth and indulged herself by rubbing her cheek over the satin while running her tongue around the edge of the bra. Ellie's fingernails scraped her scalp as she kissed and licked a path to her other breast and gave it the same treatment. She ran her thumb over the breast she'd just left until she felt Ellie's nipple harden through the material.

She wanted to lie down and worship at the feet of this amazing woman who wanted to be hers. She'd never felt possessive over anything, yet she wanted to possess every inch of Ellie's perfect body. Every curve that she'd already memorized, she wanted to forget so she could relearn it. Again and again.

Ellie groaned and moved her chest until Hayden's tongue dipped well into the cup and grazed her nipple. She took the hint and reached behind Ellie, unclasping the bra with one hand as her other thumb still massaged Ellie's rock-hard nipple, now exposed as the bra slid to the floor.

Ellie pulled her to her full height and reclaimed her mouth. Before Hayden realized what was happening, Ellie had unclasped her bra and was sliding it down her arms, forcing Hayden's hands away from Ellie's breasts so she could pull it free. She hated breaking contact even for a second, but when Ellie dipped her head and took a nipple in her mouth, Hayden let go of the frustration.

Her muscles clenched as a flood of wetness surged between her legs. Hayden was certain her underwear was soaked. She palmed the back of Ellie's head to urge her to suck harder, lick more firmly. When she was as turned on as she was, she liked a light graze of teeth. She groaned, urging Ellie on.

She missed Ellie's lips when they released her, but the heat in her eyes when she stood upright again sent another surge of wetness between her thighs. Ellie licked her lips and said, "For the love of all things holy, I need to get you naked now."

Hayden tried to form words, but none would come. She nodded and found the button on her jeans and quickly undid it. She reached for Ellie's, not wanting to be the only one about to be completely naked. When they were both naked, Ellie's mouth fused with Hayden's again, their tongues tangling in a way that had Hayden's hips moving.

She pushed on Ellie's hips until she sat, and they shimmied up the bed until Ellie's head was on the pillow, and Hayden was lying on top of her, kissing a path from her mouth, up her jaw, to her ear. She stopped and nibbled Ellie's earlobe for a second, savoring the smell of her hair, the taste of her skin. She wasn't sure why she loved this spot so much; luckily, Ellie liked it too and started squirming below her, looking for friction.

Hayden started to move her lips again, this time down Ellie's neck where she stopped at her collarbone, bit it softly, sucked a little harder, and soothed it with gentle laps of her tongue. Ellie's hips began bucking in earnest, and Hayden didn't want to tease her anymore. She slid her hand down Ellie's torso, across her flat belly until she came to Ellie's curls. She normally liked to trace her fingers over them a few times but sensed Ellie wouldn't appreciate it tonight and slid two fingers along her hot wet crease.

Hayden groaned at how wet she was. Was there anything as erotic as that first feel of sliding her fingers between a woman's legs and finding her this wet? Fuck. Not any woman. Just this woman. Just this sexy, beautiful, amazing woman who wanted to be *with* her. She somewhat reluctantly lifted her head away from Ellie's collarbone, but she needed to see Ellie's face as she touched her.

Her gorgeous chestnut brown curls fanned out around her head like a gigantic halo. Maybe it was. She was Hayden's angel. Her eyes were closed, and her cheeks flushed in the sexiest way possible, but Hayden had this urge to see her eyes as she slid two fingers into her, so she slowed on Ellie's clit and whispered, "Ellie."

"Mmm," Ellie groaned, but her eyes remained firmly shut.

"Ellie," she whispered again. "Look at me. Please."

Ellie's eyes slowly slid open. "Hmm?"

"I want to see you when I do this." She swirled two very wet fingers around Ellie's entrance and slid in. Ellie's eyes went wide.

She gasped. Her eyes started to close, but Hayden begged. "No, stay with me. Please."

Ellie nodded, and Hayden willed her to maintain eye contact. She was so wet and soft. Hayden wanted to live right there, in that moment, forever. She tried to take a mental snapshot so she could never forget how she felt. She began moving; slowly at first, and then she gained speed as Ellie's hips started to meet her thrusts.

"More," Ellie begged.

"More fingers?" Hayden wanted to be sure.

"Yes. Please." The please finished on a groan, and Hayden desperately wanted to grind against Ellie's thigh but didn't want to do anything that might jeopardize the climb Ellie was currently taking.

She slid her fingers nearly all the way out and added a third. "Is this okay?"

"God, yes. Please. Faster." Ellie's left foot dug into the mattress as she began to move her hips faster and faster against Hayden's hand. She had a fleeting thought that she wanted to keep her like this forever, but Ellie didn't give her a choice. She looked into Hayden's soul as her movement became more frantic, and her eyes finally drifted closed. Hayden could see her fighting it, but she screamed Hayden's name as she came apart, and Hayden was certain she'd never experienced anything more beautiful in her entire life.

She fluttered kisses all over Ellie's face. Her forehead, her eyelids, her cheeks, finally, her lips. Ellie's arms tightened, pulling Hayden impossibly closer even as she left her fingers buried so deeply inside her.

"Shh," Ellie murmured. Hayden wasn't sure why. She hadn't said anything. But when Ellie squeezed tighter as Hayden wiggled her fingers ever so slightly inside her, she realized the "shh" actually meant stop moving, not stop making sounds. Could this woman be any more perfect?

She obeyed Ellie's confusing signals and kept her fingers still even as Ellie's muscles quivered around them. Her head on Ellie's shoulder, she fell quickly into a surprisingly deep sleep.

The next thing she knew, she was on her back, and Ellie was lying half on top of her, running her fingers through her short hair and down the side of her face just to lift and repeat. "You know," Ellie said. "I'm the one who's supposed to sleep after such an intense orgasm. Not you. You're supposed to be the one waking me up like this."

Hayden's lips were impossibly dry, and she sucked her bottom lip in, running her tongue along it. She hadn't meant it to be sexy—it was just impulse—but Ellie looked at her like she'd just rubbed Cool Whip all over her body and asked Ellie to lick it off. "Um. It was an accident?" It came out like a question, but Hayden had no idea what she'd really meant.

"I can't believe we're here. Starting something real. You're the most amazing person I've ever met," Ellie said.

Hayden waited for a wave of panic, but it never came. "I kind of think it's always been real. I don't think we ever had a chance of something casual, no matter what we said to each other and to ourselves. From the second I put that ice pack on your knee and touched your leg, which I'm sorry for. At least, I'm sorry I didn't have your consent first."

"I wanted all of it. Every graze, every touch, every lengthy, longing look. I used to think about you when I…touched myself at night. I told myself it wasn't abnormal to masturbate to someone I knew. Especially someone I'd never have a chance to touch. And yet…here we are. Touching each other." Ellie smiled, and Hayden's legs felt weak, even though they weren't holding her up. Ellie ran the tip of her index finger along Hayden's collarbone. She didn't realize it at first, but Ellie was running the outline of her tattoo. Tattoos, really, since there were three separate birds. "Why'd you get this? I've loved it since I saw just a peek of it all those months ago, but I feel like there's a story here."

Hayden's adrenaline response told her to evade, but she didn't want to. She wanted to be open, no secrets. If she kept anything, it would just create a wall that she didn't want to hide behind. Not anymore. Not with Ellie anyway. "It's my family. My dad, my mom, and my grandma. They're all flying up to heaven or whatever is next but always near my heart."

Ellie ran a thumb under Hayden's eye. She hadn't realized she'd teared up until Ellie caught one. She placed a kiss on the head of each bird. "I'm sorry you went through that. I can't even imagine. And so young."

Hayden's throat felt tight, unsure of what to say. "Thank you." That was the safest response she could come up with.

"What about this one?" Ellie traced a finger over Hayden's right hip. "The characters. What do they mean?"

"It's supposed to be perseverance. Chinese, long form. That's what they told me at the tattoo parlor. However, I don't think anyone there actually spoke Chinese, so it might be bullshit. Well, probably not because—"

Hayden's breath caught as Ellie's lips pressed a light kiss to that tattoo as well. "This one. The one that's like a backward J with three lines over it. I think this one is "heart" isn't it? Seems like I saw that somewhere."

It was, but Hayden couldn't form any words as the hot breath from Ellie's mouth over her tattoo drifted farther south. She tried to say yes, but it came out as nothing more than a croak.

When Ellie's perfect lips found Hayden's sex, she groaned. A stream of words of love, desire, and need wanted to flow from her, but her mind was so focused on sensation, all it could manage was a hoarse, "Please."

Thankfully, Ellie didn't need any other direction because her lips and her tongue worked in tandem to lick, suck, stroke, caress pleasure out of Hayden. Hayden didn't realize her own hand had drifted to her breast until Ellie's hand interlaced with her own. Together, they flicked, pinched, and gently pulled her nipple until it was so hard, Hayden just wanted to press her palm against it, but Ellie wouldn't let her.

Ellie ran her palm back and forth across the tight flesh as her lips and other hand coaxed her closer and closer to the peak until Hayden groaned both in relief and regret as her orgasm ripped through her. She screamed something. Maybe it was, "Ellie." Maybe it was, "Yes." Hayden doubted she'd ever know and simply didn't care as all of her thoughts scattered into the wind, and she pulled Ellie back up to her. When Ellie's head was next to hers on the pillow and her leg was wrapped possessively around Hayden's hips, she tightened her arms and fell back into the most blissful slumber she'd ever experienced.

Chapter Twenty-nine

It was Valentine's Day, and Ellie seemed to have something up her sleeve. She'd asked Hayden to meet her at Ambassador Plaza before dinner. Which was a little weird as they'd normally meet at the restaurant. But Hayden had no issue doing it.

Sometimes, she still felt panicky when she thought about getting closer to Ellie, but she couldn't deny how perfect it felt when they were together. She'd never believed herself forever material, but now she couldn't imagine a world where she wasn't with Ellie. She'd gotten an email from Dr. Prewster a few days ago that also had her panicked. Now that Britt had passed their exams and was a licensed veterinary behaviorist, Dr. Prewster was ready to nail down a real timeline.

Hayden hadn't responded to her and hadn't sent the requested return receipt because she needed time to process. What she should have done was say, "Thank you, but I've changed my mind. My personal situation has changed, and I no longer want to move," but she didn't. She ignored it and decided to string Dr. Prewster along a bit before she fully committed to staying. That caused her a fair amount of guilt. She'd sat in front of Ellie weeks ago and told her she wanted to make a go at this—which they were doing—and yet, she was still keeping her options open. Why?

The vague itchiness that she'd had last year that had guided her to look for another career opportunity, another city, was gone. And in its place was Ellie and Atlas. A few weeks ago, Ellie's dog sitter had gotten sick and had to cancel the night before a trip, so Hayden had volunteered to take care of him. Since then, she'd been watching Atlas whenever Ellie had to travel for work. She loved being in Ellie's bed when she got back late from an overnight trip. Ellie was always a little horny when she got home, and Hayden was very happy to oblige, even if Ellie woke her with cold hands on her stomach. Things felt pretty perfect, so why hadn't she shut the door on Dr. Prewster?

Hayden had resolved to email Dr. Prewster in the morning and do just that when she heard Ellie's voice echo in the lobby, though she couldn't yet see her. "That tenant lounge is looking great, Bailey. I love that roll-up door you suggested. But how are things coming along on that seventh-floor build-out for the food services company? Have you been able to crack the whip at the millwork company? We're going to incur penalties if we can't get back on track there."

Hayden leaned forward on the planter she was sitting on to try to get a look at Ellie, and when she did, her heart nearly stopped. Ellie was talking to a woman a couple of inches shorter than her in dark jeans and a navy plaid blazer with the sleeves rolled up to her forearms who looked vaguely familiar. She was stunning, but Hayden only had eyes for Ellie. She was in a typical suit, one Hayden had actually seen her put on this morning. It was a dark gray with light, narrow pinstripes, and she'd worn a red shirt underneath because it was Valentine's Day, but Hayden loved the color on her no matter the day. She was tapping her two-inch pump while waiting for the answer about the millwork. It was the combination of take-charge Ellie and that hard hat that had Hayden's stomach fluttering. It wouldn't seem like a hard hat could be sexy, but damn. It so was.

"Yes. It's still going to be about two weeks behind the initial delivery date, but we're working around that, so once the cabinets do come in, we can pop them into place and wrap this job up on time," the stranger said.

"Excellent."

Hayden didn't want to eavesdrop like a stalker, so she cleared her throat and walked out.

"Hey, Hayden," Ellie said. "You're a little early."

"I didn't have time to go home, so I just walked over. The weather is lovely for February. It just took a little less time than I'd been expecting." She shrugged. "Hope that's okay."

"Of course. Hayden, this is Bailey. She owns the construction company doing most of the work in this building. Bailey, this is my, uh, girlfriend, Hayden." Hayden's heart stuttered at the word girlfriend as Ellie stumbled over it, but it was the right term. They hadn't discussed it, but they were seeing each other for real. Seeing each other exclusively. That felt like it qualified for "girlfriend" status. Hayden had never done this before, but it felt right to her. And made her feel even worse for not telling Dr. Prewster she wasn't moving to New Orleans. She was definitely emailing her in the morning. "Bailey is actually the person who suggested I bring Atlas to see you."

"I think I met you one morning while you were out for a run, but nice to see you again."

Oh, right. "Likewise," Hayden said as she shook Bailey's hand.

"Well, I have to jet. Skye has something planned for us tonight, but I don't know what and need to go pick her up. Enjoy your evening, ladies." She shared a knowing smile with Ellie, and Hayden again wondered what Ellie had in store.

"Hi, again," Ellie said after Bailey left. She grabbed Hayden's hand and interlaced their fingers. "Thanks for meeting me over here."

"Of course." Hayden stood on her toes and kissed her. Ellie still hadn't taken off her hard hat, and it was giving Hayden heart palpitations. "Where are we heading for this made-up holiday?"

"Your cynicism wounds me, Hayden." She placed a hand on her heart. "Even if it's a made-up holiday, it gives us a reason to celebrate. And you wouldn't turn down a nice dinner someplace romantic, right?"

Her grin made Hayden swoon a little bit. She was right. And she really wouldn't turn down an evening with Ellie regardless of what it was for. "I wouldn't turn down dinner, though we eat a lot of dinners together these days. But if you want to have an extra romantic one, I'm game."

"Excellent. I love Valentine's Day. Let's get you a hard hat, and we can head up."

"We're staying here? In a construction zone? That doesn't sound particularly romantic. Not that it matters. Just curious." She couldn't help but give Ellie a little bit of a hard time.

Ellie laughed. "Ye of little faith. Just wait." She handed Hayden a hard hat from a folding table, and Hayden hoped it had been cleaned since the last person who wore it, but she dutifully put it on. Ellie's eyes widened, and a smile appeared again as she adjusted it on Hayden's head.

"What?"

"You're just cute." Ellie pursed her lips.

"I hate to break it to you, but you're *just cute* too. That suit, this hard hat…" Hayden playfully fanned her face.

"I'm not saying I wore this particular suit because I knew we were having dinner, but I'm not saying I didn't, either. Also, I know you are a fan of me in red." She shrugged and pulled them toward the elevators.

Ellie pressed the button for the top floor, and Hayden was curious about what she'd planned. They'd been spending a lot of time together, but mostly low-key. Limited planning. The only thing Hayden had planned was the Michigan trip, and that hadn't taken much. And that probably didn't count as, even though she'd planned it completely with Ellie and Atlas in mind, Ellie didn't know that.

Hayden gasped when the elevator doors opened, and a field of candles was spread in front of them. "Wha?" She looked to Ellie, who watched her with a small smile and then looked back at the room they were stepping into.

Ellie placed a hand on her lower back and guided her out of the elevator. It was clearly still a construction zone, with the concrete floor covered in drywall powder, and wires hanging from the ceiling on the other side of the room, but someone had set up little battery candles around three sides of the room. In the center along the windows was a long table with a white tablecloth and a brushed nickel candlestick with an unlit taper, a picnic basket, a bottle of wine, two glasses, and two place settings.

Despite the gorgeous setup, what really grabbed Hayden's attention was the skyline behind the table. The lights of Michigan Avenue shimmered below, and the lights along the winding paths in Millennium and Maggie Daley Parks twinkled. The sky was just barely pink, and several buildings were lit up red for the holiday.

"How did you do all this? It's amazing." Hayden finally ripped her eyes away from the sight before her and looked to Ellie, who had a satisfied smile. No one had ever cared about Hayden enough to do something so elaborate and sweet for her. Not that she'd let anyone get close enough, but still. The sheer romanticism of the moment had her knees wobbly.

"I'm the owner. I have my ways. And I wanted you to feel a little extra appreciated this year. I know you think holidays are silly, but I'm okay with a day dedicated to making us focus on our sweethearts. And you, my sweetheart, deserve all the appreciation in the world." Ellie pulled her into a loose embrace and kissed her. Not strong and passionate but sweet. Gentle. Loving.

She threaded her fingers into Ellie's hair. It was too curly to run her fingers through, but she lightly scratched Ellie's head, loving how silky the hair felt. Loving the long moan she drew out of her.

Ellie's fingers dug into her hips and pulled her closer before breaking their kiss and resting their foreheads together. "We should eat. Drink wine. Watch the sky darken as the sun sinks below the horizon."

Hayden wanted to throw caution to the wind and rip Ellie's clothes off, take her right there on the dirty floor, but she also didn't want all of Ellie's hard work to go to waste. "You're right. This is gorgeous."

"Sorry about the folding chairs. I stole them from the superintendent's meeting area. And this table is a folding table where they have construction meetings every day. But it's a lovely tablecloth, isn't it?"

Hayden found the resourcefulness adorable and a little hilarious. "It is a lovely tablecloth." She ran two fingers over it. "Truly. Though I can feel the divots in the table."

Ellie grabbed her hand and kissed each of her fingers. "Well, for goodness' sake, please keep your fingers where they belong and not searching for imperfections."

Ellie's words and her lips against Hayden's fingertips took the breath right out of her chest. "I like the imperfections. They make it perfect."

Ellie's eyes flicked to hers. She smiled. "Like Atlas."

"Exactly. Dogs are always perfect." The world was filled with a lot of horrible people but not one horrible dog.

"Let's have some wine and see what lovely treats we have in this picnic basket, shall we?"

At Hayden's nod, Ellie grabbed the corkscrew and worked on opening the bottle. Hayden's mouth went dry as she watched Ellie's long fingers bending and straightening, her forearm muscles flexing as she spun the corkscrew into the cork and levered it out. She couldn't pull her gaze away. Watching Ellie's fingers play on the top of the bottle reminded Hayden of them playing across her skin in the most delicious ways.

Little moths fluttering in her stomach transformed into monarch butterflies flying twice as fast from the heat and the want in Ellie's gaze when they finally made eye contact. Her breath caught. There was no doubt Hayden was more attracted to Ellie than she'd ever been to anyone. She was so beautiful, but in their candlelit oasis on top of the world, she was resplendent. Energy and happiness radiated around her, and Hayden felt an irresistible pull. She scooted her folding chair closer.

"What? Why are you staring at me?" Ellie asked, her hands still on the wine bottle with the cork nearly out.

Hayden couldn't stop herself from touching Ellie's face. She ran her fingertips across her cheek and her thumb along Ellie's bottom lip. "What is this power you hold over me?"

"I have no idea, but I think I'm under the same spell." Ellie turned in her seat, brushed their lips together. "But we have wine to drink, cheese to eat, who knows what else. I can't let all this planning go to waste, so we'll just have to fight through it." She grinned, and Hayden would have given her absolutely anything in that moment.

"Fine, fine. What are we drinking?"

"One of my favorite Aglianicos," Ellie said, her words laced with reverence.

"A what?"

Ellie's mouth was wide. "You've never had an Aglianico? From Italy?" When Hayden shook her head, Ellie said, "It's a bold red. Similar to a cab but maybe a little meatier. I don't know if that's the right word. It's got fairly high tannins, but this one has been aged to mellow them. I'm pretty sure you'll love it."

Never one to shy away from trying new things—especially these days—Hayden said, "I'll give it a whirl and let you know."

Ellie stared eagerly as Hayden took a sip. However, once the wine hit her mouth, she couldn't deny Ellie knew her. "This is delicious. A little spicy but strong black cherry. I love it."

"Yes!" Ellie threw her fist in the air, which made her shirt gape in the most intriguing way. Hayden could see the peek of a black lacy bra. She tried to tell herself to look away, but it was like her eyes had a mind of their own. Ellie clearing her throat broke through the fog, and she realized she'd been caught.

She hoped fessing up would earn her a little grace. Or at least a laugh. "Sorry, I was trying to figure out the pattern of your bra." She flashed what she thought was her charming grin. It wasn't like she was ashamed to be checking out Ellie's chest.

"You, madame, are a rapscallion," Ellie said with a terrible fake British accent.

"A rapscallion?" Hayden also tried to use her best British accent, which she judged to be slightly better than Ellie's but not by much. "Would you like to challenge me to a duel with the weapon of your choice? Swords perhaps?" Hayden tried to hold a straight face but broke into laughter.

"Fortunately for you, I don't have any swords. I do have a small knife for some cheese, but I'd rather eat than duel, wouldn't you?" Ellie started pulling things out of the picnic basket. A granite slab that didn't look like it should have fit had about seven different cheeses on it and was covered in plastic wrap. Several bowls of fruit also came out, along with a baguette and a container with crackers.

"That picnic basket is like Mary Poppins's carpetbag." She was in awe as Ellie kept pulling out more food, including a little plate with a decadent-looking chocolate lava cake.

"It *is* a miracle basket, isn't it?" Ellie looked pleased with the spread, lit the taper, and started taking off the plastic wrap and lids. "Don't tell anyone about this open flame. My insurance provider would probably cancel the property policy, but I felt a real candle would be the final touch to set the mood."

"It does bring a little something to the space, doesn't it? Even if it's for a fake holiday."

"We are celebrating romance. The start of our romance. It doesn't matter if it's a fake holiday or not. Which, for the record, it is. The St. Valentines—there were a few, apparently—were martyred. I have no idea how that is supposed to be romantic, so I get your cynicism for *this* holiday. But I still like an excuse to plan something romantic."

"Well, you should feel free to plan romantic nights whenever the mood strikes. This is amazing." She squeezed Ellie's thigh. "Thank you. Truly." She'd never had a Valentine's Day worth remembering, but she wanted to tuck this one away in a special box to be pulled out anytime she was having a bad day or needed to remind herself that putting her heart at risk was worth it. She hoped that if she ever got scared and tried to run, this would be one of the moments she could use to talk herself off the ledge.

They finished the cheese and the wine as the sky turned fully dark, and they could look at all the twinkly lights over the parks.

"Shall we take this party back to my place? I had a sitter give Atlas dinner, but I don't want to leave him alone for too long. Plus, I got him a heart-shaped cookie for his Valentine's Day treat."

"Sure. Do we need to clean up?" Hayden would absolutely help but really hoped Ellie had someone else to do it. She just wanted to get her home, peel her out of that suit, and show her how much she appreciated the planning.

"Nope. I have someone coming first thing in the morning before the job site opens again. I just need to put out this candle. And take it with me so there isn't any evidence."

"We definitely can't let anyone know the boss has been breaking the rules," Hayden said. She stood and rubbed her stomach.

"Are you okay?" Ellie asked. "You look like you're uncomfortable."

Hayden applied a little more pressure right below her belly button, hoping that would relieve the sudden discomfort. "Just a little stomachache. I probably ate too much cheese."

"Well, let's get you home." Ellie kissed her and placed the hard hat on her head again. "Safety first. Can't risk someone seeing us downstairs without appropriate safety attire. Plus, you look so cute in it."

Ellie put her own hard hat on again, and, wow, someone could remove Hayden's stomach, and she probably wouldn't have felt it with as good as Ellie looked. What was it about a woman in a hard hat that was so damn sexy?

CHAPTER THIRTY

D id you *have sex* with her at Ambassador Plaza the other night, Ellie?" Skye said in a voice that was a lot more talk than whisper as they walked around a newly vacant floor at the Maxwell building.

"Don't be ridiculous. Of course not." Although Ellie had desperately wanted to, having sex on the floor of an active construction site seemed ill-advised. "We went back to my place. Though Hayden's stomach was a little upset, so it wasn't quite as energetic as normal. But still lovely. What about you? How was your Valentine's Day with Bailey?"

"Wonderful. She cooked for me, which was perfect because I'm a disaster in the kitchen." She pointed at a line of perimeter offices.

"There are probably too many of them," Ellie said.

"I agree. This is your showpiece wall, so we don't want it to be divided so that prospects miss it."

"Let's price out opening it up."

"How are things going with you and Hayden now that you've been official for more than a month?"

Ellie's insides felt melty and wonderful. She wanted to yell perfect but feared that was a little too overenthusiastic. "Incredible." She weighed the word before she said, "Phenomenal. For someone as terrified of commitment as she was, Hayden has really embraced it. It almost feels like we U-Hauled on the second date except we were basically dating for months before we officially started, so it's kind of like we've been together for four months. But everything just feels so easy. She's been taking care of Atlas when I travel, which secretly I think she loves as much as he does. He's been smitten with her since the beginning, and I'm pretty sure she's been smitten too."

Skye bumped her shoulder into Ellie's. "She's been smitten with you or Atlas?"

"Both, I think." Ellie shrugged. She had certainly been smitten from the first second she'd seen Hayden. "She's just slotted into my life so easily. I was so angry after I ran into Jessie, but I've since realized that it's…like I was always trying to force relationships that were never right because I wanted to find *someone*, even though deep down I knew they were wrong, and so I still put work first, even though I said I wasn't. But Atlas helped me start to reprioritize my life, and…I don't know. Hayden and Atlas make me *want to* reprioritize. And that's new."

Skye squeezed Ellie's arm and pulled her into a hug. "I'm so happy for you. You deserve someone who makes you happy, and I'm so happy that you're figuring out who you need to be to make it work."

"Thanks, Skye. I know it's still really early, but I think I'm starting to fall for her. We just click in a way I've never felt before. It's not perfect, but sometimes, the imperfections are what creates the beauty. Sorry, that's corny."

"Not at all. Now let's wrap up this walk so we can both get back to the sexy women in our lives. We're already running way late."

❖

Hayden let herself into Ellie's condo and greeted Atlas. It was becoming their thing a lot of evenings when she beat Ellie home. Not that they spent every evening together—in fact, they hadn't spent the previous night together because Hayden hadn't been feeling well—but they spent a lot of them together, and they'd slipped into spending more time at Ellie's place during the week and more time at Hayden's on the weekends. Though it was a lot faster to take Atlas out from the houseboat than Ellie's condo. Which would've been nice today. He seemed eager to pee, so she clipped his leash on and took him down the elevator and out to the street.

The dull pain from two evenings before had gotten worse yesterday, but she'd been feeling better for most of the day today.

Unfortunately, it had morphed into a much sharper pain as it traveled to the lower right side of her stomach that evening and was getting worse as she walked Atlas and had to tense her muscles to keep him from wandering too far or pulling on the leash. What the hell was going on?

"Come on, buddy. It's cold out here, and I'm not feeling good," Hayden said, feeling desperate. By the time he finally did his business and they went back upstairs, she could barely stay on her feet without doubling over. She thought about calling her doctor, but at six, the office was already closed. She'd have to call first thing in the morning because something was definitely wrong.

"Are you ready for some dinner, Atlas?" She bent to pick up his bowl and was struck by a wave of dizziness. She barely caught herself on the edge of the counter to keep from falling.

When her head cleared, Hayden stood and grabbed a glass of water from the counter. She took a sip and a few long, slow, meditative breaths to try to settle her stomach and head. When she thought she could manage a few steps, she filled Atlas's bowl with kibble and topped it with wet food, but the smell sent a wave of nausea rolling through her, and she barely set the bowl on the ground before she ran to the bathroom and emptied the contents of her stomach into Ellie's toilet.

She fell back onto her bottom and leaned her head on the edge of the tub. Her throat was impossibly tight as terror seized her. She didn't think she'd ever been this sick in her life, though her brain was floating in a fog, so she couldn't remember for certain. She tried to channel her meditative breath again as she had in the kitchen. She'd been meditating for the majority of her life, but the panicked thoughts of, *am I dying*, and, *will Ellie find me here on the guest bathroom floor* took up all the space. She couldn't force them away and silence her mind the way she'd been doing for decades.

She reached for her phone and realized she'd left it on the kitchen counter but didn't have the strength to go get it. The last thing she felt before succumbing to darkness was something wet pressing against her neck.

❖

Ellie had a bad feeling in the pit of her stomach as she rode the elevator up to her condo. Hayden hadn't texted back, which was abnormal on an evening she wasn't seeing late patients. Ellie had been running late, so she'd texted when she left the Maxwell and asked if she wanted her to pick up dinner.

When Hayden hadn't responded within a few minutes, Ellie had tried calling her. Twice. No answer.

The sound of Atlas's frantic barks when she stepped off the elevator caused her to break out into a cold sweat. Her fingers shook as she tried to slide the key into the lock, and she missed twice before it finally slid home.

"Hayden? Are you here?" she called as she walked into the living room. No Atlas or call back from Hayden. Had she even made it to the condo? Yes, her shoes were on the floor next to the door. Something had to be terribly wrong. Bile rose up in her throat as she started to imagine the worst.

"Hayden?" she cried again, running toward the sound of Atlas's barks. She didn't have to run far; they were in the guest bathroom just off the kitchen. Hayden was slumped over on the bathroom floor. Ellie's blood went icy. Atlas was barking frantically when she appeared in the doorway, but as soon as she ran into the bathroom, he went to Hayden and pressed his nose into her neck.

Ellie dropped to her knees. "Hayden, baby? Are you okay?" She placed her hand on her shoulder. No response. *Dear God, please no.* This couldn't be happening. She couldn't lose her. Ellie felt for a pulse; there but weak.

She fumbled for her phone as she shook Hayden again. She was definitely breathing, but it was shallow, and her face was gray.

Ellie called 9-1-1, and when they were on the way, she caressed Hayden's ashy face and whispered, "Please be okay."

Atlas was lying on the floor between them, his head on Hayden's arm on the floor and a paw against Ellie's thigh. Her teeth were chattering so hard, she could barely manage words.

Her heart was racing, and she was struggling not to throw up. When the fire department knocked on the door, she struggled to stand and answered on wobbly legs. She took the three firefighters to Hayden, but when Atlas saw them, he jumped up, hackles at attention, and started growling.

"Ma'am, you're going to need to control your dog so we can get in there."

"Fuck. It's okay, Atlas," Ellie said in the calmest voice she could manage. "These people are here to help, but you have to let them near her."

He growled again.

The firefighters ended up stepping into the kitchen so Ellie could lure Atlas into her bedroom. "It's okay. I know you're scared. I am too."

She desperately wanted to go back to the bathroom to see what was going on but was afraid to leave him. She got him on his bed and went through their calming protocol. She texted her parents and brother and his family, praying someone—anyone—was available to come sit with him. She had to go to the hospital with Hayden, but Atlas was going to need someone too.

Thankfully, her sister-in-law was working late a few blocks away and could leave right away. Ellie gave Atlas a handful of treats and asked him to stay on the bed and closed him in the bedroom as calmly as possible.

Ellie channeled composure she didn't realize she had to keep from breaking down in a puddle on the floor. "How's she doing, what's going on?" She squeezed the fingers of her left hand with her right, trying to find something to hold on to.

"Her heart rate is a little slow, but she's breathing okay on her own. The stretcher is on its way up. Do you want to ride with us?"

"Yes. I need to stay with her." Ellie's life, her future with Hayden, everything important was flashing before her eyes as she panicked over whether Hayden was going to be okay. But there was no way she was going to leave Hayden's side. Not after she'd finally found the woman who had captured her heart.

CHAPTER THIRTY-ONE

Every second since Ellie had found Hayden on the floor of the bathroom felt like the longest of her life. The ambulance ride, where they wouldn't even let Ellie ride in the back, seemed to take hours. Now she was in the waiting room. She wanted to throw chairs when they told her she couldn't see Hayden yet. She wasn't a relative, and Hayden was unconscious. Ellie had tried rationally explaining that she was her girlfriend, and the only family she had, but they wouldn't budge.

She had told them that two nights ago, Hayden had a weird stomachache that was worse yesterday but somewhat better today. But they still wouldn't let her back. So she paced. Chewed her lip. Waited. Envisioned throwing things like the Hulk. Paced some more.

Her phone buzzed. It was her sister-in-law giving her an update on Atlas. He was fine. She'd taken him for a walk. She asked how Hayden was doing, and Ellie wanted to cry because she didn't know.

"Someone here for Brandt?"

Finally. "Right here." Ellie nearly sprinted to her.

"What's your name?"

"Ellie. Efron." Apparently, the right answer.

"Follow me," the surly woman in scrubs said as she turned and started walking down the hall. Ellie had to nearly run to catch up.

The woman pushed open the door and motioned her to go through. When she saw Hayden lying in the hospital bed, still looking ashen but hooked up to what seemed like thirty-seven machines, tears pricked at the backs of her eyes again. Ellie sank into a visitor chair next to Hayden and took her hand. At the contact, Hayden's eyes fluttered open.

"Hey, you," Ellie said, not knowing what to say but flooded with relief.

"Hey," she rasped.

"How're you feeling?"

"Like I should be in a hospital. But they just gave me morphine, so the pain is supposed to get better soon. Though it's also making it hard for me to stay awake." Her eyes drifted closed for a moment before she opened them again. "But I wanted to see you. I told them to let you back."

"I'm glad you did. I've been wearing a hole in the shitty vinyl tile in the waiting room. Do they have any idea what's going on?" Although seeing Hayden had slowed Ellie's heart rate to a brisk climb up multiple flights of stairs—down from beating so fast, it felt about to short-circuit—Hayden still looked terrible, and Ellie was trying not to imagine the worst. She wasn't good at it. It was one of her most toxic traits.

Hayden's eyes were losing the battle to sleep, and Ellie wanted to let her rest but also needed to know if there was any news. "They think…maybe…appendicitis." Her eyes closed, and Ellie wondered if she'd fallen back asleep. She was torn about which she hoped for. "Running tests to see. May need surgery. Don't go. Please?"

Her breathing slowed, and Ellie was certain she was asleep that time. Appendicitis wasn't that bad, right? It was a pretty routine surgery. While waiting for a doctor or nurse to give her better information, she pulled out her phone to google it. It didn't seem too bad, as long as it wasn't a complicated case, but Ellie was starting to fall down the rabbit hole of appendectomies gone wrong when the door opened.

A tall Black woman who looked a lot like a young Tyra Banks walked in with an air like she owned the hospital but in a competent, not cocky, way. Ellie liked her immediately. "Hi, I'm Dr. Hunt. I'm one of the surgeons on duty this evening. You must be Ellie?"

A little puzzled at why Dr. Hunt would know her name, Ellie said, "Yes, that's me."

"Dr. Brandt here was very adamant that you be let back and kept informed." She smiled.

"Ah, thank you. I wasn't sure if anyone would tell me anything, and they locked me out in the waiting room. I don't know what the protocol is, but…"

"Dr. Brandt definitely asked for you. I don't know how much she was able to tell you before the morphine took her back under—"

"Basically nothing." Ellie was hungry to understand what the prognosis was.

"Okay, I suspect she has a ruptured appendix. We did a blood test that indicated she has an infection, and the urine test indicated it isn't in her bladder. Based on the symptoms she was able to describe and where on her abdomen she reacts to pressure, I think her appendicitis began a few days ago and likely ruptured this afternoon when the pain became intolerable. We need to take her back for a CT scan and an ultrasound. Depending on what we find, I'll have them prep her for surgery. If her appendix is ruptured, we need to get it out and cleaned up as quickly as possible."

If it was so serious, Ellie really wished they'd just take her back and get going. But she also wanted to understand what was next. And Dr. Hunt didn't seem to be frantic. "Is the surgery dangerous?" She felt like it was an asinine question, but how could she not ask?

"All surgeries have inherent risks. However, in the grand scheme of things, appendectomies are relatively…I don't want to say routine, but that really is the word. I've done four already this week."

"And everyone survived?"

Dr. Hunt laughed. "Yes, everyone survived and has been discharged."

Encouraging, but Ellie wouldn't be able to relax until Hayden was safely in recovery. Possibly not until she was home. "How long will she have to be in the hospital?"

"Best case scenario, a few days. Possibly up to a week, but it will all depend on how she's recovering and if she has an infection."

"Okay. Thank you. I'll be anxiously awaiting news."

Dr. Hunt squeezed her forearm. "She's in excellent hands. The staff in the hospital are some of the best I've ever worked with. I'll send in the CNA to take her back for tests. I'll be back to let you know when I'm about to scrub in, okay?"

Ellie struggled to swallow. It felt like there was a boulder lodged in her throat. She blinked back tears, knowing they were foolish.

There was nothing to cry about, but she had a hard time not letting them flow. No matter what happened, she was going to have to stay calm enough to strategize.

She needed to talk to Hayden's practice partner. She needed to make sure someone could continue staying with Atlas. She needed to let her work know she wouldn't be in and have her assistant reschedule any calls or meetings tomorrow. She was scheduled to go to Houston later that week, but that trip was going to have to get moved. She definitely wasn't leaving Hayden's side any more than the hospital forced her to.

Dr. Hunt gave her the kindest smile. "We'll take it one step at a time, and we'll take excellent care of her."

When she left, Ellie stood and kissed Hayden's forehead. "You'd better come back to me. You can't leave me now that I just found you. Now that I just realized I might be falling in love with you. Okay?"

❖

Hayden's mouth was dryer than it had ever been in her life. It felt like the entire Sahara Desert had been transplanted into there. She tried to swallow, but with no saliva in the zip code, that just hurt. She had no idea where she was and tried to pry one eye open to see, but it felt like they were glued shut. She kept trying because she needed to know who was holding her hand. With that incessant beeping, it sounded like she was surrounded by trucks backing up.

She finally managed and realized she was in a hospital. And the beeping was from her heart and other vitals. The warm presence on her hand was Ellie, who was sitting in what appeared to be a very uncomfortable plastic chair with her head resting on the bed against Hayden's hip, all while holding her hand.

A feeling of love flooded through her so great, it scared her. Ellie hadn't left. She'd found Hayden and rescued her and hadn't left her. Her face was so peaceful despite being on the uncomfortable hospital bed that felt like it had seven broken springs digging into her back and butt. Hayden wished she could run her fingers across Ellie's sleeping face.

She didn't have much recollection of how she'd ended up here. Her brain felt like a jumble of threads, but there were so many, she couldn't quite grab any because they were blowing around too quickly. She could remember being at Ellie's place when she'd gotten so sick. She remembered sitting on the floor of the bathroom. But after that, the threads got trickier. She remembered snippets of getting to the hospital and asking for Ellie. Maybe something about appendicitis and signing a form, but that thread was a slippery son of a bitch, and she really couldn't pull it in.

Was she dying? Already dead? She was so disoriented. The last time she'd been in a hospital, it was with her grandma, who had already passed away. But she'd still gone to the hospital with them. Had to figure out how to make funeral arrangements at seventeen.

Hayden tried to pry her other eye open with her hand but wasn't successful. Her arms had barely twitched. Was she paralyzed? She still had feeling in her hand because she could tell Ellie was holding it. Or was her mind playing tricks on her? How close to dying had she been? Was she okay now? Her dad had been about her age when he'd had his massive heart attack, and her family didn't have a history of longevity. Fuck.

Ellie must have felt her restlessness as she lifted her head. She blinked sleepily and reached for her glasses on the side table. "Good morning."

Hayden used all of her strength to manage, "Hi." Her throat felt like it was on fire with the effort. She then tried for, "Water," but it sounded like, "Ah-er."

Ellie thankfully seemed to understand. "I'm sorry, baby, I'm not sure if you can have water. Let me call the nurse, okay?"

Within seconds, a bubbly blonde named Brittany came in. "You're awake. Welcome back, Hayden. What can I help you with?"

"Is she able to have some water or anything?" Hayden was beyond grateful Ellie asked so she didn't have to.

"Let's start with some ice chips, and we'll go from there. I am going to let the floor doctor as well as your surgeon know you're awake and see if they're available."

Hayden would have traded her 401k for a real sip of water, but the ice chips still felt like a balm on the rawest skin. She sighed as the cool water slid down her fiery throat. After three ice chips, she finally felt like she might be able to squeak a few words out. "What happened?" Her words were still rough but distinguishable.

"You passed out at my house. Apparently, your appendix burst, and the pain caused you to lose consciousness. You were on the floor of the bathroom when I got home, so I called 9-1-1, and here we are. You had emergency surgery to remove your appendix and clean the abscess that had formed or something like that." Ellie rubbed a thumb over her knuckles.

She wished she could crawl into Ellie's arms so she could rub her back and make everything feel better. "Jesus." She tried to lift her right arm and rub her face, but it felt like her skin was made of lead. "What day is it?"

"Friday." So she'd been unconscious for either a day or a week. She was pretty sure. "We brought you in yesterday evening, you had surgery overnight, and it's now morning. Midmorning," Ellie said before Hayden had a chance to ask.

Not having lost an entire week was a relief. Eighteen hours wasn't that bad. She blinked twice, certain Tyra Banks had just stepped out of a time machine and into her hospital room.

"Good morning, Dr. Brandt. I'm Dr. Hunt. I performed your surgery last night. How are you feeling?"

Hayden swallowed hard and tried to prepare herself. She managed to say, "Like my innards went through a blender and then got run over by a truck."

Dr. Hunt laughed loudly. "That sounds about right. Well, the surgery went well. Unfortunately, because your appendix ruptured before we could remove it, you did have peritonitis. Essentially, an infection in the lining of your abdomen, which is probably some of the reason you feel as though your *innards went through a blender*. But I'm happy to see you're awake and alert. We're going to keep you here for a few days on some IV antibiotics and monitor you, but if all looks good, we'll send you home early to midweek next week. Okay?"

Hayden nodded. It was easier than talking.

"What about diet? Drinking?" Ellie asked. She was a queen.

"Are you thirsty? Hungry?" Hayden nodded to both. "You can absolutely drink and start eating again. You've got ice chips, but we'll get you some water and at least some broth. Probably bland foods and clear liquids for the first part of the day today, but we can get you started on whole foods again around dinnertime. Sound good?"

Hayden nodded. *Absolutely, Tyra.* It sounded like heaven. Tyra checked her incision, said it looked good, and left.

The days in the hospital passed in a blur. Hayden was tired, so she slept a lot, but Ellie brought her everything she needed. She even brought her a pair of pajamas so she didn't have to wear a drafty hospital gown and her electric toothbrush because she just didn't think a standard one got her teeth sufficiently clean. She started feeling stronger and was able to eat more and walk around without help, not that Ellie wasn't right there if needed.

And yet, Hayden found herself emotionally distancing from Ellie. She was right there every day, every night, every step of the way. She'd taken off work and had family rotating staying with Atlas, though she did go home and feed him dinner every night so he knew she hadn't abandoned him.

Hayden continued to focus on how she'd felt when she'd woken up and seen Ellie lying there, sleeping so peacefully while she watched over Hayden. She couldn't imagine the terror Ellie must have felt when she'd found Hayden lying on her bathroom floor, but she'd been so amazing since.

So why was Hayden feeling itchy again? That had completely gone away since she and Ellie had gotten together, but it was suddenly back. When she needed Ellie more than ever. Maybe it was because the desperate need scared her. It made her want to run. She hadn't been able to rely on someone since she was seventeen. Scratch that. She hadn't chosen to rely on anyone since she was seventeen. She knew if she allowed herself to, she could absolutely rely on Ellie, but having to stare her own mortality in the face had her considering if relying on someone was actually the wisest choice. It wasn't nearly as clear as it had been a few days ago.

CHAPTER THIRTY-TWO

A nd you're completely sure you want to stay here and not at my place?" Ellie asked, a little exasperated as she helped Hayden onto her boat and kept her from slipping on a little ice.

"Yes, I want to sleep in my own bed. Feel normal again," Hayden said.

"I hate that I can't stay here with you, but Atlas needs a night or two of normalcy too, and I want to be able to be with him all night in *his* home." Ellie couldn't feel more guilty about taking Hayden to the boat and just leaving her there. A few days after major surgery. But why was she refusing to go back to Ellie's place where she practically lived half the time?

"I'll be fine, I promise. And you have given up an entire week with me at the hospital. Please go home and be with Atlas. I just need a little time to decompress. With a book. And silence. Staying in that hospital was constant stimulation all the time, and my little introverted battery needs some time to recharge. Everything's fine. I'm fine here. Go see your boy."

Ellie couldn't figure out if Hayden really wanted to be alone to recharge or if she wanted to be alone because something else was going on. She had been really quiet in the hospital and not like herself. At least not the Hayden Ellie had grown used to over the last few months. This felt like pre-everything Hayden. Then again, she'd just had emergency surgery, and her life had been upended. She certainly had reason to be quiet, but Ellie was trying not to freak out about why she was pushing her away. "If you're sure that you're sure?"

"I know you're worried, but I'm sure. And you're only a phone call away. Atlas is going to need a few days of bonding time." Hayden shooed her, and Ellie again had a feeling that something wasn't right, but what could she do?

"Okay. Call me if you need me. And please text regularly to let me know you're okay. I'll be back tomorrow to check on you, okay?" She gave her a light kiss and stared until Hayden acquiesced.

"Yes, I'll see you tomorrow."

But when tomorrow came, Hayden texted: *No need to come over. I'm fine. Sleeping a lot...all I really do is sleep and eat. Stay with Atlas and give him a kiss for me. Talk later.*

What the hell was that? How could Ellie go from seeing her every day, staying at her hospital bedside, to not seeing her at all? It was driving her to the edge.

Ellie had to go back to work on Wednesday, and Hayden seemed to use that as the reason she shouldn't come over. Hayden was restless and couldn't sleep well, so Ellie shouldn't bother coming and not be able to sleep. Ellie tried to say she didn't mind. Or that she could sleep in one of the guest rooms, but Hayden wasn't swayed.

She was clearly asking Ellie to stay away. Ellie tried not to feel incredibly hurt about it, but it wasn't working. She wanted to text in all caps and with twenty question marks, *Why are you avoiding me?* But she hadn't. She had, however, decided that she was going to go see Hayden without texting first. She needed to see her. She needed to ask her in person what was wrong and why she was pulling away. None of it made any sense. But she wasn't going down without a fight.

❖

Hayden hated herself. It was the only thing that could explain her behavior. She loved Ellie. At least a little. Or maybe she was hovering at the precipice, but she was pretty sure she was already over it. And yet, she kept avoiding her. Kept pushing her away every time she tried to reach out or come over.

Every time Ellie texted, Hayden picked up her phone with the intention of telling her to come, but then fear seized her. She flashed back to finding her grandma, already gone, on their living room couch. How Grandma had looked when she'd kissed her cold forehead and said good-bye. She remembered that everyone was mortal. Her brush with death—and maybe that was a little dramatic, but it was what it had felt like when she'd been lying on Ellie's bathroom floor—had her constantly thinking about how fragile humans were. She thought about how Ellie could be killed at any moment—Ellie's best friend had died just months earlier—or about how she could be.

She kept having this waking nightmare that the situations had been reversed, and she'd walked in on Ellie on the floor. But unlike real life, Ellie was dead with Atlas curled up next to her. She cried every time. And given how short this life was, how it could be gone in an instant, it was selfish to be in a relationship with anyone. Everything was impermanent.

And so, she'd told Ellie not to come for some barely plausible excuse or another. When Ellie had tried to call, she'd pretended to be asleep. She did answer once and had faked being groggy. After that, Ellie had stopped calling. Hayden assumed it was because she was afraid of disturbing her.

She hated herself for all of it, and yet, she couldn't stop. She was paralyzed by the fear and couldn't move forward.

Then came the call. Dr. Prewster was following up since Hayden hadn't responded. She had apologized and told her about her hospital stay, though she'd played it up as the primary reason for the delay. If she'd wanted to figure things out with Ellie, she had needed to say something like, "I appreciate the offer, but my situation has changed, and I no longer want to leave Chicago." But she hadn't. She'd said she was still interested but needed a few more days to commit.

At least she hadn't accepted, but she'd left the door open. Because she clearly hated herself and didn't want to be happy.

She knew Ellie had to be feeling terrible and confused, and it was completely Hayden's fault. But paralyzed by indecision and fear, she continued *not* calling, reaching out, or responding in any way other than telling Ellie not to come.

She had lost track of the days when she heard a knock at the door. She'd been curled up on the couch with a good murder mystery with a queer female lead—but definitely not a romance—without a clue what day it was, only that she had at least two weeks before she would be released to go back to work, when the sharp crack of knuckles on her glass door jarred her from book world.

She slid the sheer curtain to the side. Ellie, looking like a dark angel in the fading light of the day, stood on the other side of the door, a look of determination on her face. Hayden's knees went weak with need and love and guilt. Her head was at war with her heart as they stared at each other. She wanted to pull her close and tell her she loved her. And she also wanted to tell her it was never going to work because nothing in life was permanent, and they'd run their course. The glass made it impossible to do either of those things, and part of her wanted to leave it that way so she couldn't make a mistake.

But the look of unbridled hurt became more and more pronounced on Ellie's face the longer Hayden went without opening the door. She slid it open and braced herself as she tried to figure out her fate.

Ellie stepped through on her impossibly high heels, looking as sexy as ever in a pantsuit. Hayden almost melted on the spot. She kissed Ellie on the cheek and squeezed her hand. "Hi." Her voice was shaky. She wasn't sure if it was because she'd only talked to one person within the last week or nerves.

"Hi," Ellie said, a tremor in her voice as well. "I hope you don't mind, but I knew if I texted or called, you'd tell me not to come."

Hayden looked down, ashamed. None of that was a lie, but she hated it. She hated who she was right then. "I'm sorry." She looked back up but couldn't bring herself to meet Ellie's eyes. She was a shit.

"Can I come in? Can we sit and talk for a bit?" Ellie was gnawing her lip, and Hayden's eyes were, of course, drawn to the movement. Those lips that she'd kissed a thousand times.

"Yeah, of course. Do you want some water?" She wanted to put off talking for as long as possible, still not sure what she could say. What she should say.

"Sure, thanks." Ellie sat on the couch and stared at her hands while Hayden got them both glasses.

She handed Ellie one and sank into the corner of the couch, wanting to give her sore abdominal muscles a break. "So," she said.

Ellie looked at her with an expression that broke her heart. "Will you please tell me what's going on? I don't understand what happened, but I'd like to try to fix it. I miss you. I hate that you're shutting me out."

The earnestness and openness were like truth serum. "I've never felt so strongly for anyone as I feel for you, and it scares the shit out of me. I never got involved with anyone before you, but there's something about you that made me break my rules. But I had those rules for a reason."

❖

Rules? She wants to talk about bullshit rules? Rules that Hayden had made up to give herself a false sense of security? But Ellie didn't want to interrupt, so she squeezed her glass until her fingertips turned white and went cold.

"I know it sounds foolish, but my childhood was defined by loss. My dad had a fatal heart attack when I was eight, my mom was killed in a car accident, and my grandma had a stroke at sixty-two and died alone at home. I was an orphan before I turned eighteen. I never had any close friends. I was always an outsider with all my moving around. And that taught me that life is fragile. And impermanent. And no one can or will stick around forever." Hayden shifted uncomfortably in her seat, and Ellie felt a little guilty for forcing this conversation and getting so angry while listening to all the reasons Hayden was a coward. She was just recovering from surgery.

"Do you need anything? Pain medication or anything?" She didn't want her to be in pain, but she needed them to continue this conversation because avoidance was breaking her heart.

"I'm fine. When I had to make funeral arrangements for my grandma, I resolved to never let myself get attached again. Never let myself get hurt. And for more than fifteen years, that completely served me. I relied on myself for everything. I never let anyone get close, not even a friend. Only Chelsea, really. And then I met you. And you thawed something in me that had frozen a long time ago. You opened that part of me up. I found myself daydreaming about you and what being with you would be like. First as friends and then as lovers. I wanted to dream and plan and be with you. And in Michigan, you pushed me to make that decision."

Panic gripped Ellie's throat. Seeing Hayden in the hospital and realizing she wasn't just falling in love with her, that she was there, had made Ellie truly start to believe that Hayden might be the person she would spend the rest of her life with. She knew it was premature, but she'd had enough relationships to know that what they had was real. Was Hayden going to dump her now? Waste her time? Leave her crying on the curb? She wouldn't have been able to find any words in the dictionary with a magnifying glass in that moment, so she continued to let Hayden talk.

"I've been all in with you. I hope you've seen that. Felt it." She waited until Ellie nodded. "And then all this happened. And all that the merry-go-round from hell that is my thoughts can obsess about is how I almost died. Dying young is in my blood. And it would be selfish of me to get you to fall for me, to rely on me as a partner, and then die."

Ellie wanted to vomit both from what she was saying and wasn't. "You've been avoiding me, pretending like what's between us can simply be ignored because you're afraid of dying and leaving me alone? That is a serious amount of self-importance, Hayden. And it's really fucked-up that you're unilaterally deciding what is or isn't fair to me."

Hayden sighed and buried her face in her hands. "It's not just that. I'm afraid to rely too much on you too. I keep having this nightmare of finding you dead on the floor in that bathroom. I know it's irrational, and I didn't die, but the thought of getting closer to you—building a life together—and having it all snatched away when something terrible inevitably happens…I just don't know if I can do it. I don't know if I'm strong enough." Her eyes were glassy as tears started to leak.

Ellie grabbed her hand, hoping a physical connection would help her get through. "No one knows how long we have on this earth. But doesn't it make sense to live every minute of it? Do the things you love? Spend time—real, meaningful time—with the ones you *love*? Embrace all the good things because you don't know how long you have?"

"That's easy for you to say. You've lost one person in your adult life. And it was hard, but you had so many other people. It's a lot harder when you're on an island and don't have anyone else. If I get used to having someone to rely on, and you're suddenly gone, how do I go back? How could I make my way through life alone after that?" Hayden's chest was rising and falling so fast, she had to be hyperventilating.

Ellie wished there was a way she could comfort her. She had to make her see that what she was saying didn't make sense, that there was no logic. "Experiencing love is never a bad thing. It's special. It should be cherished. If I were to die tomorrow, I would be so grateful for every moment of love and laughter I shared with the ones I am closest to. If you died in three decades or three days, I would cherish every moment we'd spent together. That's what life is about. It's not about surviving. It's about gratitude and love and friendship. If there is one thing my great-grandparents passed to later generations after surviving the Holocaust, it was that family and the people you love are to be cherished. Branches of my family tree were eradicated well before their time. My grandparents kept them in our memories and taught us to treasure everything that we do have as the gifts that they are."

Hayden seemed taken aback before she said, "It still seems pretty easy for someone who has *never* had to focus solely on surviving to describe what life is about. You have no idea how hard just surviving can be."

"But you're not *just surviving* anymore. We have something real. Something that feels like it could be forever. No matter how long we have, I will cherish and embrace every day. No matter what. I hope you can do the same. Please, Hayden, please tell me you can do the same. That you're willing to take this risk with me."

The look in Hayden's eyes, the thin line of her lips pressed so tightly together, told Ellie everything she needed to know. But she still waited, praying she was wrong. Hayden looked everywhere but at Ellie as she said, "I want to, Ellie, but I don't think that I can. I've been talking to a vet behaviorist in New Orleans about taking over her practice when she retires, and I think I'm going to do it."

Ellie felt like she'd taken a punch to the solar plexus. "You're what? Why haven't you talked about this before? Have you been planning this the whole time we've been seeing each other?" She couldn't sit still. She started to pace as Hayden's betrayal lanced her.

"Since before we met. I didn't mention it because what we had wasn't serious at first, and once we started dating, I didn't plan to go through with it, but…"

Ellie felt like she was watching this conversation from above, hovering on a drone as her heart was ripped out and torn to pieces. "What changed? Why do you suddenly need to move a thousand miles away?" She tried to modulate her voice but was hanging by a thread.

"I just…I started talking to her because I get this itchy feeling sometimes. Where I have to move on. It went away when we first started seeing each other, but when I was in the hospital, it came back. Like it was reminding me of all the reasons I don't do this. Why I can't do this. Why I'm not *strong enough* to do this. I'm sorry, Ellie. I want to so badly, but I…I can't. I have to protect myself, and so I'm going to go." She started to cry, and Ellie wanted to join her, but she needed to get out before she let go.

She felt dead inside but might never stop if she started crying now. "How long?"

Hayden hiccupped. "What?"

"Until you leave." Did it really matter?

"Probably a month or a month and a half. I need to be completely healed to sail *Mobile Home* by myself to New Orleans. The weather will be better for it in April too."

She'd already thought far enough ahead to know when the best time to sail into the sunset was. It felt heartless. Not at all the woman Ellie had fallen for.

"If you're worried about Atlas," Hayden said. "I expect Britt to take over the practice, and Atlas is done except for annual maintenance visits, which Britt can handle. You should consider advanced training—like nose work or agility—now."

"Great." Ellie sat her glass down. "I guess that's all there is, then. I'll see myself out after I grab my favorite Malibu of the Midwest hoodie if that's okay." She was already heading down the hall to find it before Hayden spoke.

"Of course."

Ellie yanked the hoodie out of the closet hard enough that the hanger swung wildly until it fell and hit the ground. Like Ellie's heart.

"See you around." She stalked back into the living room. "Or not." She walked out without a backward glance.

It was a long way, but she decided to walk home, despite the bitter cold in the air and the wind off the lake. The sharp sting of sleet against her face helped her acknowledge that what just happened wasn't a nightmare.

How could Hayden be such a fucking coward? The odds of a healthy forty-something woman dying had to be a fraction of a percent. Yet Hayden refused to try for a chance at true happiness because of that. It was so ridiculous, Ellie should have been able to change her mind, but she was so adamant, Ellie didn't know how.

By the time she made it to her condo, Ellie was soaking wet and moving from angry back to hurt. She managed to hold off her breakdown until she was able to bury her face in Atlas's neck, but when it came, it was like a tsunami of hurt washing her away.

Chapter Thirty-three

Hayden had always known talking to Britt about leaving was going to be hard. Second only to breaking up with Ellie. She'd been putting it off, but she had to talk to them because they had to agree to take over, or there wasn't going to be a practice anymore. Hayden hated the thought of that.

Britt was going to feel as blindsided as Ellie. Maybe more. They'd worked together for years, and Hayden had never mentioned leaving. Then again, she'd never told Britt anything even remotely personal until recently. Another reason she *needed* to get away, so she had to put on her big girl pants and just do it.

She walked into their office holding her standard low-ball glasses of rye on a big rock. But this time, it was more of a peace offering. She'd been back in the office for a week and wasn't drinking much, but this conversation called for booze. There was no other way to emotionally handle it.

"How are you feeling, Hayden?" Britt said when she walked in.

"Not one hundred percent—hell, not even eighty—but hanging in there. Thank you for doing such a great job holding everything down while I was out. I'm sorry if it was a shit show." She took a sip, and the burn helped her gear up for the rest of the conversation.

"I mean, we missed you, but Shirley did a great job of tap dancing to reschedule your clients and schedule the ones who needed urgent visits with me. We should give her a bonus this year for sure."

It had been a great test run. And that was an opening if she'd ever heard one. Dammit. "I'm happy to hear that because there's something I wanted to talk to you about."

Britt's brows furrowed.

Hayden reluctantly continued. "I was approached by a colleague in New Orleans a few months ago about buying her out of her practice. I've been dancing around it for a while, but I'm going to take her up on it."

Britt's jaw dropped. "You what? What about the sexy mom?"

Hayden's throat tightened. Of course, romantic Britt went directly to Ellie. "We…" She cleared her throat, searching for her voice again. "We broke up."

Britt jumped up out of their chair. "That bitch broke up with you while you were sick and in the hospital? Where is she?"

"Easy there. It was mutual." Okay, that was a complete lie, but Britt didn't need to know that. "It just wasn't going to work. Sometimes things don't, you know?" She shrugged, feigning a nonchalance she didn't feel. Every word she said felt like a cheese grater scraping her tongue.

"Is she why you're leaving?" They looked as crestfallen as a puppy in an ASPCA commercial.

"It's complicated. But you've passed your boards, my little smartie, so you don't need me anymore. I thought you could take a trial running it, and if you like it, you can buy me out. Or maybe I'll come back some day. Who knows?" Unlikely. She tried an encouraging smile, but Britt seemed to see through it.

"You don't look happy. Leaving on a new adventure should be exciting. You look…sad."

"I'm just not feeling well still. It's been a long day, and the little things tire me out."

"Okay, but we make a great team. I don't want you to go. Who else am I going to talk tough cases with? Or girlfriends? Or amazing weekends?"

"I'll only be a phone call away. But I've already agreed, so there's no turning back. And I'm a nomad. I'm like Mary Poppins. I go where the wind blows me."

"How can you ever establish a life if you keep moving? Make friends, find a wife, maybe get a dog?"

She had a life. She had a career she loved that she could do anywhere and the financial security to establish a practice in a new place. And she loved her peace and solitude, where she didn't have to answer to anyone.

Those words felt a little emptier than they used to, but she ignored the feeling. Pushed it to the side. "I have a life, and I don't need a wife or a dog. I'm fine." *Just fine.*

She took a sip, held the liquid on her tongue for so long that the burn turned to numbness before swallowing. She'd made it more than a decade and a half without relying on anyone. Without being weak.

❖

Ellie tried to focus on Atlas. She was in a private session with a trainer doing nose work. Apparently, sniffing out boxes and finding the one with an extra delicious treat would help him develop more confidence, so maybe he wouldn't be fearful of so many things. Ellie needed something to take her mind off her broken heart, and this was it. Even if it was Hayden's recommendation.

She'd been taking a risk when they'd started dating. She'd known Hayden's commitment issues were so deeply rooted that they probably needed a backhoe to get them completely eradicated. But despite her reservations—and when Hayden was so earnest at the cabin in Michigan begging for her to give them a try—there was no way she could resist. As Hayden had also said, they could pretend, but it had never just been innocent between them. They'd never just been a doctor and dog mom.

All bullshit. Hayden had also said that she wouldn't run if she got scared, and she'd talk to Ellie. Clearly, more bullshit since the first thing had spooked her into running away. To the other side of the country, for fuck's sake.

It had been almost a month since Hayden had pushed her away, and she was still wandering around in a fog when she wasn't focused on work or Atlas. Though those generally monopolized so much of her brain that there wasn't room for the Hayden fog to roll in. She wondered if Hayden was already gone or if she'd waited a little longer to heal before leaving. She'd thought about going to the marina to see if the boat was still there, but that felt way too stalkerish. Especially since she didn't plan to try to talk. She just wanted to know if they were still in the same city or not.

"Ellie?" Her name dragged her out of her musings.

Shit. So much for Atlas commanding her full attention. "Sorry, Greg. What were you saying?"

"I asked if you were okay. Then I said your name three more times."

"Sorry, got a little lost for a second. What did I miss?"

He looked down pointedly. When Ellie followed his gaze, she saw Atlas sitting in front of her like a good boy. Oops.

"Sorry, buddy." She gave him the treat he deserved for sniffing out the hidden treat and coming back to her.

"Are you sure you're okay? Do you want to keep going or call it a night?" Greg was a nice guy and seemed genuinely concerned, but she didn't want to leave early and go back to her empty house. One of the reasons she was coming here was because she wanted to spend as little time in her cavernously empty condo as possible. It had never been like this after a breakup before. She'd been sad and mopey but not the deep-seated hatred to be in places that she'd gone with exes. The need to avoid anywhere that held a reminder of how happy they'd been. It was a wonder spending time with Atlas didn't make her feel that way. But something about him always calmed her.

"No, thank you. I'm fine. I just got lost there for a sec. Shall I take Atlas out of the ring while you stash another piece of hot dog?"

❖

Hayden couldn't believe her last day was here. First thing tomorrow, she was pulling out and heading south. It was supposed to be a gorgeous May day, perfect for traveling. She'd stayed a little longer than anticipated, not wanting to push herself too hard, given she was going to be by herself on this two-week journey. That was how she liked it, but she wanted to be certain she was healthy enough to do it.

She'd surprised herself by inviting Britt and Shauna over for a little farewell round of drinks. She'd never actually had them over before, and it was surprisingly fun.

Until Britt got on their soapbox again about her leaving. "Are you sure that you're sure you want to do this, Hayden? I'm fine running the practice—I mean, it'd be better with you—but I'm going to miss you. I hate that you're deserting me." Their voice was light but laced with sadness.

Hayden thought it was in jest but admitted that it might not be. "I'm sorry. I've enjoyed working together, but it's simply time for me to move on. *Past* time. I've been here longer than I've ever lived anywhere so..." She shrugged as she ignored the longing to stay. To find Ellie and beg her forgiveness. She shoved all those emotions into an invisible trunk and forced the lid closed. That used to be a lot easier. She didn't allow herself to think about why that had changed. Or who might have changed it.

"You keep saying that, but what does it even mean? Why do you feel like you *always* have to keep moving? Are you that afraid of feeling something? Of learning to rely on someone?" Their eyes flashed, and Hayden wondered why she felt the need to keep moving too.

No. It was just what she did, part of her identity. She didn't want or need to change it.

"Babe." Shauna sat next to Britt again and grabbed their hand. "Let her be. She clearly has her reasons. And it's too late."

Hayden imagined her squeezing Britt's hand as a silent suggestion to get them to back off. She was grateful. She didn't want to spend her last night arguing.

Britt leaned into Shauna's side and seemed to sigh. Hayden's chest felt tight. She missed that type of easy contact "I'm sorry, Hayden. I want to be okay with you leaving, but I hate it. I've been trying to force you to become my friend for years, and now that I feel like we're finally growing closer, and you've seen that I'm cooler than you thought, you're leaving." They laughed. "Plus, without you, we won't be able to help nearly as many animals."

"I'm sorry you felt like you had to force me to be your friend. I... don't normally do friends. It's just not my thing. Moving around as much as I did as a kid, I eventually stopped trying, I guess. I became the island I am today." She looked at the bourbon swirling around the big rock in her glass and swallowed something she couldn't quite put her finger on, but it hurt. A lot.

"I'm sorry, Hayden. Moving around so much as a kid had to suck. I don't know why a parent would do that to their kid."

Hayden really hadn't told Britt anything about her childhood, had she? "It wasn't like that. My dad was in the military, but after he passed away...I don't know. Mom moved us a lot because moving to a new city, a new home, a new job, kept her from missing Dad too much. She never dated again. She always told me she'd had her one true love, and there was no way any man could ever compete or replace Dad in her heart, so she'd rather focus on me and work. Apparently, those were the only loves she would have for the rest of her life because it wasn't that much longer." The back of her nose and throat burned with tears she wasn't willing to shed. She took a sip and tried to replace the tear burn with a bourbon burn. It was only marginally successful. She stared into her drink so she wouldn't have to make eye contact.

She was staring so hard that she didn't realize Britt had moved until she felt the couch dip. "I'm really sorry. I didn't realize...any of that. I understand why leaving is ingrained in you, but I want you to know that you can choose to break the cycle. You don't *have* to always run when things get real. Or hard. I won't bug you any more about leaving. But know that you always have a friend in me, no matter how far you run. And you *always* have a place to come home to if you need it. And I'll still be your friend no matter where you live."

Hayden surprised herself when she wrapped her arms around Britt and pulled them in tightly. The powers of a simple hug were... surprising.

Chapter Thirty-four

Hayden had only been gone for two days, but they'd been two of the worst days of her life. She'd been so sure she was making the right decision in leaving, but the farther she got from Chicago, the more her stomach began to hurt. At first, she'd been scared that it was a complication from the appendicitis but was now pretty sure it was mostly psychosomatic from stress and the heartbreak of leaving a life she'd actually grown to like and people she'd grown to love. She continued to tell herself she was making the right decision—the crushing pain she felt now would be a drop in the bucket compared to how she'd feel if she lost Ellie or Britt in a few years—but, fuck, it hurt.

She couldn't help but wonder if Britt had a point when they'd said just because Hayden had never grown roots didn't mean she couldn't. Was her happiness limited due to a mistaken belief that she *needed* to move around? She'd always thought that her wanderlust was part of her personality, but maybe it was learned behavior from her family that wasn't even what they had wanted. She thought her mom had kept moving because of the grief over losing her father versus a true desire to move, but her grandmother had stayed put her entire life.

She hated feeling like this. She walked around her boat, and everywhere she looked had an imprint from Ellie, Atlas, and Chelsea. There wasn't an inch that she couldn't see her and Ellie making love on. She'd written off being in the same room as the hot tub or the couch. The primary bedroom also held way too many tender memories.

She'd also written off Chelsea's bedroom. She'd been doing better with that loss while she was in Chicago; however, the longer she was gone—the longer she was alone on the boat—the more poignant Chelsea's absence became. She'd felt as heartbroken that morning as she had the day she'd passed. While stopped to refuel yesterday, Hayden had found herself lying on Chelsea's bed crying because the boat felt so empty without her. And thus, that room was blacklisted too. She basically had the spare bedroom and the flybridge. Though even the flybridge reminded her of helping Ellie fix the straps on her life jacket.

Everything was too hard.

As Hayden was having her coffee and preparing to pull out of the marina she'd stayed in overnight, it hit her. She'd been with Chelsea for fifteen years, and it hurt like hell losing her—it still hurt like hell almost six months later—but she wouldn't go back and not take Chelsea in if she had the choice to rewrite history. Chelsea had been a pain in the ass, but she'd given Hayden so much. These last fifteen years would have been a lot bleaker if they hadn't had Chelsea in them.

And it wasn't like she would rather have lost her parents and grandmother at birth. They'd had a lot of good times together. Of course, she would have liked to have had them for longer, but...

Her mug slipped out of her hands and broke on the floor as she realized just how much of a prison she'd built around herself. *Oh God.*

She scrambled to grab paper towels and a dustpan to clean up the mess that felt like a metaphor for the mess she'd made of her own life. She thought she'd had things figured out, but none of the decisions she'd made lately felt like the right ones anymore.

If she didn't regret the time she'd spent with her family and Chelsea despite the pain of losing them, how could she run away from Ellie like a coward? Because she was terrified of getting hurt? She was disgusted with herself for the pain she'd caused and for not having the courage to fight her way through the fear.

She had a hole in her heart that was entirely her own making, but could she do something about it now? Could she find the courage to turn around and beg forgiveness? If she did, would Ellie talk to her, or would she tell her to fuck off, as she rightly could—and maybe should?

Hayden had promised her when they'd decided to give their relationship a go that she wouldn't run. That she'd talk to Ellie if she got scared. She hadn't lived up to any of it and hated herself for her cowardice. How could she have been so cruel and so shortsighted? She felt compelled to turn and fight for Ellie like she should have before, but how could she? How could she regain Ellie's trust? She didn't deserve forgiveness, so did it even make sense to try?

If she was Ellie, she wouldn't forgive her. But she also couldn't imagine a life without Ellie in it.

She sat on the kitchen floor amidst the broken porcelain and tried not to cry. She was so fucked, and it was all of her own making.

❖

"Over here, Ellie!" Skye waved from a table in the back of Once Upon a Wine.

Ellie hadn't wanted to go out that evening. In fact, she'd told Skye several times that she wasn't feeling up to it, but Skye wouldn't let it go. Ellie had finally given in just so Skye would leave her alone. She didn't have time to dodge her calls all day, every day. Plus, she couldn't ignore her in case they had a lease prospect to discuss. That was how Skye had gotten her today.

Ellie walked over, the heaviness of dread weighing each foot down until she could barely lift them. As though hundred-pound dumbbells were strapped to them. She mustered a smile she didn't feel and prayed it would pass Skye's scrutiny. Everything just felt too hard.

Skye jumped up to give her a hug. "It's good to see you." She squeezed a little longer than normal. Thankfully, she didn't say anything about…the other.

Ellie had been trying to throw herself into the rest of her life with gusto. She'd even reactivated her Tinder and Hinge dating profiles, but she just found herself swiping left and rejecting everyone who liked her. No one held any appeal. The terror that she'd never find someone to spend the rest of her life with had threatened to swallow her whole, but the worst part of it was, she was pretty sure she'd found that person, and that person had rejected her. Told her she wasn't worth the risk.

How could she come back from that? It had been two months, but her heart hadn't healed even a little. Atlas tried. He didn't understand why Hayden had simply gone away and never come back. She wished she could explain on those evenings where he lay on the couch but jumped up every time there was a hint of sound. Sometimes, he would lie on the floor next to the couch just watching the door.

It broke her heart even more.

"Do you want to split a bottle?" Skye asked, forcing Ellie to discard her maudlin thoughts and pay attention.

"Sure. Whatever you'd like is fine." There was a small gouge on the table that Ellie traced back and forth. The wood was smooth against her fingertip, as though the imperfection had been there for a long time. Maybe eventually, that was what the gouge in her heart would feel like. But how long would it take? Months? Years? They'd only been together a few months, but she'd known Hayden longer than that as they were coming up on Iris's anniversary. *Fuck.* Iris.

Ellie vaguely heard Skye ordering a bottle of something cabernet and a cheese platter. She didn't feel much like eating, but perhaps the wine would spark some hunger. Also, cheese was good for the soul.

"So." Skye let the word hang in the air.

Ellie looked up just in time for the server to bring the bottle, open it, and give a small sample to them to taste. "So what?" she said when he walked away.

"I know you only came out because I was so annoying. I'm a squeaky wheel, and I'm not ashamed. But how are you? And don't lie to me." Skye stared, eyes wide and waiting.

"I'm struggling. Still. I just keep thinking, what if she was my only chance at love, my soulmate, and she was too scared to take a chance on us, and now I'll be alone forever?" She couldn't even enjoy the delicious wine.

"I don't mean to sound glib, but are you sad because she's gone? Or because you just don't want to be alone?"

Ellie knew the answer was that she missed Hayden, the woman, the person. Not the idea of a random someone. But the question had her thinking back on her other relationships. After each of those breakups, she could easily see that she'd missed the idea of the women more than the women themselves. This time, she was broken over the loss of the person who was going to be her forever. "Hayden. Without question. I miss everything about her. Her laugh. Her dry sense of humor. The twinkle in her eye when she was flirting. The way the wind ruffled her hair—"

"Okay, okay, I get it. Does she know how heartbroken you are? Did you tell her how you feel?"

Ellie knew the interrogation was coming from a place of love, but this was ridiculous. "Of course I told her. I told her I thought we were worth taking a risk. She disagreed. End of story." Ellie felt snappy, but she didn't care to try to modulate it.

"If you love her, and I'm pretty certain that you do, I don't understand why you didn't try to talk to her a few days or a week later, after you'd both had some time to think. Maybe let clearer heads prevail." Her tone was a little softer that time.

"She made her position very clear. She isn't willing to risk the potential heartbreak in the unlikely event that I die. And didn't want to put me in that position if she died. How do you have a rational conversation when that is the other person's point of view?" Ellie shook out her hair and reminded herself not to clench her jaw. "I tried reasoning with her, but she insisted she had to leave. That she just isn't capable of a relationship. And now I'm going to die an old spinster."

"Okay, firstly, you aren't. If you can't make her see reason, she definitely isn't, wasn't, the one. But if there's a chance, however slim, I don't think you can *not* give it one more shot. From everything you've told me, she seemed like a completely different person after your trip to Michigan. If realizing she was going to lose you made her change so much, maybe after a little time, she might be able to change again. Like tuning a piano. You can't just tune it once if it hasn't been tuned in a long time. You have to keep working on it, or it goes back. Maybe Hayden is the same. She tuned herself into realizing she wanted a relationship, but the appendicitis jolted her back to her untuned ways."

"First, that analogy is horrible. Secondly, if she gets so *untuned* at the first sign of a headwind, what's to say she can ever be trusted?

She might get scared again and run away." That was the main reason she hadn't even tried. She'd wanted to—agonized over it for weeks—but if Hayden was that skittish after one little health scare, what was to keep her from wasting months or even years of Ellie's time and then cutting and running the next moment things got tough? "At this point, she's already gone, so it doesn't matter. It's too late."

"Do you know for sure? Have you tried seeing if she's still there? Talking to her again?"

"She's gone. I know it."

"For a self-proclaimed hopeless romantic, you are very quick to give up on love, you know that? What if she stayed longer because she's having second thoughts but hasn't mustered the courage to come see you? What if she couldn't get things in order and stayed a little longer? What if she's getting ready to leave right now, and you miss her because you're too busy dawdling with me? I think you owe it to yourself—to your romantic heart—to see if she's still here. To see if she'll talk to you. Hell, even if she *is* gone, you should try calling her. Something. If it's love—true love—it's worth fighting for."

Ellie was speechless. Hadn't she tried fighting for it? She felt like she'd stood in front of Hayden begging for her to love her. But she hadn't said the words. She'd told her they were worth the risk, but had she said everything in her heart? Had she said and done everything she could to convince her to stay, to convince her they had something? She was certain now that she hadn't. She couldn't believe that it took Skye to make her realize that she'd given up without much of a fight. *Shit.* Was there a chance Hayden hadn't gone yet? The fog Ellie had been living within for weeks suddenly cleared. "I have to go."

Skye had a small smile on her face. "Go. I'll take care of this."

Ellie barely heard as she grabbed her suit jacket and swung it back on. "Thank you." She checked her watch. She couldn't leave Atlas alone for much longer, so she ran home, leashed him up and walked to the marina.

The nearer they got, however, the higher her anxiety ramped up. She had no idea what she was going to say *if* Hayden was there. And that was an awfully big if. Maybe this was a fool's errand. Even if it wasn't, how was she going to convince Hayden they had something worth fighting for? Something worth risking their hearts for?

Every time she started to hyperventilate while swimming in uncertainty, Atlas pressed into her leg. Just the feel of his big warm body sent an air of calmness through her. She petted his head, scratched his ears. A dog crossed the street in the block ahead, and Atlas didn't blink. Even if Hayden was gone or totally shot her down, she had at least given her the gift of Atlas. Or at least, the gift of an Atlas who could thrive in an uncertain world. Without Hayden, she'd probably live like a recluse with Atlas in a country home with no neighbors.

A ridiculous thought, but the vision made Ellie laugh for a second. Until she saw the entrance to the marina looming in front of them, and her heart clutched. Her steps faltered, but Atlas pulled at the end of the leash. He looked back at her as though wondering what her hesitation was.

"Coming, buddy." Standing outside the marina certainly wasn't going to make anything easier, and she couldn't see any of the boat slips from there, so she had no idea if Hayden's was still docked or not. With every step, she angled her head to try to figure out if Hayden's slip was empty or occupied by another boat. But looking down a straight aisle of boats felt like an optical illusion. Every other step, she thought she could see the tip of the boat, but the next step, she wasn't sure if she was even looking at the right slip. It felt like the dock was three thousand feet long.

When she finally got to the right slip, her heart sunk. It was empty. She was too late.

Atlas seemed confused as he sniffed around the edge of the dock. "Come here, Atlas." She sat on a wooden bench built into the dock, rough from years of weathering, and contemplated her next move.

Perhaps it was a sign. Perhaps she should just head home and lick her wounds. Try to write off this period as a life lesson and move on. Hayden was gone, after all.

CHAPTER THIRTY-FIVE

Ellie wasn't sure how long she'd been sitting listening to the quiet tap of boats against their bumpers, the soft splash as waves lapped against the sides of the boats, the creak of the ropes against the cleats as the boats shifted subtly in the water. Nothing really registered, yet everything contributed to the soundtrack of this moment.

Atlas had climbed onto the bench next to her at some point and was lying with his head in her lap. He was probably getting drool on her pants, but she wasn't that concerned. They were going to the dry cleaners that weekend anyway.

The sun had gone down while she sat out there, and the wind had picked up. It wasn't cold, but Ellie was a little chilled, though Atlas across her lap certainly helped warm her. She knew she should head home, but something had her stuck in place. Inertia had set in, and she kept telling herself she'd give herself five more minutes to brood, and then she'd rally Atlas and head home.

Yet five minutes would come, and five minutes would go, and thirty minutes later, Ellie would tell herself the same thing again.

"Ellie?"

The voice sounded like it was coming from far away. Perhaps it was just the wind. Since Hayden was gone, there was no way someone knew her name here at the marina.

"Ellie?" Louder this time.

Atlas's ear twitched, but he didn't get up. Ellie looked up and down the dock but didn't see anyone in the darkness. The lights only created small pools of orange in the immediate vicinity of the poles. Atlas grumbled when she gently lifted his head to slide out. She stood and turned.

"Over here."

And she saw her. Standing on the bow of her boat on the third deck, waving. Parked in a different slip.

How had she even recognized Ellie on the bench in the darkness? Ellie waved back. Her heart did somersaults. Her entire body had come alive with shivers, and she hoped Hayden couldn't see the trembling from that distance.

"Will you…come over?"

Atlas jumped up and looked toward Hayden's voice, his butt wiggles starting, though more muted than normal.

Ellie wanted to run to her but also didn't want to appear pathetic. "Yes," she yelled back and got Atlas to jump off the bench. She took measured steps and even breaths, trying to get her nervous energy under control. Hayden being there had to be a good sign. Had she left and come back? Just decided she wanted a different slip?

What was Ellie going to say? What was Hayden? Before she had anything planned out, she was standing in front of Hayden, who had come out onto the other dock to meet them. "What are you doing here?" she asked as Ellie approached. Not a great start. She squatted to greet Atlas as usual. "Hey, Atlas. My main man. How are you?" He licked her chin and tried to push her over in his special Atlas style. She scratched his back just above his tail. His favorite spot.

"I was trying to come see you, but your slip was empty, so I thought you were gone. I wasn't ready to walk home yet, so we sat for a bit." She shrugged. She knew it sounded weird, but she hadn't been able to convince herself to move. She wasn't going to tell Hayden that, though. "Why are you in a different slip?"

She looked up from where she was squatting with Atlas two feet in front of her. "Do you want to come inside? Warm up? Atlas's ears feel a little cool, so I'm guessing you might be cold too. Perhaps have a hot toddy. May seems a little late in the year for one, but the chill in the air says otherwise." She stood, a couple of inches shorter since Ellie was in heels. Her eyes were wide and earnest. She scratched her neck and ran her thumb along her bottom lip as she often did while thinking.

"That'd be great. Thank you." It was what Ellie had come for anyway. Well, she'd come to talk, but it would be more comfortable inside rather than standing on the dock. "And a hot toddy sounds perfect." She rubbed her hands together as she realized how cold they actually were.

❖

Once they were settled, hot toddies in hand and Atlas lying at Ellie's feet, Hayden drew a deep breath and said, "I'm in a different slip because I left a few days ago. I made it to a little past Joliet and couldn't do it. I realized I was making a terrible mistake and turned around."

"You came back," Ellie whispered.

Hayden took a sip of her too hot toddy and tried not to choke. "I was going down the river, and everywhere I looked, I saw you and Atlas. Or Chelsea. Or all of you. There's nothing on this boat that you haven't put an imprint on. I felt completely empty. I would look at the couch and see us sitting here having drinks and relaxing. I would look at the hot tub and see us sitting in it with a glass of wine. Or me straddling your lap. I would look at my bed, and…well, I slept in one of the spare rooms." She had laughed at herself, but it was easier sleeping in the bedroom that wasn't the one they'd shared so many times or the one that had belonged to Chelsea for so long. "The bedroom with no baggage," she'd nicknamed it.

"I want to say I'm sorry I tainted your house, but I don't actually feel that way, so…" Ellie shrugged.

Hayden laughed. "I wouldn't say tainted. I just, I felt miserable leaving, but I was so afraid of getting hurt. So afraid because I knew that eventually, I would get hurt, or you would, whether or not we meant to do it. But when I think about Chelsea, I'd had her for fifteen years. And, yeah, it hurt when she passed away, but I wouldn't get rid of those fifteen years because of it. I wouldn't trade the four years I had with my grandma or the first thirteen years of my life with my mom just because they died. I had created this prison for myself with rules about not wanting anyone to mean anything to me. This prison I told myself wasn't a prison but the way I kept myself safe. But it was all bullshit." She wanted to stand and go to Ellie, take her hand, but she wanted to make sure she could get all the words out first.

"I've never been happier than in the last few months. You and Atlas have been the biggest part of it, but I've had other changes too, prompted by you. I actually became friends with Britt. I mentored them, and yet I'd always held them at arm's length, even as they tried to make them my friend. But I never really shared with them. Until you and I met. I turned to them for advice without realizing it. I relied on you as a friend when Chelsea passed away before we were officially a thing. You were always what I needed, and I didn't even realize it."

Hayden stood and started walking, needing to release some of the nervous energy. She was terrified that Ellie was still going to tell her to take a hike. That she wasn't reliable. That she wasn't long-term material anymore because she'd run away scared. And Ellie hadn't said anything, which was more terrifying.

"I'm sorry I was so afraid and ran. That I felt like it was the only way to protect my heart. I was so hardheaded, but it took hours of boating down the river alone with nothing to think about other than my now sad life for me to realize I was making the biggest mistake. Why would I throw away the best life I've had since my dad died out of fear? It didn't make sense. Everything you said about cherishing every moment of love and laughter would be worth it if you died tomorrow was true. Looking back, I was content living on my island and not letting anyone in. Sitting at home alone most nights with a book, a glass of wine, and Chelsea. Occasionally fucking a stranger I'd met in a bar. I was content. But not happy. I can see that now because now I know what being happy feels like. Finally. And I know that because of you. Please tell me you'll give me a chance to try again. To show you that I'll never run again." Hayden felt like she'd pulled her heart out of her chest, held it in her hands, and was offering it to Ellie. She'd never felt so exposed, but she hoped that also showed Ellie how sincere she was. She'd never opened herself up like this before.

"I want to trust you, Hayden." She played with the pendant on her necklace. "I want to give us another chance. It's why I came over. I knew I needed to talk to you. To try to convince you that we have something worth taking a chance on." The words sounded good, but Ellie looked sad as she said them, which didn't make sense. Hayden's heart felt like it was going to beat out of her chest waiting for Ellie to continue.

"But?" she prompted.

"But now that I'm sitting here listening to you, *my* fear is back. How do I know you aren't going to run at the first sign of adversity? What happens if you get scared again?" Her face was pale. She looked like she wanted to throw up.

Hayden had to reassure her somehow that she'd never run again. She knew it in her own heart, but her only way to keep Ellie was to make sure she understood that. "Something happened to me as I was heading downriver. I'd never before examined why I always felt the need to move—to never plant roots—but Britt said something about not always having to be a nomad. How what I was doing wasn't really living because life was about friends and family. Relying on people wasn't a show of weakness.

"I brushed it off at the time, but after all those hours alone, it started to sink in. I realized I'd been moving around so much because it's all I'd ever known as a child. After my dad died, we moved from New Orleans to San Francisco to Seattle. Then my mom died, and I moved to Cleveland. I'd never lived in one place longer than four years until I moved to Chicago. A nomadic lifestyle was ingrained in me, and I'd never realized it until that moment. It was like a tumbler fell into place. Living like this doesn't serve me. I know in my heart I'm never going to be afraid like I was again. And I swear to you." She dropped to her knees and grabbed both of Ellie's hands, squeezed them. "I swear to you, if I ever get scared again, I won't run. I'll come talk to you, and we can figure it out together."

"But you said that before. In Michigan. You said if you got scared, you'd talk to me. You wouldn't run. And when things got tough, you ran. Sure, you talked to me. No. You talked *at* me. It didn't matter what I said." Ellie's eyes sparkled with tears that she wasn't yet allowing to fall.

Hayden prayed she could turn this around. She had to make Ellie see. "Do you remember that tattoo on my hip? You asked what the Chinese characters meant, and I said perseverance?"

"Yes." Ellie said it slowly, as though unsure whether she remembered or not. Hayden knew she did. She'd kissed it tenderly after she'd asked, her lips on a path to the juncture of Hayden's thighs.

"I didn't know this when I got it, but I met this woman from Beijing one night at the Scarlett Lounge and went back to her hotel. She asked me about it, so I told her I'd had to get through a lot of stuff in my life. But she laughed and told me the exact translation of those characters meant 'permanent heart.' We'd laughed about it at the time because I told her my heart was permanently mine, and I was never giving it away. But the thing is, it's not mine. It's yours. It's been yours, I think, from about the moment we met in my office, you so harried and trying to drag Atlas in. I was in physical pain as I sailed south, and I realized it was because I was making the whole journey without my heart. Because I'd left it here. With you. And Atlas. Please, give me another shot. I promise, I'll spend the rest of my life showing you that you weren't wrong trying again. I love you. I haven't said those words in more than fifteen years, but I love you. And I don't want to live another day without you."

Hayden had laid herself completely bare. She prayed that this worked because if it didn't, if those words didn't sway Ellie, she didn't know what could. The corner of Ellie's mouth curved into a hint of a smile. Hayden felt like someone had just taken paddles to her chest and restarted her heart. But Ellie's words would determine if her erratic beat normalized or flatlined after the jolt.

"Do you mean that? Really mean all of that?" Ellie said softly.

"Every word."

"Even the 'I love you' part?"

Hayden squeezed her hands again. "I love you so much. I'm sorry it took me so long to admit it."

Ellie pushed her glasses up with her arm when Hayden wouldn't release her hand. "Well, that's very good. Because I love you too."

And just like that, the vise that was squeezing Hayden's chest evaporated, and joy filled all the newly opened space. She thought she might burst with it. Ellie loved her too. Her cheeks hurt, she was smiling so hard.

She released Ellie's hands so she could wrap her arms around her neck and pull her down. When their lips met, it felt like the final tumbler fell into place. Her scent, her feel…Hayden's hands belonged in Ellie's hair. Everything was complete. At least, she thought so until Atlas barked and ran in half circles behind her legs.

"Must be Atlas's stamp of approval," Hayden said.

"As if he'd hold out on us," Ellie said. She bent and scratched his head. "We love you too, buddy."

"Thanks for being our Atlas, Atlas. Without you, we never would have met."

"You really are our guiding star. Our atlas to forever," Ellie said.

Ellie kissed her again, and Hayden was more than ready to start their forever that second.

EPILOGUE

"A re you almost ready?" Ellie yelled. She couldn't believe how long it was taking.

Hayden's head popped out from around the corner. "I'm nervous, okay? I know I've met them before, but I want to make sure that I make a good impression during today's formal 'double date.'" She ducked back around the corner.

"They think you're great." Ellie walked down the hall and into the bedroom to see what the holdup actually was.

A massive pile of clothes was on the bed, and Hayden stood there in her underwear looking delicious. "Shit, Hayden. Did you try on every single piece of clothing that you have here?"

She looked at Ellie sheepishly. "Maybe." That chagrined smile pretty much always did Ellie in. "Help. Please."

"Why didn't you ask me before? I didn't know what you were doing back here." She picked through the pile. What she wanted to do was throw Hayden on top and have her way with her. But she'd told Skye they'd be there around six, and it was already five thirty. And technically, she'd *already* had her way with Hayden three times that day. So rather than delaying them further, Ellie grabbed a pair of skinny jeans, a gray flowing top that had long sleeves but would be airy enough that it wasn't too much for the August evening, and tossed them to her. "I think you should wear these with your black ankle boots."

By the time Ellie talked Hayden off the ledge and kept her from changing her clothes again and said good-bye to Atlas, it was nearly five fifty, but luckily, they were only ten minutes late.

Skye arched an eyebrow when Ellie made an excuse. "So glad you two were finally able to make it over," Bailey said as Patsy came tearing around the corner, her body seemingly moving in three directions all at once, and her feet moving faster than her body as they searched for purchase on Skye's hardwood floors. "Ah, Patsy, my second love."

Hayden dropped to her knees to greet the miniature hippo barreling toward them. "Hi, sweet girl. You're so pretty, aren't you?"

Ellie leaned over to pet her, but she didn't gush over every dog the way Hayden did. She mostly just loved Atlas.

"Don't say that too loudly, Hayden, or it'll go to her head. She already knows she's the most beautiful girl in every room," Bailey said.

Everyone laughed. "Well, you are, Patsy. There's no shame in knowing it," Hayden said. Ellie loved how much she adored dogs. All of them.

"Well, truth is truth." Bailey shrugged. "Anyway, I've got veggie kabobs ready to go on the grill, mostly from my own garden. It's sad this is going to be my last summer harvesting there." Bailey frowned, and Skye walked to her, interlaced their fingers.

"But we're building you an even bigger garden on the roof here. And there are no trees to block it, so it will get loads of sun. More than at your current place. Roxy thinks it's going to be the perfect location." Skye only had eyes for Bailey as she lovingly reassured her.

"I know. And I'm happy we are officially moving in, but I'm a little nostalgic for the old place. It was my first house. My first garden. But you're first in my heart, and I can't wait until we officially live together all the time." They kissed. Just a quick peck, but Ellie could feel the love radiating between them.

Hayden squeezed her hand. "They are awfully cute," she whispered directly in Ellie's ear.

"You're cuter. I love you," Ellie whispered back.

Hayden kissed her, but it was interrupted when Skye said, "Get a room, you two."

Ellie laughed. "As if you have room to talk. And anyway, are you going to give us the grand tour or what?" It was a little odd that

Ellie hadn't ever been there before, but Skye had been a lot more closed off before she met Bailey.

"This is my favorite part of the condo here." Bailey gestured at the entire wall of windows off the living room that opened onto a huge balcony. "We spend a lot of time just hanging out here. Honestly, I think this balcony is the reason I agreed to move in. This view, right? The zoo, the lake. It's quintessential Chicago."

"It *is* amazing," Hayden said.

"If it wasn't so hot outside, I'd open the wall, but it would get stifling. But we can step out there to give you the full experience," Skye said.

"We just replaced the furniture," Bailey said. "It was nice but didn't quite have enough room, so we bought this larger sectional."

"Aren't there only two of you?"

"It just didn't quite fill the space right, you know?" Bailey answered.

Skye tried to smother a laugh but didn't quite succeed.

"What?" Ellie asked. "What's so funny?"

"Nothing," Skye said and laughed again, this time not trying to hide it. Bailey narrowed her eyes. "We just wanted more space." Something was definitely going on, but they weren't talking, so Ellie decided she'd press Skye later when they were alone.

A lion from the zoo roared. "That's wild," Hayden said, her eyes going wide. "Can you hear them all the time?"

"Yes." Skye smiled. "The seals and sea lions are regular contributors at night, but my absolute favorite is when the wolves howl. It's chilling but amazing. It's one of the reasons I bought this condo."

Ellie was wowed by everything. She loved her condo, but this was next level. "Maybe I'm paying you too much, Skye." She laughed at Skye's shocked expression. "Just kidding. I know you work your ass off for me and a lot of other people too."

"Damn right," Skye said, her mouth open in mock horror. "Though you haven't even seen the roof yet. We put in a huge play area for Patsy so she can run around, we can take her through agility equipment, and there is even irrigation to keep it rinsed off. It's pretty amazing."

"It sealed the deal for us consolidating here. We thought about looking for someplace that we picked out together, but everything we brainstormed already existed here or could be added, so here we are." Bailey practically radiated happiness as she spoke.

"Well, this is fantastic." The lengths that Skye had gone to in order to modify the condo to suit all their needs warmed Ellie. She pulled Hayden tighter. She could imagine doing all of this with Hayden. Figuring out where they wanted to live as a couple. Making sure wherever they picked had all the amenities they both wanted.

"What are you thinking?" Hayden said when Skye and Bailey got distracted talking about their garden plans, and she and Hayden had drifted over to the east side of the rooftop balcony so they could again look out over the zoo and the lake beyond.

"Mmm." Ellie turned and pulled Hayden into her arms. "How sweet all of this is. I love how Skye and Bailey have figured out how to make this place the place of their shared dreams."

"It is very nice. The view is great—not that your balcony view isn't great too—but do you know what I need to have the place of my dreams?" She pursed her lips but made no move to kiss Ellie.

"What?" Ellie would give Hayden anything if it were within her power.

"You. Just you and me."

Hayden smiled, and Ellie's lips curved in response with her full permission. "Sounds about perfect to me. I love you so very much."

"I love you too," Hayden said. "And I can't wait to experience every day between now and forever with you, no matter where we live."

"Thank goodness Atlas showed us the way."

About the Author

Krystina has been a lover of romance novels since she was probably too young to read them and developed an affinity for sapphic romance after she found her first one on a shelf in a used bookstore in 2001. Despite a lifelong desire, she never made the time to write her own until the COVID-19 pandemic struck, and she had extra time with no daily commute or work travel.

Krystina grew up in Florida but, after spending six years in the military, finds herself now calling Chicago home—though she frequently travels so often for work that she forgets what city she's in. She works in real estate and lives with her wife and their two pit bulls and one cantankerously perfect cat. When not working, traveling, or writing, Krystina can be found reading with a glass of wine in hand, doing yoga (occasionally with a glass of wine in hand), snuggling with her fur-babies, or trying to convince herself that it's not too cold to go for a jog outside.

Books Available from Bold Strokes Books

A Talent Ignited by Suzanne Lenoir. When Evelyne is abducted and Annika believes she has been abandoned, they must risk everything to find each other again. (978-1-63679-483-9)

All Things Beautiful by Alaina Erdell. Casey Norford only planned to learn to paint like her mentor, Leighton Vaughn, not sleep with her. (978-1-63679-479-2)

An Atlas to Forever by Krystina Rivers. Can Atlas, a difficult dog Ellie inherits after the death of her best friend, help the busy hopeless romantic find forever love with commitment-phobic animal behaviorist Hayden Brandt? (978-1-63679-451-8)

Bait and Witch by Clifford Mae Henderson. When Zeddi gets an unexpected inheritance from her client Mags, she discovers that Mags served as high priestess to a dwindling coven of old witches—who are positive that Mags was murdered. Zeddi owes it to her to uncover the truth. (978-1-63679-535-5)

Buried Secrets by Sheri Lewis Wohl. Tuesday and Addie, along with Tuesday's dog, Tripper, struggle to solve a twenty-five-year-old mystery while searching for love and redemption along the way. (978-1-63679-396-2)

Come Find Me in the Midnight Sun by Bailey Bridgewater. In Alaska, disappearing is the easy part. When two men go missing, state trooper Louisa Linebach must solve the case, and when she thinks she's coming close, she's wrong. (978-1-63679-566-9)

Death on the Water by CJ Birch. The Ocean Summit's authorities have ruled a death on board its inaugural cruise as a suicide, but Claire suspects murder and with the help of Assistant Cruise Director Moira, Claire conducts her own investigation. (978-1-63679-497-6)

Living For You by Jenny Frame. Can Sera Debrek face real and personal demons to help save the world from darkness and open her heart to love? (978-1-63679-491-4)

Mississippi River Mischief by Greg Herren. When a politician turns up dead and Scotty's client is the most obvious suspect, Scotty and his friends set out to prove his client's innocence. (978-1-63679-353-5)

Ride with Me by Jenna Jarvis. When Lucy's vacation to find herself becomes Emma's chance to remember herself, they realize that everything they're looking for might already be sitting right next to them—if they're willing to reach for it. (978-1-63679-499-0)

Whiskey & Wine by Kelly & Tana Fireside. Winemaker Tessa Williams and sex toy shop owner Lace Reynolds are both used to taking risks, but will they be willing to put their friendship on the line if it gives them a shot at finding forever love? (978-1-63679-531-7)

Hands of the Morri by Heather K O'Malley. Discovering she is a Lost Sister and growing acquainted with her new body, Asche learns how to be a warrior and commune with the Goddess the Hands serve, the Morri. (978-1-63679-465-5)

I Know About You by Erin Kaste. With her stalker inching closer to the truth, Cary Smith is forced to face the past she's tried desperately to forget. (978-1-63679-513-3)

Mate of Her Own by Elena Abbott. When Heather McKenna finally confronts the family who cursed her, her werewolf is shocked to discover her one true mate, and that's only the beginning. (978-1-63679-481-5)

Pumpkin Spice by Tagan Shepard. For Nicki, new love is making this pumpkin spice season sweeter than expected. (978-1-63679-388-7)

Rivals for Love by Ali Vali. Brooks Boseman's brother Curtis is getting married, and Brooks needs to be at the engagement party. Only she can't possibly go, not with Curtis set to marry the secret love of her youth, Fallon Goodwin. (978-1-63679-384-9)

Sweat Equity by Aurora Rey. When cheesemaker Sy Travino takes a job in rural Vermont and hires contractor Maddie Barrow to rehab a house she buys sight unseen, they both wind up with a lot more than they bargained for. (978-1-63679-487-7)

Taking the Plunge by Amanda Radley. When Regina Avery meets model Grace Holland—the most beautiful woman she's ever seen—she doesn't have a clue how to flirt, date, or hold on to a relationship. But Regina must take the plunge with Grace and hope she manages to swim. (978-1-63679-400-6)

We Met in a Bar by Claire Forsythe. Wealthy nightclub owner Erica turns undercover bartender on a mission to catch a thief where she meets no-strings, no-commitments Charlie, who couldn't be further from Erica's type. Right? (978-1-63679-521-8)

Western Blue by Suzie Clarke. Step back in time to this historic western filled with heroism, loyalty, friendship, and love. The odds are against this unlikely group—but never underestimate women who have nothing to lose. (978-1-63679-095-4)

Windswept by Patricia Evans. The windswept shores of the Scottish Highlands weave magic for two people convinced they'd never fall in love again. (978-1-63679-382-5)

An Independent Woman by Kit Meredith. Alex and Rebecca's attraction won't stop smoldering, despite their reluctance to act on it and incompatible poly relationship styles. (978-1-63679-553-9)

Cherish by Kris Bryant. Josie and Olivia cherish the time spent together, but when the summer ends and their temporary romance melts into the real deal, reality gets complicated. (978-1-63679-567-6)

Cold Case Heat by Mary P. Burns. Sydney Hansen receives a threat in a very cold murder case that sends her to the police for help where she finds more than justice with Detective Gale Sterling. (978-1-63679-374-0)

Proximity by Jordan Meadows. Joan really likes Ellie, but being alone with her could turn deadly unless she can keep her dangerous powers under control. (978-1-63679-476-1)

Sweet Spot by Kimberly Cooper Griffin. Pro surfer Shia Turning will have to take a chance if she wants to find the sweet spot. (978-1-63679-418-1)

The Haunting of Oak Springs by Crin Claxton. Ghosts and the past haunt the supernatural detective in a race to save the lesbians of Oak Springs farm. (978-1-63679-432-7)

Transitory by J.M. Redmann. The cops blow it off as a customer surprised by what was under the dress, but PI Micky Knight knows they're wrong—she either makes it her case or lets a murderer go free to kill again. (978-1-63679-251-4)

Unexpectedly Yours by Toni Logan. A private resort on a tropical island, a feisty old chief, and a kleptomaniac pet pig bring Suzanne and Allie together for unexpected love. (978-1-63679-160-9)

Bones of Boothbay Harbor by Michelle Larkin. Small-town police chief Frankie Stone and FBI Special Agent Eve Huxley must set aside their differences and combine their skills to find a killer after a burial site is discovered in Boothbay Harbor, Maine. (978-1-63679-267-5)

Crush by Ana Hartnett Reichardt. Josie Sanchez worked for years for the opportunity to create her own wine label, and nothing will stand in her way. Not even Mac, the owner's annoyingly beautiful niece Josie's forced to hire as her harvest intern. (978-1-63679-330-6)

Decadence by Ronica Black, Renee Roman, and Piper Jordan. You are cordially invited to Decadence, Las Vegas's most talked about invitation-only Masquerade Ball. Come for the entertainment and stay for the erotic indulgence. We guarantee it'll be a party that lives up to its name. (978-1-63679-361-0)

Gimmicks and Glamour by Lauren Melissa Ellzey. Ashly has learned to hide her Sight, but as she speeds toward high school graduation she must protect the classmates she claims to hate from an evil that no one else sees. (978-1-63679-401-3)

Heart of Stone by Sam Ledel. Princess Keeva Glantor meets Maeve, a gorgon forced to live alone thanks to a decades-old lie, and together the two women battle forces they formerly thought to be good in the hopes of leading lives they can finally call their own. (978-1-63679-407-5)

Murder at the Oasis by David S. Pederson. Palm trees, sunshine, and murder await Mason Adler and his friend Walter as they travel from Phoenix to Palm Springs for what was supposed to be a relaxing vacation but ends up being a trip of mystery and intrigue. (978-1-63679-416-7)

Peaches and Cream by Georgia Beers. Adley Purcell is living her dreams owning Get the Scoop ice cream shop until national dessert chain Sweet Heaven opens less than two blocks away and Adley has to compete with the far too heavenly Sabrina James. (978-1-63679-412-9)

The Only Fish in the Sea by Angie Williams. Will love overcome years of bitter rivalry for the daughters of two crab fishing families in this queer modern-day spin on Romeo and Juliet? (978-1-63679-444-0)

Wildflower by Cathleen Collins. When a plane crash leaves eleven-year-old Lily Andrews stranded in the vast wilderness of Arkansas, will she be able to overcome the odds and make it back to civilization and the one person who holds the key to her future? (978-1-63679-621-5)

Witch Finder by Sheri Lewis Wohl. Tamsin, the Keeper of the Book of Darkness, is in terrible danger, and as a Witch Finder, Morrigan must protect her and the secrets she guards even if it costs Morrigan her life. (978-1-63679-335-1)